STEPHEN LEATHER

nightfall

HODDER

First published in Great Britain in 2010 by Hodder & Stoughton
An Hachette UK company

First published in paperback in 2010

11

Copyright © Stephen Leather 2010

A CIP catalogue record for this title is available from the
British Library

B format paperback ISBN 978 1 444 70064 0
A format paperback ISBN 978 1 444 70065 7

Typeset in Plantin Light by Palimpsest Book Production Ltd,
Grangemouth, Stirlingshire

Printed and bound by Clays Ltd, St Ives plc

Hodder & Stoughton policy is to use papers that are natural,
renewable and recyclable products and made from wood grown in
sustainable forests. The logging and manufacturing processes are
expected to conform to the environmental regulations of
the country of origin.

Hodder & Stoughton Ltd
338 Euston Road
London NW1 3BH

www.hodder.co.uk

nightfall

I

Jack Nightingale didn't intend to kill anyone when he woke up on that chilly November morning. He shaved, showered and dressed, made himself coffee and a bacon sandwich, and at no point did he even contemplate the taking of a human life, even though he had spent the last five years training to do just that. As a serving member of the Metropolitan Police's elite CO19 armed-response unit he was more than capable of putting a bullet in a man's head or chest if it was necessary and provided he had been given the necessary authorisation by a senior officer.

His mobile phone rang just as he was pouring the coffee from his cafetiere. It was the Co-ordinator of the Metropolitan Police's negotiating team. 'Jack, I've just had a call from the Duty Officer at Fulham. They have a person in crisis down at Chelsea Harbour. Can you get there?'

'No problem,' said Nightingale. After two courses at the Met's Bramshill Officer Training College he was now one of several dozen officers qualified to talk to hostage-takers and potential suicides in addition to his regular duties.

'I'm told it's a jumper on a ledge but that's all I have. I'm trying to get back up for you but we've got four guys tied up with a domestic in Brixton.'

'Give me the address,' said Nightingale, reaching for a pen.

He ate his bacon sandwich as he drove his MGB Roadster to Chelsea Harbour. During the three years he had worked as a negotiator he had been called to more than forty attempted suicides but on only three occasions had he seen someone take their own life. In his experience, people either wanted to kill themselves or they wanted to talk. They rarely wanted to do both. Suicide was a relatively easy matter. You climbed to the top of a high building or a bridge and you jumped. Or you swallowed a lot of tablets. Or you tied a rope around your neck and stepped off a chair. Or you took a razor blade and made deep cuts in your wrist or throat. If you were lucky enough to have a gun you put it in your mouth or against your temple and pulled the trigger. What you didn't do if you really wanted to kill yourself was say you were going to do it, then wait for a trained police negotiator to arrive. People who did that usually just wanted someone to listen to their problems and reassure them that their lives were worth living. Once they'd got whatever was worrying them off their chests they came off the ledge, or put down the gun or lowered the knife, and everyone cheered, patted Nightingale on the back and told him 'job well done'.

When he reached the address that the Duty Officer had given him, his way was blocked by a police car and two Community Support Officers in police-type uniforms and yellow fluorescent jackets. One pointed the way Nightingale had come and told him to turn around, in a tone that suggested his motivation for becoming a CSO had more to do with wielding power than helping his fellow citizens. Nightingale wound down the window and showed them his warrant card. 'Inspector Nightingale,' he said. 'I'm the negotiator.'

'Sorry, sir,' said the CSO, suddenly all sweetness and light. He gestured at a parked ambulance. 'You can leave your car there, I'll keep an eye on it.' He and his colleague moved aside to allow Nightingale to drive through. He pulled up behind the ambulance and climbed out, stretching and yawning.

If you'd asked Nightingale what he was expecting that chilly November morning, he'd probably have shrugged carelessly and said that jumpers tended to be either men the worse for drink, women the worse for anti-depressants or druggies the worse for their Class-A drug of choice, generally cocaine or amphetamines. Nightingale's drug of choice while working was nicotine so he lit himself a Marlboro and blew smoke at the cloudless sky.

A uniformed inspector hurried over, holding a transceiver. 'I'm glad it's you, Jack,' he said.

'And I'm glad it's you.' He'd known Colin Duggan for almost a decade. He was old school – a good reliable thief-taker who, like Nightingale, was a smoker. He offered him a Marlboro and lit it for him, even though smoking in uniform was a disciplinary offence.

'It's a kid, Jack,' said Duggan, scratching his fleshy neck.

'Gang-banger? Drug deal gone wrong?' Nightingale inhaled and held the smoke deep in his lungs.

'A kid kid,' said Duggan. 'Nine-year-old girl.'

Nightingale frowned as he blew a tight plume of smoke. Nine-year-old girls didn't kill themselves. They played with their PlayStations or Wiis, or they went rollerblading, and sometimes they were kidnapped and raped by paedophiles, but they never, ever killed themselves.

Duggan pointed up at a luxury tower block overlooking the Thames. 'Her name's Sophie, she's locked herself on the thirteenth-floor balcony and she's sitting there talking to her doll.'

'Where are the parents?' said Nightingale. There was a cold feeling of dread in the pit of his stomach.

'Father's at work, mother's shopping. She was left in the care of the au pair.' Duggan waved his cigarette at an anorexic blonde who was sitting on a bench, sobbing, as a uniformed WPC tried to comfort her. 'Polish girl. She was ironing, then saw Sophie on the balcony. She banged on the window but Sophie had locked it from the outside.'

'And what makes her think Sophie wants to jump?'

'She's talking to her doll, won't look at anyone. We sent up two WPCs but she won't talk to them.'

'You're supposed to wait for me, Colin,' said Nightingale. He dropped his cigarette onto the ground and crushed it with his heel. 'Amateurs only complicate matters, you know that.'

'She's a kid on a balcony,' said Duggan. 'We couldn't just wait.'

'You're sure she's a potential jumper?'

'She's sitting on the edge, Jack. A gust of wind and she could blow right off. We're trying to get an airbag brought out but no one seems to know where to find one.'

'How close can I get to her?'

'You could talk to her through the balcony window.'

Nightingale shook his head. 'I need to see her face, to watch how she reacts. And I don't want to be shouting.'

'Then there are two possibilities,' said Duggan. 'She's too high to use a ladder, so we can either lower you from the roof or we can get you into the flat next door.'

'Lower me?'

'We can put you in a harness and the Fire Brigade boys will drop you down.'

'And I talk to her hanging from a string like a bloody puppet? Come on, Colin, I'm a negotiator, not a bloody marionette.'

'The other balcony it is, then,' said Duggan. He flicked away his butt. 'Let's get to it.' He waved over a uniformed constable and told him to escort Nightingale up to the thirteenth floor. 'Except it isn't the thirteenth, it's the fourteenth,' said Duggan.

'What?'

'It's a superstitious thing. Don't ask me why. It is the thirteenth floor, but the lift says fourteen. It goes from twelve to fourteen. No thirteen.'

'That's ridiculous,' said Nightingale.

'Tell the developer, not me,' said Duggan. 'Besides, you're talking to the wrong person. You won't catch me walking under a ladder or breaking a mirror. I can understand people not wanting to live on the thirteenth floor.' He grinned at Nightingale. 'Break a leg, yeah?'

'Yeah,' said Nightingale. He nodded at the constable, a lanky specimen whose uniform seemed a couple of sizes too small for him. 'Lead on, Macduff.'

The constable frowned. 'My name's not Macduff,' he said.

Nightingale patted him on the back. 'Let's go,' he said. 'But first I want a word with the au pair.'

The two men went to the sobbing woman, who was still being comforted by the WPC. At least fifty people had gathered to stare up at the little girl. There were pensioners, huddled together like penguins on an ice floe, mothers with toddlers in pushchairs, teenagers chewing gum and sniggering, a girl in Goth clothing with a collie that grinned at Nightingale as he walked by, workmen in overalls, and a group of waitresses from a nearby pizza restaurant.

'Why aren't you up there, getting her down?' shouted a bald man, holding a metal tool box. He pointed at Nightingale and the young constable. 'You should do something instead of pissing about down here.'

'Can't you Taser him?' asked Nightingale.

'We're not issued with Tasers, sir,' said the constable.

'Use your truncheon, then.'

'We're not . . .' He grimaced as he realised that Nightingale was joking.

They reached the au pair, who was blowing her nose into a large white handkerchief. Nightingale acknowledged the WPC. 'I'm the negotiator,' he said.

'Yes, sir,' she said.

Nightingale smiled at the au pair. 'Hi, what's your name?' he asked.

'Inga.' The girl sniffed, dabbing her eyes with the handkerchief. 'Are you a policeman?'

'I'm Jack Nightingale,' he said, showing her his warrant card. 'I'm the one who's going to talk to Sophie.'

'Am I in trouble?'

'No, of course you're not,' said Nightingale. 'You did the right thing, calling the police.'

'Her parents will kill me,' said the au pair.

'They won't,' said Nightingale.

'They'll send me back to Poland.'

'They can't do that – Poland's in the EU. You have every right to be here.'

'They'll send me to prison, I know they will.'

Nightingale's heart hardened. The au pair seemed more concerned about her own future than about what was happening thirteen storeys up. 'They won't,' he said. 'Tell me, Inga, why isn't Sophie at school today?'

'She said she had a stomach-ache. She didn't feel well. Her mother said she could stay at home.'

'Her mother's shopping?'

The au pair nodded. 'I phoned her and she's coming back now. Her father's mobile phone is switched off so I left a message on his voicemail.'

'Where does he work?'

'In Canary Wharf.' Still sniffing, she took a wallet out of the back pocket of her jeans and fished out a business card. She gave it to Nightingale. 'This is him.'

Nightingale looked at it. Simon Underwood was a vice president at a large American bank. 'Inga, has Sophie done anything like this before?'

The au pair shook her head fiercely. 'Never. She's a quiet child. As good as gold.'

'Tell me what happened. How did she come to be on the balcony?'

'I don't know,' said the au pair. 'I was ironing. She was watching a Hannah Montana DVD but when I looked up she was on the balcony and she'd locked the door.'

'You can lock it from the outside?'

'There's only one key and she had it. I shouted at her to open the door but it was like she couldn't hear me. I banged on the window but she didn't look at me. That was when I called the police.'

'And she wasn't sad this morning? Or angry? Upset by something or somebody?'

'She was quiet,' said the au pair, 'but she's always quiet.'

'You didn't argue with her about anything?'

The au pair's eyes flashed. 'You're going to blame me, aren't you? You're going to send me to prison?' she wailed.

'No one's blaming you, Inga.'

The au pair buried her face in her handkerchief and sobbed.

'Let's go,' Nightingale said to the constable.

'What will you do?' the officer asked, as they walked past the crowd of onlookers.

'Talk to her. See if I can find out what's troubling her, see what it is she wants.'

'She wants something?'

'They always want something. If they didn't they'd just go ahead and do it. The key is to find out what it is they want.'

'Wankers!' shouted the bald man with the tool box.

Nightingale stopped and glared at him. 'What's your problem, pal?'

'My problem is that there's a little girl up there and you tossers aren't doing anything about it.'

'And what exactly are you doing? Gawping in case she takes a dive off the balcony? Is that what you want? You want to see her slap into the ground, do you? You want to hear her bones break and her skull smash and see her blood splatter over the concrete? Because that's the only reason you could have for standing there. You're sure as hell not helping by shouting abuse and making a tit of yourself. I'm here to help, you're here on the off-chance that you might see a child die so I'd say that makes you the tosser. I'm going up there now to see how I can help her, and if you're still here when I get down I'll shove your tools so far up your arse that you'll be coughing up spanners for months. Are we clear, *tosser?'*

The bald man's face reddened. Nightingale sneered at him and made for the entrance. The constable hurried after him.

The reception area was plush with overstuffed sofas and a large coffee-table covered with glossy magazines. A doorman in a green uniform was talking to two PCs. 'Where are the stairs?' asked Nightingale.

The doorman pointed to three lift doors. 'The lifts are there, sir,' he said.

'I need the stairs,' said Nightingale.

'It's thirteen floors, sir,' said the constable at his side.

'I know it's thirteen floors, Macduff,' said Nightingale. He jerked his chin at the doorman. 'Stairs?'

The doorman pointed to the left. 'Around the side there, sir,' he said.

Nightingale hurried towards them, followed by the constable. He pushed through the doors and started up, taking the steps two at a time. The number of each floor was painted on the white wall in green, and by the time they'd reached the tenth floor both men were panting like dogs. 'Why can't we use the lift, sir?' gasped the constable. 'Is it procedure with jumpers?'

'It's because I hate lifts,' said Nightingale.

'Claustrophobia?'

'Nothing to do with confined spaces,' said Nightingale. 'I just don't like dangling over nothing.'

'So it's fear of heights?'

'It's fear of lifts,' said Nightingale. 'I'm fine with heights. As you're about to find out.'

They reached the twelfth floor. The policeman had taken off his helmet and unbuttoned his tunic. Nightingale's overcoat was draped over his shoulder.

They reached the thirteenth floor, though the number stencilled on the wall was '14'. Nightingale pulled open the door and went into the corridor. 'What number is her flat?' he asked.

'Fourteen C,' said the constable. 'We can get into Fourteen D. A Mr and Mrs Wilson live there and they've agreed to give us access.'

'Okay, when we get in there, keep the Wilsons away from the balcony. The girl mustn't see them and she sure as hell mustn't see you. Nothing personal, but the uniform could spook her.'

'Got you,' said the policeman.

'You'll be just fine, Macduff,' said Nightingale. He knocked on the door of Fourteen D. It was opened by a man in his early sixties, grey-haired and slightly stooped. Nightingale flashed his warrant card. 'Mr Wilson, I'm Jack Nightingale. I gather you're happy for me to go out on your balcony.'

'I wouldn't exactly say that I was happy, but we need to get that little girl back inside.'

He opened the door wide and Nightingale walked in with the constable. The man's wife was sitting on a flower-print sofa, her hands in her lap. She was also grey-haired, and when she stood up to greet Nightingale he saw that she had the same curved spine. 'Please don't get up, Mrs Wilson,' he said.

'What's going to happen?' she said anxiously. Like her husband she was well-spoken, with an accent that would have done credit to a Radio 4 announcer. They were good, middle-class people, the sort who would rarely cross paths with a policeman – Nightingale sensed their unease at having him and the constable in their home.

'I'm just going to talk to her, Mrs Wilson, that's all.'

'Would you like a cup of tea?' she asked.

Nightingale smiled. More often than not as a member of CO19 he was treated with contempt, if not open hostility, and the Wilsons were a breath of fresh air. 'You could certainly put the kettle on, Wilson' he said. 'Now, do you know Sophie?'

'We say hello to her, but she's a shy little thing, wouldn't say boo to a goose.'

'A happy girl?'

'I wouldn't say so,' said Mrs Wilson.

'She cries sometimes,' said her husband quietly. 'At night.'

'What sort of crying?' asked Nightingale. 'Screaming?'

'Sobbing,' said Mr Wilson. 'Her bedroom's next to our bathroom, and sometimes when I'm getting ready for bed I can hear her.'

'We've both heard her,' added Mrs Wilson. Her husband walked over to her and put his arm around her.

For a brief moment Nightingale flashed back to his own parents. His father had been equally protective of his mother, never scared to hold her hand in public or to demonstrate his affection in other ways. In his last memory of them they were standing at the door of their house in Manchester, his arm around her shoulders, as they waved him off to start his second year at university. His mother had looked up at Nightingale's father with the same adoration he saw now in Mrs Wilson's eyes.

'Any idea why she'd be unhappy?' Nightingale asked. 'Did you see her with her parents?'

'Rarely,' said Mr Wilson. 'They've been here – what, five years?' he asked his wife.

'Six,' she said.

'Six years, and I can count on the fingers of one hand the number of times I've seen Sophie with her mother or father. It's always an au pair, and they seem to change them every six months or so.' He looked at his wife and she nodded almost imperceptibly. 'One doesn't like to talk out of school but they don't seem the most attentive of parents.'

'I understand,' Nightingale said. He took his lighter and cigarettes from the pocket of his overcoat and gave it to the constable. 'Why don't you take a seat while I go out and talk to her?' he said to the Wilsons.

Mr Wilson helped his wife onto the sofa while Nightingale went to the glass door that led on to the balcony. It was actually a terrace, with terracotta tiles and space for a small circular white metal table, four chairs and several pots of flowering shrubs, and was surrounded by a waist-high wall.

The door slid to the side and Nightingale could hear traffic in the distance and the crackle of police radios. He stepped out slowly, then looked to the right.

The little girl was sitting on the wall of the balcony

next door. She was holding a Barbie doll and seemed to be whispering to it. She was wearing a white sweatshirt with a blue cotton skirt and silver trainers with blue stars on them. She had porcelain-white skin and shoulder-length blonde hair that she'd tucked behind her ears.

There was a gap of about six feet between the terrace where he was and the one where she was sitting. Nightingale figured that he could just about jump across but only as a last resort. He walked slowly to the side of the terrace and stood next to a tall, thin conifer in a concrete pot. In the distance he could see the river Thames and far off to his left the London Eye. The child didn't seem to have noticed him, but Nightingale knew she must have heard the door slide open. 'Hi,' he said.

Sophie looked at him but didn't say anything. Nightingale stared out over the Thames as he slid a cigarette between his lips and flicked his lighter.

'Cigarettes are bad for you,' said Sophie.

'I know,' said Nightingale. He lit it and inhaled deeply.

'You can get cancer,' said Sophie.

Nightingale tilted his head back and blew two perfect smoke-rings. 'I know that too,' he said.

'How do you do that?' she asked.

'Do what?'

'Blow those rings.'

Nightingale shrugged. 'You just blow and stick your tongue out a bit,' he said. He grinned amiably and held out the cigarette. 'Do you want to try?'

She shook her head solemnly. 'I'm a child and children can't smoke, and even if I could smoke I wouldn't because it gives you cancer.'

Nightingale took another drag on the cigarette. 'It's a beautiful day, isn't it?' he said, his eyes on the river again.

'Who are you?' Sophie asked.

'My name's Jack.'

'Like *Jack and the Beanstalk*?'

'Yeah, but I don't have my beanstalk with me today. I had to use the stairs.'

'Why didn't you use the lift?'

'I don't like lifts.'

Sophie put the doll to her ear and frowned as if she was listening intently. Then she nodded. 'Jessica doesn't like lifts, either.'

'Nice name – Jessica.'

'Jessica Lovely – that's her full name. What's your full name?'

'Nightingale. Jack Nightingale.'

'Like the bird?'

'That's right. Like the bird.'

'I wish I was a bird.' She cuddled the doll as she stared across the river with unseeing eyes.

'I wish I could fly.'

Nightingale blew two more smoke-rings. This time they held together for less than a second before the wind whipped them apart. 'It's not so much fun, being a bird. They can't watch TV, they can't play video games or play with dolls, and they have to eat off the floor.'

Below a siren kicked into life, and Sophie flinched as if she'd been struck. 'It's okay,' said Nightingale. 'It's a fire engine.'

'I thought it was the police.'

'The police siren sounds different.' Nightingale made the woo-woo-woo sound, and Sophie giggled. He leaned against the terrace wall. He had set his phone to vibrate and felt it judder in his inside pocket. He took it out and peered at the screen. It was Robbie Hoyle, one of his negotiator colleagues. He'd known Hoyle for more than a decade. He was an inspector with the Territorial Support Group, the force's heavy mob who went in with riot shields, truncheons and Tasers when necessary. Hoyle was a big man, well over six feet tall with the build of a rugby player, but he had a soft voice and was one of the Met's most able negotiators. 'Sorry, Sophie, I'm going to have to take this,' he said. He pressed the green button. 'Hi, Robbie.'

'I've just arrived, do you want me up there?'

'I'm not sure that's a good idea,' said Nightingale. Whenever possible the negotiators preferred to act in teams of three, one doing the talking, another listening and the third gathering intelligence, but Nightingale figured that too many men on the balcony would only spook the little girl.

'How's it going?' asked Hoyle.

'Calm,' said Nightingale. 'I'll get back to you, okay? Try to get rid of the onlookers, but softly-softly.' He ended the call and put the phone away.

'You're a policeman, aren't you?' said Sophie.

Nightingale smiled. 'How did you know?'

Sophie pointed down at Colin Duggan, who was staring up at them, shielding his eyes from the sun with a hand. Robbie Hoyle was standing next to him. 'That policeman there spoke to you when you got out of your car.'

'You saw me arrive, yeah?'

'I like sports cars,' she said. 'It's an MGB.'

'That's right,' said Nightingale, 'an old one. How old are you?'

'Nine,' she said.

'Well my car's twenty-six years old. How about that?'

'That's old,' she said. 'Very old.'

'There's another thing birds can't do,' said

Nightingale. 'When was the last time you saw a bird driving a car? They can't do it. No hands.'

Sophie pressed the doll to her ear as if she was listening to it, then took it away and looked at Nightingale. 'Am I in trouble?' she said.

'No, Sophie. We just want to be sure you're okay.'

Sophie shuddered, as if icy water had trickled down her spine.

'The girl who looks after you, what's her name?' asked Nightingale.

'Inga. She's from Poland.'

'She's worried about you.'

'She's stupid.'

'Why do you say that?'

'She can't even use the microwave properly.'

'I have trouble getting my video recorder to work,' Nightingale told her.

'Videoplus,' said Sophie.

'What?'

'Videoplus. You just put in the number from the newspaper. The machine does it for you. Everyone knows that.'

'I didn't.' A gust blew across from the river and Sophie put a hand on her skirt to stop it billowing up. Nightingale caught a glimpse of a dark bruise above her knee. 'What happened to your leg?' he asked.

'Nothing,' she said quickly.

Too quickly, Nightingale noticed. He blew smoke and avoided looking at her. 'Why didn't you go to school today?'

'Mummy said I didn't have to.'

'Are you poorly?'

'Not really.' She bit her lower lip and cuddled her doll. 'I *am* in trouble, aren't I?'

'No, you're not,' said Nightingale. He made the sign of the cross over his heart. 'Cross my heart you're not.'

Sophie forced a smile. 'Do you have children?'

Nightingale dropped the butt of his cigarette and ground it with his heel. 'I'm not married.'

'You don't have to be married to have children.' Tears ran down her cheeks.

'What's wrong, Sophie?'

'Nothing.' She sniffed and wiped her eyes on her doll.

'Sophie, let's go inside. It's cold out here.'

She sniffed again but didn't look at him. Nightingale started to pull himself up onto the wall but his foot scraped against the concrete and she flinched. 'Don't come near me,' she said.

'I just wanted to sit like you,' said Nightingale. 'I'm tired of standing.'

She glared at him. 'You were going to jump over,' she said. 'You were going to try to grab me.'

'I wasn't, I swear,' lied Nightingale. He sat down, swinging his legs as if he didn't have a care in the world but his heart was pounding. 'Sophie, whatever's wrong, maybe I can help you.'

'No one can help me.'

'I can try.'

'He said I mustn't tell anyone.'

'Why? Why can't you tell anyone?'

'He said they'd take me away. Put me in a home.'

'Your father?'

Sophie pressed her doll to her face. 'He said they'd blame me. He said they'd take me away and make me live in a home and that everyone would say it was my fault.'

The wind whipped up her skirt again. The bruise was a good six inches long. 'Did he do that?' said Nightingale.

Sophie pushed her skirt down and nodded.

'Let's go inside, Sophie – we can talk to your mummy.'

Sophie closed her eyes. 'She already knows.'

Nightingale's stomach lurched. His hands were palm down on the wall, his fingers gripping the concrete, but he felt as if something was pushing the small of his back. 'I can help you, Sophie. Just come inside and we'll talk about it. I can help you, honestly I can. Cross my heart.'

'You can't help me,' she said, her voice a monotone. 'No one can.' She lifted her doll, kissed the top of its head, and slid off the balcony without a sound.

Horrified, Nightingale thrust himself forward and reached out with his right hand even though he knew there was nothing he could do. 'Sophie!' he screamed. Her golden hair was whipping in the wind as she dropped straight down, still hugging the doll. 'Sophie!' He closed his eyes at the last second but he couldn't blot out the sound she made as she hit the ground, a dull, wet thud as if a wall had been slapped with a wet blanket.

Nightingale slid down the wall. He lit a cigarette with trembling hands and smoked it as he crouched there, his back against the concrete, his legs drawn up against his stomach.

The uniformed constable who had escorted him up the stairs appeared at the balcony door. 'Are you okay, sir?'

Nightingale ignored him.

'Sir, are you okay?' The constable's radio crackled and a female voice asked him for a situation report.

Nightingale stood up and pushed him out of the way.

'Sir, your coat!' the constable called after him.

The elderly couple were standing in the middle of the living room, holding each other. They looked at

Nightingale expectantly but he said nothing as he rushed past them. He took the stairs three at a time, his fingers brushing the handrail as he hurtled down, his footsteps echoing off the concrete walls.

There were two paramedics and half a dozen uniformed officers in the reception area, all talking into their radios. Duggan was there and opened his mouth to speak, but Nightingale silenced him with a pointed finger and walked past.

Two female paramedics were crouched over the little girl's body. The younger of them was crying. Four firemen in bulky fluorescent jackets were standing behind the paramedics. One was wiping tears from his eyes with the back of a glove. Nightingale knew there was nothing anyone could do. No one survived a fall from thirteen floors. As he turned away he saw blood glistening around the body.

Hoyle was standing next to a PC, frowning as he spoke into his mobile. He put it away as Nightingale came up to him. 'Superintendent Chalmers wants you in his office, Jack,' he said. 'Now.'

Nightingale said nothing. He brushed past Hoyle and headed for his MGB.

'Now, Jack. He wants to see you now.'

'I'm busy,' said Nightingale.

'He'll want you to see the shrink, too,' said Hoyle,

hurrying after him. It was standard procedure after a death.

'I don't need to see the shrink,' said Nightingale.

Hoyle put a hand on Nightingale's shoulder. 'It wasn't your fault, Jack. It's natural to feel guilty, to feel that you've failed.'

Nightingale glared at him. 'Don't try to empathise with me and don't sympathise. I don't need it, Robbie.'

'And what do I tell Chalmers?'

'Tell him whatever you want,' said Nightingale, twisting out of Hoyle's grip. He climbed into the MGB and drove off.

2

What happened later that chilly November morning really depends on whom you talk to. Jack Nightingale never spoke about it and refused to answer any questions put to him by the two investigators assigned to the case. They were from the Metropolitan Police's Professional Standards Department, and they questioned him for more than eighteen hours over three days. During that time he said not one word to them about what had happened. If you'd asked the two detectives they'd have said they were pretty sure that Nightingale had thrown Simon Underwood through the window. If they'd been speaking off the record they would probably have said they had every sympathy with Nightingale and that, given the chance, they would probably have done the same. Like policemen the world over, they knew that paedophiles never stopped offending. You could put them in prison so that they couldn't get near children or you could kill them but you could never change their nature.

The post-mortem on the little girl had shown signs of sexual activity and there were bruises and bite marks on her legs and stomach. A forensic dentistry expert was able to match two of the clearer ones to the father's dental records. A swab of the child's vagina showed up the father's sperm. The evidence was conclusive. According to the coroner, he had been raping her for years. The investigating officers presented the evidence to the mother, but she denied all knowledge of any abuse. They didn't believe her.

Underwood had been in a meeting with six employees from the bank's marketing department when Nightingale walked out of the stairwell on the twentieth floor of the bank in Canary Wharf. He had shown his warrant card to a young receptionist and demanded to be told where Underwood was. The receptionist later told investigators that Nightingale had a strange look in his eyes. 'Manic,' she told them. She had pointed down the corridor to Underwood's office and he had walked away. She had called security but by the time they had arrived it was all over.

Nightingale had burst into Underwood's office but he wasn't there. His terrified secretary told him that her boss was down the corridor. She later told the investigators that Nightingale had been icy cold and there had been no emotion in his voice. 'It was like he was a robot, or on autopilot or something,' she said.

There were differing descriptions from the six witnesses who were in the meeting room with Underwood. One said Nightingale looked crazed, two repeated the secretary's assertion that he was icy cold, two women said he seemed confused, and the senior marketing manager said he reminded her of the Terminator in the second movie, the one Arnold Schwarzenegger was trying to kill. The investigators knew that personal recollections were the most unreliable form of evidence but the one thing that all the witnesses agreed on was that Nightingale had told everyone to leave, that he had closed the door behind them and a few seconds later there was an almighty crash as Simon Underwood exited through the window.

Was he pushed? Did he trip? Did Nightingale hit him and he fell accidentally? Was Underwood so stricken by guilt that he threw himself out of the window? The investigators put every possible scenario to Nightingale, with a few impossible ones for good measure, but Nightingale refused to say anything. He didn't even say, 'No comment.' He just sat staring at the investigators with a look of bored indifference on his face. They asked him several times if he wanted the services of his Police Federation representative, but Nightingale shook his head. He spoke only to ask to go to the toilet or outside to smoke a cigarette.

For the first couple of days the newspapers were after Nightingale's blood, crying police brutality, but when a sympathetic clerk in the coroner's office leaked the post-mortem details to a journalist on the *Sunday Times* and it became known that Underwood had been molesting his daughter, the tide turned and the tabloids called for Nightingale to be honoured rather than persecuted.

The Independent Police Complaints Commission sent two more investigators to talk to him but he was as uncommunicative with them as he had been with the PSD detectives. The IPCC officers offered Nightingale a deal: if he told them that Underwood had jumped there would be no charges. If he told them that Underwood had slipped and fallen through the window, there would be no charges. All they wanted was to close the file on the man's death. Nightingale said nothing.

There were some in the Met who said Nightingale had his head screwed on right, that the IPCC and the PSD were lying sons of bitches and that, no matter what he said, they'd hang him out to dry. There were others who said that Nightingale was an honourable man, that he'd killed Underwood and wasn't prepared to lie about what he'd done. Whatever the reason, whatever had happened to Underwood, Nightingale simply refused to talk about it, and after a week the investigators gave up.

Nightingale went to Sophie's funeral but kept his distance, not wanting to intrude on the family's grief. A photographer from one of the Sunday tabloids tried to take his picture but Nightingale grabbed his camera and smashed it against a gravestone. He left before Sophie's coffin was lowered into the cold, damp soil.

There were two reports into the death, by the PSD and the IPCC. Both were inconclusive and criticised Nightingale for refusing to co-operate. Without his statement, there was no way anyone could know what had happened in the meeting room that day. Two eyewitnesses had seen the body fall to the Tarmac, close enough to hear Sophie's father shout, 'No!' all the way down, but not close enough to see if he had jumped or if he had been pushed. There was CCTV footage of the reception area, which clearly showed Nightingale arriving and leaving, but there was no coverage of the room and no CCTV cameras covering the area where Underwood had hit the ground. Both reports went to the Crown Prosecution Service at Ludgate, and they decided there wasn't enough evidence to prosecute Nightingale.

He had been on suspension until the reports were published, when he was called into the office of his superintendent who told him that his career was over and the best thing for everyone was for him to resign. Superintendent Chalmers had the letter already typed out and Nightingale signed it there and then, handed over his warrant card and walked out of New Scotland Yard, never to return.

Sophie's mother killed herself two weeks after the funeral. She swallowed a bottle of sleeping tablets with a quantity of paracetamol, and left a note saying she was so, so sorry she hadn't been a better mother.

3

Two years later

Nightingale knew he was dreaming, but there was nothing he could do to stop it. He knew he wasn't really climbing the stairs to the twentieth floor of the tower block in Canary Wharf where Simon Underwood worked. He was moving too slowly, for a start, and there was no exertion, no sweat, no shortness of breath. He walked out of the stairwell, showed his warrant card to a faceless receptionist, who shook her head but didn't say anything, and moved silently down a corridor to Underwood's office, even though he knew the banker wasn't there. Then he was going down another corridor, the sound of his heartbeat echoing off the walls, towards a set of double doors. They burst open and Underwood was there, standing in front of a group of suits. His mouth moved but made no sound. Nightingale pointed at the doorway and the suits hurried out, leaving him alone with the banker. 'You're going to hell, Jack Nightingale,' said Underwood, his eyes blazing with hatred. Then, in slow motion, he turned to the floor-to-ceiling window behind him.

Nightingale opened his mouth to shout at the man but his alarm went off and he woke, bathed in sweat. He lay on his bed, staring at the ceiling. He had had the nightmare at least once a week since the day that Simon Underwood had fallen to his death. He groped for his packet of Marlboro and smoked one to the filter before getting up and showering.

His flat was a third-floor walk-up in Bayswater, two bedrooms, a bathroom and a kitchen he hardly ever used. On the ground floor a Chinese restaurant did a great bowl of duck noodles and it was a short walk to the tube station. Nightingale had bought the flat when he'd been promoted to inspector and in another twenty-one years he'd own it outright. He liked Bayswater. Day and night it was lively and buzzing – there were always people around and shops open – and on the days when he felt like jogging, Hyde Park was only a few minutes away. Not that he felt much like jogging, these days. He went downstairs, bought himself a cup of Costa coffee, then walked to the lock-up where he kept his MGB and drove to the office of Nightingale

Investigations. It was in South Kensington, another walk-up but this time above a hairdresser's that offered him a fifty per cent discount, provided he allowed a trainee to cut his hair.

Nightingale arrived shortly after nine o'clock and his secretary was already at her desk. Jenny McLean was in her mid twenties, with short blonde hair and blue eyes that always reminded Nightingale of Cameron Diaz. Jenny was shorter than the actress and smarter, educated at Cheltenham Ladies' College, then Cambridge, and fluent in German, French and Japanese. Her family owned a country pile with five hundred bedrooms and twelve acres, or vice versa, chased foxes and shot wild birds at the weekend. Nightingale had absolutely no idea why she worked for him. He'd placed an advert in the local paper and she'd walked off the street with her CV and told him she'd always wanted to work for a private investigator, that she could type and knew her way around Microsoft Office. He'd wondered at first if she was an undercover agent for the Inland Revenue, checking on his tax returns, but she'd worked for him for more than a year and now he didn't know how he'd manage without her. She smiled brightly and nodded at the door to his office. 'Mrs Brierley's already here,' she said.

'Can't wait to hear the bad news, huh?' said

Nightingale. He didn't like divorce work. He didn't like following unfaithful husbands or wayward wives, and he didn't like breaking bad news to women who cried or men who threatened violence. He didn't like it, but it paid the bills and he had a lot of bills to pay.

'Can I get you a coffee or a tea, Mrs Brierley?' he asked, as he walked into his office.

Joan Brierley was in her early fifties, a heavy-set woman with dyed blonde hair, too much makeup and lines around her mouth from years of smoking. She declined and held up a packet of Benson & Hedges. 'Do you mind if I . . . ?' she said.

Nightingale showed her his Marlboro. 'I'm a smoker too,' he said.

'There aren't many of us left,' she said.

'Strictly speaking, this is my workplace so I should fine myself a thousand pounds every time I light up,' said Nightingale. 'I'm lucky that my secretary doesn't mind or she'd sue me for all I'm worth.' He reached over to light her cigarette, then his own.

'On the phone you said you had bad news,' said Mrs Brierley. 'He's been cheating, has he?'

'I'm afraid so,' said Nightingale.

'I knew it,' she said, her voice shaking. 'When money started disappearing from our joint account, I knew it.'

'I filmed them,' said Nightingale, 'so you could see

for yourself. I followed them to a hotel but he's also visited her house when her husband was away.'

'She's married?'

Nightingale nodded.

'Why would a married woman want to steal another woman's husband?' said Mrs Brierley.

It was a question Nightingale couldn't answer. 'I've got his mobile-phone records. He calls her three or four times a day and sends her text messages.' He slid over a stack of photocopies. 'The messages say it all, pretty much.'

Mrs Brierley picked them up. 'How did you get these?'

'Trade secret, I'm afraid,' said Nightingale. He had contacts working for most of the mobile-phone companies; they would give him anything he wanted, at a price.

She scanned them. 'He loves her?' she hissed. 'He's been married to me for twenty-four years and he loves her?'

Nightingale went to his DVD player and slotted in a disk. He sat down again as Mrs Brierley eyed the screen. The camerawork wasn't great but Nightingale had been hired to do surveillance, not produce a Hollywood movie. He'd taken the first shot from behind a tree. Brierley arrived in his dark blue Toyota,

a nondescript man in a nondescript car. He had a
spring in his step as he walked to the hotel's reception desk, holding a carrier-bag from a local off-
licence. Nightingale had managed to get closer to the
hotel entrance and had filmed Brierley signing in and
being given a key.

The next shot was of the woman arriving. He'd got
a good shot of her parking her BMW and had followed
her to the entrance. Like Brierley, she didn't look around
and clearly wasn't worried that she might have been
followed.

Mrs Brierley stared at the screen, her mouth a tight
line.

The final shot was of Mr Brierley and the woman
leaving the hotel together. He walked her to her car,
kissed her, then went to his Toyota.

Nightingale pressed the remote control to switch off
the DVD player. 'Your husband paid in cash but I have
a copy of the receipt.' He slid it across the desk towards
his client, but she was still staring at the blank television screen, the cigarette burning between her fingers.
'The woman's name is Brenda Lynch. She's—'

'I know who she is,' said Mrs Brierley.

'You know her?'

'She's my sister.'

Nightingale's jaw dropped. 'Your sister?'

'Didn't you know?' said Mrs Brierley. She forced a smile. 'Some detective you are. Lynch was my maiden name.' She took a long drag on her cigarette, held the smoke in her lungs, then exhaled slowly.

'I'm sorry,' said Nightingale.

She waved away his apology, as if it was an annoying insect. 'How much do I owe you, Mr Nightingale?'

'Miss McLean outside has your bill,' said Nightingale.

Mrs Brierley stubbed out what remained of her cigarette in the ashtray on his desk.

'I'm sorry,' said Nightingale, again.

'There's nothing for you to be sorry about,' she said, and stood up. 'You did a very professional job, Mr Nightingale.' There were tears in her eyes. 'Thank you.'

Nightingale opened his door for her. 'Mrs Brierley would like her bill, Jenny,' he said.

'I have it here,' she said, and handed it to her. Mrs Brierley took out her cheque book as Nightingale went back into his office.

He flopped into his chair and stubbed out the remains of his cigarette. He might not enjoy breaking bad news to people, but it was part of the job. If a husband or a wife suspected that their spouse was up to no good, ninety-nine times out of a hundred they were right. In Mrs Brierley's case it had been unexpected withdrawals from their current account, late nights supposedly at

the office and a new brand of aftershave in the bathroom. He noticed that she had left the phone records
and the hotel receipt and thought about going after her
but decided against it – perhaps she didn't want them.
He wondered what she would do now that she knew
the truth. She would almost certainly divorce her
husband, and probably split up her sister's family as
well. She had three children and two still lived at home
so she'd probably keep the house and Mr Brierley would
end up in a rented flat somewhere, either with or without
his sister-in-law for company.

Nightingale went back to his desk and started reading
Metro, the free newspaper that Jenny had brought with
her. Shortly afterwards he heard Mrs Brierley leave.
There was a soft knock on his door and Jenny pushed
it open. She was holding a pot of coffee. 'You read my
mind,' he said.

'It's not difficult,' she said. 'You don't ask much from
life. Curries, cigarettes, coffee.'

'The breakfast of champions,' he said.

She poured coffee into his mug. 'She took it quite
well, didn't she?'

'She cried, which is a good sign. It's when they go
quiet that I start thinking about knives and hammers
and things that go bump in the night.'

'I gave her the card of a good divorce lawyer.'

'Very thoughtful of you.' Nightingale sipped his coffee. Jenny made great coffee. She bought the beans from a shop in Mayfair and ground them herself.

'I felt sorry for her,' said Jenny, sitting on the edge of his desk.

'There are two sides to every case,' said Nightingale. 'We only get to hear the one that pays us.'

'Even so,' said Jenny.

'Maybe she made his life a misery. Maybe the sister was kind to him. Maybe she let him wear her stockings and suspenders and the wife wouldn't.'

'Jack . . .' Jenny shook her head.

'I'm just saying, you can't go feeling sorry for the clients. They're just jobs.'

'Speaking of which, a solicitor in Surrey wants to see you.' She handed him a scribbled note.

Nightingale studied it. 'Can't he just email us the info?'

'He said he wants to see you in his office. He's got gout so he has trouble getting about. I figured you wouldn't mind as you don't have much on at the moment.'

Nightingale flashed her a tight smile. He didn't need reminding of how light his caseload was. 'This place, Hamdale. Never heard of it.'

'I've got the postcode – you can use the GPS on your phone.'

'You know I can never get it to work.'

Jenny grinned and held out her hand. 'I'll do it for you, you Luddite.' Nightingale gave her his Nokia and she programmed in the location. 'You'll be fine,' she said.

'And how do I get back?'

'Leave a trail of breadcrumbs,' she said, sliding off the desk. 'If you go now you should be there by two o'clock.'

4

Nightingale cursed as he squinted at his phone's GPS display. The autumn sun was glinting off the screen and he couldn't make out which way he was supposed to go. He peered through the windscreen and saw a signpost ahead. He braked. It said, 'Hamdale 5', and pointed to the left.

He slid the phone into his pocket and followed the sign. Hamdale was a tiny village, a cluster of houses around a thatched pub and a row of half a dozen shops. The solicitor's office was wedged between a cake shop and a post office. There were double yellow lines along both sides of the road so Nightingale did a U-turn and left the MGB in the pub's car park.

When he pushed open the door, a bell dinged and a grey-haired secretary looked up from an electric typewriter. She peered at him over gold-framed spectacles. 'Can I help you?' she asked.

'Jack Nightingale.' He looked at the piece of paper Jenny had given him. 'I'm here to see a Mr Turtledove.'

'Ah, he's expecting you,' said the woman. 'I'll tell him you're here. Would you like a cup of tea?'

'I'm fine, thanks.'

She placed both hands on her desk and grunted as she pushed herself up, but a door to the inner office opened and she sank down again into her chair. 'I was just going to show Mr Nightingale in,' she said.

The man who had appeared was in his sixties, almost bald with heavy jowls and watery eyes. He was wearing a heavy tweed suit and leaning on a wooden walking-stick. He was a good head shorter than Nightingale and he smiled, showing yellowing teeth, as he held out his hand. Nightingale shook it gently, afraid he might break the bones, but Turtledove's grip was deceptively strong. 'Come in, please,' he said.

The office was little more than a box with a small window overlooking a back yard. The room was lined from floor to ceiling with legal books and there was a damp, dusty smell that reminded Nightingale of the shed he'd used for a den when he was a kid. There were two chairs in front of the desk, both buried under piles of dusty files, all tied up with red ribbon. 'Please put them on the floor,' said the solicitor, as he limped around his desk and sat down in a high-backed leather chair. He placed his stick against the window-sill behind him, then turned sombrely to Nightingale. 'First let me say how sorry I am for your loss,' he said.

Nightingale moved the files as instructed and sat down. 'My loss?' he said.

'Your father.'

'My father?' Nightingale had no idea what he was talking about. He took out his wallet and gave Turtledove one of his business cards. 'I'm Jack Nightingale. I'm here about a job.'

Turtledove frowned, looked around for his spectacles, then realised they were perched on top of his head. He pushed them down and read the card, then smiled amiably at Nightingale. 'There's no job, Mr Nightingale. I'm sorry about the confusion. I'm the executor of your late father's will.'

Nightingale raised his eyebrows. Now he was even more confused. 'My parents' estate was finalised more than a decade ago.'

Turtledove tutted. He rifled through a stack of files on his desk and pulled one out. 'Your father passed away three weeks ago,' he said.

'My parents died in a car crash a couple of days after my nineteenth birthday,' said Nightingale. It had been a senseless accident. They had stopped at a red traffic-light and a truck had ploughed into the back of them.

The car was crushed and burst into flames and, according to the young constable who had broken the news to Nightingale, they had died instantly. Over the years, he'd grasped that the officer had said that to make the news more bearable. In all probability they had died in the flames, screaming in agony. Policemen had to lie – or at least bend the truth – to make bad news less painful. He knew from experience that people rarely died instantly in accidents. There was, more often than not, a lot of pain and blood and screaming involved.

'Your adoptive parents,' said Turtledove, nodding sagely. 'Bill and Irene Nightingale.'

'I wasn't adopted,' said Nightingale. 'They were my parents – their names are on my birth certificate. And they never said I was adopted.'

'That may well be, but they were not your biological parents.' He opened the file and slid out a sheet of paper, which he passed across the desk. 'These are your details, aren't they? Correct date of birth, national insurance number, schools attended, your university?'

Nightingale scanned the sheet. 'That's me,' he said.

'Then your father was Ainsley Gosling, and it has fallen to me to administer his last will and testament.' He smiled. 'It's just occurred to me that I'm a Turtledove, you're a Nightingale and your father was a Gosling. What a coincidence.'

'Isn't it?' said Nightingale. 'But I've never heard of this Ainsley Gosling. And I'm damn sure I wasn't adopted.'

'You were adopted at birth, which is why I assume your adoptive parents' names went down on the certificate. It would never happen these days, of course.'

'Bollocks,' said Nightingale.

Turtledove's lips tightened. 'There's no need for profanity, Mr Nightingale. I understand that this has come as a shock to you, but I am only the messenger. I was never given to understand you were unaware that Mr Gosling was your biological father.'

'I apologise,' said Nightingale. 'If he's my father, then who is my mother?'

'I'm not privy to that information, I'm afraid.'

Nightingale fished out his packet of Marlboro. 'Can I smoke?'

'I'm afraid not,' said Turtledove. 'It's against the law, you know, to smoke in a place of employment.'

'Yes, I know,' said Nightingale. He put away the cigarettes. 'How did he die, this Gosling?'

'I don't know,' said Turtledove. 'The case came to me from another lawyer, a firm in the City. I was told that Mr Gosling had passed away and that I was to act as executor to the will.'

'That's a bit unusual, isn't it?'

'Very,' said Turtledove. 'I had no dealings with Mr Gosling, and I never met the man. I was merely sent his last will and testament and your details and told to contact you as his sole heir and beneficiary.'

'But usually wouldn't the solicitor who drew up the will also administer it?'

'Of course,' said Turtledove. 'But I suppose my being local meant it would be easier for me to deal with the house. But, as you say, it is unusual.'

'House? What house?'

Turtledove took the will out of the file and gave it to Nightingale. 'There isn't much in the way of money, I'm afraid, but there is a substantial property, a country house, by the name of Gosling Manor. It's about six miles outside Hamdale.' He opened a drawer and gave Nightingale a key-ring with two keys on it. 'I've some paperwork for you to sign and then it's all yours. I've a map here with the house marked on it.'

'Burglar-alarm code?'

The solicitor shook his head. 'I assume there isn't one.'

Nightingale put the key and the map into his coat pocket. 'You said there was cash?'

'A few hundred pounds,' said Turtledove. 'We'll have to get the house valued in case there are inheritance tax issues.'

'You mean I'll have to pay for it?'

'It depends on its value. But once the tax liability has been assessed, yes, you will most certainly have to pay it. Death and taxes are the only two certainties in life, as Mark Twain once said. Or was it Benjamin Franklin?' He put a hand to his forehead. 'My memory just isn't what it was.'

'You don't know what the house is worth?'

The solicitor looked over the rims of his glasses at Nightingale. 'I'm just the middle man, I haven't seen the house. I was just told that it's substantial.'

'Mr Turtledove, this is all very unusual, isn't it?'

'Mr Nightingale,' said the solicitor, 'I've never had a case like it.'

5

Nightingale drove slowly down the narrow country road. The sky had darkened while he had been in the solicitor's office, and it was starting to rain. He switched on the wipers, which swished back and forth leaving greasy streaks on the glass. He glanced down at the map Turtledove had given him. When he looked up he saw a tractor pulling out in front of him and jammed on the brakes. The tyres couldn't grip the wet road and the car slid to the right. Nightingale took his foot off the brake pedal, then pumped it and brought the skid under control, managing to stop just inches from the back of the tractor. The driver was wearing headphones, his head bobbing up and down in time to whatever music he was listening to, totally oblivious to how close he'd come to killing Nightingale. As Nightingale sat with his hands on the steering-wheel, heart pounding, the tractor roared off, leaving a plume of black smoke behind it. His mind hadn't been on the road, he realised. He'd been too busy thinking about his meeting with the solicitor.

It didn't make sense. Nightingale had never suspected that Bill and Irene Nightingale weren't his real parents. Even the phrase 'real parents' sounded wrong. Of course they were his real parents. In every childhood memory he had, they were there – his mum teaching him the alphabet, his father helping him ride his bike for the first time, clapping as he blew out birthday candles, the pride on their faces when he'd told them he'd been accepted by King's College, London. There had been tears in his father's eyes when he'd told Nightingale that he was the first member of the family ever to go to university. Nightingale was sure that if he really had been adopted, his parents would have said something.

Nightingale took deep breaths to steady himself, then put the car into first gear and headed off. To the right there was a field that had been recently ploughed, to the left a six-foot-high stone wall. Ahead, he saw a break in it and a large circular metal mirror attached to a tree. He slowed the car. He saw metal gates and a sign: Gosling Manor. He pulled up alongside the gates and climbed out of the MGB. On the other side of them a narrow paved road curved to the right through thick woodland, mainly deciduous trees that had lost most of their leaves, their bare branches outlined like skeletons against the grey November sky. A thick chain linked the gates, with a brass padlock. Nightingale took out the keys Turtledove had given him. One fitted the padlock. He unravelled the chain, pushed open the gates and got back into his car.

He drove slowly as the road curved to the right, then to the left. When the trees thinned he saw the house and brought the car to a halt. It was a stunning mansion, the sort of grand house you'd see on the cover of *Country Life* magazine or on a box of chocolates you'd give to an elderly relative at Christmas. The main part of the house was built of sandstone with upper façades of weathered bricks. It was two-storeys high, topped with a steepled tiled roof that was almost the same colour as the bricks, and four towering chimney stacks, which gave it the impression of an ocean-going liner. Vibrant green ivy had been trained to climb the walls, reaching from the ground to the roof, the main vines as thick as a man's wrist. The entrance, too, was shrouded in ivy, a massive oak door with ornate black hinges. The window-frames were painted white, and to the left of the main building there was a brick garage with four doors, also painted white, and a matching tiled roof. To the left of the house, a magnificent conservatory and, beyond it, another wing seemed to have been added as an after-thought. The house appeared somehow to have grown out of the ground rather than having being built, as if it had pushed itself out of the earth as a living, breathing entity.

Nightingale drove slowly towards it. The paved road merged into a parking area large enough for several dozen vehicles, now littered with dead leaves, and in the middle stood a massive stone fountain, whose centrepiece was a weathered stone mermaid surrounded by dolphins and fish. There was no water in it. He parked the MGB and climbed out. He looked back down the road that disappeared into the woodland. There was no sign of the main road, no sound other than birdsong and the occasional bark of a far-off dog. He turned back to the house. 'And it's mine, all mine,' he muttered to himself. When Turtledove had given him the keys Nightingale had assumed there had been some mistake, but as he stood looking at the grand house he realised such mistakes didn't happen – people weren't accidentally handed multi-million-pound mansions. Checks would have been carried out, assurances given, and the only way that the house could be his was if Ainsley Gosling really had been his father.

The thought that his parents had lied to him so completely made his head spin. If he really had been adopted, they couldn't have kept the secret to themselves, surely. Other members of the family must have known – babies didn't just appear from nowhere. He took out his mobile phone, scrolled through his address book and called his uncle Tommy. He hadn't spoken to him since the previous Christmas when he'd driven up to Altrincham to spend the day with him and his aunt.

His aunt answered the phone. 'Auntie Linda? It's Jack.'

There was a moment's hesitation as if she wasn't sure who Jack was, then she almost yelped: 'Jack!'

'Hi, how's things?'

'Jack, it's so good to hear from you. Is everything okay?'

'Everything's fine. And Uncle Tommy, how is he?' He looked around as he talked, and frowned when he saw a CCTV camera half hidden in the ivy over the front door.

'He's taken the dog out for a walk. He'll be so sorry that he missed you. How's work? Are you married yet?'

'No, I'm not married yet.' Jack laughed. 'Look, I know this is a strange thing to ask out of the blue, but do you by any chance know if I was adopted?' He spotted another CCTV camera on the side of one of the chimneys, and a third atop the conservatory. There was a long silence and Nightingale thought for a moment he'd lost the connection. 'Aunty Linda, did you hear me?'

'What a question, Jack. We don't hear from you for almost a year and you ask a question like that.'

'I know, I'm sorry, but something very strange has happened. You'd know, wouldn't you? You'd know if I was adopted?'

'Jack, I can't . . .'

'You can't what, Aunty Linda?'

There was another long silence.

'Aunty Linda?'

'Jack, this is really something you'd have to talk to your uncle about.'

'Why can't you tell me?'

'Because Uncle Tommy was your father's brother – he's blood. I'm just Tommy's wife. You have to talk to him.'

'Aunty Linda?'

'I have to go, Jack. I'll get your uncle to call you. Goodbye now.' The line went dead.

Nightingale put away the phone. She'd sounded nervous, scared even, and he'd never known his aunt to be scared of anything before. He stood back and scrutinised the front of the house. He spotted another three CCTV cameras. He took out the keys Turtledove had given him and walked up to the door. There were two locks, which opened with the same key. The door creaked as he pushed it open. He stepped into a hallway with wood-panelled walls and a marble floor, dominated by a massive chandelier hanging from the ceiling. He looked around for a burglar-alarm console but couldn't see one and there was no beeping to suggest that a system was working. There was no furniture and no pictures or mirrors on the wall. The house had been cleared but he had no way of knowing if professional burglars or a removal firm had taken everything away. There was a light switch by the door but nothing happened when Nightingale flicked it. He walked across the hallway, his black leather shoes squeaking on the marble, and tried another switch but that didn't work either.

Three oak doors led off the hallway. Nightingale pushed one open and stepped into a room the size of a basketball court with a vaulted ceiling and a massive white marble fireplace. The room was also devoid of furniture and the carpets had been taken up to reveal oak floorboards. Patches of underlay were stuck to them, like flaking skin, and around the edge, close to the skirting-board, he noted the metal tacks that had been used to keep the carpet in place. Whoever had lifted the carpets had simply ripped them up.

Along one wall a line of windows looked over ornamental gardens with bushes that had been trained into the shapes of exotic animals. Nightingale saw a giraffe, an elephant and a line of horses, and beyond them what looked like a hedge maze. The curtains had been removed but the brass rods from which they had hung were still in place. Nightingale frowned when he saw a small CCTV camera in one corner of the room, aimed at the windows. He could understand the need for security on the exterior of the building but having them inside seemed like overkill.

He saw something on the mantelpiece and walked over to it, the floorboards creaking underfoot. It was an envelope, with his name printed on it in slightly uneven typing. As he reached for it he heard a bang upstairs and flinched. He listened intently but heard nothing. He picked up the envelope. Something shifted inside it. He was about to open it when he heard another noise from the upper floor, this time a scratching sound that lasted a second or two. He put the envelope into his jacket pocket and walked on tiptoe to the door. He listened, but heard nothing.

The staircase that curved upwards was marble and he made no sound as he crept up it. He put his hand on the wooden banister as he craned his neck to look around the curve. The wall to the left was panelled and there were brass picture hooks from which large paintings had once hung.

The stairway opened onto a landing that ran the length of the building. There were small chandeliers hanging every twelve feet or so, miniature replicas of the one in the downstairs hallway. To the left the landing would be above the large room he had been into so that was where he headed, still on tiptoe. There were CCTV cameras at either end and doors to left and right. He eased open the first on the left. The room was empty and, as in the room downstairs, the curtains had been removed. He closed the door quietly and opened the one opposite. That room, too, was empty.

He pulled the door closed and moved silently down the corridor. He listened carefully at the next door before he put his hand on the brass handle and turned it. Inside this room there was furniture: a large four-poster bed and a green leather winged armchair. Dark green curtains were tied back with gold ropes. The bed was made, and didn't appear to have been slept in, and the bathroom was spotless.

He checked another nine bedrooms, all of which were empty, then went back downstairs. There was a large dining room, a study, another reception room, a huge kitchen, from which all the appliances had been removed, and a walk-in larder with bare shelves. Even the conservatory had been stripped. Nightingale looked out across a sweeping lawn to a small lake and a stable beside a large paddock. He shivered. There were cast-iron radiators dotted around the house but the heating system wasn't working.

He tried opening the conservatory door but it was locked and he could see no key for it. He walked slowly back through the kitchen and into the main hallway. He heard a soft scratching upstairs. 'If you want to get out before I lock up, now's the time,' he called. The scratching stopped immediately. 'Stupid cat,' Nightingale muttered, under his breath. He pulled open the front door and gasped when he saw two men standing there. He took a step back as they came towards him.

They were wearing uniforms, he realised, police uniforms, and the older man was a sergeant. The younger of the two grabbed his arm. 'What are you doing here?' he asked. Nightingale was too surprised to speak and he just shook his head. The policeman tightened his grip. 'Right. Come on, in the car.'

'It's my house,' said Nightingale.

The policeman let go of him, He was in his early twenties, skinny, with a rash of acne across his fore-head. 'What's your name?' he asked.

'Jack Nightingale,' he said. 'Look, I used to be in the job, and now I'm a private investigator.'

'Let's see your ID, then.'

Nightingale took out his wallet, showed them his licence and gave them one of his business cards. He patted his chest and sighed. 'You scared the shit out of me,' he said.

'The house has been locked up since old man Gosling died,' said the sergeant. He had grey hair and broken veins across his cheeks. An old scar under his chin looked as if it had been caused by a broken bottle. 'We were told the house was going up for auction.'

'He left it to me,' said Nightingale. 'A solicitor in Hamdale's handling probate or whatever they call it. I'm the sole heir.'

'Are you a relative?'

'Apparently,' said Nightingale. 'If you don't mind me asking, how did you know I was here? The power's off so I assume the alarm's not working.'

'There's no alarm link to our station. Gosling had his own security arrangements. We saw the gate open as we were driving past, that's all. What's the name of the solicitor?'

'Turtledove.' He took the business card out of his wallet and showed it to them. 'You guys local?'

'Depends what you mean,' said the sergeant. 'There used to be a police house in Hamdale but that went in the seventies. The nearest station now is in Hastings.

But we took the call when it happened. Well, I did anyway. Gosling killed himself. Blew his head off with a shotgun in the master bedroom.'

'There's no doubt it was suicide?' asked Nightingale.

'Shotgun was still in his hands. And there was some weird stuff in the room that suggested he was a bit not right in the head, if you get my drift.'

'I don't,' said Nightingale. 'What do you mean?'

'There were lots of candles burning. And he was in some sort of magic circle, one of those star things.'

'There's no sign of it now,' said Nightingale.

'A team of cleaners went in. Crime-scene specialists. They do a good job, those guys. You wouldn't get me doing it for love or money.'

'How did you get in the house?' asked Nightingale. 'Security seems pretty tight.'

'Gosling's driver found the body. He let us in.'

'But there was no note?'

The sergeant shook his head. 'They don't always leave notes.'

'They usually do,' said Nightingale. 'They want to explain themselves, maybe ask for forgiveness.'

'You know a lot about suicides, then?' said the PC.

'I was a negotiator, back in the day,' said Nightingale.

The sergeant frowned. 'Jack Nightingale? Aren't you the guy who killed that paedophile?'

'Allegedly,' said Nightingale. He took out his packet of Marlboro. The PC shook his head as if Nightingale was trying to sell him a wrap of heroin, but the older man took one. Nightingale lit it, and one for himself.

'Mr Nightingale here's a bit of a legend,' said the sergeant. 'Threw a banker out of a window down Canary Wharf.'

'Allegedly,' said Nightingale. He took a long drag on his cigarette and blew smoke into sky.

'The bastard was fiddling with his daughter,' said the sergeant. 'She topped herself, right?'

'Right,' said Nightingale. He shivered and took another drag on his cigarette.

'The bastard got what was coming to him.' The sergeant flicked ash onto the ground.

'Allegedly,' said Nightingale.

'So, are you going to be moving in?' asked the younger man.

Nightingale laughed and looked up at the imposing façade. 'You've got to be joking,' he said. 'I'd rattle around in a place this big.'

'Must be worth a fortune. What do you think, Sarge?'

'Five million, six maybe.'

'Before the property crash.'

'What happened to all the furniture and stuff?' asked Nightingale. 'Who took it away?'

The sergeant shrugged. 'It was gone when we got here. The only room that had furniture was the bedroom where he died.' His radio crackled and he walked away, talking into the microphone.

'You're going to hell, Jack Nightingale,' said the PC, his voice dull and lifeless, almost robotic.

Nightingale turned to him. 'What?' he said.

'I said, are you going to sell up?'

Nightingale wondered if he'd simply misheard.

'You could make even more money dividing it up into flats.'

'I guess so,' said Nightingale. He was sure he hadn't misheard. But the policeman didn't appear to be messing with him: he was smiling good-naturedly, just making conversation with a former cop while he waited for his colleague to finish on the radio. 'I haven't really had time to think about it.'

'Was he a close relative, old man Gosling?' He had an Essex accent, with long vowels and clipped consonants, slightly high-pitched as if his voice hadn't fully broken. It sounded nothing like the one that had told Nightingale he was going to hell.

'Not really,' said Nightingale. 'He was my father. Allegedly.'

The sergeant was on his way back to them. 'Landlord of the Fox and Goose has got a problem with gypsies,' he said. He grinned at Nightingale. 'Not that we can call them gypsies these days. "Citizens of no fixed abode" is probably the politically correct term. Anyway, one's just glassed a waitress so we've got to get over there. Good luck with the house.' He reached into his pocket and gave Nightingale a Neighbourhood Watch card. 'My number's on there. Give me a call if you need anything.'

Nightingale read his name: Sergeant Harry Wilde. 'Thanks,' he said. 'Look, something I don't understand. The house is old, right? More than a hundred years, I'd guess.'

'A lot more,' said the policeman. 'The main part dates back to the sixteenth century but a lot of additions were made during the nineteen thirties. Then the family who sold it to Gosling were into horses so they built the stable and paddocks.'

'So why's it called Gosling Manor? Has it been in the family for generations?'

'Mr Gosling bought it in the eighties, cash on the nail, they say. Used to be called Willborough Manor, after the family who built it. They were the local squires here for a couple of hundred years. Mr Gosling put a few noses out of joint by renaming it and there's a lot of folk around here still call it by its old name. They've got a point. Houses are like boats – you only bring bad luck by renaming them.'

'Yeah, well, it was certainly unlucky for Gosling,' said Nightingale.

Wilde's radio crackled again. 'We've got to go,' said the sergeant. He stuck out his hand and Nightingale shook it. 'What you did back then, fair play to you. It was the right thing.'

Nightingale smiled thinly but he didn't say anything. He had long since given up trying to justify to himself what he'd done that November morning and he'd never tried to justify it to anyone else.

He watched the two policemen walk to their patrol car before he climbed into the MGB. He took the envelope out of his pocket. Inside there was a key and the business card of a safe-deposit company. 'The plot thickens,' he muttered. He looked at the envelope again. Other than his name there was nothing on it, no indication of who had left it for him in the house. He doubted it had been Ainsley Gosling because if it had been there when the police had entered they'd have opened it in case it was a suicide note. That meant someone else had been in the house after the police had taken away the body.

6

The safe-deposit company was in Mayfair and Nightingale travelled there by tube because he figured parking the car would be a nightmare. He went straight from home after phoning Jenny to say that he would be late in. She was full of questions about his visit to the Hamdale solicitor but Nightingale said it would have to wait until he was back in the office.

The company's office was discreet with just a small brass plate on a black door and a single brass bell-push. He pressed it and looked up at a CCTV camera. The door buzzed and Nightingale went in. The reception area was equally discreet, grey walls and carpet, glass and metal furniture, and no inkling of what services were on offer. Nightingale told a receptionist why he was there and two minutes later a female clerk in a grey suit was leading him down a steel staircase to a large room lined with metal doors of varying sizes. The

clerk took Nightingale's key, then used it with a key of
her own to open the two locks on one of the larger
doors. She pulled out a metal box and placed it on a
table, had him sign a form attached to a clipboard, then
went back upstairs. Nightingale wondered what it
contained. The clerk hadn't strained as she'd lifted it
so if there was cash inside there wouldn't be much.
Diamonds would be nice, he decided. Or a few
Krugerrands. Or maybe even an explanation of who
Ainsley Gosling was and why he had given up his son
for adoption and never made any attempt to contact
him until after he'd blown off his head with a shotgun.
He took a deep breath and opened the lid. It was empty.
Nightingale groaned. What was the point of leaving him
the key if there was nothing in the box? Was someone
playing a sick trick on him? He started to close the lid
but stopped. There was something at the bottom of the
box. A brown envelope. He took it out and opened it.
Inside he found a single DVD.

7

Jenny was on the phone when Nightingale opened the office door. 'I'm sure the cheque was sent out on Tuesday and it's only Thursday today so it could still be in the post,' she said, wagging a warning finger at him as he went over to the DVD player. 'He isn't in at the moment, but as soon as he arrives I'll tell him to call you.'

Nightingale slotted in the DVD and turned on the television. 'Remote?' he mouthed at Jenny.

She pointed at his desk. 'Absolutely,' she said, into the phone. 'Goodbye.' She replaced the receiver and wagged the finger at him again. 'You can't mess around with Customs and Excise like this,' she said. 'They send people to jail for not paying their VAT.'

'While they let murderers and rapists roam the streets,' he said, picking up the remote control. 'You should write a letter to the editor of the *Daily Mail*.'

'How did it go yesterday? What's the job?'

'There's no job,' said Nightingale, 'but I do have a house. A bloody big one. And a father I never knew that I had.'

'Jack, what on earth are you talking about?'

'Get me a coffee and I'll tell you,' he said. As Jenny made it, Nightingale filled her in on the events of the past twenty-four hours.

'A mansion?' she said, when he'd finished.

'Right out of *Country Life*,' he told her. 'Land as far as the eye can see, stables, a conservatory, more bedrooms than you can shake a stick at.'

'And it's yours?'

'Seems to be. Unless this is all some *Candid Camera* stunt.'

'And this Gosling was your father?'

'According to the solicitor, yes. My biological father. I was adopted at birth. He killed himself a few weeks ago. I've asked Robbie to get me the case file.'

He pointed the remote at the DVD player and pressed 'play'. 'He left me this, too, in a safe-deposit box.'

The screen flickered into life. A bald, elderly man, his scalp flecked with liver spots and scabs, was frowning and cursing as he adjusted the lens of the camera. Then he went to sit on a bed – it was the one in the master

bedroom at Gosling Manor, Nightingale noticed. Where
Ainsley Gosling had killed himself.

The man was overweight, with heavy jowls and a
swollen belly that strained at the crimson dressing-gown
he was wearing. He adjusted it and Nightingale caught
a glimpse of milky-white skin, blue-veined like ripe
Stilton. There were dark patches under his eyes as if
he hadn't slept in days. He took a deep breath to
compose himself, then forced a smile and began to
speak. 'Hello, Jack,' he said, his voice a deep, wheezy
growl. 'I wish this could have been under more fortu-
itous circumstances but . . .' He shrugged. 'As you will
probably already know I'm Ainsley Gosling, your father.'
He readjusted the dressing-gown. 'Your biological
father, that is.' Gosling sighed. 'I've not been much of
a father, obviously. And there's not much I can do to
rectify that now.' He held up his hands. '*Mea culpa*,
Jack. It's all my fault.'

'What's his fault?' asked Jenny. 'What's he talking
about?'

Nightingale didn't answer but motioned for her to
be quiet as he stared intently at the screen. Gosling was
in his seventies and grossly overweight, but he had
Nightingale's slightly hooked nose and the same frown
lines across his forehead.

Gosling sighed again, then coughed. Nightingale

recognised a smoker's cough and smiled. His adoptive parents had never smoked and they couldn't understand why their son had taken up the habit. Maybe it was in his genes.

'So, to business,' Gosling continued. 'The fact that you're watching this means that I'm dead and that you've been to the house. Nothing that I can say will ever make up for what I've condemned you to.'

'What does he mean, Jack?' said Jenny.

'Sssh,' hissed Nightingale.

'But you must believe me, Jack,' Gosling continued, 'I do regret my actions, and if I could turn back time . . . But even I can't do that. What's done is done.' Gosling took a deep breath, then coughed. The cough turned into a splutter. Belly trembling and shoulders shaking, he fought to control it. 'I'm your father, Jack. Not that my being your father means anything in the traditional sense. I've given you nothing over the last thirty-three years. Not even your name.'

Gosling bent down. When he straightened he was holding a bottle of brandy. He took a swig, then wiped his fleshy mouth with the back of his hand. 'I gave you away when you were a few hours old, Jack, to a man who passed you on to the Nightingales. He knew they were good people and that they were desperate for a baby so they'd take you, no questions asked.' He took another swig, then cleared his throat. 'So, where do I start?' he said, looking at the bottle in his hand as if he was seeing it for the first time. 'At the beginning or at the end? Do I tell you what's happened, or what's going to happen?' He had another slug of brandy, then closed his eyes. He shuddered, opened his eyes again and looked straight into the lens. He took a deep breath and licked his lips.

'Get on with it,' Nightingale muttered.

'On your thirty-third birthday, Jack, a demon from hell is coming to claim your soul.' Gosling closed his eyes, took a deep breath, and sighed. When he opened them, they were burning with a fierce intensity and he began to speak faster. 'I did a deal with a devil thirty-three years ago. Not *the* devil. A devil. One of his minions. A nasty piece of work.'

'This is a joke, right?' said Jenny. 'Somebody's messing with you?'

'The deal was simple enough,' continued Gosling. 'I got power, almost unlimited power – power over women, power to amass money, more money than a man could spend in a dozen lifetimes. The only thing I couldn't get was immortality. That wasn't up for nego-tiation.' He forced a smile, showing uneven teeth. 'Even a newborn's soul wouldn't buy me that.'

'He's insane,' said Jenny. 'Look how his hands are shaking. Look at his eyes. He's mad as a hatter, Jack.'

Nightingale ignored her and blew smoke at the television screen.

'In exchange for your immortal soul, I got the keys to the kingdom here on earth. And now it's time to pay the piper.' He took another swig of brandy and looked at his wristwatch. 'I've tried to put this right, Jack. I've tried to renegotiate, but there's nothing I can do. What's done is done. Your soul and your sister's soul are forfeit.'

Jenny frowned in confusion. 'You don't have a sister,' she said. She turned to him. 'Do you?'

'Not that I know of,' said Nightingale. 'But I'm getting a lot of surprises this week.'

'You said you were an only child.'

'I am.'

'Your sister was born two years after you,' growled Gosling, almost as if he was answering Jenny's question. 'Another child, another deal. Another soul. I tried to trace her but she's vanished.' Gosling tried to smile at the camera but it came across as a snarl – the snarl of an animal that knew it was trapped. 'I just wanted you to know that I'm sorry, Jack. Sorry for what I did, sorry for what happened, and sorry for what's going to happen to you.' Gosling got to his feet unsteadily. His dressing-gown flapped open and he grabbed at it with his free hand as he lurched over to the camera, still clutching the bottle. His swollen belly filled the screen and then it went blank.

'Jack, what the hell is going on?'

Nightingale put his hands behind his neck. 'I have absolutely no idea,' he said. And that was the truth. Jack Nightingale didn't believe he had a soul, and he certainly didn't believe that a soul was something to be bartered or traded like a sack of beans. He reached for his cigarettes.

'You smoke too much,' admonished Jenny.

'Can't argue with you there,' said Nightingale, taking one out and lighting it.

'Your birthday's the week after next, isn't it?' she said.

'Friday the twenty-seventh,' he said. 'What is it today?'

'Thursday the fifth.'

'Three weeks, then. But you don't need to get me anything.'

'I wasn't planning to,' she said. 'What are you going to do?'

'Few beers and a curry,' said Nightingale. 'Same as I do every year. Birthdays are no big deal.'

Jenny jerked her thumb at the DVD player. 'You know what I mean.'

'It's a wind-up, Jenny. Some sort of practical joke.'

'He left you his house. And his money. He made you his sole heir, according to the solicitor.'

'So?'

'So why would he do that unless you were his son?'

'Maybe he is my father, maybe he isn't. I'll talk to Robbie, see if he can run a DNA check for me. But even if he is my biological father . . .' He gestured at the television. '. . . even if what he just said is true, that was nonsense.' He flicked ash into the ashtray. 'Did you hear what he said? He sold my soul for the keys to the kingdom. He was mad, Jenny. Deranged.' He checked his watch. 'Tell you what, can you hold the fort? I'm going to have a chat with Turtledove.'

8

Turtledove was dipping a digestive biscuit into a cup of tea when Nightingale burst into his office. His jaw dropped and a chunk of biscuit fell into his tea.

'Mr Turtledove, I need you tell me what's going on,' said Nightingale.

Turtledove's glasses were perched on top of his head but now they dropped onto his nose. 'Excuse me?' he said.

The secretary appeared at Nightingale's shoulder. 'I'm so sorry, Mr Turtledove, I said you were busy but he barged straight past me.'

'You didn't even get out of your chair,' said Nightingale, without looking at her. He closed the door on her and sat down. 'I don't think you've told me everything, Mr Turtledove.'

'I've told you all I know,' said Turtledove, putting the remains of his biscuit on the saucer.

'Just who was Ainsley Gosling?'

'I told you yesterday. He was your genetic father.'

'What did he do for a living? How did he make his money? How could he afford that house? Have you seen it? It's a mansion, Mr Turtledove, a huge mansion.'

'I never met Mr Gosling and I never visited the house,' said the solicitor. 'I've told you that already.'

Nightingale took out his cigarettes. Turtledove opened his mouth to protest but closed it when Nightingale glared at him. He lit one and blew smoke, trying to calm himself.

'I understand how stressful it must be, losing your father,' began Turtledove, but Nightingale cut him short with a wave of his hand.

'Please don't try to empathise with me,' said Nightingale. 'I've been trained to empathise and I can spot a fake a mile off. Now, you said you never met Gosling. How can that be if you're the executor of his will?'

'I didn't draw up the will. It was delivered to me by courier,' said the solicitor. 'After he died.'

'So you didn't witness the signature?'

'Mr Nightingale, how many times do you want me to repeat myself? I never went to the house, and I never met Mr Gosling. I was simply asked to execute the will.'

'So you have no idea if the will is genuine or not?'

'I assume the firm that drew it up made all the necessary checks,' said Turtledove. 'My understanding is that he was a client of theirs for many years.'

Nightingale flicked ash onto the floor. 'Who was he? What did Gosling do for a living?'

'I have absolutely no idea,' said the solicitor. 'Obviously, being local, I'd heard of him, but I gather he kept himself to himself. He was a very private man.'

'He died three weeks ago,' said Nightingale. 'Why did it take you so long to contact me?'

'I was only sent the file on Monday. On Wednesday I called your office.'

'Did you know that he committed suicide?'

Turtledove's jaw dropped.

'I assume from the look on your face that you didn't,' said Nightingale.

'Good Lord, what happened?'

'He blew his head off with a shotgun,' said Nightingale. 'I don't suppose he left a note with you, did he, anything that you were supposed to give me?'

'There was nothing,' said the solicitor. 'He killed himself, you say? That's terrible. That's simply terrible.'

'And you never went to Gosling Manor?'

'Never.'

'And so you didn't leave an envelope on the mantel-piece?'

The solicitor frowned. 'I'm sorry, I don't understand.'

Nightingale waved his cigarette dismissively. 'It doesn't matter,' he said. 'You're being paid for your work, I assume. You're not doing this out of the good-ness of your heart.'

'Of course I'm being paid,' said Turtledove.

'By whom? Specifically,' said Nightingale. 'I want a name.'

Turtledove flicked through a case containing busi-ness cards. He took one out, squinted at it and handed it to Nightingale. 'This is the gentleman who handled your father's finances. He's the manager of a bank in Brighton.'

'But you haven't met him?'

'No. He sent me a retainer and a promise to pay my bill in full once the will had been executed.'

'Why are you being paid by a bank in Brighton and not by the lawyer who sent you the file?'

Turtledove looked pained. 'I'm afraid I can't answer that, Mr Nightingale. As I keep telling you, everything about this matter has been irregular and, frankly, I'm starting to wish that I'd never heard of Ainsley Gosling.'

'You and me both, Mr Turtledove,' said Nightingale.

9

The bank manager was a middle-aged man in a dark blue pinstriped suit. His office was a windowless cube in a featureless block a stone's throw from the Brighton seafront. 'My name's Mr Collinson,' he said. 'I'm the manager here, but I'm not sure how I can help you.'

Nightingale never trusted men who introduced themselves as 'Mr'. It suggested that they wanted to impose their authority on you from the start. There was a brass nameplate on the desk that announced his full name – Phillip Collinson – but even that was preceded by 'Mr'. Collinson waved him to a small, uncomfortable plastic chair with metal legs while he himself took the massive leather executive model, with large arms and a high back, the type favoured by shaven-headed villains in James Bond films.

The bank manager was balding but had artfully

combed his hair across the top of his head and used gel to keep it in place. He leaned back and pursed his thin lips as he scrutinised Nightingale's business card. 'Mr Nightingale, if you are Ainsley Gosling's son, why the different surname?'

'I was adopted, apparently,' said Nightingale. 'But surely you know that. Didn't you instruct Turtledove?'

'I didn't actually instruct him,' said Collinson, placing the card on his desk and steepling his fingers under his chin. 'The instructions regarding the execution of the will came from a law firm in the City. I'll be paying Mr Turtledove for his work, but that's the end of my involvement.'

'But you met Mr Gosling?'

'Of course, several times. He was a valued customer.'

'Did he come here or did you go out to Gosling Manor?'

'We went to his house,' said Collinson. 'Mr Gosling was reluctant to travel so either I or the deputy manager would go to see him.'

'Do you do that for all of your customers?' asked Nightingale. 'My bank manager won't even see me to talk about my overdraft.'

Collinson smiled without warmth. 'As I said, Mr Gosling was a valued customer.'

'Rich, you mean?'

'Rich is relative,' said Collinson. 'But let's just say it was worth our while to keep him happy. But I don't understand why you're here now, Mr Nightingale. Mr Turtledove will be handling the will and the distribution of assets. It's nothing to do with the bank.'

'Did he ever mention me?'

'No, he didn't.'

'He didn't mention that he had a son?'

'Never.'

'You said he was a valued customer,' said Nightingale. 'Exactly how much was he worth?'

Collinson sat back in his executive chair and patted his hair, as if he was checking that the comb-over was still in place. 'That's confidential, I'm afraid. I can't reveal details of a client's account.'

Nightingale reached into his jacket pocket, took out a photocopy of Ainsley Gosling's will and gave it to him. 'I'm his sole beneficiary, so anything he has will come to me.'

Collinson licked his upper lip as he studied the document. Then he put it on the desk and leaned back in his chair again. 'To be honest, Mr Nightingale, I don't think there will be much coming your way. During the last years of his life, Mr Gosling spent most of his funds.'

'On what?'

Collinson chuckled. 'We don't ask our customers what they spend their money on,' he said.

'The house is worth a lot.'

'It's heavily mortgaged,' said the bank manager.

'But you said Gosling was rich.'

'That's what you inferred, Mr Nightingale,' said Collinson.

'All right, a valued customer, you said. But you're saying he died penniless?'

'Not penniless, no,' said Collinson. 'But last year he took out a large mortgage on the house and during the two years prior to that he withdrew the bulk of the funds he was holding with us. The credit crunch didn't help, of course – the house fell in value, as did his stock portfolio.'

'There was no furniture in the house, did you know that?'

'It was fully furnished the last time I visited. Beautiful things, mostly antiques. And a very valuable collection of paintings.'

'Well, it's all gone now,' said Nightingale. 'How much money did he have with you before he started withdrawing it?'

'I wouldn't be able to get the figure without looking at his file,' said the bank manager. 'I'm not sure I can do that, even with you being his heir.'

'Approximately,' said Nightingale. 'A ballpark figure.'

'Ballpark?' Collinson stared up at the ceiling as if the numbers were written there. 'I'd say twelve million pounds in cash. A million or so in Krugerrands and gold bullion. A stock portfolio amounting to some fifteen million pounds, give or take.' He looked back at Nightingale. 'I'd say somewhere in the region of twenty-eight million pounds.'

'And the mortgage?'

'Two million,' said Collinson.

'So you're saying that in just a few years Ainsley Gosling went through thirty million pounds and you've no idea what he spent it on?'

'More than that, I'm afraid,' said the bank manager. 'We only handled his UK assets. My understanding is that there were funds in the United States, Central Europe and Asia, notably Hong Kong and Singapore.'

'Amounting to how much exactly?'

Collinson shrugged. 'I don't have exact figures for his overseas assets, but it would certainly be in excess of one hundred million pounds.'

Nightingale sat stunned. 'A hundred million?'

'In excess of.'

'And it's all gone?'

'I'm afraid so, yes.'

'There's no suggestion that he was being blackmailed or had a drug or gambling problem?'

'We don't make a habit of prying into the private lives of our clients, Mr Nightingale,' said Collinson, disdainfully, as if Nightingale had just accused him of shop-lifting.

'Just so long as you have their money?'

'Exactly,' said the bank manager, missing the sarcasm.

Nightingale wanted a drink and time to think. He drove back to London, left the MGB in the multi-storey car park close to his office, then slipped into one of his favourite local pubs. It was a gloomy place that had yet to be given a corporate makeover – no fruit machine, no olde-worlde menu with microwaved lamb shanks and chilli con carne, just a long bar and a few tables and a grizzled old barman who didn't look at him or try to start a conversation. As he walked to the bar he called Jenny on his mobile. 'I'm in the Nag's Head,' he said. 'I need some thinking time.'

'Yeah, alcohol is renowned for helping the thought process,' she said acidly.

'Come and join me.'

'I'm trying to sort out our accounts due,' said Jenny. 'If we don't get the cash-flow sorted we won't be able to pay our VAT.'

'Now you're making me feel guilty,' said Nightingale.

'I doubt that,' she said. 'Keep your mobile on. If anything crops up I'll give you a call.'

Nightingale ordered a bottle of Corona and sat at the bar. If what Gosling had said was true, his parents had lied to him virtually from the day he was born. There had never been so much as a hint from them that he wasn't their child. Two boys in his class at primary school had been adopted, and he had talked to his mother about it, but she had never given any indication that she wasn't his biological mother. Nightingale couldn't understand why they hadn't told him he was adopted. There was no shame in it, and he wouldn't have loved them any the less, but now the truth had come out and he wasn't able to ask them why they had lied because they were dead and gone. Or was it all a massive confidence trick? Was Turtledove part of it? Was the idea to convince Nightingale that the house was his, then ask him to put money up front? He smiled to himself. If it was a con, it would be a waste of time because Nightingale had little in the way of cash to be parted from.

He sipped his Corona. He was drinking it from the bottle with a slice of lime shoved down the neck. Someone had told him once that the lime was there to keep away the flies, but Nightingale liked the bite it gave the beer.

A hand fell on his shoulder and he jumped. Beer sloshed over his hand and he cursed. He turned to see Robbie Hoyle grinning at him. 'Bloody hell, Robbie, do you have to creep up on me like that?'

Hoyle slid onto the stool next to him. 'Jumpy,' he said.

'I'm not jumpy. I just don't like being crept up on that's all. How did you know I was here?'

'The lovely Jenny said you were drowning your sorrows.' He took a manila envelope from his inside pocket and waved it in front of Nightingale's face. 'I was going to drop off the stuff you wanted but then I figured I could do with a drink myself. I didn't realise you were so skittish.'

'What do you want, Robbie?' asked Nightingale.

'A Porsche, a villa in Málaga, a mistress with huge tits and a dad who owns a brewery, all the normal sort of crap.'

'To drink, you soft bastard. What do you want to drink?'

Hoyle nodded at the barman. 'I'll have a red wine, preferably from a bottle with a cork.' He slid the envelope across the bar to Nightingale. 'Here's the info about the Gosling suicide,' he said. 'It was a strange one and no mistake. You were right about the magic circle. It's called a pentagram and it's supposed to offer you protection against things that go bump in the night.

That's what the report says, anyway. They ran it by an occult expert. Apparently quite a few people who dabble in the occult end up topping themselves.'

Nightingale opened the envelope and slid out four large photographs. It was the bedroom in Gosling Manor, but not as he'd seen it when he went to the house. The bed was there, and the chair, but sprawled between the two was the bloated body of the man in the DVD, his head a bloody mess, a shotgun across his legs. The bed, the chair and the body were surrounded by a five-pointed white star that had been drawn on the floor, and at the points of the star there were large church candles. Wax had dripped down them and solidified in pools around their brass holders. Inside the pentagram, brass bowls contained what looked like ashes.

One photograph was of the wall near the window, showing a spray of blood. There was dried blood on the windows, too, and on the ceiling. A lot of it.

'None of that spooky stuff is there now, I take it?' said Hoyle.

'The cops said a crime-scene clean-up crew had been in,' said Nightingale, 'and they'd done a hell of a job. I didn't see any blood spatter or anything.'

'So what's the story, morning glory?'

'You won't believe it,' said Nightingale. 'I'm not sure I believe it myself.'

The barman gave Hoyle a glass of red wine. He sniffed it and nodded his thanks. 'So tell me.'

Nightingale told him about the meeting with Turtledove, about Gosling Manor, the safe-deposit box and the DVD. 'What I can't work out is why my parents lied,' he said. 'Why didn't they just tell me?'

'If you were adopted at birth, and your biological parents didn't want to see you again, then what would be the point?'

Nightingale frowned at his friend. 'What?'

'If your real parents, your biological parents, weren't going to see you, there'd be no point in telling you.'

'Bollocks,' said Nightingale. 'There's all sorts of reasons you need to know you're adopted.'

'For instance?'

Nightingale shrugged. 'I don't know. Blood groups, maybe. Inherited disorders. I don't have DNA, Robbie. I deserved to know that.' He sipped his beer. 'He was bald.'

'Who was bald?'

'Gosling. My biological father. Bald as a coot. My dad – the man that I thought was my dad – had a great head of hair. I always thought I'd inherited my hair from him but now I find out that my dad was bald.'

Hoyle laughed. 'Is that what's got you all riled up? The fact that you might be bald one day?'

'It's not about baldness, it's about me not being who I thought I was. Robbie, my biological father made a DVD saying he'd sold my soul to the devil and then he blew his head off with a shotgun, which suggests, if nothing else, that he might have had a few sanity issues. What if I take after him? Nature and nurture, right? We're a combination of our genes and our environment, and now I've found out that my genes have come from a nutter.'

'A bald nutter, to boot.'

'Exactly,' said Nightingale.

Hoyle sipped his wine. 'It's a joke, right? Some sort of sick practical joke?'

'I'm just telling you what happened,' said Nightingale.

'I mean this Gosling character, he's just playing with you.'

'But he killed himself, Robbie. Blew his head off with a shotgun. Bit extreme for a jape, don't you think?' He pulled out some photocopied sheets from the envelope: the police report and a copy of the conclusions of the inquest that had been held a week after the death. The verdict was suicide. 'Just a thought, there's no doubt that it was Gosling who died, is there? Shotgun blasts don't leave much to identify.'

'It's all in there,' said Hoyle. 'His fingerprints matched

the ones in the house. Nothing useful dental-wise so they did a DNA match. It's definitely him.'

'Can you do me a favour?'

'Within limits,' said Hoyle, cautiously.

'I want to know if I really am his son. Can you check my DNA against his?'

'Shouldn't be a problem,' said Hoyle. 'Do you want to give me a sample now?'

Nightingale took a small plastic bag from his jacket. Inside were half a dozen hairs that he'd plucked from his scalp, the roots intact.

Hoyle took it. 'I was hoping for blood.' He slid it into his jacket pocket. 'It might take a day or two,' he said. 'I'll have to wait until there's a friendly face in the lab.'

'I can't believe the way my parents lied to me,' said Nightingale. 'And my uncle and aunt. My aunt and uncle must have known too.'

'Have you spoken to them?'

'My aunt was all jittery, and my uncle's going to call me back.'

'What about other family?'

'That's it, pretty much. Mum was an only child, all my grandparents died years ago, and Uncle Tommy and Auntie Linda never had kids. She has a few rela- tives but I hardly know them.' He looked up from the papers he was reading. 'What happened to the body?'

'Cremated.' Hoyle rubbed his finger around the rim of his wine glass. 'You're not taking this selling-your-soul-to-the-devil thing seriously, are you? People don't sell their souls to the devil.'

'He didn't say he sold his soul. He said he sold my soul. And my sister's.'

'You don't have a sister, Jack. You were an only child, remember? Which, incidentally, explains a lot.'

'What?'

'Only kids tend to be self-centred, used to getting their own way, have difficulty in forming lasting friendships.'

'Screw you.'

'See? That proves my point. Now me, one of four kids, you couldn't wish for a more sociable fellow.'

'I say again, screw you. And the rest of the Waltons.'

'Easy enough to check if you had a sister,' said Hoyle. 'There'd be a birth certificate.'

'Gosling's not down on mine,' said Nightingale. 'Just my mum and dad. If Gosling did have a daughter, she'd be almost impossible to trace.'

'It's bollocks, the whole thing.'

'Yeah, maybe,' said Nightingale. He drained his bottle of Corona.

'You know it's bollocks, right?' said Hoyle. 'There's no such thing as the devil.'

'Not *the* devil, *a* devil. He was very clear on that.'

'So now you believe in devils?'

'I'm not saying that. If there was a devil there'd be a God, and I've seen nothing over the past thirty-two years that's convinced me there is. No God, no devil, end of story.'

'There you go, then. It's bollocks.'

'He's left me a huge bloody house in the sticks, Robbie. A mansion.'

'So you're going up in the world.'

'Why would he do that if I wasn't his flesh and blood? It's one hell of an expensive joke, don't you think?'

'Okay, show it to me.'

'What?'

'The house. Spooky Towers.'

'At night?'

'You *are* jumpy.' Hoyle grinned and finished his wine.

'The power's off. Gosling stopped paying his bills a month before he died.'

'I've got torches in the car. You scared?'

'Don't be stupid. And it's not in the least bit spooky. It's bloody gorgeous in fact.'

'I double dare you,' said Hoyle, grinning. He waggled his fingers and made a ghostly wailing sound.

'Screw you,' said Nightingale again.

11

It was just before nine o'clock when they pulled up outside Gosling Manor in Hoyle's Ford Mondeo. Hoyle climbed out of the car. 'Bloody hell, Jack, it's huge. It's got to be worth millions.'

'It would have been worth a lot more before the property crash,' said Nightingale. 'And it's mortgaged to the hilt, apparently.'

'How many bedrooms?'

'A lot.'

'And four garages. How cool is that?' Hoyle walked around to the boot of the car, his feet squelching on dead leaves. He opened it, took out two torches and tossed one to Nightingale. 'Come on, give me the tour, then.'

Nightingale took out his key and opened the front door. 'Wipe your feet,' he said.

'You sound just like my wife,' said Hoyle.

'I just don't want you walking dead leaves around my house,' said Nightingale.

'Now you definitely sound like her.' Hoyle laughed and wiped his feet on the large mat in front of the door. 'Happy now?'

They walked inside, playing their beams around the hallway. Nightingale led the way to the huge drawing room and pointed his at the massive fireplace. 'That's where the envelope was,' he said. 'It wasn't there when the cops came so someone else must have a key.'

'Where's all the furniture?' asked Hoyle.

'He must have sold it,' said Nightingale. 'I'm guessing he sold everything before he died, except the furniture in the bedroom.'

'You could have some great parties in here.'

'You could have a half-decent game of five-a-side football,' said Nightingale.

Something scraped across the floor upstairs and both men jumped. 'What the hell was that?' said Hoyle.

'Probably a cat,' said Nightingale. 'There was a cat upstairs last time I was here.'

'Didn't sound like a cat,' said Hoyle.

'Do you want to leave?'

'Hell, no, we're here now,' said Hoyle. 'Show me where he topped himself.'

Nightingale led him back into the hallway and up the staircase. 'What are you going to do with the place?' asked Hoyle.

'Sell it, I guess,' said Nightingale. 'Pay off the mortgage, see what's left. Why – do you want to make me an offer?'

'You could think about developing it,' said Hoyle. 'Turn it into flats. There's a big market for these old buildings when they're done right.'

'It'd be sacrilege to split it into flats, a beautiful house like this,' said Nightingale. 'I don't know how easy it'll be to find a buyer, though.'

'The rich are always rich,' said Hoyle. 'Recession or boom, they always have money. Sell it to a Russian oligarch or a Saudi prince and let them enjoy it.'

'I was thinking, back in the bar, it might be a con.'

'A con?'

'They're setting me up for something. Telling me the house is mine, then hitting me for money somehow.'

'Have you got any money?'

Nightingale laughed. 'No,' he said. 'But maybe they don't know that. Can you do me a favour and check out the solicitor for me? His name's Ernest Turtledove. He's based in a village called Hamdale.'

Something screamed out in the fields and both men stopped dead. 'Fox?' said Hoyle, hopefully.

'I hope so,' said Nightingale. He shone his torch along the landing. 'This way.' He headed down the corridor towards the master bedroom.

Hoyle ran his beam along the ceiling, the light making

the miniature chandeliers sparkle. He stopped when he saw the CCTV camera. 'Smile,' he said. 'We're on *Candid Camera*.'

'They're all over the place,' said Nightingale, 'but no alarms from what I can see. Just the cameras.'

'Which means what, do you think?'

The two men paused, their torches pointing at the camera.

'Which means he wasn't worried about burglars. It was more about watching the house, inside and out.'

'Maybe not,' said Hoyle. 'If you've got comprehensive CCTV coverage, you don't need an alarm. Any burglar worth his salt would know he'd be filmed and give the place a wide berth.'

'Unless they wore masks,' said Nightingale. 'You're missing the point, Robbie. He was scared of someone, but it wasn't burglars. And whoever he was scared of wouldn't be put off by an alarm.'

Hoyle walked down the corridor to take a closer look at the camera. 'It's not working,' he said.

'Why would it be?' said Nightingale. 'The power's off.' He went to stand next to Hoyle. There was a small red light on the side of the unit but it wasn't glowing.

Hoyle ran his torch along the ceiling and down the wall. 'I don't see any wiring,' he said. 'Could be a wireless system. I wonder where the monitors are?'

'I didn't see any downstairs, and there was nothing in the bedroom.'

'Must be somewhere,' said Hoyle. 'They wouldn't take them away and leave the cameras behind.'

Nightingale walked back to the master bedroom and opened the door. 'This is where he killed himself.'

Hoyle flashed his torch across the ceiling. 'Two CCTV cameras in here,' he said. He went into the bedroom, his torch lighting the walls and ceiling. 'They've done a hell of a job cleaning this up, haven't they?'

'It was a professional clean-up crew,' said Nightingale, following him into the room.

'If ever I kill anyone, I'll use them to clean up afterwards,' said Hoyle. 'They've got rid of all the splatter. And there's no staining on the floor at all.' He frowned. 'What about the pentagram?'

'I guess that was chalk and they just rubbed it off,' he said. 'I think this is where he lived, during his last few days. There was no furniture anywhere else in the house. This was the nerve centre, I guess.'

'So, why no monitors?' said Hoyle. 'If he was holed up here, he'd need the monitors close by. Otherwise they'd be useless.'

'What are you thinking, Robbie? He was here under siege, waiting for somebody?'

Hoyle grinned. 'Somebody,' he said. 'Or something.'

He made a ghostly face, waggled his hands in the air and moaned.

'A man died here, Robbie, let's not forget that.'

'He killed himself,' said Hoyle, suddenly serious. 'And anyone who does that loses any sympathy I might have had. Killing yourself is the coward's way out, Jack, because it leaves the living to clear up the mess you've made.'

'You don't know the facts,' said Nightingale.

'I know that he's dumped a whole load of grief on you,' said Hoyle. 'He claimed to be your father but didn't have the decency to tell you face to face. He could at least have had a sit-down with you, answered any questions that you had and then gone ahead and done the dirty deed.'

'Yeah, maybe.'

'There's no maybe about it,' said Hoyle. 'Only cowards commit suicide.'

'Sometimes it takes guts,' said Nightingale, quietly. 'Sometimes it's the only way out.'

'Well, there's no way I'd top myself and leave my girls wondering why,' said Hoyle.

'He did explain,' said Nightingale. 'That's what the DVD was for.'

'You're not buying this, are you?' said Hoyle, scornfully. 'You don't really think that on your birthday a devil's going to come and take your soul?'

Nightingale scowled. 'Of course not.'

'There you are, then. The DVD's a load of crap. He was a nutter and, genetic father or not, he's just trying to screw with your mind from beyond the grave.'

'Because?'

'He was a nutter, Jack. There's no "because" with a nutter.' He nodded at the door. 'Come on, let's have a look downstairs.'

Nightingale followed Hoyle down the staircase. Hoyle ran his hands over the panelled wall. 'This is quality workmanship,' he said. 'No Polish builders here – it's the real thing. The wood alone's worth thousands. How old do you think it is?'

'The cops said sixteenth century,' said Nightingale. 'It was called something else then, named after the local squires.'

'Hey, do you think owning this makes you the new squire? Maybe you'll get to deflower the local virgins. Any idea how much land goes with it?'

'I didn't ask,' said Nightingale.

'Could turn it into a golf course, maybe,' said Hoyle. 'This would make a great clubhouse.'

They went into the kitchen. Hoyle opened a door to find a pantry lined with empty shelves while Nightingale opened another to reveal a tiled room that had been plumbed for a washing-machine but, like the rest, had been stripped bare. Beyond the pantry there were three small rooms. There were marks on the walls where posters and pictures had once been fixed, and Nightingale decided they had been staff quarters. A door led to the back garden. There were three locks, two bolts and a CCTV camera aimed at it. 'That one's not wireless,' said Hoyle, aiming his torch at the camera. 'See the wire there?'

Nightingale squinted up at it. A black wire at the rear of the camera unit burrowed into the plaster. 'Which means what?' he asked.

'Which means that the monitors are somewhere downstairs, probably,' said Hoyle. 'Have you checked all the rooms?'

'Not yet,' said Nightingale.

'Let's have a look-see,' said Hoyle. They went back to the drawing room, then along a corridor to a large room lined with teak bookshelves and cabinets. 'The library?' said Hoyle.

'Looks like it,' said Nightingale.

Beyond it there was another drawing room with a huge fireplace and then a smaller room that must have once contained a snooker table because the wooden scoreboard was still on one wall and a rectangular light fitting hung from the centre of the ceiling. There was a CCTV camera over the door.

Hoyle went back into the corridor. 'The house is

old, so the cameras must have gone in after the panelling, right?'

'Obviously,' said Nightingale.

Hoyle turned his torch on him, and he held up a hand to shield his eyes. 'So they couldn't have pulled the panelling away without damaging the wood, could they?' He ran his torch along the pristine walnut panels. 'This is all quality joinery,' he said. 'You can't just pull them off and stick them back.'

'So?'

'So I don't think they can have run the wires from the downstairs cameras along the hallway. They couldn't have done it without damaging the panelling.'

Nightingale frowned. 'Okay. So, wireless upstairs and wired down here. But the wires don't run along the corridor.' Realisation dawned. 'There's a basement,' he said.

'Exactly,' said Hoyle. 'They ran the wiring straight down.'

They went back to the main hallway. 'If there were stairs to the basement, wouldn't they be here?' asked Nightingale.

Hoyle walked along the panelling, tapping it every few feet. Each tap produced the same dull thud.

'Are you looking for a secret panel?' asked Nightingale.

'Have you got any better ideas?' Hoyle carried on tapping.

'Why would he need to hide the entrance to his own basement?'

'Who knows what was going through his head? We've already decided he was a nutter, right?' He carried on tapping the panelling.

'We don't even know if there is a basement,' said Nightingale.

'Old place like this is bound to have one,' said Hoyle. 'They used to build their foundations really deep.' He moved along the hallway and tapped again. This time the sound was hollow. Hoyle grinned and tapped again. There was definitely a different timbre, almost an echo.

'You've got to be kidding me,' said Nightingale. He tapped the wall near him. A dull thud. Hoyle tapped. The hollow echo.

Hoyle ran the tips of his fingers around the panelling, then pushed. Nothing moved.

'Try pulling,' said Nightingale.

Hoyle did so. There was a click and a section of the wall swung open. 'Open, Sesame,' he whispered. He grinned at Nightingale in triumph. 'What would you do without me, Jack?'

12

Nightingale followed Hoyle down to the basement. The stairs were wooden and there was a brass banister on the left. He kept his hand on it and felt for each stair with his foot before trusting his weight on it. Their torches picked out books, shelves and shelves of them, mostly leather-bound.

'Why did he put his library here?' said Nightingale.

'Because he was a nutter,' said Hoyle. 'Nutters do nutty things.'

They stopped halfway down and shone their torches around. The basement appeared to run the full length of one wing of the house. The bookshelves continued and, running down the centre of the space, there were two lines of display cabinets. There was a sitting area with two large red leather chesterfields and a coffee-table piled with more books. A huge desk was covered with newspapers. There was an antique globe that was almost four feet high and a vast oak table with more than a dozen candles on it. Molten wax had dripped down it and pooled on the floor.

'This is just weird,' said Nightingale.

'It looks like he spent a lot of time down here,' said Hoyle. 'Come on, let's have a look around.'

Hoyle headed down the stairs. Nightingale wrinkled his nose. There was a musty smell in the air that left a nasty taste in his mouth. It wasn't just the smell of old books or soot from the candles, it was bitter and acrid. When he swallowed, his stomach lurched and he had to fight to stop himself throwing up.

Hoyle reached the bottom and walked between the two rows of cabinets. 'Jack, you've got to see this,' he called.

Nightingale joined him beside a glass-sided cabinet, whose shelves were filled with human skulls of different sizes, some so small they could have come only from infants, others adult-sized, yellowed with age, the teeth stained brown and ground down from years of wear and tear.

'How sick is this?' said Hoyle. 'He collected skulls.'

Nightingale bent down to peer at them. Most of the skulls had small irregular holes in the back as if they had been pierced with a chisel or smashed with a hammer. 'They didn't die of natural causes,' he said.

'Could have been done post-mortem,' said Hoyle.

'I hope so,' said Nightingale.

They walked along to the next cabinet. It was filled with knives – knives with curved blades, knives with handles carved in the form of exotic creatures, knives with twin blades, knives made of wood, ivory, every sort of metal. Some had what appeared to be dried blood on their blades, others were chipped and scratched. A few were decorated with strange writing. 'Most of these are illegal, antiques or not,' said Nightingale.

Hoyle went to the next cabinet, which held crystal balls. He shone his torch over them and the light refracted into a dozen rainbows. Nightingale moved to the wall and ran his light across some books. Only a few had titles on their spines. He pulled one out at random. A title was etched into the front cover: *Sacrifice and Self-Mutilation*. He opened it. It had been printed in 1816 in Edinburgh. He flicked through. There were illustration plates that made his stomach turn – black-and-white drawings of people being tortured and butchered. He put the book back and took out the one next to it. It was in Spanish, and bound in what looked like lizard skin. He couldn't make sense of what it was about but the illustrations inside were of strange and mythical creatures, winged dragons and twin-headed snakes. He pulled out a few more volumes. All were old, their pages well thumbed and creased, and many bore handwritten notes in the margins. Most were concerned with witchcraft or black magic.

Nightingale flinched as something crashed behind him. He whirled around, dropping the book he'd been holding. Hoyle was gazing down at dozens of glass fragments. 'Bloody hell, Robbie, what are you playing at?' Hoyle didn't reply. Nightingale picked up the book and put it back on the shelf. 'What happened?' he asked.

'It was one of the crystal balls,' said Hoyle. 'I dropped it.'

'I can see that,' said Nightingale. He picked up one of the smaller balls and weighed it in the palm of his hand. 'But these are solid crystal,' he said. 'They shouldn't shatter.'

'That one was different,' he said. 'It was full of smoke or mist, like it was moving all the time.'

'Are you okay?'

'I saw something,' said Hoyle, quietly, 'in the mist.'

'What? What did you see?'

Hoyle prodded one of the curved splinters with his shoe.

'Robbie, what did you see?'

'It's stupid. Nothing.'

'Robbie?'

Hoyle swallowed. 'I saw myself.'

'Your reflection?'

'No, like I was inside the glass. In the mist. I was standing in the middle of a road . . .'

'Come on, Robbie, you're winding me up.'

Hoyle shook his head. 'I was standing in the middle of the road and a taxi hit me. A black cab.'

'Robbie . . .'

Hoyle looked at him. 'I'm serious, Jack. The cab went right over me.'

'It's dark down here, Robbie. You were shining the torch on it – the light must have played tricks on you.'

'I know what I saw,' said Hoyle.

'Crystal balls are mumbo-jumbo nonsense,' said Nightingale. He stared at the one he was holding. 'Show me the future, O Magic Ball,' he moaned. 'Tell me what lies ahead.' He ran his torch across the ball and the light fractured into a rainbow. 'Nothing,' he said. 'Maybe I should try another channel.' He grinned at Hoyle. 'Do you think I could get Sky Sports on this?' Hoyle tried to smile, but Nightingale could see that his friend was unsettled. He put the crystal ball back into the display case. 'How many books do you think there are? Thousands? Tens of thousands?'

'A lot,' said Hoyle.

'He can't have read them all, surely.'

'Maybe he was a speed reader,' said Hoyle. 'Maybe they're investments. Maybe he bought them by the yard and never read them.'

They walked along the display cases. 'He was a collector, that's for sure,' said Nightingale. There was a case of what appeared to be shrunken heads, leathery fist-sized lumps with straggly hair and pig-like noses. In the next they found chunks of rock, which Nightingale realised were fossils. He peered closer. They looked like birds but had long claws and teeth.

'Vampire bats?' asked Hoyle, only half joking.

'I don't know what the hell they are,' said Nightingale. 'They're fossils so they've got to be old. But I don't think birds ever had teeth, did they?'

'They look more like lizards than birds,' said Hoyle. He played the beam of his torch down the basement to the end furthest from the stairs. 'That looks like the security system,' he said. There were half a dozen LCD screens on the wall in two banks of three.

The two men walked through the display cases towards them. As they got closer they saw a black wooden desk with a straight-backed chair and a large stainless-steel console dotted with labelled buttons. Nightingale ran his finger along it. 'This picks up the feeds from the CCTV cameras,' he said. 'Look at this. There's – what? Twenty-four cameras?'

'Twenty-eight,' said Hoyle. 'Overkill, wouldn't you say?'

'He'd sit down here watching the screens. But watching for what?'

'Scared that someone would rip off his collection?'

'I don't think he was scared,' said Nightingale. 'I think he just wanted to know what was going on in the house. He couldn't have been alone. He'd have needed a staff – cleaners, gardeners, a driver, an estate manager. Maybe he didn't trust them. Maybe he didn't trust anybody.'

'But when he died, he was alone in the house,' said Hoyle. 'That's what it said in the file.'

'He must have let the staff go,' said Nightingale.

Hoyle waved a hand at the rows of display cases behind them. 'And what is this place? What was Gosling doing down here? It's not a display or an exhibition. He kept it all hidden away.'

'You know what it is,' said Nightingale. 'It's Witchcraft R Us, that's what it is. A shrine to black magic. Ainsley Gosling was a Satanist and this was where he plied his trade.'

'There's no such thing as magic,' said Hoyle. 'Smoke and mirrors and superstition, that's all there is. This is the twenty-first century, Jack, the third millennium. Magic belongs back in the Dark Ages.'

'You got the heebie-jeebies over that crystal ball, didn't you?'

'That was different. That wasn't magic – it was . . .' He paused, lost for words. 'I don't know what it was. Maybe you were right, maybe the light was playing tricks with my reflection.'

'Okay, but you got married in church, didn't you?'

'So?'

'So that was a religious ceremony, before God.'

'That's different,' said Hoyle, rubbing his wedding band.

'No, it's the same. What you did in church with Anna was a ceremony with all the paraphernalia of religion. And remember Sarah's christening? I had to renounce Satan and all his works.'

'They're just words, Jack. Everyone says "until death us do part", but most marriages end in divorce. They're words, not spells.' He waved his arm at the shelves of books. 'This is bollocks. All of it. And you know it's bollocks.'

'I'm not saying it's not bollocks,' said Nightingale, 'I'm just saying that Gosling obviously believed in it, that's all. And maybe that belief is what drove him to kill himself.' He moved towards the stairs. 'Come on, let's get the hell out of here. We can't see properly with the torches – I'll get the power switched on and we'll come back.'

They walked past an oak desk on the way to the staircase. Unlike the others in the basement it wasn't heaped with books or papers: there was just a single leather-bound volume open with a Mont Blanc fountain pen next to it. The pages were filled with a handwritten scrawl, but Nightingale couldn't read it in the torchlight. He picked it up and took it with him.

13

Robbie Hoyle lived in a neat semi-detached house in Raynes Park that he'd bought a couple of years before property prices crashed and was now worth less than the mortgage he'd taken out to pay for it. His wife's black VW Golf was already in the driveway so he parked in the street.

'Maybe we should sell this place and move into Chez Nightingale,' said Hoyle, as they walked down the driveway to the house.

'I don't think you could afford the rent, mate.'

'You could cut me a deal,' said Hoyle. He unlocked the door. 'We're going to need a bigger place – we bought this before we knew we were having twins.'

'Twin girls, they can share a room,' said Nightingale.

'Spoken like an only child,' said Hoyle, pushing the front door open. 'Trust me, kids need their own space.'

Anna Hoyle came out of the kitchen, holding a bottle

of red wine. 'Keep the noise down, boys. I've only just got the twins to sleep and Sarah's got an exam tomorrow.'

'I love you too,' said Hoyle. He pecked her on the cheek.

'I'm serious,' said Anna. She smiled at Nightingale and held up the wine bottle. 'Hi, Jack. Red okay?' Nightingale and Hoyle had met Anna at the same time ten years earlier. She had been a probationer at the south London station they were working at and they had both asked her out. She'd said yes to Nightingale first but on the evening they were due to meet he'd been called away to an armed siege at a bank in Clapham. The following evening she'd gone for a drink with Hoyle and things had gone so well that they had married six months later. After three children she was still a stunner, with shoulder-length blonde hair, a trim figure and green eyes that always seemed amused.

'Red's fine. Sorry I kept your man out,' said Nightingale, taking off his raincoat. He dropped it on the back of an armchair and gave her a brotherly peck on the cheek. He'd long ago come to terms with the fact that she'd never be more than a friend, though he still caught himself looking at her legs whenever she left a room.

'I'll get the glasses,' said Hoyle. 'You sit yourself down. I know you gumshoes spend all your day pounding the streets.'

'Great,' said Nightingale. He collapsed onto the sofa and stretched out his legs.

'How's business?' asked Anna, sitting opposite him.

'Getting by,' he said, trying not to look at her cleavage. 'The divorce rate always goes up during a recession. More arguments about money, I guess.'

'And Jenny?'

'She's fine.'

'Asked her out yet?'

Nightingale groaned. 'Anna, she's an employee. She's staff. Start anything with your staff these days and you end up in an industrial tribunal.'

'She fancies you something rotten, Jack. It's as plain as the nose on your face. Why else do you think she works for you?'

Nightingale grinned. 'We're a dynamic company with growth prospects,' he said.

Hoyle returned from the kitchen with three glasses. He put them on the coffee-table and flopped into an armchair while Anna poured the wine. 'So, did Jack tell you he's a man of property now?'

'Really?' said Anna. 'Property?'

'I've been left a house.'

'A mansion,' said Hoyle. 'It's fantastic, babe. You have to see it to believe it. Dozens of bedrooms, a library – the kitchen alone is the size of this place.'

'Lucky you,' said Anna. 'How come?'

'A relative died,' said Nightingale.

'Close?' asked Anna.

'My father.'

Anna's eyebrows shot skywards. 'Jack!'

'Okay, somebody claiming to be my father.'

Hoyle sipped his wine. 'Some sort of Satanist, apparently.'

'A devil-worshipper?' said Anna. 'This is a joke, right?'

'I don't know about devil-worship, but he was definitely disturbed. He blew his head off with a shotgun.'

Anna drew her legs up underneath her and held her glass with both hands. 'I thought your parents died years ago,' she said.

'They did, but apparently I was adopted and Gosling was my genetic father.'

'But you'd know if you were adopted, surely.'

'It happened at birth. I was given to the Nightingales and registered as if I was their natural child. Anyway, it might all be bollocks. Some sort of scam.'

'You should be able to prove if he was your father or not. DNA, right?'

'I'm on the case,' said Hoyle.

'We could ask him now, if you like,' said Anna.

Nightingale and Hoyle looked at her in amazement.

'What?' said Nightingale. 'What on earth are you talking about?'

'What was his name – your father?'

'My genetic father? Ainsley Gosling.'

'Well, let's ask Mr Gosling. Let's go right to the source.'

'Anna, what's going on?' asked her husband.

'Let's have a séance,' she said. 'Fingers on a glass and you talk to the dead – the spirits. Robbie and I used to do it years ago.'

'It was a joke, a party game,' said Hoyle.

'We had some pretty weird messages.'

'There's always someone pushing the glass,' said Hoyle.

'Anna, you don't really believe that you can talk to the dead?' said Nightingale.

'It works! I can't explain why it works but you can get messages from people who've passed over.'

Nightingale frowned. 'You're serious?'

'I'm just saying it's worth a try. And they say that spirits who passed over violently, like when they've been murdered or committed suicide, tend to hang around – I suppose because there's unfinished business.'

'Well, Jack is certainly that,' said Hoyle.

Anna smiled brightly at Nightingale. 'Want to give it a go?'

14

Nightingale, Hoyle and Anna sat at the dining-table. Anna had written the letters of the alphabet on squares of paper, with the words 'Yes' and 'No'. She arranged the letters in a circle with A at the top, and put 'Yes' and 'No' inside. Hoyle fetched another wine glass from the kitchen and placed it upside down, also inside the circle. 'Now what?' asked Nightingale. 'We stare at it and make spooky sounds?'

'We have to place our right index fingers on the bottom of the glass,' said Anna, 'but first we have to cleanse our auras.'

'We have to what?' said Nightingale.

'I think she's saying you need a shower,' said Hoyle.

'It's about making the area safe and comfortable for spirits,' said Anna, ignoring her husband's sarcasm. She went over to the fireplace, lit three candles and carried one over to the sideboard, close to the dining-table.

Then she switched off the lights. 'The spirits feel more comfortable in the shadows,' she said.

'Don't we all?' said Nightingale. 'Why can't I have my wine?'

'There must be no alcohol at the table, no cigarettes, no impurities,' said Anna.

'Because?'

'Because impurities attract bad spirits,' she said.

'Where do you pick up this stuff?' asked Nightingale.

'She reads,' said Hoyle.

Anna took her seat and held out her hands. 'Now we form a circle and say the Lord's Prayer,' she said.

'Strictly speaking, it's a triangle,' said Nightingale.

'Don't quibble,' said Anna. 'Now, hold my hands and close your eyes.'

The two men did as they were told and Anna led them in the Lord's Prayer. It had been a long time since Nightingale had said it and he stumbled twice, mumbling over the words he'd forgotten. When they'd finished they opened their eyes. Anna kept hold of their hands. 'Let all spirits here within know that we mean you no harm and that we are here solely to do God's will,' she said.

'Amen,' said Hoyle.

'Good grief,' said Nightingale.

Anna looked at him disapprovingly. 'You have to take

it seriously,' she said. 'Now, place the index finger of your right hand on the bottom of the glass.' She did so gently and the two men followed. 'Right, here we go,' she said. 'Is anybody there?' They sat in silence for ten seconds. 'Is anybody there?' Anna repeated.

'You're mad, you know that,' said Nightingale.

'I'd be careful if I were you,' said Hoyle. 'The last person who said she was mad is buried in our back garden.'

Anna glared at him. 'Is anybody there?' she said, her voice lower this time.

Hoyle grinned at Nightingale and waggled his eyebrows. Nightingale tried not to laugh. They stiffened as the glass jerked under their fingers.

'Is anyone there?' repeated Anna.

Slowly but surely the glass scraped across the table top, heading for the piece of paper with 'Yes' written on it.

'No way,' said Nightingale, under his breath.

'Sssh!' hissed Anna.

The glass stopped next to 'Yes', then moved back slowly to the middle of the circle. Nightingale looked at Hoyle, who shook his head as if to say he wasn't pushing the glass.

'What was your father's name again?' whispered Anna.

'Ainsley Gosling,' said Nightingale, his eyes on the glass.

'We want to speak with Ainsley Gosling,' said Anna. She tilted her head back. 'Is Ainsley Gosling there?'

The glass jerked again, and moved inexorably towards 'Yes'. It stopped halfway, but a few seconds later it began to move again until it nudged the piece of paper.

'I don't believe this,' whispered Nightingale. 'Someone's pushing it.'

'Jack!' hissed Anna. 'The spirits sense negativity.' The glass moved back to the centre of the table. Nightingale knew he wasn't applying any pressure to it and it didn't feel as if either Anna or Hoyle were either. 'Do you have a message for us?' asked Anna, and even before she had finished the question the glass shot across to 'Yes', then slid back to the centre.

'This is amazing,' whispered Hoyle. 'You're not pissing around, are you, Jack?'

Nightingale shook his head. His finger was aching but he didn't want to take it off the glass, afraid that he would put a stop to whatever was happening. 'Now what, Anna?' he said.

She was still staring at the ceiling. 'What do you want to say to us?' she said.

The glass didn't move. Nightingale willed it to do

something, but it stayed defiantly where it was. 'You're among friends,' said Anna, softly. 'We only want to hear what you have to say.'

The glass moved quickly and, in rapid succession, touched the letters J A C and K.

'Jack!' said Hoyle, excitedly. 'It spelled out your name.'

'We can all read, honey,' said Anna. She took a deep breath. 'Yes, Jack is here with us. Do you have a message for him?'

The glass moved slowly towards 'Yes', touched the piece of paper and drifted back to the middle of the table. Then it began to move in small circles, slowly at first and then faster – so fast that Nightingale's finger almost slipped off it. It raced to the letter I and stayed there for several seconds, slid back to the centre and, almost immediately went to the opposite side of the circle and nudged W. Slowly it spelled out I – W – A – N – T, and stopped.

'"I want,"' said Hoyle. 'Did you see that?'

'What do you want?' asked Anna. 'Please tell us what you want.'

The glass began to move again. It slid over to Y, then O, and slowly spelled out 'YOU TO'.

It stopped. 'What?' said Hoyle, staring at it. 'What is it you want Jack to do?'

The glass began to move again in a series of jerks,

and in rapid succession it picked out S-H-A-G-J-E-N-N.

'Shag Jenn?' said Nightingale, then realisation dawned. He cursed and pulled away his finger. Anna and her husband burst out laughing.

'You two are a couple of kids,' said Nightingale, folding his arms and leaning back in his chair.

'Your face,' said Hoyle.

'Come on, admit it, we had you going,' said Anna.

'It's not funny,' said Nightingale.

'It is from where we're sitting,' said Hoyle. 'I want you to shag Jenny . . .' he said, in a spooky voice, waggling his fingers. 'That's what we want in the spirit world. We want Jack Nightingale to get laid.' He stood, retrieved his wine and returned to the sofa. 'You bought it, hook, line and sinker.'

'Only because I trusted you,' said Nightingale. 'Which isn't a mistake I'll make again.'

Anna gathered up the pieces of paper, screwed them into a ball and threw it at Nightingale. It bounced off his head and fell onto the floor. 'I'm going home,' he said.

'Don't sulk,' said Anna.

Nightingale laughed as he stood up. He held out his arms and hugged Anna. 'Bitch,' he said.

'Sticks and stones,' said Anna.

Nightingale kissed her cheek and waved to Hoyle. 'I'll get you back, you know that.'

'I wouldn't have it any other way,' said Hoyle, raising his glass in salute.

15

Nightingale woke up early on Friday morning with Simon Underwood's words ringing in his ears. It was the second night in a row that he'd had the dream. He sat up and ran his hands through his hair, then caught sight of his reflection in the mirrored door of the wardrobe on the far wall. His face was bathed in sweat and there were dark patches under his eyes as if he hadn't slept for a week. He groaned and lit a cigarette, smoked it all the way down, then showered and padded to the kitchen naked to make himself a black coffee. As he sipped it, he phoned his uncle Tommy. It was just after six thirty but his aunt and uncle had always been early risers.

His aunt answered again but she didn't say anything to him, just called for her husband.

Uncle Tommy sounded hesitant. 'Yes, Jack, how's things?'

'Everything's fine, Uncle. I called you a couple of days ago.'

'Aye, I'm sorry, lad, I've been busy.'

'I need to talk to you about Mum and Dad.'

'Aye, Linda said. But it's complicated, and I'm not sure your dad would want me talking about it.'

'He's dead, so I can't ask him or Mum, but I have to know the truth. You can understand that, can't you?'

His uncle sighed but didn't answer.

'We have to talk about this, Uncle Tommy,' said Nightingale.

'Aye, lad. I guess so.'

'How about I drive up to Altrincham on Sunday? About ten in the morning?'

His uncle put his hand over the receiver and said something to his wife. 'Linda says come for lunch, Jack. She'll do one of her roasts.'

'Lunch it is.'

'Jack, look . . . I'm sorry about all this.'

'Let's talk on Sunday, Uncle Tommy. It'll be easier face to face.'

Nightingale was already at his desk when Jenny walked in. She waved through the doorway as she dropped her bag onto her desk, slipped off her trainers and changed into a pair of Chanel high heels with pretty bows on the back. 'The early worm,' she said.

He was studying the book he'd taken from the basement in Gosling Manor and looked disapprovingly over the top. 'A bit of respect would be nice,' he said, 'me being management and all. I couldn't sleep. Came back to watch the DVD again.'

'Are you worrying about it?'

'My father tells me he's sold my soul to a devil and blows his head? Don't you think I should be a bit concerned?'

'He was probably deranged.'

'And I'm his offspring. What if it's hereditary?'

'What if what's hereditary?'

'He went mad. Maybe he was schizophrenic. Manic-depressive. I don't know. But if he was my father then maybe I'll go crazy too.'

Jenny gestured at the dirty mugs on his desk. 'I think you might be suffering from an excess of caffeine, Jack.'

'It's not the coffee,' said Nightingale. 'The more I look at the man in the DVD the more I see myself in him.'

'That's ridiculous,' said Jenny.

'It's the eyes. I look into his eyes and it's like staring into a mirror.'

'He doesn't look anything like you.'

'You don't know what I'll look like when I'm his age.'

'He was fat, he looked like he'd spent a lifetime boozing and taking God knows what drugs, and he looked sick.'

'And bald,' said Nightingale.

'And bald. Though I don't see what that's got to do with it.'

'Gosling was bald. That means I'll go bald, too.'

Jenny grinned. 'No, it doesn't,' she said. 'The baldness gene crosses the sexes. Didn't you do biology at school?'

'I must have been off on the day we did baldness. How does it go again?'

Jenny sighed and picked up the dirty mugs. 'You'll inherit the hair of your mother's father,' she said.

'Are you sure?'

'Yes,' she said. 'Do you have any idea who your real mum was? If what Gosling said is true, she might be out there.'

'I know,' said Nightingale, 'but I wouldn't have the first idea how to find her. I doubt he went through an agency.'

'We could try hospital records for the day you were born. That would be a start.'

'If Gosling was doing this secretly, he wouldn't have used a hospital,' said Nightingale. 'For all we know I could have been born in Gosling Manor. Oh, yeah, while I remember, how much is in the company account?'

'Not a lot.'

'I'm going to use the credit card to pay the electricity bill at Gosling Manor. Just under a grand. Can we cover it?'

'Barely,' said Jenny. 'We dipped into the red again last month.'

'We've got an overdraft facility of five hundred quid, right?'

'We used that, then went into the red,' said Jenny.

'Mrs Brierley's cheque should clear tomorrow.'

'Assuming it doesn't bounce like last time,' said Jenny.

'That was because her shit of a husband emptied their account,' said Nightingale. 'The new cheque was on hers. It'll be fine.'

'You're not planning to live there, are you?'

Nightingale laughed. 'If you'd seen the size of the place, you wouldn't even ask,' he said. 'It's huge. It's a couple of hundred yards from the kitchen to the main bedroom.'

'Gosling lived there alone, didn't he?'

'I'm not sure. I think he must have had staff living in, for cleaning if nothing else. And it needs a team of gardeners. That's another reason I couldn't live there – I couldn't afford the upkeep.'

'So why have the power connected?'

'Robbie and I found the basement and I want to go through it properly. It was hard by torchlight. And the estate agents will need the electricity on when they start showing people around.'

'That's the plan? Sell it?'

'I'm going to have to because there'll be inheritance tax to pay. Turtledove doesn't know how much but it'll be a lot.'

Jenny looked at the clock on the wall. 'You haven't forgotten Mr McBride, have you?'

'McBride?'

'The gentleman whose wife's having an affair with her boss, remember?'

'What time's he due?'

'Ten.'

'Time for another coffee, then,' he said.

'What are you reading?' asked Jenny, as she went over to the machine. She put down the dirty mugs and picked up a clean one.

'A book,' said Nightingale. 'And I'm not reading it, I'm staring at it, trying to make sense of the letters, which isn't the same thing.'

'What are you talking about?' said Jenny. She poured him some coffee and brought it through to his office.

Nightingale handed it to her. 'See for yourself,' he said.

Jenny opened it. It was full of handwritten scrawl, some in dark blue ink, some in black, and some in what looked disconcertingly like dried blood. Dotted among the text there were sketches of circles and pentagrams. Jenny tried reading a sentence at random but she couldn't make any sense of it. It certainly wasn't English, or any other language she recognised.

'At first I thought I might have caught dyslexia,' said Nightingale. He sipped his coffee, then reached for the whisky bottle.

Jenny moved it out of his reach without taking her eyes off the book. 'You don't catch dyslexia,' she said, frowning over the spidery writing. 'Where did you get this from?'

'I picked it up in the house last night,' said Nightingale. 'Old man Gosling's basement is packed with books and stuff . . . weird stuff. I thought that might have been his diary but I can't make head or tail of it. I thought it must have been written backwards, but even if you read it from right to left it still doesn't make sense.'

Jenny looked up. 'I've got it,' she said.

'The suspense is killing me,' said Nightingale. 'What have you got?'

'It's not written backwards, it's mirror writing. There's a difference.'

'So you have to read it in a mirror? How on earth did he manage that?'

'You can teach yourself to write that way. Leonardo da Vinci used to do it, so that no one could read his papers.' Jenny fetched a small mirror from her bag, sat down opposite Nightingale and held the book so that a page was reflected.

Nightingale shook his head. 'It still doesn't make sense.'

'It's not English, that's why.'

He took the mirror from her and tried to read a sentence. 'What is it? Italian?'

'Latin.'

'My comprehensive was a bit light on dead languages,' said Nightingale. 'Can you translate it?'

Jenny rolled her eyes. 'Didn't you read my CV when you hired me?'

'I was too busy looking at your legs,' said Nightingale. 'Can you tell me what it says?'

'Eventually,' said Jenny.

A sudden knock at the door startled them. Jenny hurried to open it. Joel McBride, a middle-aged man in a wheelchair, looked up at her. He was in his late forties with lank brown hair, flecked with grey, that kept falling into his eyes. He was wearing a scarlet wind-breaker and black leather gloves with the fingers cut off. Nightingale decided that his bulging arm muscles were the result of pushing himself around. 'I'm sorry I'm early but the taxi got the pick-up time wrong,' said McBride.

'No problem,' said Nightingale, getting up from his chair. 'As my lovely assistant just reminded me, the early worm catches the bird. There's something we need to discuss.'

'About my wife?' said McBride.

'I'm afraid so,' said Nightingale.

16

Nightingale ordered another Corona, his third, and wondered whether it was worth going outside the wine bar for a cigarette but decided that on balance he'd prefer to continue to watch a recording of a Manchester United–Liverpool match on a big LCD TV with the sound turned down. Nightingale's father, his real father, the man who had brought him up, had been a big United fan and had taken him to hundreds of games over the years. Bill Nightingale had been a season-ticket holder for as long as he could remember and Jack's yearly birthday present from the age of ten had been his own season ticket. It was father-and-son time, and going to the games had marked some of the happiest times of his childhood. His father had helped him collect autographs of the first-team players, standing with him in all weathers outside the players' entrance, passing the time by testing each other on the

names of all the squads going back to the early nineteen fifties. Nightingale had gone once or twice after
his parents had died, but it had never felt the same and
he hadn't renewed his ticket. 'I knew I'd find you here,'
said a voice at his shoulder. It was Jenny.

'I wasn't exactly hiding, and it's the closest bar to
the office,' he said. He checked his watch. It was just
before eight o'clock. 'Why aren't you home?'

She held up the Waitrose carrier-bag. 'I was in the
office, reading the Gosling diary,' she said. 'I got caught
up in it.' She put the bag down on the bar and ordered
a glass of white wine from the barman. 'Can we sit at
a table?' she asked Nightingale. 'I always feel like a lush
standing at the bar.'

'I feel like a lush too, but where am I going to find
one at this time of night?' said Nightingale. He grinned
and indicated an empty table. 'You grab yourself a seat
and I'll get your drink.'

Jenny threaded her way through the tables and sat
down. She put the bag in front of her and helped herself
to a breadstick. Nightingale took her wine and his bottle
of Corona to the table and sat opposite her.

'Are you okay?' she asked.

'Of course. Why wouldn't I be?'

'You've been quiet, that's all.'

'I've been working.'

'How many beers have you had?'

Nightingale chuckled. 'What are you, the alcohol police?'

'You're not driving, are you?'

Nightingale raised his glass. 'No, Jenny, I'm not driving.'

'And you're sure you're okay?'

He sipped some beer. 'I'm fine,' he said. 'Fine and dandy.' He nodded at the Waitrose bag. 'Have you managed to make sense of that?'

Four women in power suits burst into laughter at the table next to them. They were all in their early thirties, wearing too much makeup and jewellery, and weighing each other up with humourless eyes. Nightingale had them pegged as office colleagues, not friends. He made eye contact with one and she sneered at him dismissively. Nightingale smiled to himself, unfazed by her contempt.

'What are you grinning at?' asked Jenny.

'I'm just happy that you're the way you are and not like those harpies over there.'

'Harpies?'

'Those hard-faced bitches in their power suits, drinking bubbly and baring their fangs.'

'That sounds a tad misogynistic,' said Jenny.

'I love women,' said Nightingale.

'That's so not true,' said Jenny. 'You like some women, you tolerate the rest.'

'I open doors for them, I give up my seat on buses.'

'On behalf of womankind, thank you so very much.' She sipped her wine. The women at the other table laughed again and one shouted at a waiter to bring another bottle of champagne. 'Having said that, I do see what you mean,' she said. She put down her glass and took the book out of the carrier-bag. 'So, here's the scoop. This wasn't written by Ainsley Gosling. He would have been reading it.'

Nightingale raised an eyebrow. 'So, who did write it?'

'So far as I can tell it's the diary of somebody called Sebastian Mitchell. The first entry is in 1946. The most recent was twelve years ago. There are notes in the margin that aren't in mirror Latin so I'm guessing Gosling wrote them.' She put it on the table. 'I've only read bits – it'll take for ever to read the whole thing. My Latin's rusty and it's a pain having to read it in the mirror. But I can tell you that this guy Mitchell was some sort of Satanist. You've heard of Aleister Crowley, right?'

'Vaguely.'

'He was a big-time Satanist. Mitchell studied under him. Crowley died in 1947, the year after Mitchell started writing his diary, but while Crowley enjoyed his infamy, Mitchell preferred to hide his light under a bushel and this was never meant for publication.'

'It says all that in the diary?'

'It mentions Crowley, yes, but the diary isn't about him. It's about how Mitchell was trying to summon devils. A sort of "how to" book, detailing what he did, the pitfalls and perils, what worked and what didn't.'

'This keeps getting better and better, doesn't it?'

'Just because it's written down it doesn't mean it's true. I kept a diary until I was fifteen, full of adolescent ramblings.'

'Now, that I'd like to read,' said Nightingale. 'Gosling was using this book. It was open on his desk – it might well have been the last thing he read. I need to know what he was thinking about before he killed himself.' He ran a hand through his hair. 'Is there stuff in there about selling souls?'

'Jack, you know that's nonsense.'

'I need to know what he believed,' said Nightingale. 'It doesn't matter whether or not it's nonsense, what matters is what he believed. Is there stuff in there about selling the souls of children?'

'It's a handwritten diary, Jack. Mitchell could have been as crazy as . . .' She left the sentence unfinished and reached for her glass.

'As my genetic father?'

Jenny avoided his eyes. 'I'm not saying he was crazy. But he did kill himself – there's no getting away from that.'

'What does it say about selling souls, Jenny?'

Jenny sighed. 'You have to summon a devil,' she said. 'Not *the* devil, but one of his minions. In the book, Mitchell describes the different sorts of devils and what they do. So, if you want to sell a soul you have to call up one of his minions.'

'How do you know which devil to summon?'

'You're not taking this seriously, are you?'

'Just tell me what the book says.'

Jenny nodded slowly. 'Okay. According to Mitchell, there are sixty-six princes under the devil, each commanding 6,666 legions. And each legion is made up of 6,666 devils.'

Nightingale frowned as he struggled to do the calculation in his head. 'There are three billion devils in hell?'

'It's a big place,' said Jenny. 'Look, Jack, Mitchell was delusional – the book's proof of that. No one in their right mind believes in a hell full of devils.'

Nightingale drained his beer and waved at a waitress for another bottle. 'Here's the thing, Jenny. The way I see it, there are two possibilities. One, he sold my soul to a devil, and on my thirty-third birthday my life as I know it will be over.'

'Which is nonsense.'

The waitress arrived with his next Corona. Nightingale took the bottle and raised it to Jenny. 'Which is nonsense,' he agreed. 'Two, he was as mad as a hatter. There was something wrong with him, paranoid schizophrenia, early Alzheimer's, bipolar, I don't know.' He tapped the side of his head. 'A few bricks short of a wall.'

'You're still worrying about the heredity thing?'

'And you think I shouldn't be?'

'I think it's obvious he was having problems,' said Jenny. 'That doesn't mean you will.'

'Mental problems, Jenny. And mental problems can be hereditary. My father was mad so I might be headed that way too.' He pointed at the book in front of her. 'Anyone who wrote that must be crazy, and anyone who believed in it must have been even crazier. My dad blew his head off with a shotgun. Maybe . . .' His voice tailed off.

'What, Jack? What is it?'

'I was a negotiator – you know that. Everyone thinks that negotiators are like they are on TV, running around talking to hostage-takers, getting villains out of banks and persuading them to hand over their guns before anyone gets hurt. But it's not like that. Most of the time it's domestics that have got out of hand or it's sad buggers wanting to kill themselves – or to be talked out of killing themselves.' He took a long pull on his beer. 'Christ, I want a cigarette.'

'That's the beauty of the legislation,' said Jenny. 'You're only allowed one pleasure at a time.'

'Sometimes they just want someone to talk to,' Nightingale went on. 'There was one woman out in Tower Hamlets – every time she had a fight with her husband she'd pick up a knife, sit in her garden and threaten to cut herself. A negotiating team would go out, and after an hour or two and a few cigarettes she'd give us the knife and start crying and saying she loved her husband even though he belted her every time he had a few drinks inside him.'

'She wasn't really suicidal?'

'She just wanted someone to talk to, and by threatening to harm herself, she got it. I saw her three times over the years. Knew what brand of fags to take her and what buttons to press when I got there. Emma, her name was. She's probably still at it.' He sipped his beer, then took another long pull. 'It wasn't hard to empathise with her. She was trapped in a life she hated, with a man who showed emotion through violence, and she'd had half a dozen miscarriages that were probably because of the drink, the drugs and the smoking. You could understand what was upsetting her. And once you understand you can negotiate. You can tell them what they want to hear.'

'And she wanted someone to care?'

'That was all she wanted. Someone to listen to her, to prove that she mattered, that her life amounted to something.'

'And did you really care or were you faking it?'

'I cared – of course I cared. She was a human being in pain. How could I not care?' He finished his Corona and signalled to the waitress again. 'But the ones who really want to kill themselves, they're a different ball game. You could look into their eyes and you'd know, just know, that something wasn't right. You'd know without a shadow of a doubt that they were going to do it, and that the only reason you were there was because they wanted an audience.'

'Why would they want an audience?'

Nightingale shrugged. 'Who knows? There's no logic to what a crazy person does. That's what crazy is.'

'Crazy is as crazy does?' said Jenny. 'Very Forrest Gump.'

'Yeah, life is a box of chocolates,' said Nightingale. 'In my father's case, Black Magic.'

'That's funny,' said Jenny. 'Good to see you haven't lost your sense of humour.'

The waitress brought over Nightingale's beer. Jenny's wine glass was still half full.

'Some people want to kill themselves and do it in private,' said Nightingale. 'It's easy enough – you swallow a bottle of sleeping tablets, hang yourself or jump off a very tall building when no one's looking. But sometimes they want a reaction so they'll throw themselves in front of a train or stand on a ledge and wait for a crowd to gather. They're the really sick ones.'

'You've seen a lot of people commit suicide?'

Nightingale grimaced. 'Not too many, but enough,' he said. 'The one thing they had in common was the look in their eyes. Once you've seen it, you never forget it. And I can see it in Gosling's eyes when I look at that DVD – I can see it, Jenny.'

'Jack . . .'

Nightingale stood up. 'Jack, are you okay?'

'I need some fresh air.'

'You mean you need a cigarette, right?'

Nightingale shook his head. 'I've got to walk for a while, clear my head.'

'Do you want company?'

'Thanks, but I'd rather be on my own for a bit. Can you keep a hold of that diary for me, see if you can turn up anything else I should know?'

'You're not going to drive, are you?'

'Of course not.'

'You've been drinking, Jack.'

'I know I've been drinking. And I'm not going to drive. I just need some air.'

17

Nightingale lit a cigarette as he walked down the street. He passed a dozen or so shops, three of which had gone out of business while the rest were trying desperately to drum up trade by offering sales of up to ninety per cent off and free credit. The only ones that seemed to be thriving were the charity outlets offering second-hand clothes, household goods and toys. A cold wind blew at his back and he raised the collar of his raincoat.

'Hey, Mister, got a cigarette?'

A girl was sitting in the doorway of an Oxfam shop, a sleeping-bag wrapped around her legs. She was dressed in Goth black, with thick mascara and black eye-shadow. Her dyed black hair was unkempt and there were chunky silver rings on all of her fingers. A black-and-white Border collie lay on the ground next to her. She mimed smoking just in case he'd missed the question.

Nightingale held up his burning cigarette. 'You know these things'll give you cancer?' he said.

'Everybody dies,' said the girl. She can't be more than twenty-five, thought Nightingale. 'Sooner or later.'

'But some sooner than others.' Nightingale took out his pack of Marlboro and offered her one. 'Don't say I didn't warn you.'

She helped herself and smiled up at him. 'Got a light?'

Nightingale flicked a flame. She cupped it with her left hand as she inhaled. One of her rings was a strange cross, curved into a loop at the top.

'You're going to hell, Jack Nightingale,' said the girl, her hand touching his.

Nightingale jerked it away. The dog flinched, then looked at Nightingale mournfully, his tail twitching from side to side. 'What did you say?'

'It opens the gates of hell,' she said. 'The ring. It's an ankh. The symbol of eternal life. Do you want to buy it? You can give it to your girlfriend.'

'I don't have one.'

'Boyfriend, then.'

'I'm not gay.'

'Just lonely?'

Nightingale straightened and took a long drag on

his cigarette. 'I'm not so lonely that I need a dog for company,' he said.

The girl stroked the collie. 'He's not company, he's protection,' she said.

'He doesn't look that fierce,' said Nightingale.

'You'd be surprised,' she said. 'Things aren't always the way they seem. Where are you going?'

'I don't know.'

'Don't know, or won't tell?'

Nightingale flicked ash on the pavement. 'I've a lot on my mind,' he said.

'You can think too much, you know,' she said. 'Sometimes you've just got to go with the flow. *Que sera, sera*. Whatever will be, will be.'

Nightingale took out his wallet. 'You sleep rough?' he asked.

'I don't sleep much, really,' she said. Nightingale handed her a twenty-pound note, but she refused it. 'I'm not begging,' she said.

'Buy the dog something. A bone. Whatever.'

The collie's tail twitched again as if he understood what Nightingale was saying. 'He's not begging, either.' The girl flashed him a grin and evidently changed her mind. She grabbed the note. 'But there's no point in looking a gift horse in the mouth, is there?' It disappeared into her leather jacket.

'I never understood that saying,' said Nightingale.

'It's about checking teeth, to see if the horse you've been given is a good one or not. It'd be like me checking that the money you've just given me isn't fake. That'd be looking a gift horse in the mouth.' She stroked the dog as she talked. Her fingernails were painted black – they were long and pointed, almost talons. She saw him looking at them and held up her right hand. 'You like?'

'They're distinctive.'

She curled her fingertips and admired them. 'Do you want me to scratch you?' she said.

'What?'

'That's what guys say when they see my nails. They wonder what it would be like to have their backs scratched with them. Is that what you were thinking?'

It was exactly what Nightingale had been thinking, but he shook his head.

'Why is it, do you think, that guys really want girls to hurt them?'

'I'm not sure that's true,' said Nightingale.

'It is, believe me,' said the girl. She was stroking the dog again. 'I think guys like to be treated like dogs. You stroke them, feed them and exercise them, but you have to punish them every now and again to show them who's boss.'

Nightingale chuckled. 'Well, good luck with philosophy,' he said, and walked on.

'You take care,' she called after him.

'You too,' said Nightingale. He smoked as he walked, deep in thought. That was twice now that he'd heard someone tell him he was going to hell. The constable at Gosling Manor, and now the girl with the dog. Was he imagining it? It was what Simon Underwood had screamed in the dream, just before he went through the window. But that had been a dream, or a nightmare, and now he was wide awake, albeit a bit drunk. 'Maybe I'm just going crazy,' he muttered to himself.

'We're all crazy,' said a gruff voice.

Nightingale jumped. A homeless man was sitting in the doorway of a hardware shop, nursing a bottle of cider. He was in his sixties with long grey hair, a straggly beard dotted with crumbs, and wads of newspaper tied around his legs with string.

'The whole world's gone crazy,' he said, waving the bottle at Nightingale. 'God's abandoned us and the Lord Jesus doesn't care any more. They're letting us wallow in our sins until the end of days.'

'Sounds about right,' said Nightingale. He took out his wallet, gave the man ten pounds and carried on down the road.

18

Nightingale hadn't lied when he'd told Jenny he wasn't going to drive. And he'd meant what he'd said about wanting some fresh air, even though the first thing he'd done when he'd left the wine bar was light a cigarette. Neither had he been lying when he'd told the girl in the shop doorway that he didn't know where he was going. So far as he was concerned, he was doing just as he'd said he would: taking a walk while he collected his thoughts. But his subconscious had other plans for him. It took him to his car, and three hours later he was driving through Manchester, and ten minutes after that he was parking outside the grave-yard where his parents were buried and wondering why he had never visited since the funeral.

He climbed out of the MGB and locked the door, then stuck his hands into the pockets of his raincoat and walked towards the ivy-covered stone arch that led into the churchyard. The house where he had been brought up was a mile from the weathered grey stone church but the only time he had been there was for the funeral. His parents had never shown any interest in religion and Nightingale had been surprised to discover that they had bought the twin burial plot just three years before their untimely death. They had been crushed in their car by a petrol-tanker. Later the driver had sworn he hadn't seen the red traffic-lights or their car. He hadn't been drinking, he'd tested negative for drugs and his tachometer showed that he'd only been driving for four hours before the accident. The coroner put it down to a fatal lapse in concentration and the driver ended up serving two years in prison for causing death by careless driving. It was just one of those things, everyone had said at the funeral and the reception after-wards – Nightingale's parents had been in the wrong place at the wrong time.

There was a wooden gate set into the arch and it creaked as Nightingale pushed it open. A black-painted sign topped with a cross announced the name of the church, that the vicar was the Reverend T. Smith and that there would be a bring-and-buy sale in aid of the church roof restoration fund the following Wednesday.

It was starting to get dark and there were no lights on inside the church. As Nightingale followed the path to the right of the building a halogen security light clicked on, illuminating the graves to his right. A second light came on as he continued to walk, and elongated shadows writhed over the gravestones. The stained-glass windows were covered with wire mesh and there was anti-climbing paint on the drainpipes. Nightingale suspected that local thieves had more to do with the need to restore the roof than simple wear and tear.

His parents' graves were at the far end, close to the boundary wall and shaded by a spreading willow tree. There was a single black marble headstone with the names William and Irene Nightingale, their dates of birth and the date they'd died, and above them, optimistically, 'Living together in eternity'. It was the first time Nightingale had seen it. At the funeral there had just been a hole in the ground, Astroturf strips over the pile of earth ready to be shovelled back in. He had been nineteen and if someone had asked back then whether he believed in God he'd have laughed scornfully and probably refused to answer. If he was asked the same question now, fourteen years later, the laugh would be more ironic and he still probably wouldn't bother to answer.

He looked down at the grave. 'Funny old world, innit?' he said aloud. In the distance an owl hooted. The two security lights clicked off. There was an almost full moon overhead and the sky was clear of clouds so there was enough light to see by. A cold breeze from behind made him shiver so he turned up his coat collar and put his hands back in his pockets. His right hand found his cigarette lighter and he held it like a talisman. 'Why did you never tell me you weren't my real parents?' he said softly, to the gravestone. His breath feathered in the cold night air. 'I wouldn't have loved you any less. You'll always be Mum and Dad to me, no matter what.'

The owl hooted again. Nightingale sighed. What he was doing made no sense to him. He didn't believe in ghosts, he didn't believe in an afterlife, and he sure as hell didn't believe that he could talk to his long-dead parents. 'This is crazy,' he said. 'I'm crazy. The whole thing is crazy.' He took out his lighter and the packet of Marlboro and lit a cigarette. 'I know, I smoke too much,' he said. 'And I drink. I'm a big boy now.' He took a deep lungful of smoke, held it, then exhaled slowly, aiming at the marble headstone. 'Did you know Gosling? Did you know he was my real father? Is that why you never said anything? Is that why you never told me I was adopted?'

High overhead a passenger jet was moving across the night sky, its red and green navigation lights flashing. Nightingale gazed up at it, rubbing the back of his neck with his left hand. He could feel the tension in the muscles, the tendons as taut as steel cables.

'Can I help you?' asked a voice.

Nightingale started. His left foot slipped on the grass and he stumbled sideways. His arms flailed as he fought to keep his balance and he cursed loudly. He turned to see a middle-aged vicar in a cassock, with a brass cross around his neck. He seemed as shocked as Nightingale was. 'You almost scared the life out of me,' said Nightingale, patting his chest.

'I'm sorry,' said the vicar. 'I thought you'd heard me walking along the path. I wasn't exactly on tiptoe.' He had the look of an ex-boxer, with a squarish jaw and a slightly flattened nose. While he was a good six inches shorter than Nightingale he was heavy-set and had thick forearms that bulged through his clerical garb. His light grey-brown hair was receding, and while he studied Nightingale with unflinching pale blue eyes, his smile was that of a kindly uncle.

'I was . . . deep in thought,' said Nightingale. 'Miles away.'

'I saw the lights go on and we've had a lot of problems recently,' said the vicar. 'When times are good, we have vandalism most weekends, but when they're bad it's all we can do to keep the lead on the roof.'

'I'm sorry, I guess I shouldn't be here,' said Nightingale. He pointed at the grave. 'My parents. I wanted to . . .' He shrugged. 'Actually, I'm not sure what I wanted.'

'You're not a regular at my church, are you?'

'I'm afraid not. Sorry. A lost sheep.'

'No one is ever truly lost,' said the vicar. 'The shepherd will always welcome you back.' He extended his hand. 'Timothy Smith.'

Nightingale shook it. 'Jack Nightingale.'

The vicar looked at the headstone. 'Fourteen years ago,' he said. 'How time passes.'

Nightingale peered at the man, but his face wasn't familiar. He didn't remember much about the funeral. He'd sat on a hard pew next to his aunt and uncle and after the service, when they were outside, Uncle Tommy had shown him how to drop a handful of earth into the grave. It had been muddy and he hadn't been able to bring himself to clean his shoes for at least a month. But he couldn't summon the face of the man who had conducted the funeral, or recall anything he'd said. 'You knew my parents?'

'Of course,' said the vicar. 'They were regular church-goers.'

'Not while I was at home,' said Nightingale. 'I don't remember them taking me.'

The vicar nodded. 'They'd been coming for about a year before they died.'

'I would have been at university,' said Nightingale. 'It's funny, I never knew they were religious.'

'People tend to turn more to the Church as they get older,' said the vicar. 'As they become aware of their own mortality, they start looking for solutions.'

'Lifelines?' said Nightingale.

'Perhaps,' said the vicar. 'We take our converts where we can.'

Nightingale held up his cigarette. 'Is it okay to smoke?'

The vicar smiled. 'Of course.' He gestured at the church. 'But not inside, we're covered by health and safety regulations these days.' He looked wistfully at the cigarette in Nightingale's hand.

'You smoke?' asked Nightingale.

'I try not to,' said the vicar, 'and every year I give it up for Lent.' Nightingale offered him the packet and he took one. Nightingale lit it for him. 'Marlboro always make me feel like a cowboy' he said.

'It was the packet that got me started on them,' said Nightingale. 'Took me a while to get used to the smoke.'

The two men exhaled.

'Can I ask you a question?' said Nightingale.

'Of course,' said the vicar. 'Anything but geography – I was always bad at it. How's anyone supposed to remember all those capital cities?'

Nightingale chuckled. 'It's a bit more esoteric than that,' he said. 'I wanted to ask you if you believed in the devil.'

The vicar frowned. 'If one believes in the Lord, one has to believe in the devil. The two come as a package deal, if you like.'

'Horns, a forked tail and a pitchfork?'

'Not necessarily,' said the vicar. 'But who can doubt that there's evil in the world?'

'I believe in evil. But is evil within men or is it an outside force that corrupts?'

'When there was only Adam and Eve there was no evil. Evil came from without.'

'Because Satan introduced the serpent into Paradise? You believe in all that?'

'It's not my faith that needs examining, is it? What's troubling you, Jack?'

Nightingale smiled ruefully. 'You don't want to go there.'

'Try me,' said the vicar. 'One smoker to another.'

Nightingale sighed. 'I'm not sure I know what's going on, what's real and what's an irrational fear.' He took a drag on his cigarette. 'Is it possible to sell your soul?'

'To the devil?'

Nightingale nodded.

'Tough question,' he said. 'Tougher than geography.'

'Is that your way of saying you don't have an answer?'

'I'll have a stab at it,' said the vicar, flicking ash on the path. He took a deep breath. 'We talk of giving our

lives to Christ, so there must also be misguided indi-
viduals who give themselves over to evil.'

'And would such a deal be irrevocable?'

'A person can always change his mind. The history
of the Church is filled with conversions.' He took a
drag on his cigarette. 'Looks like I'm a smoker again.'

'Once a smoker, always a smoker,' said Nightingale.
'What if there was a contract with the devil?'

The vicar looked pained. 'It's more a case of coming
to believe that Jesus Christ is our Lord and Saviour.'

'I understand that, but I'm not talking about a
contract with Christ. I'm talking about doing a deal
with the other side. The dark side. What if your soul is
promised to the devil?'

'I think you're being too literal, Jack,' said the vicar.
'One no more makes a contract with the devil than one
does with Jesus. It's not a matter of signing on the
dotted line. It's a matter of belief.' He dropped his cigarette butt and squashed it with his foot.

'And do you believe in hell?'

'As a concept?'

'As a place.'

The vicar laughed. 'There! I told you not to go asking
me about geography.'

'You've very good at avoiding questions,' said
Nightingale. 'You'd be a nightmare to interrogate.'

'You're a police officer?' asked the vicar.

'In a previous life,' said Nightingale. 'So, is there a hell, or not? And if there is, where is it?'

'Scripture doesn't give us an exact location,' said the vicar. 'It's a place of real torment that may or may not have a physical location in this universe. A black hole, maybe. Or it might be in another dimension, a place we move to after death.'

'You believe that?'

'I believe in God, of course. It'd be difficult to do this job if I didn't. And I believe that we go from this life to be with God.'

'But where?' asked Nightingale. 'Where do we go?'

'Heaven,' said the vicar. 'That's what the Bible says.'

'But where is heaven?'

The vicar smiled. 'There you go,' he said. 'Geography again.' He put a hand on Nightingale's shoulder. 'I'm sorry I can't answer all your questions. I know how frustrating that can be. So far as I'm concerned, as a Christian, it's less important where heaven is than to know that one day I'll be there.'

'I suppose so,' said Nightingale.

'The Church doesn't have all the answers,' said the vicar. 'There has to be faith. Belief is about faith.'

'And that's the problem,' said Nightingale. 'I'm a bit short of both at the moment.'

19

Nightingale lit a cigarette as he steered the MGB with one hand. The vicar hadn't been much help but, then, Nightingale hadn't expected he would be. He hadn't gone to the graveyard for spiritual guidance. Truth be told, he had no idea why he'd felt the need to be there. His questions could only be answered by his parents, and they were dead. Dead and buried.

He wound down his window and blew smoke as he drove. There was no proof that he was adopted. It might turn out to be some perverse mistake, that Ainsley Gosling had simply been wrong, or that he had chosen Nightingale as the victim of some beyond-the-grave hoax. Fathers didn't sell the souls of their children to the devil, not in the twentieth or twenty-first century. Not in any century. But until Hoyle came back with the results of the DNA analysis, Nightingale had no way of knowing whether Gosling really had been his biological father.

A blue light flashed in his rear-view mirror and Nightingale swore. He hadn't been speeding but the car had woven a little while he was lighting the cigarette. The siren blipped and Nightingale swore again. He indicated, pulled over and switched off the engine. The police car pulled up behind him and two constables got out. Nightingale gritted his teeth and stubbed out his cigarette. They'd smell the alcohol on his breath. He leaned over, flicked open the glove compartment and groped for the packet of Wrigley's chewing gum he always kept there. He unwrapped two sticks and slotted them into his mouth, then opened the door and climbed out, keeping his hands where the officers could see them. 'Sorry, guys, I wasn't speeding, was I?'

The younger of the two was in his mid-twenties and holding a breathalyser machine. The older man did the talking. 'Have you been drinking, sir?' he asked.

'A few beers, a few hours ago,' said Nightingale. Even with the spearmint gum he knew he wouldn't get away with a complete denial. He took out his wallet and showed them his private-investigator identification. 'Guys, I know this won't cut me any slack, but I used to be in the job.'

'If you were in the job, you'd know there's no slack to be cut,' said the policeman. 'We're going to need a sample of your breath to ascertain if you've been drinking. If you're unable or unwilling to provide such a sample we'll take you to the station where you'll have to give a blood or urine sample.'

Nightingale raised his hands in surrender. He knew there was no point in arguing. 'No problem,' he said.

The younger policeman handed him the breathalyser unit and showed him what to do. Nightingale took a deep breath, then blew slowly into the tube. A red light winked on accusingly and the officer grinned triumphantly.

The older man told Nightingale he was being arrested but Nightingale wasn't listening. It was his own fault, no one had forced him to drink and drive, and now he was going to have to pay the penalty for his stupidity.

'You're going to hell, Jack Nightingale,' said the younger policeman, putting a hand on his shoulder. His voice was cold and flat, devoid of emotion.

'What?' said Nightingale.

'I said we'll secure your car and drive you to the station, sir. Please give me the keys.' His voice had returned to normal.

Nightingale shook his head. 'What did you say just then?'

The younger constable looked at his colleague. 'Drunk as a skunk,' he said.

'I'm not drunk,' said Nightingale. 'I've been drinking

but I'm not drunk. What did you say about me going to hell?'

'There's no need for offensive language, sir,' said the older policeman, taking hold of Nightingale's left arm.

'I wasn't being offensive,' said Nightingale. 'I just want to know what he said.'

'He said we're going to have to secure your vehicle. You can come back and get it once we've done the paperwork at the station and you're fit to drive. Now, please don't give us any more trouble.' He tightened his grip.

Nightingale said nothing. He handed over his keys and let them lead him to their car.

20

A bored custody sergeant made Nightingale empty his pockets, checked his driving licence, and asked him if he suffered from any medical problems. 'I'm fine,' said Nightingale. The sergeant went through a list of diseases and illnesses, methodically ticking them off as Nightingale shook his head. 'Do you think you might self-harm?' asked the sergeant, who was in his late forties, with thick greying hair and a wide jaw.

'Do I what?' asked Nightingale.

'Do you think you might hurt yourself?' He prodded the form. 'I have to ask.'

'What if I said yes?'

'Then we'd have to leave the cell door open and I'd have to get a constable to sit outside and watch you.'

'All night?'

'For as long as you're in custody.'

'That's crazy, isn't it?'

'It's the rule,' said the sergeant. 'We've only got CCTV in two cells and they're both occupied.'

'I don't see why you need to keep me here in the first place. Can't you just bail me and send me on my way?'

'We have to be sure that you won't go back and drive your vehicle while still intoxicated.'

'What if I crossed my heart and swore to God that I'll go straight home?'

'You'll be here for a few hours,' the sergeant said. 'It's procedure. You were showing seventy micrograms, which is twice the legal limit.'

'I tell you what,' said Nightingale, 'if you let me keep my cigarettes and get me a cup of coffee, I'll promise not to self-harm.'

'No cigarettes in the cell, but I can let you have a smoke in the yard when you want one,' said the sergeant. 'The coffee isn't a problem, but I warn you, it tastes like dishwater.'

'So long as it's got caffeine in it, I'll be happy. And so long as I'm happy, I won't be self-harming.'

Both men turned as they heard a commotion at the entrance to the custody suite. Three uniformed officers were half dragging, half carrying a man who was cursing and shouting. He was in his twenties, wearing faded jeans and trainers, and a torn T-shirt that was spattered with blood. He was struggling with the three policemen, and although they were all much bigger than he was they were clearly having trouble keeping him under control. 'The devil made me do it!' shouted the man, spittle spraying from his lips. 'Don't you see? Don't you understand?'

'What's the story, lads?' asked the custody sergeant.

'Assault with a deadly weapon, Sarge,' said one of the constables. 'He was charging down the high street with a samurai sword, swiping it at anyone he saw. Cut three women and almost took the arm off a pub doorman.'

'Where's the sword now?' asked the sergeant.

'In the van,' said the oldest of the three constables. He was wearing a stab-proof vest and black gloves but there was a cut across his cheek.

'Did he do that to you?' asked the sergeant.

The constable nodded. 'With his nails, after we took the sword off him.'

The man struggled and swore and the three officers wrestled him to the floor. Two held him by the arms while the third lay across his legs.

'Has he been drinking?' asked the custody sergeant.

'Can't smell it on his breath,' said the constable who was holding down the captive's legs.

'Must be drugs, then,' said the sergeant. 'Either that

or he's just plain crazy.' He walked over and stood looking down at the man. 'What have you taken?' he asked. 'Amphetamines? Cocaine? Tell us and we can help you.'

'Fuck you!' The man spat at the sergeant and phlegm landed on his tunic. The sergeant took a step back. 'Put him in number three,' he said, 'and use restraints until he's calmed down.'

Two of the officers lifted the man, holding an arm each, while the third kept a tight grip on his belt. 'Just calm down and you walk under your own steam, right?' said the officer holding the man's belt. 'But you keep struggling and we'll have to Taser you, okay? For your own safety. You keep fighting us and you're the only one who'll get hurt.'

The man ignored the officer. He stared at Nightingale and grinned manically. 'You understand, don't you?' His eyes were red and watering. They burned with a fierce intensity. 'You believe in the devil, don't you? You know what he can do! Tell them! Tell them the devils are here, making us do their work for them!'

Nightingale looked away.

'Tell them!' screamed the man, lunging at Nightingale. 'Tell them, you bastard!'

The three constables grappled the man, lifted him off his feet and carried him, still screaming, towards the cells.

'It's a full moon in a few days,' said the custody sergeant, using a tissue to clean his tunic. 'It always brings out the nutters. They might not sprout claws and fangs but the moon sure does something to them.'

'Tell me about it,' said Nightingale. 'When I was a negotiator we always had a higher workload when the moon was full. More assaults, more rapes, more suicides, more everything.'

The sergeant picked up Nightingale's driving licence and frowned at it. 'You're not *the* Jack Nightingale, are you?' he said.

'I'm *a* Jack Nightingale.'

'Inspector, right?'

'In another life, yeah,' said Nightingale. 'Have we met?'

'You came out to a wannabe jumper when I was on the beat in Kilburn,' said the sergeant, handing back the licence. 'Asylum-seeker who said he'd kill himself if he wasn't given leave to remain. You spent the best part of five hours talking him down. You were a big smoker then – I was sent out to buy you some Marlboro.'

'Thanks for that,' said Nightingale.

The older of the two policemen who had arrested Nightingale walked in. The custody sergeant waved him over. 'Hey, Bill, did you know that Mr Nightingale here was a celebrity?'

The officer shrugged carelessly. 'He said he used to be in the job, yeah.'

'He was a negotiator, one of the best,' said the sergeant. 'And CO19 – right?'

'For my sins, yeah.'

'He's the one who threw the paedophile banker out of the window in Canary Wharf,' said the sergeant.

'Allegedly,' said Nightingale.

'Are you serious?' said the officer, suddenly interested.

'The banker was fiddling with his daughter,' said the sergeant.

'More than fiddling,' said Nightingale. 'He'd been raping her for years.'

'Bastard,' said the officer.

'The mother knew what was going on, didn't she?' asked the sergeant.

'I think so,' said Nightingale.

'How could she let that happen to her kid?' asked the sergeant.

Nightingale shook his head. 'It's beyond me.'

'What happened to the little girl?' asked the officer.

'She died,' said Nightingale, flatly.

'Topped herself,' said the sergeant. 'Poor little thing.'

He pushed Nightingale's cigarettes and lighter across the counter. 'I've a lot of respect for what you did, Jack,' he said. 'That bastard deserved it.'

Nightingale pocketed the Marlboro and slid the lighter into his trouser pocket. 'Thanks,' he said.

'I'll get you a coffee sent in and we'll have you out of here as soon as possible.'

'Thanks, Sergeant.'

True to his word, the custody sergeant brought Nightingale a cup of coffee about half an hour after he'd been placed in a cell. 'I sent one of the lads out to Starbucks,' he said. 'Thought I'd save you the canteen rubbish.'

'I appreciate it,' said Nightingale, taking the cup from him.

'Probably your first time on this side of a cell door,' observed the sergeant.

'That's true enough.' Nightingale was sitting on the bed, a concrete block on which lay a blue plastic mattress. To the right of the door there was a toilet without a seat.

'Do you want a blanket or something?'

'I'm fine,' said Nightingale.

The sergeant started to leave, then stopped. Nightingale could see that he wanted to say something. 'After the guy went through the window . . .' said the sergeant.

'Yes?'

'There were no . . . ramifications?'

'I left the force,' said Nightingale.

'But you weren't charged?'

'There was no evidence. No witnesses, no CCTV. And I said nothing.'

The sergeant smiled. 'Always the best way,' he said, 'especially when dealing with the Rubber Heels.' Rubber Heels was the nickname of the Professional Standards Department, the cops who investigated other cops. 'And now you're a private investigator. Pays well, does it?'

'Pays okay,' said Nightingale. 'But there's no pension and not much in the way of perks.'

'You miss the job?'

Nightingale sipped his coffee. 'I miss the job, but I don't miss all the crap I had to wade through to do it.'

'A lot of the guys, they're saying they wish they had the balls to do what you did.'

Nightingale didn't respond.

The sergeant looked as if he wanted to say more, but instead he nodded and left.

It was just after half past five in the morning when the custody sergeant unlocked the cell door. He gave Nightingale a printed sheet informing him of his court date and told him he was free to leave. 'Are you going home?' he asked.

'I thought I'd get my car,' said Nightingale.

'Why don't you have another puff in the breathalyser first?' said the sergeant. 'I wouldn't want you picked up again. They'd probably blame me for letting you out too soon.'

Nightingale gave another breath sample, and this time he was below the limit. 'Is there a minicab firm I can use?' he asked.

The sergeant nodded at a row of orange plastic seats. 'Sit yourself down. I'll see if I can arrange something,' he said. He went to his counter and spent a few minutes on the phone, then called Nightingale over. 'Two of our guys will run you out,' he said. Nightingale thanked him. 'All part of the service, Jack,' he said.

21

Nightingale got home at just after eight o'clock. He let himself into the house, made himself a cup of coffee and phoned Robbie Hoyle. 'What's wrong?' said Hoyle.

'Maybe I just wanted a chat.'

'It's Saturday morning – early Saturday morning. My day of rest. Yours too. So I'm guessing there's something wrong.'

'You should be a detective,' said Nightingale.

'Yeah, so should you,' said Hoyle. 'Now what's wrong?'

'I was pulled in for drink-driving last night.'

'Oh, shit,' said Hoyle. 'Did you hit anyone?'

'No, nothing like that. I'd had a few beers and they breathalysed me.'

'You stupid bastard.'

'I know, I know.'

'You'll lose your licence, you know that?'

'That's why I'm calling, Robbie.'

'Come on, Jack, you know there's nothing I can do if you're in the system. Not these days.'

'I wasn't asking you to pull strings,' said Nightingale. 'I need a brief, a good one. Who's hot on drink-driving right now? There's got to be something that could sway the court. Former officer of the law, under a lot of stress, father just committed suicide – I'm thinking mitigating circumstances.'

'I'll ask around,' said Hoyle. 'Are you okay?'

'I'm fine, just kicking myself.'

'Do you want to come to the house tomorrow? Anna's doing a roast.'

'Maybe, mate. Let me see how my hangover shapes up.'

'If you need anything, let me know,' said Hoyle.

'Just get me that lawyer, mate,' said Nightingale. 'If I lose my licence I'll be well screwed.'

22

Nightingale spent most of Saturday asleep. He woke up at six o'clock that evening, cooked himself eggs and bacon and made himself a coffee, then watched Sky News as he ate. A large computer company had sacked two thousand workers, two high-street retailers had gone into receivership, and unemployment was heading towards three million. The pound was continuing to slump, the stock market was in the doldrums, and the tame economist that Sky had wheeled out said things would get worse before they improved.

When he'd finished eating he sat with his feet on the coffee-table, flicking through a hundred or so cable channels, unable to find anything that held his attention. He switched off the television and stared at the sideboard. A dozen photographs in various-sized frames stood on it. There was his graduation picture, in which he was wearing a robe and mortar board, his passing-

out at Hendon Police College, a photograph of Robbie
and Anna Hoyle on their wedding day and, to the right
in a small group, three of his parents. He stared at the
family portraits. The middle one was a wedding photograph, his mother in white holding a spray of flowers,
his father in a grey suit, his arm around her waist. He
was thirty-two when he married, and Nightingale's
mother had just turned twenty-five. She was pretty,
with curly black hair and green eyes, which suggested
Irish ancestry, and a sprinkling of freckles across her
upturned nose. She was smiling at her husband in the
same way that Nightingale had seen her look at him
throughout his childhood. There had never been any
doubt that she had loved him with all her heart. The
photograph to the right of that one was smaller, in a
silver frame. It was the first picture of Nightingale as
a baby, wrapped in a soft white blanket, his cheeks red
and his eyes closed, clasped by his mother who was
held by his father, both gazing down at him with love
and pride.

It was, Nightingale now realised, the start of the lie.
He wasn't their child: he had been given to them. On
the day that photograph had been taken, they had been
strangers with no connection to him, no family link,
no DNA, just a man and a woman who had been given
a baby. The child they were holding could have been

anybody's. Everything that had happened to Nightingale after that day, everything he had become, was based on a lie.

The third photograph had been taken outside Manchester United's Old Trafford stadium. Nightingale was just twelve, flanked by his father and uncle, all three sporting red-and-white scarves. They were on their way to take their places in the stands. It was a few years before the stadium had been made all-seating and Nightingale's father had always preferred to watch his football on his feet. A fellow supporter had taken the photograph with a camera that Nightingale's father had given him the previous Christmas.

Nightingale stared at it. His uncle must have known. Good old Uncle Tommy. Laughing, joking Uncle Tommy, who always turned up with a present, a card and a bear-hug every birthday and Christmas, and had slipped him an envelope containing a thousand pounds the day Nightingale had headed off to university. Good old Uncle Tommy, who must have known about the lie right from the start. And Auntie Linda. They must have known because they'd have seen that his mother hadn't been pregnant and that Nightingale had appeared from nowhere – and they had never let on, not even at the funeral. They had both been there, of course, standing either side of Nightingale as the two coffins were lowered into the ground. And neither of them had ever said anything about him being adopted, not then and not since.

He stared at the photograph of the three football fans. A father, his son, and the uncle. Except that Jack Nightingale wasn't Bill Nightingale's son and Tommy wasn't his uncle. Until Nightingale found out the truth, he would never be able to look at them in the same way again.

23

Nightingale parked the MGB in the street in front of his uncle's house, a neat three-bedroom semi-detached in a tidy, predominantly middle-class area of Altrincham to the south of Manchester. It had taken him the best part of three hours to drive from London. He climbed out, stretched, and lit a cigarette. His aunt and uncle were both ex-smokers, had been for twenty years, and wouldn't let anyone light up anywhere near them. His uncle's black Renault Mégane was parked in the driveway. Nightingale locked his car and walked slowly down the path to the front door, knowing he had to extinguish the cigarette before he rang the bell. The garden was well tended, with two large rhododendron bushes at either side of a neatly mown lawn. There was also a small water feature with a twee stone wishing-well and a bearded gnome holding a fishing rod. The gnome had been there for as long as Nightingale could remember; as a child he'd always been a little scared of it, half convinced that it moved whenever he took his eyes off it. He flicked ash at it. 'Are they biting?' he asked. The gnome stared fixedly at the hook on the end of its line. 'Maybe you should try somewhere else.' He tossed his cigarette into a flowerbed, then went up to the front door and reached out to press the bell.

He heard a rustle behind him and his heart raced, his childhood fears flooding back. He spun around, half expecting to see the gnome behind him, but it was only Walter, his aunt's Persian cat. The cat brushed itself against the back of Nightingale's legs and miaowed. Nightingale bent down to rub it behind the ears. 'Long time no see, Walter,' he said. The cat arched its back and purred loudly.

Nightingale straightened and rang the bell. He heard it chime inside the house. The cat continued to purr and wind himself round Nightingale's legs. 'What's wrong, Walter? You starved of affection?' asked Nightingale. After thirty seconds he rang again, but no one came to the door. 'Where are they, Walter?' said Nightingale. 'Are they in the back garden?'

Nightingale walked around the side of the house and opened a wooden gate that led to the rear, where his uncle had a vegetable patch and grew his prize-winning roses. As Nightingale closed the gate behind him, he noticed a red smudge on his hand. He held it up, frowning. It looked like blood, but there was no cut. He checked both hands, and then the latch on the gate, but there was only the one smear.

He walked down the path to the garden. 'Uncle Tommy?' he called.

There was no answer. He knocked on the kitchen door. 'Auntie Linda, it's me – Jack.'

Walter miaowed again. Nightingale knelt down and stroked the back of the cat's neck. 'What's going on, Walter?' he said. There was a glistening red smudge on the cat's nose. Sudden panic gripped Nightingale and his heart began to pound. He looked at the kitchen door. Set into the bottom there was a cat flap, which Walter used to get into and out of the house. There were red smudges on it.

Nightingale stood up and banged on the door. 'Auntie Linda! Uncle Tommy! Are you in there?' He pressed his ear to the wood but heard nothing. He hit the door again, then moved to the kitchen window and stood on tiptoe to peer through it. Beyond the sink he could see a bare leg, a broken plate and a pool of blood. Nightingale hammered on the window. 'Auntie Linda!'

He looked around, wondering to do, spotted his uncle's shed and ran to it, throwing open the door and grabbing a spade. He dashed back to the house and used the spade to smash the window, then climbed inside. His aunt was on the kitchen floor, her head shattered, brains and blood congealing on the tile-patterned lino. Her mouth was wide open and her eyes stared glassily at the ceiling. Nightingale knew immediately that there was no point in checking for signs of life.

He walked carefully around the pool of blood. There was no sign of a murder weapon and the back door had been locked, which meant that the attacker had either left by the front entrance or was still in the house. There was a knife block by the fridge and Nightingale pulled out a large wood-handled blade. 'Uncle Tommy, are you in the house?' he shouted.

He went through to the sitting room. There was an unopened copy of the *News of the World* on the coffee-table, and an untouched cup of tea. Nightingale went over to the table and touched the cup. It was cold and there was a thick scum on the surface.

He moved slowly back into the hallway, listening intently. He started up the stairs, taking them one at time, craning to look up at the landing above. Halfway up he found an axe, the blade covered with blood. He didn't touch it but stepped carefully over it. As he reached the top he heard a soft creak and froze, the knife out in front of him. He took another step.

Something was moving on the landing. Something just out of sight. He crept up, his mouth bone dry, his heart thudding. He stopped again when he heard another gentle creak. Then he saw something move. It was a foot – a naked foot – suspended in the air. Nightingale took another step and saw two feet, then pyjama bottoms, and as he reached the top he saw his uncle hanging from the trapdoor that led to the attic. There was a rope around his throat and, from the unnatural angle of the head, it was obvious that the neck had snapped. Nightingale realised that his uncle must have sat in the trapdoor and dropped. He was naked from the waist up and there were drops of blood across his chest. Nightingale could see no wounds on him so the blood could only have been his wife's. He must have battered her to death in the kitchen, then come upstairs and killed himself.

The rope creaked as the body moved slightly. He was dead but the fluids within him were shifting as the organs settled. The pyjamas were wet at the groin and there was a pool of urine on the floor. Nightingale took out his mobile phone and dialled 999. As he waited for the operator to answer, he turned. The bathroom door was wide open and through it he saw the mirror above the sink. Scrawled across it in bloody capital letters were seven words: YOU ARE GOING TO HELL, JACK NIGHTINGALE.

24

Jenny was sitting at her desk, using a small mirror to read the handwritten diary, when Nightingale walked in. He opened the door to his office. 'Coffee would be nice,' he said. He flopped onto his chair and put his feet on the desk. A small spider had set up home in the corner by the window and there was a layer of dust on the blinds. 'When's the cleaner in next?' he called.

'She was here on Friday morning,' Jenny replied, as she poured his coffee, 'and she'll be in again tomorrow.'

'Then she's doing a shit job,' said Nightingale. 'She's Polish, right?'

'Romanian,' said Jenny. 'I'll talk to her.'

'Tell her to give the blinds a wipe.'

'I hear and obey,' said Jenny, appearing at the door with a steaming mug. 'Just like your women – hot and black.'

Nightingale frowned.

'What?'

'I was joking,' she said, putting the mug on his desk and sitting down opposite him. 'Trying to lighten the moment.'

'But I've never had a black girlfriend,' said Nightingale, reaching for the mug.

'That's what makes it funny. What's wrong, Jack? You look like—'

'Like I've seen a ghost?'

'Well, yes, actually.'

Nightingale sipped his coffee. 'My uncle killed himself yesterday – killed himself and murdered my aunt.'

Jenny's jaw dropped. 'What?'

'My uncle Tommy. He hanged himself.'

'Why?'

Nightingale shrugged. 'He didn't leave a note. I spoke to him during the week and said I'd drive up to Altrincham for Sunday lunch so they were expecting me. He sounded fine then. But when I got there, they were dead.'

'Jack, that's terrible. That's . . .' She sat down. 'I don't . . . it doesn't . . .' She shook her head. 'This is unreal.'

'It's real, all right,' said Nightingale. 'I spent yesterday talking to the Manchester cops.'

'The cops?'

'It was a murder-suicide, Jenny. The cops have to investigate, but it's open and shut. My aunt's blood was all over him and she'd scratched his face. There was no one else involved.'

'But why? Why would he kill his wife?'

'I've no idea. I'd told them I wanted to talk about my parents, whether I was adopted or not.'

'And they were okay on the phone?'

'They sounded a bit nervous, but they invited me for lunch.'

'I can't believe this,' said Jenny.

'I'm having trouble coming to terms with it myself,' said Nightingale.

'They weren't having problems or anything?'

'I don't think so.'

'Jack, you don't think this is connected to Gosling, do you?'

'It didn't occur to me, Jenny.' Actually, that was a lie because as soon as Nightingale had seen the bloody letters on Uncle Tommy's bathroom mirror he had known that he was in some way connected to the death of his aunt and uncle. But he couldn't figure out what that connection was. When he'd first seen the words scrawled in blood he'd thought he was dreaming. He'd stared at the message in horror, imagining that at any minute he'd be in

Underwood's office and the man would crash through the window and fall to his death. But it was no dream, he didn't wake up, the words were real and his uncle and aunt were dead. Nightingale had no idea why he was hearing people telling him he was going to hell, and even less why his uncle would write it on the bathroom mirror before killing himself. But until he had worked out what was going on, he didn't intend to worry Jenny.

'Did you tell the police about Gosling?' she asked.

'I thought it would just make a complicated situation even more so.' Nightingale swung his legs off his desk. 'It was one hell of a weekend,' he said. 'I spent Friday night in the cells.'

'You what?'

'I was done for drink-driving on Friday night.'

'Oh, Jack . . . You said you weren't going to drive.'

'And I wasn't. Swear to God, when I left the wine bar I had no intention of getting behind the wheel. I don't know what came over me.'

'So now what happens?'

Nightingale took another sip of his coffee. 'I didn't hit anyone but I'm going to lose my licence so I'll need to find somewhere to keep the MGB.'

'I'll look after it for you,' said Jenny.

'Have you got a garage?'

'I can leave it with my parents. My dad can take it

out every week, keep the battery charged. Those old cars seize up if you don't drive them.'

Nightingale smiled. 'We call them classics rather than old cars,' he said. 'Does he know what he's doing?'

'He's got two old Jags and a frog-eyed Sprite. Sorry, classic Jags. And a Jensen-Healey.'

'You never told me that.'

'You never asked, Jack. My dad used to work for Jaguar. He was an accountant and until he retired he was on the board.'

Nightingale put down his mug. 'You constantly amaze me,' he said.

'Mutual,' said Jenny.

'How goes the translation?'

Jenny shuddered. 'It's full of some very weird stuff.'

'How weird?'

Jenny leaned forward. 'Have you got a tattoo?'

'A tattoo? What – "I love Mum", that sort of thing?'

'A pentagram. Either a tattoo or a mark that looks like a pentagram.' She sat back in her chair. 'I know it sounds ridiculous but, according to Mitchell's diary, anyone whose soul belongs to the devil has a mark, a pentagram, hidden somewhere on their body.'

'You're right, it sounds ridiculous,' said Nightingale. 'I'm thirty-two years old, and if I had a tattoo I'd know about it.'

'So you've nothing to worry about, then,' said Jenny. She started to get up but Nightingale waved her back into her chair.

'Whoa, horsey,' he said. 'Are you saying that if I do have a mark I should worry?'

'You said you haven't.'

'But if I had, do you think I'd have something to worry about?'

'I think I'm reading the ramblings of a deeply disturbed mind. That of a sad bastard with too much time on his hands.'

Nightingale raised his mug in salute. 'That's my girl,' he said. 'You had me worried for a moment.'

'Worried about what?'

'That you were starting to take this nonsense seriously.' He took another sip of coffee. 'Do you still have that pal at the Department for Work and Pensions?'

'Sure. Why?'

'Can you get her to run a check and see if Sebastian Mitchell's still alive and kicking?'

'If he is, he'll be in his eighties. Maybe older.'

'Be nice to know if he's still around. Or if he met a sticky end, too.'

25

Nightingale unlocked the front door of Gosling Manor and flicked the light switch. The massive chandelier glowed with more than two dozen bulbs. He had paid the bill on Friday and the electricity company had promised to have the power reconnected over the weekend. 'Excellent,' he said. He switched off the light. It wasn't yet noon and the hallway was flooded with natural light from a skylight in the double-height ceiling. He walked through to the main drawing room and flicked the light switches there to check that they were working, then went back into the hall and looked up at the CCTV camera that covered the main entrance. A small red light on the side glowed weakly.

He went back into the drawing room and saw, out of the window, something move by the trees, a shadow that slipped behind a massive oak. Nightingale stared at it, wondering what it was. It was too tall to have been a dog or a fox, too small for a man. It might have been a child, but what would a child be doing in the grounds? He lit a cigarette and continued to stare at the tree. The grounds of Gosling Manor would be a magnet for local kids, he realised. Lots of trees to climb, places to build dens, and with the house empty, there'd be no one to chase them away. If it had been in a city it would have been vandalised already, windows smashed and graffiti sprayed across the doors and walls. Even though country children were different from their inner-city counterparts, Nightingale knew it would be a matter of time before someone broke in. An empty house was just too tempting a target, even when it was in the middle of nowhere. He needed either a night watchman or a security company making regular visits. If squatters moved in, the house would be that much harder to sell. The grounds needed maintaining, too. The lawns were still immaculate but grass grew and it would need cutting before long. And someone would have to rake up all the dead leaves.

Nightingale sighed. It would cost him a small fortune to carry out even basic maintenance on the huge house, money he didn't have. And there was bound to be a sizeable inheritance-tax bill. Even if he were to sell the house quickly, he reckoned he'd be lucky to see more than a few thousand pounds once he'd paid off the mortgage, the taxman and the estate agent. He blew smoke and briefly considered setting fire to the building and claiming on the insurance. Except there probably wasn't any insurance. Gosling hadn't insured his mort-gage payments, so he almost certainly hadn't insured the house against fire.

There was no further movement around the oak tree and Nightingale turned away from the window. He went back into the hall and pulled open the panel that led down into the basement. He flicked the switch at the top of the stairs and the fluorescent lights kicked into life. He heard a scratching sound upstairs and froze, his hand still on the switch. For a few seconds there was only the sound of his own breathing. Then he heard a miaow and more scratching. 'Hey, cat, get down here and I'll let you out!' shouted Nightingale. His voice echoed in the hallway.

The scratching stopped. Nightingale had never been a great fan of cats. He didn't like the way they stared at people, the disdainful way they looked down their noses as if there was no doubt in their minds that cats were the superior species. But if cats were so smart, they'd be able to open their own cans of food. 'Or you can stay up there and starve – the choice is yours,' he shouted. Starvation wasn't an option, Nightingale knew, as there would almost certainly be a large rodent population calling Gosling Manor home. Cats, unlike humans, were natural survivors.

Nightingale went slowly down the stairs. The basement didn't look quite so large now that the lights were on, but it was still bigger than most small-town libraries. The exhibits in the display cases didn't look quite so eerie under the stark lights. For the first time Nightingale noticed the bare brick walls and the uneven tiled floor.

The six LCD screens at the far end of the basement were blank, but as Nightingale got closer to them he could see small green lights that showed they were switched on. He sat down in front of the stainless-steel console and pushed the button labelled 'Main Entrance' but nothing happened. Next he tried 'Study' but that didn't work either. He frowned. Then he noticed six buttons at the top right of the console. He pressed them and, one by one, the screens flickered into life. The two in the middle showed full-screen views while the others were divided into four, giving a total of eighteen shots of the house and its grounds.

The two full screens showed an upstairs corridor and the master bedroom. Nightingale started with the 'Study' button, then worked his way methodically through all twenty-eight cameras. There was no sign of the cat. He noticed a cupboard to the left of the desk and opened it to find a computer with slots for six

DVDs. He pressed 'eject' but all were empty. If recordings had been made of the CCTV feeds, they weren't there now.

Nightingale returned to the view of the master bedroom and leaned back in the chair. He could just make out the rust-coloured stain where Gosling's body had lain after he'd pulled the trigger. Had there been anyone in the basement when Gosling had killed himself? Probably not: he wouldn't have wanted any witnesses. A shotgun in the mouth wasn't a cry for help. He'd just wanted to end it all. He must have dismissed the staff before he did it.

Nightingale stared at the bed, the chair and the candles surrounding the circle, which had presumably offered some form of magical protection. Gosling must have believed he was safe if he stayed inside it, which implied that he would have had to remain there all the time. But there was no food in the room, and no way of getting to the bathroom without leaving the circle, so if Gosling had been inside it for any length of time he must have had someone in the house to help him, to bring him food and deal with his waste. He took out his wallet and flicked through it until he found the Neighbourhood Watch card given to him by the policeman he'd met the first time he'd come to the house. He tapped out the number on his mobile.

'Sergeant Wilde? This is Jack Nightingale – I own Gosling Manor. You were around with your colleague earlier this week.'

'You can call me Harry, Jack. You outranked me when you were in the job, so it's only fair.'

'Can you talk?'

'I just got home and my wife's burning my dinner as we speak so, yes, fire away. How can I help you?'

'You said that Gosling's driver let you into the house after he'd found the body.'

'That's right.'

'Was there anyone else in the house?'

'At the time he killed himself? No. He'd sent what staff there were home the night before.'

'So there were people still working at the house? Even though the furniture had all gone?'

'There was a skeleton staff, I think. An old woman who did the cooking and a bit of cleaning, and her husband tidied the garden. The driver doubled as butler.'

'I don't suppose you've got their phone numbers, have you?'

'Why? Is there a problem?'

'No, I just need someone to keep the place clean, I thought the old staff might be the best bet,' lied Nightingale. 'I'm not that handy with the old mop and brush, to be honest.'

'You and me both.' The policeman laughed. 'Let me have a look through my old notes. Can I call you on this number?'

'Day or night,' said Nightingale, and ended the call.

He wandered past the bookshelves, running his fingers along the spines. He stopped at one titled *The Devil and His Works* and pulled it out. It was a large leather-bound volume by Sir Nicholas Weatherby, published in 1924. Nightingale wondered what a knight was doing writing a book about the devil. He flicked to the index. There were four references to 'summoning the devil'. The first mentioned it in passing, the second and third were biblical quotes about Satan, but the fourth took up half a dozen pages in the final chapter. Nightingale carried the book to Gosling's desk and sat down to read.

Sir Nicholas began with a stern warning about the dangers of any sort of interaction with Satanic forces. Many who tried ended up dead or deranged, and only highly experienced Satanists should ever attempt to make contact with the devil or his demons. Nightingale laughed at the author's flowery language – his style seemed more suited to a Barbara Cartland romance than a serious treatise on the dark arts.

In the next paragraph Sir Nicholas detailed a spell that he said guaranteed an appearance by Satan himself.

'It is,' said Sir Nicholas, 'only to be used by a level-nine Satanist with the protection of a magic circle fortified by holy water blessed by the Pontiff.'

Nightingale couldn't see how repeating a few words, none of which made any apparent sense, could achieve anything, let alone summon the devil. He stood up and, in a loud voice, slowly recited the first sentence. '*Bagabi laca bachabe Lamc cahi achababe Karrelyos,*' he said. He stopped and listened but all was still. He smiled to himself. What had he expected? The stench of brimstone? A flash of lightning? It was nonsense. '*Lamac lamec Bachalyas,*' he continued. He paused again. Nothing had changed. It hadn't got colder or hotter, lighter or darker. There was no sign that the words were having any effect at all. His heart was racing and his mouth had dried even though he knew it was a charade. He kept his finger on the page so that he wouldn't lose his place, and continued: '*Cabahagy sabalyos Baryolas Lagoz atha cabyolas Samahac et famyolas Harrahya.*'

When he reached the end he put down the book and stood up. 'Is anybody there?' he said. His voice echoed around the basement. 'Anybody?' He grinned. 'I thought not. The whole thing's bollocks.' He held the book above his head. 'If it isn't bollocks, and if there really is a devil, then strike me down now – do your worst. Come on you bastard! Do your worst!'

He caught sight of himself in an ornate gilt mirror and realised how ridiculous he was being to even entertain the idea that a few mumbled words would summon a demon from hell. He winked at his reflection. 'Only joking,' he said.

He turned away and walked down to the bank of surveillance monitors. Something moved on one of the small screens. A car at the entrance to the estate. Nightingale leaned over the console and pressed the button to bring up the picture on one of the big screens. He doubted that the devil would turn up in a Ford Mondeo. He watched Robbie Hoyle climb out of his car and walk over to the speakerphone. A handset on the left of the console buzzed and Nightingale picked it up. 'Hi, Robbie,' he said. 'What's up?'

'How did you know it was me?' said Hoyle.

'Smile, you're on *Candid Camera*.'

Hoyle looked around until he spotted the camera and waved. 'Are you going to let me in or what?'

'You're not trying to sell me something?'

'No.'

'And you're not a Mormon or a Jehovah's Witness?'

'Definitely not.'

'You're not the devil, are you?'

'What?'

'The devil. Can you prove that you really are Robbie Hoyle and you're not the devil in disguise?'

'Don't be a prick, Jack. Jenny told me you were here and said we should talk.'

'I'll take that as a no.'

Nightingale couldn't see a button that operated the gates. He took the handset away from his head. There was a single button below the mouthpiece and he pushed it. On the screen the gates began to open. 'Thank you so much,' said Hoyle, and walked back to the car.

Hoyle was still just halfway down the drive when Nightingale opened the front door. He parked in front of the house next to the MGB and climbed out. 'Are you okay?' he asked.

'What did the lovely Miss McLean tell you?'

'That your uncle killed his wife then topped himself.'

'That's pretty much it.'

'Bloody hell, Jack. What happened?'

Nightingale shrugged. 'I've no idea. I spoke to them on the phone and they were okay. When I drove up on Sunday she was dead in the kitchen and he was hanging from the attic trapdoor.'

Hoyle walked into the hall. 'Jack, you look like shit.'

'Thanks.' Nightingale shut the door behind them. 'There was something weird, Robbie. Something I didn't tell Jenny.' Nightingale sighed. 'My uncle wrote a message on the bathroom mirror. In blood.'

'You're serious?'

'Do I look like I'm joking?' He took a deep breath. 'He wrote that I'd be going to hell.'

'You specifically?'

'"You are going to hell, Jack Nightingale."'

'In blood?'

'In blood,' repeated Nightingale. 'In my aunt's blood.'

'He wrote that in blood and then hanged himself?'

Nightingale nodded.

'That's sick.'

'The whole thing is sick.'

'Why would he write that?'

'I don't know, Robbie. But . . .'

'But what?'

Nightingale had been about to tell his friend about the dreams he'd been having and that the message written in blood had been Simon Underwood's last words before he went through his office window, but he knew how crazy that would sound so he bit his tongue. 'Nothing,' he said.

'And what did the police say about it?'

'They didn't see it. I cleaned the mirror before they got there.'

'Bloody hell, Jack. Are you mad? Tampering with

evidence in a murder case? They'll throw away the key.'

'Only if they find out. And you're the only person I've told. No one else knows.'

'Even so. You can't do that. It's evidence.'

'He killed her, Robbie, there's no doubt about it. The axe was on the stairs and there was blood spatter all over his chest. He was a big man so I don't see that anyone else could have hanged him. The message on the mirror would have muddied the waters.' He jerked a thumb at the entrance to the basement. 'Come on.' He headed for the basement and Hoyle followed.

They reached the bottom of the stairs where Hoyle stood with his hands on his hips. 'It's a lot less intimidating with the lights on, isn't it?'

'Yeah, and the CCTV's running, too, so you can check out every room without leaving your seat. You still haven't said why you're here, Robbie.'

'Don't get paranoid, mate. Jenny said you were coming out here so I said I'd swing by and see what you were up to. Check that you were all right. Oh, and the DNA results came back,' said Hoyle. 'Ainsley Gosling is definitely your father.'

'Terrific,' said Nightingale.

'Is that good news or bad?'

'I'd put it at about fifty-fifty,' said Nightingale. 'Why

would my uncle kill himself, Robbie? And why would
he batter his wife to death? He loved her. They were
peas in a pod, joined at the hip. Same as my parents.'
He grimaced. 'I suppose I should start saying "adoptive parents" now that I know Gosling was my real
father.'

'What did the Manchester cops say?'

'Murder-suicide, which is obviously what it was. The
doors were locked, her blood was on the axe, along
with his fingerprints, and there was blood spatter all
over him. Open and shut.'

'Except no motive.'

'They reckon he just snapped. It happens.'

'And what about what he wrote?'

Nightingale ran his hands through his hair. 'I don't
know, Robbie. I just don't know.'

'He must have written it for a reason,' said Hoyle.
'I understand why you didn't want the cops to see it,
but you can't pretend it wasn't there.'

'I don't know why he would have written it. He was
fine when I last spoke to him.'

'And why are you here? Jenny said you've a couple
of cases that need work.'

'Nothing that can't wait a day or two,' said
Nightingale. 'I'm trying to find my mother. My real
mother – my birth mother. I wanted to talk to my uncle

about the adoption but that avenue's been closed so I thought I'd try to track her down. If Ainsley Gosling was my genetic father, he must have known who my she was. Is.' He shrugged. 'I don't even know if she's alive.' He sat down on one of the chesterfields. 'In a way, she might be the only family I've got left. And maybe she can tell me what's going on.'

Hoyle looked around. 'I don't suppose there's a coffee machine down here?'

'Everything but,' said Nightingale.

'There must be adoption records, right? If your parents adopted you there'd have to be paperwork.'

'My birth certificate has Bill and Irene Nightingale down as my parents. There's nothing to say I was adopted. And, according to the DVD Gosling left me, I was given to them at birth. I don't think any agency was involved.'

'That's illegal.'

'It was thirty-three years ago. I don't think everything was computerised as it is now. And I get the feeling that Gosling wasn't too concerned about the legality of what he was doing. I think he just got the baby, his baby – me – gave him to the Nightingales and they passed him off as their own.' He waved his arm around the basement. 'I think the answer's somewhere here. Gosling must have kept records and this is his hidey-hole so I want to see what I can find.' He pointed to the middle of the basement. 'I'm going to start with those filing cabinets but I'll go through every book in the place if I have to.'

'Looking for what, exactly?'

'I don't know, Robbie. But he was a rich man so he must have kept a track of what he was spending. Everyone does, right? You keep receipts and bank statements and bills.'

'Anna looks after the finances,' said Hoyle. 'But, yeah, I know what you mean.'

'So, I think Gosling must have paid someone to help him with the adoption. He couldn't have done the whole thing himself. If I can find his records for the year I was born, I might turn up a clue as to who my real mother was.' He smiled ruefully. 'I keep saying that. "Real mum". As if Irene Nightingale was some sort of fake. She wasn't. She was my mum and she'll always be my mum, no matter how this pans out.' He flicked ash onto the floor. 'Shouldn't you be at work?'

'Late shift,' said Hoyle.

'Do you want to make yourself useful?'

'That's why I'm here.'

26

Nightingale found Ainsley Gosling's financial records in six beechwood filing cabinets between a display case of ivory carvings and a seaman's chest with a lock that had rusted with age and defied his attempts to open it. Gosling had been methodical with his record-keeping and there were separate files for each quarter going back to 1956. Nightingale pulled out the three most recent ones and took them to a desk where Hoyle was poring over a huge leather-bound book filled with newspaper clippings. He looked up. 'He was interested in serial killers – Fred West, the Yorkshire Ripper, Harold Shipman. He followed all the cases.'

'Everyone should have a hobby,' said Nightingale, dropping the files onto the desk. 'These are his most recent financial records. Can you see what he was up to in the months before he died?' He went back to the filing cabinets. The records for the year he was born were in the third. He pulled out the four files.

'He was buying books, big-time,' said Hoyle, holding up a receipt from a Hamburg bookstore. 'He paid a million and a half euros for something called *The Formicarius* in January.'

'A million and a half euros for a book? It's no wonder all his money went.'

'Published in 1435, according to this. But that's just one. There's a receipt here for six hundred thousand dollars, another for a quarter of a million pounds. A stack of receipts from China that I can't read. And, from the look of it, they were all about witchcraft or demonology. Occult stuff.' Hoyle gestured at the book-shelves. 'That's where all his money went. He spent millions putting this library together.'

Nightingale put the files on the desk. 'He wasn't building a library. He was buying information.'

'I don't follow,' said Hoyle.

'He didn't care about the books, he wanted the infor-mation in them.' Nightingale sat down in a leather winged chair. 'Here's what I think. He did a deal with the devil when I was born. Or, at least, he thought he did a deal.'

'Jack . . .'

Nightingale held up a hand to silence his friend. 'Whether he did or he didn't do isn't the issue. What matters is what was going through his mind. And so far as he was concerned he'd sold my soul. Then, as he said on the DVD, he had a change of heart. He wanted out of the deal, but for that he needed information.' He pointed at the bookshelves. 'He thought the answer lay somewhere in those.'

'You're not starting to believe this mumbo-jumbo, are you?'

'I'm trying to empathise with Gosling,' said Nightingale. 'I'm trying to think the way he was thinking. If I can get inside his head, maybe I can make sense of this. Maybe I can work out why he killed himself.'

'Why does it matter?'

'He was my father.'

'In name only,' said Hoyle. 'You never knew him. So why does it matter? And why are you looking for your genetic mother?'

Nightingale didn't reply.

'You think this all might be true, don't you?' asked Hoyle, quietly.

'Don't be soppy,' said Nightingale.

'You want to ask her if Ainsley Gosling sold your soul to the devil.'

Nightingale shook his head and opened a file. It was full of bank statements, used cheque books and receipts.

'I don't think he sold my soul. But I think he believed he did. There's a difference. Besides, I haven't got a mark.'

'What's that supposed to mean?'

Nightingale sighed. 'They say that if your soul belongs to the devil, you carry a mark. Like a tattoo.'

'"They"?'

'The people who believe in this crap,' said Nightingale. 'It was in that book I took with me last time. It was written by some top Satanist. In it he says that if the devil has your soul, you have a pentagram tattoo somewhere on your body. And I haven't. You've seen me in the changing rooms enough times.'

'That's true. Not a pretty sight, it has to be said.'

'But no pentagram. So, it's all bollocks.' He flicked through a cheque book. The dates in it were from the year that he had been born.

'Damn right, it's bollocks,' said Hoyle. He held up another receipt. 'He bought a dozen books from a shop in New Orleans for a total of half a million dollars – all about voodoo. You know, you should be able to sell them – you'd make a fortune.'

'Assuming I can find someone crazy enough to buy them,' said Nightingale. He handed the cheque book across the desk to Hoyle. 'Thirty-three years ago, Ainsley Gosling paid twenty thousand pounds to a woman called Rebecca Keeley.'

Hoyle studied a cheque. 'That was a lot of money back then.'

'It's a lot of money now,' said Nightingale.

'What do you think the going rate for a baby was?'

'Twenty grand sounds about right to me. I'll see if I can track her down.'

Hoyle tapped the file he'd been working through. 'What I don't see in these files are his household accounts. Utility bills and payments to staff. It's all big payments. He must have left the small stuff to a manager.'

'His driver, maybe,' said Nightingale. 'He only had three people working for him towards the end.'

Hoyle pulled out a piece of paper. 'You know he had a Bentley?'

Nightingale shook his head.

'An Arnage,' said Hoyle. 'Nice motor.'

'But nothing here for the driver?'

'No pay slips, no national insurance, no tax details.'

'He probably didn't want his staff down here so the household accounts must be somewhere else.'

Hoyle checked his watch. 'I'm going to head off,' he said. 'Gotta be in the factory by six. You sure you're okay?'

'I keep flashing back to my uncle's house. And I keep thinking that maybe if I'd gone straight around to see them . . . Yeah, I'm fine. I'm leaving now myself. I'm on a case this evening.'

Hoyle stood up. 'Anything interesting?'

'Divorce. Wife playing offside. Makes a change – usually I'm following the husband.' Hoyle was still holding a file. 'Are you going to take that with you?'

'Thought I might, yeah. If I find anything interesting I can run the names through the PNC.'

'Go ahead, knock yourself out,' said Nightingale.

They went up the stairs together and Nightingale switched off the lights, then shut the panel behind them. He locked the front door and they stood looking up at the building.

'It's an awesome house, Jack,' said Hoyle. 'Be a great place to raise a family.'

'Bloody hell, Robbie! Can you imagine the upkeep? I'll have to sell it, pay off whatever taxes they hit me with and the mortgage, and if I'm lucky I'll have enough left to buy a packet of fags.'

'I'm just saying, it must be nice to be rich.'

'No argument there.'

'How did old man Gosling make his money?'

'No idea,' Nightingale said. 'Maybe we'll find out somewhere in his records.'

'I never said I was sorry, about your dad dying.'

'No great loss,' said Nightingale. 'I didn't know him.

Never met him. He was nothing to me so there's no grieving to be done. I did that when my parents died – for a long time. With Gosling it's confusion rather than grief. I just don't understand what was going through his mind, why he gave me up for adoption – why he did what he did.'

Hoyle held up the file he was holding. 'Maybe we'll find the answer in one of these.'

Nightingale nodded. 'I hope so,' he said. 'I really hope so.'

27

The problem with divorce work, as Nightingale knew all too well, was that the deceived spouse always wanted proof. It wasn't enough just to say that he'd seen a man and woman enter a hotel and that they'd stayed there for an hour. The client wanted photographs or a video, hard evidence that could be waved in the face of the guilty party. The problem with photographs was that good cameras were bulky, and you needed a telephoto lens for decent shots – hotels, even cheap ones, didn't take kindly to men in raincoats skulking around their reception areas with them.

Nightingale's green MGB was too conspicuous for surveillance work and the company credit card was close to its limit, so he had borrowed Jenny McLean's Audi A4. He wasn't sure how his assistant could afford such an expensive car, but he couldn't bring himself to ask her directly in case she mistook his curiosity for jealousy. He'd parked outside the hotel and listened to a radio discussion programme while he waited for Mrs McBride to arrive for her assignation. She was as regular as clockwork, using the same hotel on the second and last Monday of each month. She always drove there with her lover and parked in a multi-storey a short distance away. She would check in and get the key to the room, then phone the man on his mobile. Nightingale had watched them two weeks earlier but Joel McBride wouldn't take his word for it and was insisting on photographic evidence.

Nightingale saw Mrs McBride coming around the corner and switched off the radio. He climbed out of the Audi and locked it. He was holding a black-leather attaché case and pointed it at her as he pressed a hidden button in the handle. A lens in the side was connected to a digital video recorder inside the case.

Mrs McBride was smiling as she talked into her mobile phone, her high heels clicking on the pavement. She was an attractive blonde in her thirties, about five feet six with good legs. She was so engrossed in her call that she didn't give Nightingale a second glance as she walked past him. The briefcase recorded sound and vision and he was close enough to hear her say 'darling' and tell whoever it was that she would see them soon.

She pushed through the double doors into Reception

and Nightingale followed her. As she walked up to the desk, he moved to a sofa and sat down, keeping the lens pointed at her. She handed over her credit card and filled in the registration form, then took her room key and headed for the lifts. Nightingale got up and walked slowly after her, pretending to have a conversation into his mobile. He waited until the lift doors were about to close after her before he stepped in. 'I'm just getting into the lift,' he said into his phone. 'I'll call you back.' He put it into his pocket and looked at the button she'd pressed. 'Same floor,' he said. He smiled but he didn't feel like smiling. He hated lifts with a vengeance but there were times when he had no other choice than to trust his fate to the wires and pulleys that kept him suspended above the ground.

She flashed him an uninterested smile and watched the numbers as they winked on and off. When they reached the floor she walked quickly down the corridor. Nightingale followed, keeping well back. She had a room in the middle of the corridor so he walked past her, tilting the case to keep her in the camera's view. He heard her unlock the door and close it. He walked to the end of the corridor, turned and stepped around the corner, keeping the briefcase aimed at the room where Mrs McBride was. He didn't have to wait long. He heard the lift doors open and took out his phone, held it to his ear with his left hand and aimed the attaché case down the corridor with the right.

Mrs McBride's lover walked briskly down the corridor, tapping a copy of the *Evening Standard* against his leg. He was wearing a dark blue pinstripe suit that had the look of Savile Row and carrying a cashmere coat over one arm.

Nightingale walked towards him slowly, muttering into his phone, keeping the case pointing towards the man as he knocked on Mrs McBride's door. She opened it and kissed him, then dragged him inside just as Nightingale drew level with the door. His timing was perfect.

He went back outside and sat in the Audi. Two hours later he videoed the man leaving on his own and walking along the street towards the tube station. Five minutes after that he got a nice shot of Mrs McBride walking out of the hotel, looking like the cat that had got the cream.

28

Jenny looked up from her computer when Nightingale walked in, swinging his attaché case. 'How did it go?' she asked.

'Perfect,' said Nightingale. He put the case on her desk, clicked the double locks and opened it. He removed the memory card from the side of the camera and gave it to Jenny. 'Run off a couple of DVDs, might need a bit of editing.'

'No problem,' said Jenny. 'How's my car, by the way?'

'I had a bit of a run-in with a delivery van, scraped the side.'

'You did not!'

Nightingale grinned. 'Joke,' he said. 'Would I take any risks with your pride and joy? Now, did you get the credit-card records? They were obviously regulars at the Hilton. Be handy to show how often they go there.'

'Yes, but my contact's asking for more money.'

'Because?'

'Because he says they're clamping down – Data Protection Act and all that. Now he wants three hundred a go.'

'There's enough in petty cash, right?' said Nightingale, lighting a cigarette.

Jenny flashed him a sarcastic smile. 'We haven't had any petty cash for the last three months. I paid him myself.'

'Put it on Mr McBride's bill,' he said.

'My DWP pal wants more too.'

'What is it with these people?' Nightingale sighed. 'They shouldn't even be selling us information in the first place.'

'I think that's why the price keeps going up,' said Jenny.

'But she came through, did she?'

'She managed to track down Rebecca Keeley. She's in a nursing home, apparently. But nothing on Mitchell. He isn't on any of the databases. Never paid tax, never been on the electoral roll, never seen a doctor. The original invisible man.'

'Well, I hope we're not paying for that,' said Nightingale.

'We're paying for the checks, Jack, not the results.'

'So what's the story on Keeley? It's an old folks' home, is it?'

'Hardly,' said Jenny. 'She's only fifty.'

Nightingale's brow furrowed. 'Fifty? That means she was seventeen when she gave birth.'

'You're assuming she's your mother, Jack. And that's a very big assumption. All you have is that Gosling gave her some money at about the time you were born.'

'Twenty thousand pounds was a lot of money back then,' said Nightingale. 'He must have been paying her for something important.'

'She could have sold him a painting. Or a piece of furniture.'

'He was meticulous with his records. Every cheque stub was filled in with either a reference number or a description of what he'd paid for. But the one for Keeley just had the amount with no explanation.'

'I'm just saying, don't get too excited. It might turn out to be nothing.'

'Message received and understood,' said Nightingale. 'So why's she in a home if she's only fifty?'

'I don't know, but I've got an address,' she said, handing him a sheet of paper. 'Shall I get Mr McBride in so that you can give him the bad news – and his bill?'

'Might as well,' said Nightingale, studying the piece

of paper she'd given him. The Hillingdon Home was in Hampshire, and there was no indication of what sort of outfit it was. Underneath the address there was a phone number, and the name of the administrator, a Mrs Elizabeth Fraser.

'His wife paid for the hotel room, did you realise that?' asked Jenny.

'Yeah, I saw her handing over her card. Unbelievable, isn't it? She sleeps with the boss and pays for it. What's he got that I haven't?'

'Charm for a start,' said Jenny.

29

'Go on, number five!' bellowed Nightingale, waving his betting slip. 'Go on, my son!'

'His name's Red Rover,' said Hoyle, at his shoulder.

'He doesn't know his name,' said Nightingale. 'Go on, number five!'

The greyhounds reached the second bend in a tight pack with number five somewhere in the middle. Nightingale had put twenty pounds on it to win for no other reason than that he'd liked the way the dog seemed to be smiling as it was walked around by its trainer.

Hoyle had put fifty pounds on number six, and as the dogs sped into the final stretch he cursed: number six was bringing up the rear.

'Come on, number five!' shouted Nightingale.

A black dog, its tongue lolling out of the side of its mouth, seemed to hit a second wind and hurtled into the lead. It crossed the finishing line just yards behind the mechanical hare. Number five came in third. Nightingale screwed up his betting slip. They were at Wimbledon Stadium in south London. It had been Hoyle's idea – he had been a regular visitor before he was married but now he barely managed two or three evenings a year. 'Which do you fancy in the next race?' asked Nightingale, studying his race card

'Old Kentucky,' said Hoyle.

'I think having the word "old" in his name isn't a great start,' said Nightingale.

'Won his last four races,' said Hoyle. 'Come on, drinks are on me if he loses.'

They joined a queue to place their bets. 'I got an address for that woman, the one Gosling gave twenty grand to,' said Nightingale. 'Some sort of home in Hampshire.'

'You really think she might be your mother?'

'She's the only lead I've got.'

'Are you going to see her?

'I've got to, Robbie.'

'You don't have to, you could let sleeping dogs lie.' He grinned. 'No pun intended.'

Nightingale kept his eyes on the list of runners.

'Are you going to see her because she's your mother? Or because of this devil's contract thing?' asked Hoyle, lowering his voice to a whisper.

'I just want to meet her.'

'What if she doesn't want to meet you?'

Nightingale frowned at him. 'What do you mean?'

'She gave you up for adoption thirty-three years ago. She hasn't made any attempt to contact you during that time, and the last thing she's going to expect is you turning up on her doorstep.'

Nightingale reached the front of the queue and handed a twenty-pound note to the cashier, a rotund woman in her fifties with blue-rinsed hair and green eye-shadow. 'Old Kentucky in the next race,' he said.

The woman smiled at him through the protective Perspex screen. 'You're going to hell, Jack Nightingale.'

'What?' said Nightingale, his fingers gripping the race card so tightly that his knuckles whitened. 'What did you say?' He knew what she'd said – he'd heard her quite distinctly. There was no mistake.

'Win or place?' said the woman.

Nightingale was sure he hadn't misheard the first time – she hadn't mumbled and had looked him right in the eye as she'd spoken. Her voice had been flat and cold, the voice of something not quite alive. But, like everyone else who had told him he was going to hell, she didn't seem to be aware that she'd said it.

'Win or place, young man,' said the cashier. 'I don't have all day.'

'Win,' said Nightingale. Had he imagined it? Was his subconscious playing tricks on him? It had started with the dreams of Simon Underwood falling to his death, but maybe now his subconscious had decided that the dreams weren't enough, that it wanted to torment him while he was awake. Or maybe he was going crazy.

The cashier handed him a betting slip and Nightingale walked away.

'Jack, are you okay?' Hoyle called.

Nightingale reached for his cigarettes. No, he wasn't okay. He was a long, long way from it. He lit a cigarette but had taken only one drag when an official in a blazer tapped him on the shoulder and told him that smoking wasn't allowed. 'But we're outside,' he said, waving at the sky.

'It's a place of work,' said the man. 'Health and safety.'

'It's bloody nonsense,' said Nightingale.

'It's the law,' said the man. He had short, wiry hair and its dark brown hue was so uniform that it had to have been dyed. His cheeks were threaded with burst veins and he had the look of a former sergeant major hankering for the days when he could make life a misery for men who couldn't answer back. 'Don't give me a hard time, sonny.'

'You're not going to tell me I'm going to hell, are you?'

'I don't have to use bad language,' said the man, holding up a small transceiver. 'All I have to do is call Security.'

Nightingale dropped the cigarette onto the ground, stamped on it and headed for the bar. He was about to order a beer but changed his mind and asked for a whisky instead. It had just arrived when Hoyle appeared at his shoulder. Nightingale handed the barman a ten-pound note and ordered Hoyle a glass of red wine.

'What's wrong, mate?' asked Hoyle.

'Nothing,' said Nightingale. He downed his whisky in one gulp, and when the barman returned with Hoyle's wine, he pointed at his empty glass and asked for a refill.

'Clearly,' said Hoyle. 'Since when have you been knocking back the whisky like that?'

'What's happening to me, Robbie? My bloody life's turned upside down in less than a week. My parents aren't my parents. The man who was my father claimed he'd sold my soul to the devil. My uncle killed my aunt and himself and . . .' He shook his head and picked up his glass.

'And what?'

'That message – the one my uncle wrote in blood. People keep saying it to me.'

'They *what*?'

'I keep hearing people tell me I'm going to hell.'

'You're under a lot of stress, that's all. Have you heard me say it?'

'No.'

'That's a relief.' His face went blank and he stared at Nightingale. 'You're going to hell,' he said, his voice a low whisper.

'Screw you, Robbie. It's not like that.'

Hoyle grinned. 'Just trying to lighten the moment,' he said.

'Cheers, mate.' Nightingale drained his glass.

'But, seriously, you should lay off the booze,' said Hoyle. 'You were never a big drinker. Strictly amateur.'

'I can drink you under the table,' said Nightingale. 'And look who's talking! You're a bloody wine drinker.'

Hoyle picked up his glass. 'You're just upset because you thought you were a Nightingale, but you turned out to be a Gosling,' he said. 'How the mighty have fallen.'

'It's not funny,' said Nightingale. 'My whole life has been a lie, Robbie. My parents lied to me from the day I was born. My uncle and aunt lied. Probably everyone I knew as a kid lied to me.'

'They didn't lie to you, they just didn't tell you the whole truth. There's a difference,' said Hoyle.

'That's lying by omission,' said Nightingale. 'Which is still lying.'

'You were adopted. Loads of people adopt and don't tell their kids. It's just . . . simpler.'

'Simpler? Or do you think that the fact they bought me from a Satanist might have had something to do with their reticence?' Hoyle didn't answer. 'Anyway, can we change the subject?' said Nightingale. 'I've had it up to here with Ainsley bloody Gosling.'

Hoyle sipped some wine. 'Jenny said business hasn't been so good recently.'

'She did, did she?'

'She said it was a bit quiet, yeah.'

'It's a dry spell, that's all,' said Nightingale. 'It happens. Peaks and troughs. Swings and roundabouts. Everyone's cutting back because of the recession, so the corporate side is down – but divorce work's up. We're doing okay.'

'I don't know why you're bothering with the marital-strife stuff. You're better than that, Jack.'

'Like I've got a choice.'

'You were a great negotiator – the best. You should be working for one of the kidnapping insurance firms. Or in-house security for a multinational.'

'The last guy I negotiated with exited through a twenty-storey window, let's not forget,' said Nightingale. 'That doesn't look great on the old CV.'

'I'm serious,' said Hoyle. 'You're better than this. You

know you are. Two years in the wilderness is enough. It's time to come back in.'

'Maybe.'

Hoyle slapped him on the back. 'You know I'm right, mate. Oh, one bit of good news for you. Your man Turtledove is the real McCoy, he's been a solicitor for nearly forty years and there's never been a complaint against him. So, whatever's going on, it's not a con. Now, come on, the next race is about to start.'

'Do you believe in hell, Robbie?'

'Who was it said that hell is other people?'

'I'm serious,' said Nightingale. 'Do you believe in a place called hell?'

'I've been to Harlesden, mate. That's as close to hell as I ever want to go.' Hoyle put his arm around Nightingale's shoulders. 'No, Jack, there is no such place as hell. You can trust me on that.'

Nightingale finished his whisky. 'Let's go see these dogs run,' he said.

30

Joel McBride had thought long and hard before he decided to kill himself. He had no children, his parents were long dead, and most of his friends were his wife's and he was sure they would side with her. McBride loved his wife and had done since the day they'd met, when she was a sales representative for a children's books publisher and he had been working in the Trafalgar Square branch of Waterstones. She'd walked in wearing a short skirt and a low-cut top ready to extol the merits of her firm's three new authors, and within an hour they were having coffee at Starbucks over the road. Two nights later they were in Leicester Square and on the next they were in bed together.

They had been married less than six months when McBride had injured himself. They had been on a riding holiday in Spain. His wife was a keen horsewoman but it had been his first time. His first and last. They had gone trekking through sand dunes, six holidaymakers and two girls from the stable, and had rounded off the afternoon with a gallop along the beach. The stable girls knew McBride was a novice and had told him to hold back, but he'd wanted to show off to his wife so he'd given the horse its head. It had been a combination of bad luck and bad judgement: the rein had snapped, McBride had fallen and the horse had trodden on him when he'd hit the sand. His spinal cord had been severed. The holiday insurance paid for the hospital in Spain and the flight back to London, but he had never walked again and never would.

Things had changed after the accident, of course. He could get himself in and out of his wheelchair and manage the toilet, and he could drive a specially adapted car, but he was still a cripple and, worse, a cripple who couldn't get an erection. Sex was out of the question – or, at least, the sort of sex they'd enjoyed before the accident. He did his best to please her with his hands and tongue but it wasn't enough. He'd known that one day she would take a lover but had hoped she'd be honest enough to tell him, and reassure him that she still loved him, that she was his wife and would be for ever.

He'd suspected for weeks that she'd embarked on an affair, but she'd denied it when he'd asked. But he knew in his heart that she was planning to leave him. She might stay for a few more weeks, maybe months, but there had been a growing coldness in her eyes and long silences in front of the television, so he had asked Jack Nightingale to check up on her.

McBride had confronted her with the evidence – the phone records and the video of her checking into the hotel – and had asked if she was planning to leave him. She hadn't said anything. Instead she'd put on her coat and walked out of their house. He had waited all evening and all night but she hadn't returned – and she'd switched off her mobile phone. McBride knew he couldn't bear to live without her.

His house, their house, the house they'd lived in for more than six years, was just a mile from the canal. That was the best way, he'd decided. He had painkillers but he'd checked on the Internet and an overdose wouldn't kill him straight away. He'd die, but from liver failure, and it would be a long, lingering death over several days. His doctor would probably prescribe sleeping pills but it usually took at least three days to get an appointment with him. He thought of cutting his wrists but the idea of slicing through his flesh with a knife made him feel sick. The canal would be simple and quick.

McBride's wheelchair wasn't powered so he used his

hands to propel it along the pavement. He hadn't bothered to put on the fingerless leather gloves that usually protected them and his palms were soon muddy and sore. It had rained earlier that evening and the wheels made a swishing sound as he rolled along. The canal wasn't deep, McBride knew, five feet at most, but standing up wasn't an option for him. He'd found a length of chain in his garage, left there by the man who had sold them the house. It was heavy, the links the thickness of his thumb, and he had wrapped it around his waist, fastened with a padlock, in case he changed his mind at the last minute.

He rolled up the steep concrete ramp from the pavement to the muddy towpath. To his left there were banks of nettles and beyond them a tall hedge threaded with blackberry bushes. The canal was to his right. A narrow-boat was moored there, dark blue with circular brass-framed portholes and skylights. McBride kept going until it was out of sight, then pulled the chair around so that he was facing the water. He closed his eyes and swallowed. 'Our Father, who art in heaven,' he whispered. He hadn't been inside a church since his wedding day, and had never thought of himself as religious, but he wanted to die with the Lord's Prayer on his lips. He continued to mumble it as he propelled himself forward. He had to push hard to get the wheels over the edge but he rocked himself back and forth until he pitched head first into the cold, dark water.

McBride had thought he was alone, but there was one witness – two if you counted her dog, which would be reasonable because the dog was watching as McBride wheeled himself to the edge of the canal and into the water. She was wearing Goth black and had upside-down black crosses dangling from her ears and an Egyptian ankh around her neck. She wore a black leather motorcycle jacket, black leather jeans and high-heeled black boots. The dog barked and looked up at his mistress. She smiled down at him and stroked his head, concentrating on the spot he liked, just behind his ear. 'Not one of ours,' she said. The dog panted, drooling a little and showing a fleshy pink tongue. He was wearing a black leather collar with a silver buckle and studs, and hanging from it was a small silver penta-gram.

31

The Hillingdon Home sounded grand but it wasn't. It was a sixties-built concrete block with rusted metal-framed windows and graffiti spray-painted across the doors. As Nightingale finished his cigarette, he peered up at the top floors. Blank faces stared from some of the windows, white smudges behind the glass. It was a local-authority home on the outskirts of Basingstoke, about fifty miles south of London. The car park was full so he had left the MGB in the street, a short walk away. In his left hand he held a bunch of flowers. He had decided he ought to bring something and that flowers were the best bet. He dropped the butt of his cigarette onto the ground and pushed open the double doors that led to the reception area.

He'd phoned ahead to let the home know he was coming and an overweight West Indian woman in a floral dress took him to the office. The administrator was stick-thin with dyed chestnut hair and thick-lensed spectacles perched on her nose. She sat behind a large desk that bore an old-fashioned computer and a plastic nameplate – Elizabeth Fraser. 'I have to say, it was a bolt from the blue when you called,' said Mrs Fraser. 'Miss Keeley hasn't had a visitor in the ten years she's been here.'

'We lost touch,' said Nightingale.

'I'll say,' said Mrs Fraser. She tapped on her keyboard and frowned. 'We don't have anyone down as her next of kin.'

'As I said, we've been out of touch.'

She peered at him through her glasses. 'And the different surname is a concern,' she said.

'I think she gave me up for adoption when I was born.'

'I see,' said Mrs Fraser. 'Would you have any paperwork to substantiate that?'

Nightingale shrugged. 'I'm afraid not, it was a private adoption.'

'I have to say, Mr Nightingale, I'm a little reluctant to allow you access to Miss Keeley without some sort of evidence that you're a family member.'

Nightingale took out his wallet and removed his driving licence. He gave it to the administrator. 'This proves who I am, Mrs Fraser,' he said. 'As to proving that I'm her son, well, short of a DNA test, I'm not sure how I'd go about doing that. But I'm guessing that if she's in a local-authority home she doesn't have any money so it's not as if I'm here to rip her off. I don't have any proof that she's my mother but I was hoping that if I talked to her . . . I don't know, Mrs Fraser. My life's been pretty much turned upside-down over the last week and I just want some answers. I'm hoping I might get them from Miss Keeley.'

Mrs Fraser smiled. 'You're correct about the money,' she said. 'Miss Keeley doesn't have a penny to her name.' She fed Nightingale's details into the computer, then gave him back his driving licence. 'I must warn you not to expect too much,' she said. 'Miss Keeley was in a psychiatric hospital before she came here, and while she isn't what we'd classify as mentally ill now, she is uncommunicative. In fact, she hasn't said a word since she was brought here. From what we were told, she didn't speak in her last institution either. Not a word. The reason she was moved here was because there was no suitable medical treatment available and she was no longer considered a danger to herself or others.'

'How long has she been in care?' asked Nightingale.

'Well, as I said, she's been with us for around ten years, and in the hospital for six years, but prior to that her records are patchy. Apparently there was a fire in the home where she lived before she went into the hospital.'

'So she might have been institutionalised all her life,' said Nightingale.

'That's a definite possibility,' said Mrs Fraser. She stood up. 'I think you'll understand once you've seen her.'

She led Nightingale out of her office and down a corridor to a flight of stairs and walked up to the third floor where a male nurse was sitting at a desk reading the *Daily Express*. He nodded at Mrs Fraser.

'Everything okay, Darren?' she asked.

'No worries, Mrs Fraser,' he said. He had an Australian accent. He was in his late twenties, well over six feet tall, with wavy blond hair, a fading tan and a small diamond earring in his right lobe.

'We're here to see Miss Keeley. Is she okay?'

The man smiled. 'She never changes,' he said. 'I wish they were all as amenable.'

Mrs Fraser took Nightingale along the corridor and stopped outside a door on which a clear plastic box contained a white card. She took it out and looked at it, then put it back and knocked on the door. She opened it. 'It's only me, Miss Keeley,' she said. 'I have a visitor for you.'

As she opened the door wide, Nightingale saw a hospital bed, neatly made, and a bedside table with a water glass and a paperback book. It was the New English Bible, he realised, and it was well thumbed.

'This is Jack Nightingale,' said Mrs Fraser. 'He's come to have a chat with you. That's nice, isn't it?'

The woman was sitting in an armchair. Her hair was grey and tied back in a ponytail. She was wearing a shapeless pale blue dress and fluffy pink slippers. Her hands were clasped in her lap and she was staring out of the window, her lips pursed as if she was about to blow a kiss.

Nightingale stepped into the room and Mrs Fraser closed the door. 'He's just come to say hello, and he's brought you some flowers,' said Mrs Fraser.

Nightingale held them out but the woman didn't react. Her face was lined, there were dark patches under her eyes and her hands were wrinkled and hooked, like claws. 'She's only fifty, right?' said Nightingale.

'Yes,' said Mrs Fraser.

'But she looks so . . . so old.'

'The drugs can have that effect, I'm afraid.'

'Drugs?'

'She's had a lifetime of tranquillisers, anti-depressants and anti-schizophrenia medication.'

'But she's not on medication now?'

'She's still on anti-depressants, and she has developed diabetes so she has to have regular insulin injections. There's also a high-cholesterol problem and she takes medication for low blood pressure.' She patted the woman's arm. 'I'll leave you alone with Jack for a while, Miss Keeley,' she said. She smiled at Nightingale. 'I did warn you not to expect too much,' she said. 'They'll bring her a meal at four o'clock, and you're welcome to stay until then. Just let Darren know that you're leaving.'

'Thank you,' said Nightingale. Mrs Fraser let herself out and he sat on the bed, the flowers beside him, facing the woman. She continued to gaze out of the window, across the road to the discount carpet warehouse opposite. 'Do you know who I am?' he asked quietly.

The woman showed no sign that she had heard him.

'My name's Jack – Jack Nightingale.' He smiled. 'Though my name probably won't mean anything to you.'

She continued to stare outside, as if she was alone.

'Rebecca, did you have a baby thirty-three years ago? Because if you did, I'm your son. I'm the baby you gave away.' Nightingale smiled again, but this time it was more of a grimace. 'Or sold. Did you sell me, Rebecca? Did you sell me for twenty thousand pounds?

The woman's hands moved. She scratched her left wrist with the yellowed fingernail of her right index finger. Nightingale could hear the sound, a dry rasp like two sticks being rubbed together.

Nightingale tried to see in her some sort of resemblance to himself. She had a tight, pinched face and a sharp, almost pointed nose. She was nothing like him.

'Are you my mother?' he asked. 'Just answer me that. Did you give birth to me thirty-three years ago?' He smiled. 'It's Friday,' he said. 'Friday the thirteenth. That's funny, isn't it? Of all the days I should come to see you, it's Friday the thirteenth. And two weeks today I'll be thirty-three years old. Do you know what's supposed to happen to me on my thirty-third birthday, Rebecca? Do you?'

He couldn't tell if she'd heard a single word he'd said to her. He stood up and walked to the door. He grabbed the handle, but before he pulled it open he turned to look at her.

'Can't you even say goodbye to me?' he said.

The woman didn't move.

'Mum?' The word felt strange on his lips. 'If you are my mum, can't you even say goodbye? This will be the last time you see me.' He thought he detected a slight movement of her head, but then she was perfectly still again. He went to her chair and squatted so that his head was level with hers. He noticed she was wearing a small gold crucifix around her neck on a fine gold chain. 'Mum, can you hear me?'

Her eyes were glistening with tears but her cheeks were dry, as dry and wrinkled as old parchment.

'Why did you do it? Why did you sell me to Ainsley Gosling? I know he gave you twenty thousand pounds. Did he buy me from you?'

The woman's right hand twitched and her eyes widened. It was the first reaction she'd shown since he'd walked into the room. Her mouth opened and he saw she had no teeth, just ulcerated gums.

'Ainsley Gosling, you know that name, don't you?'

The woman's mouth opened wider. Her tongue was coated with white fur and he could smell her breath, sour and vinegary, like stale vomit.

'Ainsley Gosling,' repeated Nightingale. 'He was the man you sold me to, wasn't he? Tell me.'

The woman's hands bunched into arthritic fists and she stared at Nightingale, seeing him for the first time. She took a deep breath, opened her mouth and began to scream as if she was being burned at the stake.

32

Robbie Hoyle sipped his coffee and flicked through the file he had taken from the basement at Gosling Manor. Ainsley Gosling seemed never to have thrown away a single receipt or invoice. There were travel inventories that showed he had travelled the world, invoices from antiques shops and auction houses that showed he had been an avid collector, and one with a Harley Street address, written in an almost illegible scrawl. Hoyle screwed up his eyes and made out some of the words but not all. It related to treatment at a private clinic, and one word was quite clear – 'ultrasound'.

He looked at the heading again. 'Dr Geoffrey Griffith, paediatrician'. It was dated twenty months after Nightingale had been born. 'Got you,' he whispered. He couldn't see the name of the patient but he was fairly sure it involved Nightingale's missing sister. He took out his mobile phone and scrolled through the address book until he found his friend's number. The call connected but after half a dozen rings it went to voicemail. Hoyle looked at his watch. His shift was due to start in fifteen minutes so he drained his cup, paid his bill and headed out of the coffee shop. The Starbucks was across the road from the police station. He looked left and right. A double-decker bus drove past, then an *Evening Standard* delivery van. Cars rushed by on both sides of the road. He pressed redial but the call went to Nightingale's voicemail again. A Tesco truck drove past, a motorcycle courier, then a line of cars, bumper to bumper. 'Jack, it's Robbie. I'm just heading into work but I've found something in Gosling's file about your sister.' There was a gap in the traffic and Hoyle stepped off the pavement. 'I'll give you a call when my shift's over . . .'

A girl in Goth clothes was standing in the doorway of a florist's. Her Border collie was sitting next to her, its ears pricked. She ran a hand through her spiky jet black hair as she watched Hoyle step off the pavement.

'Hey, Robbie!' she shouted. Her voice cut through the hum of the traffic and Hoyle stopped in his tracks. 'Hey, Robbie, have you got a light?' she called.

Hoyle turned, frowning, the phone still at his ear. The girl waved and blew him a kiss. He took a step towards her and the black cab hit him full on at thirty-five miles an hour, breaking his legs, hip and spine, bursting his spleen and splintering his ribs, which punctured his lungs. The driver said later that he'd been distracted by something in the back of his cab, which was empty at the time. Something had been fluttering around like a trapped bird, he told police, but when he'd turned there was nothing. He hadn't had time to brake before the impact.

Hoyle bled out quickly as he lay on the Tarmac and he was dead before the paramedics arrived. The contents of the file were scattered across the road. The wind picked them up and blew them in all directions. The invoice from the paediatrician was caught in an updraught, spun into the air, then slapped against a lamppost. The wind snatched it again and it swirled back into the road. It blew under a parked car and settled in a puddle of oily water.

The girl and the dog watched as Hoyle's life ebbed away, then disappeared into the crowds pouring out of nearby shops, some staring in horror, others reaching for their mobile phones to photograph and video Hoyle as he lay dying in the road.

33

The male nurse straightened the quilt over Rebecca Keeley and took the thermometer from her mouth. 'I'm not sure you should still be here,' he said to Nightingale. He put the thermometer into the top pocket of his tunic. 'I think it'd be better if you left now.'

'It wasn't anything I did,' said Nightingale. The woman had only screamed once, but the mournful wail had gone on for more than a minute and it was only when she ran out of breath that she had stopped. Her hands had tensed into fists and she had grabbed her crucifix and held it in front of her as if she was warding off a vampire.

The nurse had burst into the room expecting the worst, but the woman had remained in her chair even when she was screaming. When she quietened he had helped her onto the bed and draped the quilt over her.

Nightingale tried to help but the nurse pushed him away. His mobile phone had rung while the nurse was comforting Rebecca Keeley, but he had reached into his pocket and switched it off.

The nurse took his stethoscope from around his neck and listened to her chest, then took her pulse. 'I really think you should go,' he said to Nightingale.

'We were just talking and she started to scream,' said Nightingale. 'I didn't do anything.'

'Miss Keeley doesn't talk,' said the nurse. 'I've been here eighteen months and she's not said one word to me.' He stood up and faced Nightingale with his hands on his hips. 'It would be best if you left now.'

'She's never done that before? Screamed like that?'

The nurse shook his head. 'She's normally as good as gold. What did you say to her?'

'Nothing,' lied Nightingale. 'I just told her who I was and showed her the flowers. Are you sure she isn't in pain or something?'

'No, she's fine.'

'Look, I'd really like to sit with her for a while,' said Nightingale.

'She needs rest,' said the nurse. 'She'd be better off sleeping.'

'If it's a question of money . . .' said Nightingale, taking out his wallet.

The nurse held up a hand. 'It isn't,' he said. 'It's a question of my patient's wellbeing. She needs her rest, Mr Nightingale. You can come and see her tomorrow.'

He was adamant, so Nightingale thanked the man for his help and left. As he went out of the room he picked up a hairbrush from the dressing-table and slipped it into his pocket.

34

Jenny smiled as Nightingale walked into the office. 'How did it go?' she asked.

'Difficult to say.'

'Was she pleased to see you?'

'Not really,' said Nightingale. He went over and made himself a coffee. 'Want one?' he asked.

'I'm okay,' she said. 'Come on, Jack, tell me what happened. Is she your mother or not? What did she say?'

'Not much,' said Nightingale. 'She's been on all sorts of anti-depressants for years. She's in a hell of a state.'

'But she's your mother. There's no doubt?'

'I don't know,' said Nightingale. 'She screamed like a banshee when I mentioned Gosling but all in all I couldn't get much sense out of her.' He pulled a Ziploc bag from the pocket of his coat. Inside was the hair-brush. 'But I did get a DNA sample.'

'You stole her brush?'

'I borrowed it,' said Nightingale. 'She can have it back when I'm done with it. You remember that private forensics laboratory we used on the paternity case? The one out by the airport?'

'Applied Forensics,' she said, taking the bag from him.

'Courier the brush over. I'll give you a few of my hairs, too. Get them to run a comparison on the DNA to see if we're related. Ask them to do a rush job.'

'You have to pay double for their forty-eight hour service,' said Jenny.

'Then let's do it,' he said. 'The sooner I know, the better.'

'Okay, but remember that it's Friday. Even if I get it to them today, it'll be Tuesday at the earliest before we have the results.'

'I need to know quickly,' said Nightingale. He perched on the corner of her desk. 'If she really is my mother then I have to go back to her.'

'Was she pleased to see you?'

'Horrified, more like.' He sipped his coffee. 'Screamed the place down, actually. They threw me out.'

'Why?'

'Well, they were quite nice about it, but I had to

leave.' The door opened. Two men in raincoats came in and even before they opened their mouths Nightingale knew they were cops.

'Jack Nightingale?' said the older of the two.

'That's what it says on the door.'

The one who had spoken produced his warrant card. 'I'm Inspector Dan Evans. This is DC Neil Derbyshire.'

'Is this about my aunt and uncle?' asked Nightingale, putting down his coffee and getting up.

Evans frowned. 'I'm sorry, I don't understand.'

'Tommy Nightingale. And Linda. Up in Altrincham.'

'It's a Jack Nightingale we're here to see,' said Evans.

'That's me,' said Nightingale. 'What's it about?'

'Do you know Inspector Robert Hoyle?' asked Evans.

'Robbie? Sure.'

'In what capacity?'

'He's a friend and a former colleague. What's happened?'

'I'm sorry, Mr Nightingale. Inspector Hoyle died this morning.'

The news hit Nightingale like a punch to the solar plexus. 'He what?'

'RTA, just after eleven o'clock. He was crossing the road, got hit by a taxi.'

Nightingale sat down heavily. 'My God. Oh, my God.'

'It was an accident,' said Derbyshire. 'He stepped off the pavement and the taxi ploughed into him.'

'We got your name and number off his mobile,' said Evans, frowning at the detective constable. 'Yours was the last number he called.'

'Had the driver been drinking?' asked Nightingale.

'Stone-cold sober. Says he was distracted by something in the cab but that Inspector Hoyle had just stopped in the middle of the road.'

Nightingale fumbled for a cigarette.

'Can I get you coffee or tea?' Jenny asked the detectives. She moved across the room to Nightingale and put a hand on his shoulder.

'We're fine, thank you,' said Evans.

'What's happening about Anna? Who's telling her?' said Nightingale.

'Superintendent Chalmers is with her now,' said Evans.

'Chalmers?' said Nightingale. 'She hates him.'

'You used to work in hostage negotiation, right?' asked Derbyshire.

'In another life.'

'You're the one who killed the paedophile, right? The banker who was molesting his daughter?'

'Allegedly,' said Nightingale.

'They said you threw him out of a ten-storey window,' said Derbyshire.

'They?' echoed Nightingale.

'I'd have done the same in your place,' said Derbyshire.

'Most of us would,' agreed Evans. 'If we had the balls. I'm a dad myself. Two girls. If anyone touched them . . .'

Nightingale straightened. 'Is there anything else, guys? Anything you need from me?'

'We're just clearing up loose ends,' said Evans.

'But there's nothing untoward, right? It was an accident, pure and simple?'

'Is there something else we should know about?' asked Evans.

Nightingale shrugged but didn't say anything.

'Was he doing something on the side for you?' asked Evans.

'Robbie was a straight arrow,' said Nightingale.

'We all do favours for friends, especially those who used to be in the job,' said Derbyshire.

'I never asked him for favours like that. I didn't have to.'

'No offence,' said Evans.

'None taken,' said Nightingale. 'Thanks for . . .' He

left the sentence unfinished. There was no reason to thank them: they were just doing their job.

When the two detectives had left Nightingale went into his office and pulled open the bottom drawer of his desk. He kept a bottle of brandy there for clients who needed a stiff drink after hearing bad news. He took it out now. 'Do you want one?' he asked Jenny.

Jenny nodded. 'I don't believe this,' she said.

Nightingale sloshed brandy into two glasses and gave one to her. 'I've got to go and see Anna,' he said.

'She must be in pieces. Three children. Oh, those poor kids.' She gulped some brandy, her hand shaking. 'This doesn't feel real.'

It never did, Nightingale knew. As a police officer he'd broken news of fatalities to families more than a dozen times, and rarely was it greeted with anything but disbelief. Mothers, fathers, children, the first reaction was always complete denial. Their loved one couldn't be dead: they'd only just seen them, talked to them, they were on their way home, they had just left for work. Then, once they had acknowledged the death, came the questions – how, why, when – as if understanding would lead to acceptance. More often than not it didn't. Acceptance came only with time.

Two young policemen had broken the news to Nightingale that his parents had died. They had turned up at his university hall of residence with one of his lecturers, asked him to sit down and told him they had bad news about his parents. Even when they had explained what had happened, Nightingale had still called home to check because he hadn't wanted to believe that his mum and dad were dead. Then when he had gone home and stood in the empty house, he had still half thought that they would be back at any moment, that he'd hear their car in the drive and they would rush in, laughing and saying it had all been a terrible mistake and they weren't the ones who had died in the accident. Even at the funeral it hadn't seemed real: the coffins were closed and part of him clung to the hope that someone else was inside them and that his parents were still alive.

'Why, Jack?' she asked. 'Why Robbie?'

'There's no reason,' said Nightingale. 'Wrong place, wrong time. A stupid accident. And accidents happen.' He smiled thinly. 'It's Friday the thirteenth, remember. Shit happens on Friday the thirteenth.'

'But why to Robbie?'

It wasn't a question he could answer. Bad things happened to good people. That was the way of the world. He stood up, went to his raincoat and took out his mobile phone, then sat down at his desk and switched it on. 'I was the last number he called, but my phone was off while I was with my mother,' he said. He looked at the little screen. He had a voicemail message. He pressed the button to pick it up and put the phone to his ear. 'Jack, it's Robbie. I'm just heading into work but I've found something in Gosling's file about your sister.' Nightingale could hear traffic in the background. 'I'll give you a call when my shift's over . . .' There was more traffic noise, then a girl's voice in the distance. 'Hey, Robbie!' And a second or two later, 'Hey, Robbie, have you got a light?' Then there was a sickening thud and silence.

Nightingale took the phone away from his ear and stared at it in horror.

'What's wrong?' asked Jenny.

'I just heard Robbie being run over,' he said.

'No way,' said Jenny.

'He'd rung to say he had information for me. Some girl called his name and then . . .'

Jenny held out her hand. 'Can I?'

'I don't think you should, kid,' said Nightingale.

'Please. I want to.'

Nightingale gave her the phone and she listened to the message. 'Who's the girl?' she asked. 'Did you recognise her voice?'

Nightingale shook his head. 'I don't think so.'

'She knew Robbie, she called him by name.'

'I guess so.'

'But if she knew him, why did she ask him for a light? She must have known he didn't smoke.'

Nightingale took the phone from her. 'Maybe she was calling someone else and Robbie thought she was talking to him.' He sipped his brandy. 'I'll go and see Anna.'

'Can I come?'

Nightingale opened his mouth to say that she should stay and mind the office, but she had known Robbie well. She'd been to his home and met Anna and the kids. 'Of course,' he said. 'Just leave a note on our door saying we'll be shut for a couple of hours.' He put the bottle back into his bottom drawer. 'On second thoughts, let's just close up for the day. If it's important they can call me on my mobile.'

35

A dozen large nondescript saloon cars were parked outside the Hoyle house and a single police patrol car. Nightingale found a space about a hundred yards from the house. It was starting to rain but Jenny had brought an umbrella with her so they sheltered under it as they walked along the pavement. 'What do you say to someone whose husband has died?' she asked.

'There's nothing you can say,' said Nightingale. 'You've just got to show that you're there for them.'

'Will she be all right? You know, financially.'

'Sure. He'd have insured the mortgage so the house will be paid for and there'll be a pension. The job will have people helping her.'

'Poor Anna. Poor, poor Anna.'

'Has anyone close to you died, Jenny?'

'Touch wood, I've been lucky so far,' she said. 'My

granddad passed away a few years ago but he was
ninety-seven. My family live for ever, pretty much.'

'You're lucky,' said Nightingale.

Jenny put her arm through his. 'Sorry,' she said. 'I
wasn't thinking.'

'You don't have to walk on eggshells with me,' said
Nightingale. 'I was a cop for almost ten years and I've
seen more than my share of dead bodies. I'm well over
my parents and Gosling – well, he was just a name.
My aunt and uncle . . . I don't know. That still hasn't
really hit me. I think it's because I was in London and
they were up in Altrincham. I didn't get to see them
much so in a way nothing's changed. I mean, I know
they're dead . . .' He shrugged. 'It's difficult to explain.
I was just about coming to terms with it but now this.
Now Robbie's dead too.'

'Are you okay?'

'You don't have to keep asking if I'm okay,' said
Nightingale. 'You're as bad as Robbie.' He groaned.
'God, listen to me. Talking as if he was still . . .' He
swore savagely.

Jenny squeezed his arm. 'Do you want to go for a
walk? We can come back later.'

'No, we have to go in – we have to see her now.'

They walked up the path to the front door and
Nightingale rang the bell. Anna's older sister, Marie,

opened the door. Her cheeks were wet from crying but she forced a smile when she saw Nightingale. 'Jack, hello.'

'I'm so sorry, Marie,' said Nightingale. He hugged her and gave her a light peck on each cheek. 'This is Jenny – she works with me.'

Marie smiled. 'Come on in – let me take your coats. Anna's in the sitting room.'

She was on the sofa, her arm around her eight-year-old daughter, Sarah. There were a dozen people in the room, drinking tea and making small-talk. An elderly woman Nightingale didn't recognise was walking around with a plate of chocolate biscuits. Superintendent Chalmers was standing by the window in conversation with Hoyle's immediate superior, a chief inspector whom Nightingale had met a couple of times. Both men nodded at him and carried on talking to each other.

Anna wiped her eyes with a handkerchief but started sobbing again when she saw Nightingale. She whispered to her daughter, got up and hurried over to him.

'I'm so sorry, Anna,' he said. 'If there's anything . . . you know . . . just ask.'

Anna hugged him and rested her head on his shoulder. 'I still haven't told the twins. I don't know what to say.'

'They're too young to understand,' said Nightingale.

'They're asking for him. Last time I said he was at work. They're asleep now.' She put her hands on his chest and looked into his eyes. 'What do I say, Jack? How do I tell them that they'll never see their father again?'

Nightingale bit his lower lip. He was finding it difficult enough to come to terms with Hoyle's death, and couldn't imagine how two three-year-olds would react. 'I don't know, Anna. All you can say is that Robbie loved them more than anything and that he's in heaven looking down on them.'

'Do you believe that, Jack? Do you believe he's up there somewhere, watching us?'

'I'd really like to think so, Anna,' said Nightingale. He had heard the uncertainty in his voice. 'But kids believe, and that's what's important.'

'I can't live without him, Jack.'

'Yes, you can, Anna. We're all here for you. We'll get you through this.'

Tears rolled down Anna's cheeks and she wiped her face with the handkerchief. Then she realised that Jenny was beside Nightingale. 'Oh, Jenny, thanks for coming.'

'If there's anything I can do, Anna, if you need help taking care of the kids or shopping or if you need driving anywhere,' she said, and gave her a hug.

'Thanks so much,' said Anna. She gestured at the

woman with the biscuits. 'Robbie's mum was straight around and she's staying with me until . . .' She wiped her eyes again. 'Until, I don't know . . .'

'Are you okay for money, love?' asked Nightingale.

Anna nodded. 'A really nice man from the Police Federation gave me his card and said he'd handle everything – Robbie's pension, any money we need to tide us over.'

'That's good,' said Nightingale.

'Robbie didn't even have a will, did you know that?'

'Who does?' said Nightingale. 'I haven't.'

'Me neither,' agreed Jenny. 'You just don't think about it, do you?'

'I did ask him, loads of times,' said Anna, 'but he said writing your will was tempting Fate, that he had no intention of . . .' She faltered, then blew her nose. 'Stupid, stupid bastard,' she said. She touched Nightingale's arm. 'I've got to get back to Sarah. She's been so calm, so collected, so together, but I don't think it's really hit her yet.'

'She's in shock,' said Jenny. 'We all are.'

Anna went back to the sofa and sat down with her daughter. Sarah held her mother's hand, her lower lip trembling.

'I can't believe this is happening,' said Jenny. 'I keep thinking I'm going to wake up – it just doesn't feel real.'

'Can you see any whisky? I need a drink.'

'Jack . . .'

'Come on, Robbie would understand,' he said. 'If it was me, I'd expect him to have a drink.' He smiled ruefully. 'But then again, if it was me, there wouldn't be so many people grieving.' He nodded at the superintendent. 'Bloody Chalmers wouldn't be there, for a start.'

'It's good that he came, Jack,' said Jenny.

'He hated Robbie. And vice versa.'

'Which makes it all the more decent of him to have come,' said Jenny.

'Yeah, maybe,' he admitted.

Marie appeared at Jenny's shoulder. 'Would you like some coffee or tea?' she asked them.

'Coffee, please,' said Jenny.

'Me too,' said Nightingale.

'I'll put a drop of something in yours, Jack, shall I? Brandy, maybe? Or whisky?'

'You read my mind, Marie, thanks. Whisky would be great.'

'It's not mind-reading,' she said. 'Every cop in the room has got brandy or whisky in their coffee. Even the superintendent over there.'

Jenny smiled at Nightingale as Marie went off to the kitchen. 'See, Jack? He's human after all.'

36

'When did you eat last?' asked Jenny, as they walked towards Nightingale's MGB. It had stopped raining but there were still pools of water on the road. They had stayed at Anna's house for almost two hours, during which time more than a hundred police officers had called to pay their respects. Robbie Hoyle had been well liked, but even if he had been the most unpopular man on the Met, they would still have come. Police officers were a tight family and always closed ranks when one of their own died.

'Does whisky count as one of the major food groups?' asked Nightingale.

'No, it doesn't,' said Jenny.

'Yesterday then.'

'You didn't have breakfast?'

'Who has breakfast these days?' said Nightingale. 'No one has the time.'

Jenny put her arm through his. 'Come on, we're going to eat,' she said. 'My treat.'

'Your treat? Am I paying you too much?'

'You haven't paid me at all this month.' She laughed. 'How does Chinese sound?'

'If you're paying, we'll eat whatever you want,' he said.

They reached the MGB and climbed in. Nightingale headed north to London. Jenny knew a Chinese restaurant around the corner from her home in Chelsea where she was greeted like a long-lost cousin. Nightingale asked her to order and she did so in what sounded like fairly fluent Cantonese, much to his surprise. 'I didn't know you spoke Chinese,' he said.

'I sometimes wonder if you even looked at my CV,' she said. 'It did say that I spent four years in Hong Kong when I was a kid.'

'Yeah, I probably didn't get that far down it,' said Nightingale. 'You had shorthand and typing and a good phone voice.'

Two Tsingtao beers arrived. 'I'm serious, Jack. Sometimes you're a bit on the self-centred side.'

'I'm all I've got,' said Nightingale. 'I guess that comes from having my parents die when I was a teenager.'

'Maybe, but you should try opening up more.'

He raised his glass to her. 'Okay, I will.'

'No, you won't,' she said. She clinked her glass against his.

'I'll try,' he said.

Their food arrived. Half a Peking duck, scallops fried with celery, chicken with cashew nuts, pak choi in oyster sauce, and rice. An old Chinese lady, her hair held up in a bun with two scarlet chopsticks, came over, spoke to Jenny in Chinese and walked away cackling.

'What's the joke?' asked Nightingale, struggling with his chopsticks.

'She wanted to know if you were my husband.'

Rice fell onto his lap. 'And what did you say?'

'I told her you were my father.'

'What? I'm only . . . How much older than you am I?'

'You didn't read my CV, did you? I'm twenty-five. And you'll be thirty-three next week. So . . . ?'

'I'm eight years older. Which hardly makes me father material, does it?'

'Jack, I was joking. And would you like a knife and fork?'

'I can manage, thanks,' said Nightingale. He picked up a piece of chicken and got it halfway to his mouth before it slipped from his chopsticks and fell onto the tablecloth.

'There's nothing to be ashamed of in not being able

to handle chopsticks,' she said, deftly picking up a cashew nut with hers and popping it into her mouth.

'Yeah, well, you're half Chinese, apparently,' said Nightingale.

'I said I lived in Hong Kong for a few years. I wasn't born there,' she said. 'Daddy was working for one of the trading hongs.'

A scallop fell into the pak choi. 'So, my question to the Chinese expert is, now that they know how great knives and forks are, why don't they stop using these bloody things?'

'Tradition,' she said.

'Well, they've changed other traditions, haven't they? They stopped using rickshaws and wearing those Mao outfits, and they replaced donkeys with cars easily enough, so why not do the sensible thing and replace chopsticks with more user-friendly tools?' He waved for the waitress to bring them two more beers. They laughed and argued and ate and discussed everything but the one thing they were both thinking about: Robbie Hoyle.

When they had finished their meal a waitress placed a saucer on the table. On it was the bill and two fortune cookies. Nightingale picked one up and held it between his finger and thumb. 'This had better be good luck,' he said.

'Lottery numbers would be nice,' said Jenny.

Nightingale grinned. He crushed the cookie and let the pieces fall to the tablecloth. He unrolled the slip of paper and looked at the typewritten sentence. The smile froze on his face. It was as if time had stopped dead and his whole world was focused on the seven words in front of him. 'YOU ARE GOING TO HELL, JACK NIGHTINGALE.'

'Jack, what's wrong?' asked Jenny, leaning across the table towards him.

Nightingale couldn't take his eyes from the printed fortune. He was holding it so tightly that his finger and thumb had gone white.

'Jack?' said Jenny. She reached over and pulled the slip away from him. Nightingale sagged in his seat, his arms folded across his chest. She read it, and smiled. 'It's not so bad,' she said. '"Never take a stranger at his word, but remember that friends can also lie." Good advice, if you ask me.'

Nightingale snatched the piece of paper from her. 'NEVER TAKE A STRANGER AT HIS WORD, BUT REMEMBER THAT FRIENDS CAN ALSO LIE.' Nightingale wiped his face with his left hand, blinked several times and read it again.

'Jack, what is it?'

Nightingale turned the slip of paper over. The back was blank.

'You look like you've seen a ghost.'

He tossed the fortune onto the table. 'I'm just tired,' he said. 'My eyes are playing tricks on me.'

'What did you think it said?'

'Nothing.'

'Don't lie to me, Jack.'

Nightingale massaged the bridge of his nose. 'I'm just tired, kid.'

'Don't "kid" me,' she said. She picked up the scrap of paper. 'This is the normal sort of fortune rubbish you find in every cookie, but when you looked at it, it was as if you were reading your death warrant.'

'It was nothing,' said Nightingale.

'I'm serious, Jack. Don't you dare lie to me.'

'It's a long story.'

'I'm not going anywhere.'

Nightingale sighed. 'Okay. I thought it said I was going to hell. That's what it said the first time I read it.'

'That you were going to hell?'

'That's right. That I, Jack Nightingale, was going to hell.'

'So you misread it. No big deal.' She frowned. 'Those words mean something, don't they?'

'My uncle wrote them before he died. In blood. In his bathroom.'

Jenny gasped. 'Why didn't you tell me that before?'

'Because . . . I don't know, Jenny. I thought maybe I'd imagined it. Like I imagined it just now, when I read the fortune.'

'Why would your uncle tell you that you were going to hell?'

'I've no idea. But those words keep cropping up.'

'Since when?'

'Like I said, it's a long story.'

'Jack . . .'

'Okay, okay,' said Nightingale. He sighed and put his head in his hands. He had never told Jenny about Sophie Underwood, or what had happened to her father. It wasn't something he wanted to talk about, but as he sat in the Chinese restaurant and stared at the table-cloth stained with the food that had slipped from his chopsticks he told her everything that had happened on that chilly November morning. Or, at least, as much as he could remember.

'Hand on heart, Jenny, I don't remember what happened to the father. I don't remember if he jumped or if I pushed him. There's a gap in my memory, just a few seconds, but no matter how many times I replay it in my mind, I can't remember what happened. It feels like I pushed him – I know I wanted to and I know he deserved to die the way Sophie died, but I can't remember doing it. But the one thing I can remember is what he said to me. Or screamed at me, more like.' He forced a smile. 'He yelled at me that I was going to hell. Not a curse, not an insult, but like he knew it was a fact.'

'It's an expression, Jack.'

Nightingale shook his head. 'He meant it. And I remember him saying it as clear as if he was standing here right now. But I don't remember what happened after that. The next thing I do remember I was down-stairs, heading towards my car. He said it, and I saw it just then, on the fortune that came out of my cookie.'

'But it doesn't say that, Jack.'

'Not now it doesn't. But it did when I looked at it. It did, Jenny. I swear.'

'Maybe your subconscious is playing tricks. You heard about Robbie, it made you think about sudden death, and your subconscious replayed what happened two years ago and muddled things up.'

'Since when were you a psychiatrist?'

'It's common sense. We've both been under stress since we found out what happened to Robbie. And stress does funny things to people.'

Nightingale drank the rest of his beer. 'I still can't believe Robbie's dead. You know, I've known him almost ten years. We were at Hendon together.'

'He was a nice guy,' said Jenny.

'He was a better cop than me,' said Nightingale. 'A better human being, too. A husband, a father. He didn't deserve to die like that.'

'Nobody deserves to die,' said Jenny. 'It was just a stupid accident.'

'He was leaving a message for me when he was hit by the cab,' said Nightingale. 'Maybe if I'd answered the phone it wouldn't have happened. Do you want another beer? One for the road?'

Jenny shook her head. 'I'm fine,' she said. 'It was an accident, Jack. You have to stop blaming yourself. And at least it was quick. He didn't suffer.'

'That's bollocks,' said Nightingale. 'They always say that. "At least he didn't suffer. At least it was quick." One moment they're there and then they're gone. Bang. Thank you and good night.'

'But isn't that better than lying in a hospital bed wired up to a life-support machine?'

'There's too much unfinished business. There's no time to prepare yourself, or to prepare the people you care for. Sudden death just rips people away. It leaves too many unanswered questions.' Nightingale opened his wallet and dropped three twenty-pound notes onto the saucer. 'I need a smoke,' he said. 'And don't worry, I won't be driving.'

Jenny picked up the money and gave it back to him. 'My treat, remember?'

'Thanks.' He returned the notes to his wallet.

'I'll come with you.'

'Secondary smoke kills,' he said. 'I wouldn't want you on my conscience.'

Jenny opened her mouth to argue but Nightingale held up his hand to silence her. 'I just want to be on my own,' he said. 'I'm sorry. I need to think.'

'And you can't think when I'm around? Jack, you can't always push people away like this.'

'I'm not pushing anyone away,' he said.

'No, you're running away, and that's worse. You can't solve your problems by running away from them.'

Nightingale headed for the door. 'Watch me,' he said.

37

First thing on Tuesday morning the forensics lab phoned Jenny. When she'd hung up she hurried into Nightingale's office. 'The lab came back with the results,' she said. 'Rebecca Keeley's your mother.'

'There's no doubt?' said Nightingale.

'Only that one in six billion nonsense,' said Jenny. 'She's your birth-mother, no question of it. They're sending me a fax to confirm it and their bill.'

'Will petty cash cover it?' asked Nightingale, hopefully.

'It might if we had any,' said Jenny. 'We'll need a cheque.'

Jenny's computer beeped to tell her that she had received an email. She went over to her desk while Nightingale phoned Hillingdon Home and spoke to Mrs Fraser, who told him that Miss Keeley had slept through the night and now seemed much calmer.

Nightingale explained that, following a DNA test, he was now sure that Rebecca Keeley was his mother, but thought better of mentioning that he'd stolen the hairbrush. Mrs Fraser said she had no objections to Nightingale visiting again. This time he didn't take flowers, but he had with him an old photograph album.

The male nurse met him in Reception and explained that his mother was sitting in the garden. It wasn't so much a garden as a patch of grass with a couple of wooden benches, a rockery filled with heathers of various hues, and a stone birdbath covered with sparrow droppings. Nightingale's mother was on one of the benches, wearing a tweed coat and a purple headscarf. She was staring at the birdbath and stroking the crucifix around her neck.

'I like her to get some fresh air now and again,' said the nurse. 'I'll take her back inside in half an hour.' He pointed at a large picture window overlooking the garden. Three old women were sitting in armchairs, staring blankly through the glass. 'I'll be in the residents' lounge,' he said. 'If she starts getting agitated again, I'll have to end the visit.'

'I understand,' said Nightingale.

He went over to the bench and sat down next to her, unbuttoning his raincoat. He had the photograph album on his lap and said hello, but she ignored him.

'It's me, Jack,' he said. 'I've come back to see you.'

There was no sign that she was aware he was there. He opened the album. The first picture was of himself at only a few days old, wrapped in a white cloth, his eyes wide open. 'This is me, not long after I was born,' he said. He pushed the album towards her. 'Do you remember me as a baby? Did you see me when I was born or did he take me away from you straight away? I know you're my mother, Rebecca. I checked. There's no doubt. I'm your son.'

The woman looked down at the picture, still rubbing the crucifix between her thumb and first finger.

'Do you recognise me, Rebecca? Do you recognise the baby in this picture?'

'Edward?' she whispered.

'Edward? Is that the name you gave me? Is that what you called me? My name's Jack now, Jack Nightingale.' He turned the page. There were six photographs across the spread, different views of his parents holding him. 'These are the people who took care of me, Rebecca. Bill and Irene Nightingale, my parents.'

She reached out and gently touched the pictures one by one with her left hand, holding the crucifix tightly in the right.

'Do you remember, Rebecca?' asked Nightingale, in a soft whisper. 'Do you remember holding me when I was born? Did you kiss me?'

He turned the page. The next set of photographs was of himself at two weeks old, tiny and defenceless. He flicked through the pages and showed her one of him smiling. He'd always been a happy baby, according to his mother. Happy and smiling and as good as gold.

A single tear trickled down Rebecca Keeley's cheek.

Nightingale reached across and held her left hand. 'Why did you give me away?' he asked.

She shook her head slowly. Nightingale wasn't sure if she hadn't understood his question or was denying what he'd said.

'What was the money for? The twenty thousand pounds?'

'Are you a ghost?' she whispered.

'A ghost?' repeated Nightingale. 'Why would you think I'm a ghost?'

'You died,' she whispered. 'You died when you were born.'

Nightingale froze. 'Is that what he told you? Is that what Ainsley Gosling told you?'

'You were stillborn, he said. The doctor wouldn't even let me see you. They took you away and said they'd bury you but I never saw a grave.' She stared at him with tear-filled eyes. 'Why have you come back?'

'I didn't die,' said Nightingale. 'I didn't know about you. I didn't even know you existed. Gosling gave me to the Nightingales and they brought me up.'

The woman's brow furrowed even more. 'You're not a ghost?'

Nightingale stroked her wrinkled hand. 'No, I'm flesh and blood.'

'And Ainsley?'

'He died,' said Nightingale.

'What happened?'

'He got sick and died,' said Nightingale. He had no compunction about lying to the woman. He didn't think she'd react well to the news that Gosling had blown his head off with a shotgun.

'Is he a ghost now? Will he come to see me?'

'I don't think so,' said Nightingale.

'I loved him,' said the woman, her hands trembling.

'What was the money for?' asked Nightingale. 'The twenty thousand pounds he paid you?'

'He said I needed a holiday. He said he'd join me and he gave me the money and a train ticket to Blackpool and I never saw him again. I always wanted to see Blackpool. I wanted to climb the tower and walk on the pier.' She blinked. 'What's your name again?' she asked.

'Jack.'

'That's nice. I was going to call you Edward.'

'That's a good name,' said Nightingale. He smiled. 'You know, I never really felt like a Jack. But Edward? Eddie? Ed?'

'Never Eddie,' she said primly. 'Edward.'

'You can call me Edward, if you like,' said Nightingale. 'Rebecca, do you know if he had any other children? A daughter, maybe?'

'I stayed in the hospital for two days afterwards and then I went to Blackpool and the last time I saw him was at the station. He said he'd come to see me in Blackpool. But he never did.' A tear rolled down her left cheek. 'Why did he tell me that you'd died?'

'I don't know. I'm sorry.'

She sniffed. 'I'm sorry too,' she said. 'How old are you?' she asked.

'Thirty-three next week,' he said. 'On Friday the twenty-seventh.'

She gasped and clutched at the crucifix. 'My God,' she said.

'What?'

She avoided his gaze and stared at the birdbath. 'Nothing,' she whispered, rubbing the crucifix between her finger and thumb. 'Nothing, nothing, nothing, nothing.' She repeated the word like a mantra.

Nightingale narrowed his eyes, 'You know, don't you?'

She shook her head.

'You do. You know what he did, why he took me away from you when I was born.'

'I don't, I don't, I don't,' she murmured. She kissed the crucifix with her thin, bloodless lips and carried on rubbing it. 'I don't, I don't, I don't.'

'You know what's going to happen on my thirty-third birthday, don't you? On Friday next week.'

The woman didn't answer but she squeezed the crucifix harder.

'You know, don't you? You have to tell me. You owe me that much.'

Tears rolled down both her cheeks. 'He told me you died,' she muttered. 'That's what he told me.'

'But you knew what he was, didn't you? You knew he was a Satanist.'

'Not at first. I just thought he was a man who liked me, who cared about me.'

Nightingale took a deep breath. He wasn't getting anywhere by asking her directly. She was confused, clearly damaged by the years of medication. He forced himself to smile and gently stroked her hand. He knew from his years of negotiating that sometimes you had to come in from the side, to slip through the defensive barriers that people put up to protect themselves. 'I bet he was a handsome man,' he said quietly.

'Oh, yes,' she said. 'The first time I met him, he took my breath away.'

'Where did you meet him?'

'Church,' she said.

'Church?' repeated Nightingale. That didn't make sense because the last place a Satanist would go was a place of worship. 'Which one?'

'A spiritualist church in Islington,' she said. 'I wanted to contact my parents. They died when I was young and I was in a children's home. I used to go to the church trying to get a message from them.'

'And did you?'

'No.' She trembled. 'Not at the church, but later, with Ainsley, they spoke to me.'

'Ainsley helped you contact your parents?'

'He helped them contact me,' she corrected him. 'He brought their spirits to talk to me, to tell me that everything was all right, that they loved me and were watching over me.'

'And he did that at the church?'

'No, it was later, at his home. At the church I never got a message. But Ainsley did. Every time. The spirits were always talking to him.' She smiled at the memory. 'Some of the regulars were jealous because the messages were always for Ainsley. It was as if the spirits were queuing up to speak to him.'

'Then he took you to his home?'

'He had a lovely house. So big, with a huge garden. Bigger than this, with trees and flowers and a summer-house. That was where he made love to me for the first time.'

'And you got pregnant?'

'Not then. That was later. After my parents spoke to me.'

'How did they do that, Rebecca? Did you hear their voices?'

'No,' she said. 'Ainsley knew how to use a ouija board and they spoke to me through that. Every night they would talk to me about why they had died, why I had to be strong, and why I should trust Ainsley and let him take care of me.'

'Rebecca, was it your parents who said you should have a baby with Ainsley?'

She nodded fiercely. 'They said they wanted grand-children. They said I was their only child so it was up to me to give them a grandchild and that if I did they would be happy in heaven.'

'But when the baby was born, you thought it was dead?'

She put a hand up to her forehead. 'I don't know,'

she said. 'I'm not sure.' Her lower lip began to tremble. 'I remember telling the nurse that I wanted to hold the baby and Ainsley taking it and saying it was dead, but I think it was breathing.'

Nightingale closed the album. 'You never saw him again, after you had the baby?'

'I came back from Blackpool and went to his house but it was empty, and everyone I spoke to said it had been empty for years.' Tears were running down her face but she ignored them. 'Why did he leave me?' she whimpered. 'Why did he take my baby?'

'I think you know,' said Nightingale, harshly. 'I think you know what he planned to do right from the start. That's why he paid you. He paid you to have me, didn't he?'

'No!' she wailed. She grabbed the lapels of his jacket, her fingers curled like talons, and pushed her face up to his. He could smell the sourness of her breath and a sickly sweet perfume around her wrinkled neck. He tried to release her grip but her hands were locked rigid. 'No!' she shouted, and her spittle peppered his cheek. The photograph album fell on to the grass.

'Please, Rebecca,' he said. 'Calm down, it's okay.'

He heard running footsteps and twisted around to see the male nurse running towards them. 'What happened?' asked the nurse, as he gently prised the woman's fingers off Nightingale's jacket.

'I don't know,' lied Nightingale. 'I was just talking to her about the pictures and she went off again.'

The nurse sat down beside her and put an arm protectively around her. 'I think you should go.'

'You're probably right,' agreed Nightingale. He bent down and picked up the album, then stood up and put a hand on the woman's shoulder. 'Take care,' he said. She didn't react, just stared at the stone birdbath, her cheeks still wet with tears. She reached up with her right hand and began caressing the crucifix again.

38

Finding someone to buy the books from Ainsley Gosling's library was surprisingly easy. On Wednesday morning, before he showered or shaved, Nightingale made himself a mug of coffee and powered up his laptop. He entered 'shops selling second-hand books on witchcraft' into Google, which threw up more than six thousand sites. He added 'London', which brought it down to around five thousand. He scrolled through them and realised that most were regular bookshops so he put a plus sign in front of 'witchcraft' and tried again. He sipped his coffee as he studied the list of sites. One on the second page looked promising – a store called Wicca Woman in Camden Town, close to Camden Lock market. He clicked onto the website. Wicca Woman apparently sold everything that a wannabe witch could need, from clothing to potions to magic wands, and it had a comprehensive list of books, including a second-hand section. The address was on the main page with a telephone number.

Nightingale shaved, showered and put on his second-best suit, then called the number and asked to speak to the owner. Her name was Alice Steadman and she said she'd be delighted to see any books he might want to sell, and that she would be in the shop all day.

Nightingale managed to find a space in a multi-storey car park a short walk from Wicca Woman. It was in a side-street, sandwiched between a shop that sold hand-knitted sweaters and a boutique that seemed to stock only T-shirts promoting drug use. A bell chimed as he pushed open the door. A stick of incense was burning next to the cash register, filling the premises with a cloying, flowery fragrance. There were two pretty teenagers in the shop, giggling as they looked at a display of love potions. The sales assistant was a punk girl with fluorescent pink hair, a stud in her chin, two in each eyebrow and a nose-ring. 'Don't they set off metal detectors in airports?' asked Nightingale.

The girl grinned, showing perfect white teeth. 'All the time,' she said. She patted her groin. 'But this is the one I have problems with.'

'I bet,' laughed Nightingale. 'Is the boss in? Mrs Steadman? I spoke to her on the phone about some books.' He held up a carrier-bag that contained five he had taken from the basement at Gosling Manor.

'I'll get her for you.' She disappeared through a beaded curtain and returned with a tiny woman in her sixties. In a long black shirt that reached her knees, black knitted tights and black shoes that curled up at the toes, she looked like a pixie's shadow and had a bird-like, inquisitive face. Like a bird, she cocked her head to one side as she looked at him. 'Mr Nightingale?'

'Yes,' said Nightingale.

'I thought you'd be older,' she said. 'You sounded older on the phone.'

One of the girls held up a small cloth bag. 'Here – do these fings really work?'

Mrs Steadman tilted her chin and fixed her with a steely glare. 'My dear, everything in this shop works, providing you believe in it.'

'But it'll make my boyfriend fall in love with me, yeah? And not look at any other girls?'

'That's what it says on the label, my dear, and that's what it'll do. But use it sparingly. No one wants a lapdog for a husband, do they?' She smiled at Nightingale. 'Come with me, young man, and show me what you have.'

She led him through the curtain into a small room. There was a circular table, with three wooden chairs, and above them a colourful Tiffany lampshade. A gas fire was burning so Nightingale took off his raincoat and draped it over the back of one of the chairs. 'Would you like a cup of tea? I've just made a pot,' asked Mrs Steadman.

He sat down and placed the bag on the table. 'Tea would be lovely, thank you,' he said.

Mrs Steadman brought over a tray with a brown ceramic teapot, two blue-and-white striped mugs and a matching milk jug and sugar bowl. 'How do you like it?'

'Milk and no sugar,' said Nightingale, as she poured.

'Sweet enough?' she said, and giggled like a teenager. 'So, these books, they were left to you, you said?'

'Yes, by my father. His name was Ainsley Gosling. Have you heard of him?'

'Should I have done?' She passed him a mug and sat down.

'He was a collector of books on the occult. I wondered if he'd bought any from you.'

'I don't recall the name,' she said, stirring her tea. 'And, really, I don't carry a huge selection of books. I deal mainly in spells and talismans.'

'And you make a living from that?'

Mrs Steadman chuckled. 'Young man, I don't do this to make money. This is my life. This is who I am.'

'Forgive me for asking, but are you a witch?'

Mrs Steadman's eyes sparkled with amusement. 'Just show me what you have in the bag, young man,' she said.

Nightingale took the five books from the bag and put them on the table in front of her. She took a pair of reading glasses from the top pocket of her shirt and put them on. She picked up the first book, opened it carefully and studied the first page, which listed the date of publication and the publisher. 'My goodness,' she said.

'It's about witchcraft in the eighteen hundreds,' said Nightingale.

'I can see that,' she said. 'This book I've seen before, but only reproductions. This is a first edition with the original illustrations. They were changed in later editions because some people found them . . . offensive.'

'Is it valuable?'

'Oh, yes.'

'Would you buy it from me?'

She looked at him over the top of her glasses. 'Young man, if I wanted to buy this I'd have to remortgage my house. A second edition sold for fifteen thousand pounds last year. This is a first edition and it's in perfect condition.'

'But you can't buy it?'

Mrs Steadman sat back in her chair. 'It's out of my league, young man,' she said. 'If you like, you could leave it with me and I'll see if I can sell it for you. For a commission, of course. Say, ten per cent.'

'Sounds like a plan,' said Nightingale. He took out his cigarettes. 'Do you mind if I . . . ?'

The woman patted her chest. 'I'm afraid so,' she said. 'Asthma. And you know those things will give you cancer.'

'Please don't tell me I'm going to hell,' he said. 'That's the last thing I need to hear right now.'

'There's a big difference between dying of lung cancer and going to hell.'

'Do you believe in hell?' asked Nightingale.

The woman fixed him with her eyes. They were so dark brown that they were almost black, glistening like pools of oil. 'No, young man, I do not.'

'There's no such place?' The tea was very strong, the way his mother used to make it. 'Strong enough that the spoon stands up in it,' was what she'd always said.

'How could there be? Fire and brimstone and suchlike.'

'But I thought . . .' He was going to say 'witches' but caught himself just in time. '. . . people in your line were big believers in heaven and hell and devils.'

'Young man, you have a very strange idea of what my "line" entails,' she said. 'I channel energy, I use the power of the natural world to make changes for good. It has nothing to do with God or the devil, with heaven or hell, and everything to do with the natural order of things.'

'Love potions?' said Nightingale.

'Trinkets,' said the woman. 'We use the real power to help people, to cure sickness or at least to ease pain and suffering. It has nothing to do with condemning people to eternal damnation.' She picked up the second book. It was leather-bound, a history of the Salem witch trials of 1692. 'This is nice,' she said. 'Not my sort of thing but you'd get a thousand pounds or so if you can find the right collector. It would probably fetch a higher price in America.'

'Can you sell it for me, Mrs Steadman?'

She nodded thoughtfully. 'I know a lady in Boston who would probably be interested,' she said. She put it aside and picked up the third. It was a Victorian book on natural healing that Nightingale had found open on a display cabinet. It was filled with watercolour paintings of plants and flowers and appeared to offer cures for everything from earache to bunions. 'Now this I can definitely sell,' she said. 'I sold a copy over the Internet last month and I had several people chasing it. How does five hundred pounds sound?'

'Like music to my ears,' said Nightingale. 'Could you pay me now?'

'If you're happy with a cheque.'

'Delirious,' said Nightingale.

She picked up the next book and smiled. 'This one too. It's one of the best books on pagan rituals there is and I think . . .' She opened it and nodded enthusiastically. 'Yes, it's a second edition. There's a market for it here in Camden – we've got quite an active pagan community. Would you take three hundred for it?'

'Excellent,' said Nightingale.

'Tell me, is there a reason you're selling them?'

Nightingale smiled. 'I have a cash-flow problem,' he said, 'and they're not really of any interest to me.'

'Your father's books, you said. Was he a big collector?'

'I'd say so,' said Nightingale.

'And, if you don't mind me asking, why did you come to my little shop rather than trying an auction house?'

'I want to keep a low profile,' said Nightingale. 'I figured if they were in an auction there'd be publicity. My father died a short time ago and I don't want newspapers trying to drum up a story.'

'Why would that be a story?'

Mrs Steadman was as sharp as a knife and a better inquisitor than the detectives who had quizzed him after Simon Underwood had fallen to his death. 'He killed himself, Mrs Steadman.'

Her eyes widened. 'Oh, I'm so sorry. I didn't mean to pry.'

'It's okay. We weren't exactly close. Now I just want to sell a few of his books to raise some money.'

'I quite understand,' she said. She picked up the last book. 'Now this one I'll definitely buy, but I'm afraid it's not in the same league as the others,' she said. 'I sold a copy just last week, here in the shop.' It was a collection of spells and seemed more like coffee-table book than one that a witch would use, full of glossy photographs and recipes – it reminded Nightingale of a Jamie Oliver cookbook. 'It's only worth about twenty pounds, I'm afraid. Several thousand copies were published in the seventies.'

'Twenty pounds is fine,' said Nightingale. 'I really wanted to know what you thought about it. It says anyone can work a spell, that you don't have to be in a coven or be a real witch. Is that right?'

'That's a difficult question, young man.'

Nightingale pointed at the book she was holding. 'But you believe in it, don't you? That if you light a candle of a particular colour, use a particular incense and the right herb, and say the right words, something magical will happen?'

'Would you like a biscuit?' asked Mrs Steadman. 'I get the feeling that you're going to be here for a while so I think I should give you something to nibble.'

Nightingale laughed. 'A biscuit would be wonderful, thank you.'

Mrs Steadman went over to a shelf and returned with a packet of chocolate Hobnobs. 'My weakness,' she said.

Nightingale took one, wondering if it had been an attempt to distract him, or if she was simply being hospitable. 'I guess my question is, does magic work?' he said.

'Well, of course it does, young man,' she said, taking a biscuit for herself and placing it on her saucer. 'If it didn't, people would soon lose interest, wouldn't they? If those girls out there buy that potion and use it and it doesn't work, well, I'll have lost two customers and they'll tell all their friends and before long the shop will be out of business.'

'But I thought you had to believe for magic to work.'

'Well, you could say that about medicine,' said Mrs Steadman. 'With most illnesses, placebos work almost as well as the genuine article. Not for antibiotics, of course, but for the drugs that treat depression or high blood pressure or relieve pain it's more a question of belief than of a true chemical effect. People believe that paracetamol will take away their headache so it does, when in fact a sugar pill would do the job just as well.'

'You see, now you're confusing me,' said Nightingale. 'Is it the spells that do the business, or is it believing in them that makes them work?'

'Belief helps,' said Mrs Steadman, patiently. 'It probably makes the spells more efficient, but even someone who didn't believe would get results. It's like cooking. You don't necessarily understand why yeast makes bread rise, but follow a recipe for bread and you'll get a loaf.'

'And what about black magic?'

'The chocolates?

Nightingale chuckled. He was starting to like Mrs Steadman – she had a sense of humour not dissimilar to his own. 'I mean spells that perhaps aren't as well meant as the ones you sell in your shop.'

'There's no such thing as black magic,' she said earnestly. 'There's no black magic and no white magic. There's just magic.'

'But I thought—'

Mrs Steadman silenced him with a wagging finger. 'It's like electricity, young man,' she said sternly. 'You can use it to power a life-support machine, or an electric chair. One saves lives and the other takes them, but the electricity itself isn't good or bad. It's just a power to be used.'

'But stuff like selling your soul to the devil. Is that possible?'

Mrs Steadman looked concerned. She reached forward and put her hand on his. 'Is that what this is about? You want to sell your soul?'

Nightingale shook his head emphatically. 'Absolutely not,' he said.

'You swear, on all you believe in?' She stared deep into his eyes.

Nightingale met her gaze levelly. 'I swear,' he said quietly. 'I just need to know, that's all. Is it possible?'

She pulled her hand back and sipped her tea, still watching him with those intense black eyes. 'There are spells that supposedly enable you to give your soul to the devil,' she said eventually. 'One I know is actually quite simple. You go to a churchyard at night – any churchyard will do, but the older the better – you draw a magic circle on the ground, and within it you draw two crosses. You take some wormwood in each hand and hold a Bible in the left. Toss the wormwood in your right hand up and the wormwood in your left hand down taking care not to drop the Bible. Then you say the Lord's Prayer backwards.' She sipped her tea.

'And that's it?'

'That's it. Bob's your uncle. On your way home, you leave the Bible on the steps of a church.'

It sounded too easy. 'So there's no contract? You don't do a deal?'

'It's a spell,' said Mrs Steadman. 'Quite a simple one.'

'And what if you change your mind? What if you want to take it back?'

'That's just as easy,' she said. 'You renounce Satan. Three times.'

'That's it?'

'Did you expect something more dramatic?'

Nightingale reached for his cigarettes again, but remembered her no-smoking policy. 'I thought there were contracts, I don't know, signed in blood or something.'

'Ah . . .' She winced as if she'd bitten down on a bad tooth.

'So there is more?' said Nightingale.

'You asked about making a pact with the devil – with Lucifer or Satan or whatever you want to call him. That's simple. But contracts with minor devils are a much more complicated matter. There are sixty-six princes under the devil, each with 6,666 legions.'

'And each legion is made up of 6,666 devils,' said Nightingale.

'You've been doing your homework,' she said.

'I'm been doing a bit of research,' admitted

Nightingale. 'So, to do a deal, you approach one of the devils?'

'Or one of the princes. But the devil himself can't be summoned by mere mortals.'

'I know, I tried.'

Mrs Steadman's eyebrow shot skywards. 'I do hope you're being flippant, young man,' she said.

'I found a book with a spell or something. You recite the words and the devil appears.'

'I think not,' she said.

'Well, it didn't work,' said Nightingale. 'But it's possible to summon a particular devil? One of the princes?'

'I wouldn't know, young man,' she said. 'Now you're talking about Satanism and devil-worship and that's as far removed from what I do as you can get. Wicca has nothing to do with the devil or devil-worship.'

'Do you believe in it, Mrs Steadman?'

She shook her head. 'No. I don't believe in hell and I don't believe that there is an entity called Satan. But I believe in good and evil. And I believe that there is a power in the earth that can be harnessed and used.'

'But there are ways of selling a soul, aren't there? As opposed to giving yourself over to the devil.'

'Mr Nightingale, I'm not even sure I believe in souls, not in the sense you mean. My beliefs are more that everything is connected, everything flows, that we are one with the earth.'

'But for someone who did believe, there are things they could do to sell their soul? Or a soul?'

'In theory, yes.' She was clearly uncomfortable with the way the conversation was going.

'Please tell me,' said Nightingale. 'I need to know.'

'You're talking to the wrong person,' she said. 'It's like asking a doctor how to commit murder.'

'In my experience, doctors make the best murderers,' he said.

'In your experience?'

'I was a policeman in another life.'

'So you believe in reincarnation? At least that's something.'

Nightingale laughed. 'I didn't mean that literally,' he said. 'Mrs Steadman, please, how does one go about selling a soul?'

'Oh, Mr Nightingale . . .'

'Just hypothetically. What would one do?'

Mrs Steadman put her mug down. 'Hypothetically, then,' she said. 'You have to renounce God and the Church. You pay homage to the devil, drink the blood of sacrificed children, and strike your deal with whichever devil you summon. A contract is drawn up and signed with blood drawn from the left arm.

Then your name is inscribed in the Red Book of Death.'

'And if you wanted to sell the soul of a child, could you do that?'

Mrs Steadman spread her hands, palms down, on the table. 'Why are you asking these questions? You seem like a nice man, a good man. What you're asking, it's not . . .' She shivered. 'It's not right.'

'Have you ever heard of a man called Sebastian Mitchell?' asked Nightingale, quietly.

Mrs Steadman stiffened. 'You know him?'

Nightingale shook his head. 'I have a book he wrote. A diary.'

'Burn it.' Her tiny hands clenched into fists.

'It's handwritten. In Latin.'

'Burn it,' she repeated. 'Go home now and burn it.'

'You couldn't sell it for me?'

She shook her head emphatically. 'The sort of people who'd want to buy a book like that, I wouldn't want to do business with,' she said.

39

Nightingale was humming as he walked into the office. Jenny looked up from her computer. 'You sound happy,' she said.

'I've come into some money.' He dropped a cheque on her desk. 'Eight hundred and twenty quid,' he said.

'Who did you kill, Jack?'

'O ye of little faith,' said Nightingale, heading over to the coffee-maker. 'I sold some of the books in the basement at the manor to a lovely little witch in Camden.'

'You did not,' said Jenny, picking up the cheque and holding it up to the light as if she suspected it was a forgery.

'I did, and she promised to buy more. She has a shop and she sells on the Internet, too.'

'Eight hundred and twenty quid! That's brilliant,' said Jenny.

'Should keep the wolf from the door. And there's more to come,' said Nightingale, pouring himself a coffee. 'She'll sell a couple of the rarer books and thinks she'll get top dollar. I said I'd go back with a list of other books and she'll let me know what they're worth.' He sat on the edge of her desk. 'She wanted to have a look herself but I don't think I should be showing visitors around Gosling Manor.'

'You'll take me, though, right?' said Jenny.

Nightingale raised his mug to her. 'You're different,' he said. 'You're family.'

'You're so sweet.'

'I know, I know.'

He took a package out of his pocket and unwrapped it. It was a magnifying glass he'd bought at Wicca Woman. 'Looking for clues?' she said. 'It's very Sherlock Holmes.'

'Yeah, and I bought the deerstalker and the pipe on eBay.' He took the coffee and the magnifying glass into his office and sat down at his desk. He pulled open the top drawer and took out his photograph album.

'What have you got there?' asked Jenny.

'Pictures of me as a baby,' said Nightingale.

'No way,' said Jenny. 'Why've I not seen them before?'

'Because I never wanted you to see me naked,' said Nightingale.

'Show me!'

'You're shameless,' said Nightingale. He pushed the album towards her. 'Don't say I didn't warn you.'

Jenny squealed. 'Oh, my God, you were adorable,' she said, looking at the first picture. She turned the page. 'Oh – so cute! Look at your smile, those chubby little cheeks.' She turned to the next page and smiled when she saw the photographs of his parents. 'They were so proud of you,' she said. 'You can see it in their eyes.'

'Yeah, they were good people,' said Nightingale.

Jenny nodded at the magnifying glass. 'Seriously, what's that for?' she asked.

'You'll think I'm stupid.'

'Heaven forbid,' she said.

Nightingale pulled the album back across the desk and turned to the first photograph, the one taken when he was just a day old. 'I'm pretty damn sure I don't have a pentagram tattoo,' he said. 'I would have seen it at the gym or someone would have mentioned it over the years. I mean, I had four full medicals while I was with the Met and the Met's doctors are bloody thorough. Not much gets past them.'

'So?'

'So I was thinking that maybe it's somewhere that can't be seen. On my head, maybe, under my hair.'

'You're right,' said Jenny.

'I am?'

'Yeah, I do think you're stupid.'

Nightingale smiled thinly. 'Thanks.'

'Well, at least checking your baby pictures with a magnifying glass beats shaving your head,' said Jenny.

Nightingale held it over the photograph and bent close to it. 'There's nothing,' he said.

'Of course there's nothing,' said Jenny. 'The whole idea's ridiculous.'

Nightingale turned the page and began to check the rest of the photographs.

'Jack, give it a rest,' said Jenny.

Nightingale opened his mouth to reply but before he could speak the office door was thrown open by an angry woman. It took him a couple of seconds to work out who it was and that he'd last seen her through the lens of his video camera leaving the hotel where she'd met her lover. It was Mrs McBride. Before Nightingale could react she rushed over and slapped him across the face. His mug fell from his hands and hot coffee splattered across the floor. 'Hey!'

He was off balance and before he could get off the desk she slapped him again. 'You bastard!' she shrieked.

Jenny reached for the phone. 'I'm calling the police,' she said.

Mrs McBride ignored her. 'He killed himself, you bastard. Are you happy now?'

'Who?' asked Nightingale.

'Who do you think? My husband. He killed himself because of you.' She raised her hand to slap him again but then she burst into tears and slumped to the ground, racked with sobs.

Jenny put down the phone and went around the desk to comfort her. At first Mrs McBride shook her off, but eventually she allowed herself to be led to the sofa. Jenny gave her a tissue and sat down next to her. 'What happened?' she asked.

Nightingale picked up the mug and dropped a few sheets of copy paper onto the spilled coffee. It wasn't the first time he'd been attacked by an angry spouse, and he doubted it would be the last.

'He drowned himself,' said Mrs McBride. 'In the canal. He left me a note.' She dabbed her eyes. 'He said he loved me and couldn't live without me.' She looked up at Nightingale. 'Why did you do it?' she asked tearfully.

'He was a client,' said Nightingale. 'I was working for him.'

'You bastard,' she said, but this time there was no venom in her voice, only despair.

'You were being unfaithful,' said Nightingale, quietly. 'Your husband had a right to know.'

'My husband was dead below the waist,' said Mrs McBride. 'We hadn't had sex for five years. Five bloody years. What should I have done? Become a nun?'

'Mrs McBride, I'm sorry but that's not my problem. Your husband wanted to know where he stood.'

'Ha bloody ha,' said Mrs McBride.

Nightingale flushed when he realised what he'd said. 'You know what I meant,' he said. 'He suspected you were being unfaithful. He wanted to know the truth.'

'I was his wife – that's the truth. I stood by him all the time he was in the hospital. I stuck with him in sickness and in health. That's the truth.'

'You were being unfaithful,' said Nightingale.

'Jack . . .' said Jenny.

'I was having sex, that's all!' hissed Mrs McBride. 'I'm a woman, not a block of bloody wood. I needed sex and I found a man who'd give me sex and you went and told Joel. You bloody well told him and now he's dead!' She began to cry and Jenny put an arm around her.

'Mrs McBride, I'm sorry for your loss . . .' said Nightingale.

'It's your fault he's dead,' she said.

'Did he say that?' asked Nightingale.

'He didn't have to. He said in the note that he couldn't live without me, and that he knew I was going to leave him.' She looked up at him with tear-filled eyes. 'Is that what you told him? Did you tell him I was going to leave him?'

'I didn't tell him anything of the sort,' said Nightingale. 'I just gave him my report.'

'He said in his note that he couldn't bear to live without me, but I was never going to leave him.' She grabbed at Jenny's hands. 'You have to believe me.'

'I do,' said Jenny.

Mrs McBride looked at Nightingale. 'When he told me he knew, I was glad in a way. I'd been feeling as guilty as sin for weeks and wanted to tell him myself. But when he showed me the video you'd given him, I couldn't face him. I went to stay with my friend Lynn to give him time to cool down, but then I was going to explain everything and tell him I still loved him, but now I can't because he's dead and that's your fault.'

'Did he tell you about my investigation?'

'He showed me the video you gave him. And the phone records. But it wasn't until I found your name in his cheque book that I knew who'd done it.' She dabbed her eyes. 'How can you live with yourself, doing what you do?'

'It's my job, Mrs McBride.'

'You could have talked to me and I could have explained. I'd have ended it with Ronnie – he's married anyway. You knew that, didn't you? His wife makes him sleep in the spare room and he just wanted to touch someone, to share a bed with them. Ronnie was never going to leave her and I was never going to leave Joel.'

'There's nothing more I can say, Mrs McBride, other than that I'm sorry for your loss.'

'Sorry doesn't cut it,' said Mrs McBride. 'You killed my husband, and you're going to hell.'

'Your husband killed himself, Mrs McBride. You know that and so do I.'

'I don't know how you can live with yourself. You're scum – you make money from the suffering of others. You should be ashamed of yourself.'

She burst into tears and Jenny gave her a box of tissues. Mrs McBride threw it at Nightingale. 'I don't want your bloody tissues! I want my husband!' she shouted.

Nightingale looked helplessly at Jenny. 'Go away and I'll handle her,' she mouthed. Nightingale did as he was told. He went outside and lit a cigarette. A lot of what the angry woman had said was just plain wrong, he knew, but one thing she had said was definitely true: he *was* ashamed of himself.

40

Six uniformed constables carried Robbie Hoyle's coffin to the grave, followed by Anna and Sarah. They were both dressed in black and held single red roses. The twins had stayed at home with Anna's sister. More than three hundred people had crowded into the church, most of them police officers. Superintendent Chalmers gave one of the eulogies. He talked about Hoyle's career, his family and his life outside work, and told a couple of anecdotes about Hoyle's early days on the beat that had the congregation smiling and nodding. Chalmers clearly spoke from the heart, and his voice cracked a couple of times. The cynic in Nightingale wanted to think that he was faking it but he came to realise that Hoyle's death had hit the man hard.

Anna gave one of the readings, holding her head up, projecting her voice and smiling across at her daughter. Several tough CID detectives had tears in their eyes.

Nightingale was wearing a dark blue suit and a black tie and Jenny a black cashmere coat over a black dress, her hair held back with a black Alice band. They were standing on a gravel path, about fifty feet from the grave. The six officers lowered the coffin into the ground as the vicar read from the Bible.

'When I die, I don't want to be buried,' whispered Nightingale.

'You should say that in your will,' said Jenny.

'I haven't got one.'

'Well, draw one up,' she said. 'You've got your flat in Bayswater and you've got Gosling Manor. You have to leave it all to somebody.'

'I don't care who gets it,' he said. 'My parents are gone and I've no kids.' He grinned. 'I'll leave it all to you.'

'You will not,' she said.

'There's nobody else close to me,' he said.

'Find a charity, then,' she said. 'I don't want to profit from your death, Jack. It's bad enough my parents always telling me that I'll be set up for life when they go. I don't want that from you as well.'

'I don't need a will, then.'

'Yes, you do,' she said. 'Otherwise your assets get

divided up according to some legal formula. If you're married, the surviving spouse gets it. If you have kids, they get a share. And if there's no wife and kids it goes to the parents, and if they're not around any other relatives get it. Trust me, you need a will.'

'Anyway, the will isn't the point. The point is that I don't want to be buried, okay?'

'Message received,' she said. 'Do you want to donate your body to medical science instead? I'm sure your liver would be worth looking at.'

Nightingale flashed her a tight smile. 'I'm not having bloody medical students poking around with my innards,' he said. 'Cremation will do just fine.'

'Cremation it is,' said Jenny. 'What shall I do with the ashes?'

'Whatever you like,' said Nightingale. 'Speaking of which, do you think it's okay to smoke in a church-yard?'

'I think legally you'd be okay but it's pretty bad form. How about an egg-timer?'

'A what?'

'I'll have your ashes put in an egg-timer. Then you'll be one of the few men in the country who's actually useful in the kitchen.'

The policemen finished lowering the coffin. The three on the left dropped their end of the slings and the three on the right pulled them out. Anna let her rose fall onto the coffin and encouraged Sarah to do the same.

'Scatter them over the pitch at Old Trafford,' said Nightingale.

'Are you serious?'

'Yeah. I don't want to be in the ground – I don't want to rot slowly, and I don't want a gravestone for people to look at.'

'Jack, you're thirty-two, you've got years ahead of you. Provided you stop smoking and drinking.'

'Unless Gosling was telling the truth. In two weeks' time I'll be thirty-three. Two weeks today, in fact.'

'Today's Thursday,' said Jenny. 'Your birthday's Friday the twenty-seventh.'

'Yeah, but I figure that means my soul's up for grabs just after midnight on the twenty-sixth, right?'

'I don't know how prompt devils are,' said Jenny. 'Anyway, it's all nonsense and you know it. Come on, we have to go to the reception.'

'I can't face that,' said Nightingale.

'Well, at least let's say goodbye to Anna. You can't just leave without saying anything.'

Anna was being comforted by Robbie's mother. 'She's got enough on her plate,' said Nightingale. 'I'll call around tomorrow.'

As Nightingale turned to go he spotted Derbyshire and Evans, the two detectives who had called into his office. He went over to them. 'Did you guys know Robbie?' he asked.

'Met him once on an interview course at Hendon,' said Evans. 'Never worked with him, though.'

'Bloody nightmare,' said Nightingale. 'I still can't believe it. Anything happening with the taxi driver?'

The inspector shook his head. 'The way things stand at the moment, we can't even do him for careless driving. He wasn't on his mobile, he hadn't been drinking, he wasn't speeding. It really was an accident, plain and simple.'

'What's his name?'

Evans narrowed his eyes. 'Why?'

Nightingale faked a smile. 'The Federation rep asked if I'd give Anna a hand filling out the insurance forms and they need details of the accident.'

Evans nodded. 'Barry O'Brien,' he said. 'He lives out in Hammersmith. He was fully insured, clean licence and everything, so I don't see there'll be any problems.'

'How is he?'

'Physically fine – he was wearing his seatbelt – but he's really shaken.'

'He should be,' said Nightingale.

'I'm serious,' said Evans. 'He was in a right mess when we saw him. He'd never had an accident before, and he's been driving a cab for over thirty years. He's taking it really badly.'

Nightingale thanked them and headed for the exit. Jenny linked her arm through his. 'You just lied to him, didn't you?' she said. 'There are no insurance papers.'

'How do you know?'

'I just know. You can't lie to the police, Jack.'

'Yes, you can. It's practically a national pastime,' said Nightingale. 'Everyone lies to the cops.'

'But why do you need to know who the driver was?'

'I want to talk to him.'

'Because?'

Nightingale sighed. 'Because he killed my best friend and I want to know what happened.'

'They told you what happened. It was an accident. Robbie was in the wrong place at the wrong time.'

'Yeah, well, cops don't always tell the truth,' said Nightingale. 'I need to hear it from the horse's mouth.' They walked out of the graveyard. 'I can't work, Jenny, not today. Let's go and get drunk.'

'I've a better idea,' said Jenny. 'Why don't you show me Gosling Manor?'

'You're serious?'

'Why not?' said Jenny. 'I want to see if it's as big as you say it is.'

Nightingale grinned. 'Jenny, size isn't everything, you know.'

'Actually,' she smiled, 'it is, pretty much.'

41

Jenny climbed out of the MGB. 'You weren't joking – it is a mansion,' she said. 'How many rooms?'

'A lot,' said Nightingale.

'I expected gargoyles and turrets and stuff but it's really nice,' she said. 'And the gardens are spectacular.' She stood with her hands on her hips, admiring the house. 'It's chocolate-box pretty, isn't it? Not the sort of house you'd expect a Satanist to live in.'

'It was built by the local squire, apparently.'

'What is it – seventeenth century?'

'Sixteenth, the cops said. But it's been added to over the years. You should have a look around the back – there's a lake. And stables. How does it compare to the McLean ancestral pile?'

Jenny smiled. 'Ah, now you're talking,' she said. 'My parents' place is a bit special.'

'As special as this?'

'I'm not playing the who's-got-the-biggest-house

game, Jack, but this is lovely, really lovely. You're very lucky to have it.'

'Yeah, but I can't see how I can keep it,' said Nightingale. He walked over to the garage, which was to the right of the main building. There were four metal doors that opened upwards but all were locked. CCTV cameras at either end covered all the doors and the area in front of them.

'He was big on security,' observed Jenny.

'Inside and out,' said Nightingale. He went to the far side of the garage. There were two windows, dusty and covered with cobwebs. He peered through the first but all he could see was a bare concrete floor, discoloured from years of spilled oil. He moved to the second, cupped his hand over his forehead and squinted through the glass. There was a long wooden workbench but no tools. A pulley and chains hung from a metal girder running the full length of the interior and there was a dark area at the far end, which looked like a pit.

'What are you looking for?' asked Jenny, joining him at the window.

'A Bentley,' said Nightingale. 'Apparently that's what Gosling drove. Or, rather, that's what he was driven around in.' He moved away from the window. 'Empty,' he said. 'Just like the house.'

'Maybe he sold it,' said Jenny.

'He seems to have sold everything else.'

'Except the books,' said Jenny.

'Except the books,' agreed Nightingale. 'Come on, I'll give you the tour.'

They walked to the front door and Nightingale unlocked it. He bowed and waved her inside. 'Wow, would you look at that chandelier!' she said. 'And this floor is Italian marble, right?'

'Only the best for Ainsley Gosling,' said Nightingale, closing the door.

'And there's no furniture?'

'Just a bed and a chair in the master bedroom.'

'That's where he . . . ?'

'Killed himself? Yeah. But you wouldn't know by looking at the room – it's been cleaned. Not a speck of blood.' He waved his hand around the hall. 'So, can you see the secret panel?'

'The what?'

'The secret panel. Gosling was the only one who knew how to get down to the basement.'

Jenny walked slowly along the length of the hallway, running her hand along the wooden panelling. 'How did you find it, if it's so secret?'

Nightingale waxed an imaginary moustache and did his best Hercule Poirot impersonation. 'Because I am ze great detective,' he said.

'Robbie found it, right?'

'It was a joint effort,' said Nightingale. He pressed the panel that led down to the basement and it clicked open. He flicked the light switch. 'Be careful, the stairs are quite steep,' he said. 'And keep hold of the handrail.'

He followed her down the stairs. 'This is amazing,' said Jenny. 'There must be thousands of books here. Are they all witchcraft and devil stuff?'

'Seem to be.'

'Are you going to sell them all?' she asked, as she pulled one out of the middle of a shelf. 'Ah,' she said, before he could answer. 'Perhaps not.'

'What's wrong?' he asked.

She held up the book so that he could see the title. *Dissecting Humans*.

'No way,' he said.

Jenny leafed through it. 'Complete with illustrations,' she said. 'I think it's a medical text. At least, I hope it is.' She put it back on the shelf and started walking through the display cases. 'It's half library, half museum.'

Nightingale went to Gosling's desk. He sat down, opened the top drawer and pulled out a leather file. Inside, plastic folders held business cards – lawyers, businessmen, politicians, showbiz personalities, even high-ranking policemen. Ainsley Gosling had had some very important friends.

'Have you seen these crystal balls?' asked Jenny. 'Was he a fortune-teller as well?'

'Get away from there!' shouted Nightingale, leaping out of the chair.

Jenny jumped backwards. 'What's wrong?' she said.

Nightingale hurried over to her. 'Just don't touch them,' he said.

'Why? Are they valuable?' she said. 'Don't worry, I'll be careful.'

'It's not that,' he said. His shoe crunched on a piece of broken glass. 'It's just . . .' He tailed off, not sure if he could explain what he was worried about without appearing to be a complete idiot.

'Tell me, Jack.'

'The last time Robbie was here he saw himself in one of the balls.'

'His reflection, you mean?'

Nightingale took a deep breath. 'This is going to sound crazy, but he saw himself being hit by a taxi.'

Jenny's face hardened. 'That's not funny, Jack,' she said.

'I'm not joking,' said Nightingale. He pointed at the shards of glass on the floor. 'He was so shocked that he dropped it.'

'Jack, listen to yourself. You're saying Robbie saw his future. You know that's impossible.'

'I'm only telling you what he told me, Jenny. And if you'd seen the look on his face, you'd know how serious he was.'

'He saw himself being hit by a cab?'

'That's what he said.'

'It's crazy.'

'Everything about this is crazy,' said Nightingale. 'This basement is crazy, the DVD Gosling left me is crazy – killing yourself in a magic circle isn't exactly a sign of sanity.'

Jenny flopped down onto a leather sofa. 'Are you okay?'

'In what sense?'

'You've just found out your parents weren't your real parents, that your real father killed himself with a shotgun and your birth-mother has spent most of her life in a psychiatric institution. Your uncle and aunt are dead and you've just buried your best friend.'

Nightingale lit a cigarette and sat down beside her. 'Yeah. It's been a stressful few days,' he said sarcastically.

'And how are you going to deal with it all?'

Nightingale held up the cigarette. 'Nicotine and alcohol, same as usual,' he said.

'Do you want to talk about it?'

'With a therapist?'

Jenny laughed. 'With me, you idiot.'

'I'm okay,' said Nightingale. 'I'm in bits about Robbie, but I'm an adult, I can deal with it. The parents thing is confusing me a bit, but I'm not the first person to discover they were adopted, and I can deal with it.'

'And your mother?'

'She's not my mother, Jenny. She's . . .'

'She's what?'

Nightingale shook his head. 'I don't know,' he said. 'Yes, she gave birth to me, I'm sure of that now, but she's nothing to me and never will be. My mother was Irene Nightingale and she's been dead almost fifteen years. And Bill was my father. Nothing will ever change that.'

'And the DVD? Gosling's message to you?'

'The ramblings of a suicidal madman.'

She looked at him earnestly. 'You're sure that's how you feel?'

'Why do you ask?'

'Because what you've been through is traumatic. And you seem to be taking it all very calmly.'

'I was a cop for almost ten years, Jenny. It takes a lot to faze me.' He blew smoke at the ceiling. 'Trust me, I'm fine.'

42

When Nightingale woke on Friday morning he lay in bed for almost half an hour staring up at the ceiling. He had acted on impulse when he'd asked the detective inspector for the name of the man who had killed Robbie Hoyle, but once he had it he knew that nothing would stop him going to talk to him. Nightingale wanted to know if Hoyle had died immediately or if he had lain in a pool of blood, begging to be saved. He wanted to know why O'Brien hadn't stopped or swerved, why he had just mown Hoyle down. He wanted to know what had happened, even though that knowledge wouldn't change anything. Hoyle's death didn't make any sense but, in Nightingale's experience, few deaths did.

He booted up his laptop and logged on to Tracesmart, an online service that provided access to electoral rolls around the country. There was only one

Barry O'Brien living in Hammersmith. He made a note of the address and called Jenny to tell her he'd be late in. 'I've things to do at Gosling Manor,' he lied. 'I'll be with you during the afternoon. If there's anything important, I'll be on the mobile.' He ended the call, feeling suddenly guilty. He didn't like lying to Jenny, but telling her what he was really doing would only worry her. Nightingale had always been much more comfortable asking questions than answering them.

He shaved, showered and put on a clean shirt and a dark blue suit that had just come back from the dry-cleaner's. He made himself a cup of black coffee, smoked a Marlboro, then drove to Hammersmith.

O'Brien's house was in a terraced street and a black cab was parked in front of it. Nightingale found a space for the MGB about fifty yards away. He climbed out and walked over to the cab. There was no damage to the front, no blood, not even a scratch – nothing to show that the vehicle had ended the life of Robbie Hoyle. Nightingale wasn't surprised. A London cab weighed more than 1600 kilograms and flesh was no match for that amount of steel moving at speed.

A middle-aged housewife walked by with a white poodle on a lead. She was holding a screwed-up plastic bag and cajoling the animal to do its business.

Nightingale flashed her a smile and she glared at him as if he was a child-molester.

A flight of half a dozen stone steps led up to the front door of O'Brien's house. Nightingale pressed the bell and heard it buzz in the hallway. He went back to the pavement and looked up at the bedroom windows. The curtains were drawn. Nightingale wondered if O'Brien had worked through the night and was now sleeping. He rang the bell again. When there was no answer, he took out his mobile phone and dialled the number he'd been given by Directory Enquiries. He heard the phone ring inside the house. He let it continue for a full thirty seconds, then ended the call and put the phone back in his pocket.

He stood on the pavement, considering his options. If O'Brien was asleep, he'd answer the door eventually. He obviously wasn't working because his cab was in the street. Maybe he'd taken the day off and gone somewhere without it. If that was the case, then Nightingale was wasting his time.

He went back up the steps. There was a letterbox in the middle of the door. He pushed it open and bent down to shout through it. 'Mr O'Brien?' The door moved forward. Nightingale frowned. He straightened and pushed it open.

There were half a dozen envelopes on the carpet,

mainly bills, and several garish leaflets. Nightingale stepped inside. 'Mr O'Brien? Are you there?' There was no answer, but Nightingale could hear a soft buzzing, like an electronic hum, coming from upstairs. He closed the door. He knew he shouldn't be in the house, but he also knew that something was wrong. People didn't leave their front doors open in London. He walked down the hallway and checked the living room, then the kitchen. There were dirty dishes in the sink and a half-drunk cup of coffee on the draining-board. He touched the kettle. It was cold.

He went back into the hallway. 'Mr O'Brien? Are you upstairs?' A large bluebottle flew around his head and he swatted it away. He headed up the stairs, peering up at the landing above. 'Mr O'Brien, is everything okay?'

The buzzing got louder. Two more large flies circled Nightingale's head. As he reached the landing he saw that the bathroom door was ajar. There were half a dozen flies on the wall by the light switch and as he moved closer more flew out through the open door. The buzzing was much stronger now, like a faulty electric circuit.

There was a bad smell in the air, an odour Nightingale had encountered many times during his years as a police officer, a smell that was difficult to describe but could never be forgotten. Before he even pushed open the bathroom door, Nightingale knew what he would find.

The man had been in the water for at least a day, probably longer, and had already started to swell. There were deep cuts in both arms and the savage wounds were filled with flies. They were everywhere, feeding and laying their eggs, buzzing around Nightingale as if they resented his appearance at their banquet.

O'Brien had filled the bath with water and cut his wrists with a Stanley knife, which was lying on the floor, the blade covered with blood. There were smears across the wall and the floor where arterial blood had sprayed but most had gone into the bathwater. O'Brien's eyes were still open, staring up at the ceiling. Nightingale didn't know why Barry O'Brien had wanted to kill himself but one thing was for sure: it hadn't been a cry for help.

Scrawled across the tiles at the side of the bath in bloody letters was the sentence with which Nightingale had become all too familiar: 'YOU ARE GOING TO HELL, JACK NIGHTINGALE.' Dozens of flies were feeding off it.

Nightingale stared at the words in horror. 'What is going on?' he whispered. He pulled a couple of feet of toilet tissue from the roll, swatted the flies away with his hands and used it to wipe the tiles, then dropped it into the toilet. He pulled off another length, wet it under the tap and wiped the tiles a second time. They looked too clean now so he splashed bloody water from the bath over them and washed his hands in the basin. A fly came so close to his right ear that he flinched.

He dried his hands and went back into the hallway where he took out his mobile phone and started to dial 999. He stopped at the second digit. He cancelled the call and instead dialled New Scotland Yard. He asked the switchboard operator to put him through to Inspector Dan Evans, and after a couple of minutes the inspector was on the line. 'Dan, I thought I'd better tell you this before you hear it from anyone else,' he said.

'That sounds ominous,' said the inspector, jovially.

'I'm at Barry O'Brien's house and he's killed himself.'

There was a long silence. 'I hope this is some sort of sick joke,' said Evans, eventually.

'He's cut his wrists. He's been dead for a while by the look of it.'

'What the hell are you doing in his house?'

'I came to talk to him,' said Nightingale. 'The front door was open.'

'So you just walked in?'

'Like I said, the front door was open.'

'You can't just go wandering around people's houses, Nightingale. You're not in the job any more.'

'I know that, but what's done is done. I was going to call 999 but I thought I'd better let you know what had happened.'

'Do you need an ambulance?'

'He's definitely dead. Are you going to handle it or should I call 999?'

'Have you any idea of the trouble this is going to cause, Nightingale? You got O'Brien's name from me, right?'

'I've forgotten where I heard it,' said Nightingale, 'and I doubt I'm going to remember.'

'Let's keep it that way,' said Evans. 'Where's the body?'

'Upstairs bathroom,' said Nightingale.

'Wait for me downstairs, outside the house,' said Evans. 'And don't touch anything.'

43

They left him in the interview room for the best part of an hour, with just a cup of canteen coffee. Nightingale had asked if it was okay to smoke and a sullen uniformed constable had said no. He hadn't been arrested so he was free to leave whenever he wanted, but there were questions that had to be answered and Nightingale decided it would be best to get it over with. They hadn't searched him or taken his mobile phone so he rang Jenny and said he'd be later than expected. She wanted to know where he was. 'It's complicated,' he said. 'I'll explain when I get back.' Jenny pressed him for more details but Nightingale heard footsteps in the corridor. The door opened and Superintendent Chalmers, in full uniform and holding a clipboard, walked in. Nightingale hung up.

'Calling your brief?' asked Chalmers. Dan Evans and

Neil Derbyshire, both holding notebooks and ballpoint pens, were behind him.

'I didn't think I needed a lawyer,' said Nightingale. 'They told me they just wanted a chat.'

'A chat it is, then,' said Chalmers. He sat down opposite Nightingale. Evans took the chair next to him while Derbyshire moved the one that was beside Nightingale and placed it by the door so that all three policemen were facing him around a metal table that had been bolted to the floor. On a shelf on the wall above the table there was a digital voice recorder and in the far upper corner of the room a small CCTV camera.

Chalmers nodded at Evans, who switched on the recorder. 'Superintendent Ronald Chalmers, interviewing Jack Nightingale.' He looked at the clock on the wall. 'It is now a quarter past two in the afternoon on Friday the twentieth of November and with me are . . .' He nodded at Evans.

'Detective Inspector Dan Evans.'

'Detective Constable Neil Derbyshire.'

'If this is just a chat, why the recording?' asked Nightingale.

'It's procedure,' said Chalmers.

'Can I smoke?'

'No, you can't,' said the superintendent.

'But I'm not under arrest?'

'No, you're not.'

'I'm free to go whenever I want?'

'You're helping us with our enquiries into the death of Barry O'Brien.'

'Just so we're all clear on that,' said Nightingale. 'I'm here to help.'

'Date of birth,' said Chalmers.

'What?'

'Your date of birth, for the record.'

'I'm thirty-two, thirty-three on Friday the twenty-seventh. That's a week from today.'

Evans and Derbyshire scribbled in their notebooks.

'Don't feel you have to get me a present,' said Nightingale.

'What were you doing in Barry O'Brien's house this morning?'

'I wanted to talk to him.'

'So you broke in?'

'The front door was open.'

'You invited yourself in? Is that it?'

'The door was open. I pushed it and it opened. I went upstairs and found the body.'

'Why did you go upstairs?'

'To see if he was there.'

'But you'd already called his phone so you knew he wasn't in the house.'

'I thought he might be asleep.'

Chalmers sat back. 'So why didn't you just go away and come back another time?'

'I don't know,' said Nightingale. 'I just thought . . .'

'Yes? You thought what?'

'I thought that maybe something was wrong.'

'So why didn't you call the police? Why did you break into his house?'

'I didn't break in,' said Nightingale. 'I already told you, the front door was open. Then I heard the flies.'

'The flies?'

'He'd been dead for a while. He was covered with flies. I heard the buzzing from the hallway.'

'And what did you want to talk to Mr O'Brien about?'

Nightingale sighed. It was a difficult question to answer.

'You do understand the question, Mr Nightingale?'

'Yes. I just wanted to talk to him.'

'About what?'

'About what happened to Robbie.'

'You're referring to Inspector Robert Hoyle?'

'Robbie Hoyle,' corrected Nightingale. 'Nobody called him Robert.'

'You wanted to talk to Mr O'Brien because he was responsible for the death of your friend, Inspector Hoyle?'

'I guess so.'

'You guess so?'

Nightingale threw up his hands. 'You make it sound like there was something sinister going on. I just wanted to talk to him.'

'About what, specifically?'

'About what happened. How Robbie died.'

'But there's no mystery as to what happened. It was a road-traffic accident. What did you expect Mr O'Brien to say? Did you want him to apologise? Did you want him to express remorse?'

'No,' said Nightingale, flatly.

'And when he wasn't remorseful, did that make you angry?'

'He was dead when I got there,' said Nightingale.

'You're making a habit of walking in on dead people, aren't you?' said Chalmers.

Nightingale didn't reply.

'Come on, Jack, don't get all coy with me. You found your aunt and uncle dead, didn't you? Just a few days ago. Up in Manchester.'

'My uncle killed my aunt and then he hanged himself. I was supposed to be having Sunday lunch with them.'

'According to the Manchester cops, you smashed a window to get in. With a spade.'

'There was blood on the cat,' said Nightingale.

Chalmers looked confused. 'What?'

'There was blood on the cat and on the cat flap. So I knew there was something wrong. Then I saw my aunt through the window, lying on the kitchen floor.'

'And again you didn't wait for the police.'

'What do you expect?' snapped Nightingale. 'I call 999 and when and if I get through some civilian arsehole asks me a series of questions on his check list before telling me that someone will be with me at some unspecified time and then I sit on my arse and wait until they bother to show up? You know how piss poor the police response times are these days. I saw blood on the door and my aunt on the floor so I did what I had to do and I'm damn well not going to apologise to you or anyone else for that.'

'And you don't think it's a bit coincidental, discovering three bodies in less than a week?'

'I don't know.'

'Yes, you do, Jack. You know there's something strange going on here. And I think you're not telling us the whole story.'

'There's no story to tell.'

'The thing is, you've always been a bit of a vigilante, haven't you? That's why you had to leave the force.'

Nightingale sat back in his chair and folded his arms. He knew there was no point in rising to the bait –

Chalmers was only trying to provoke him.

'You threw Simon Underwood out of his office window, didn't you? And got away without even a slap on the wrist. Is that what you think, Nightingale, that you're some sort of masked avenger who can go around murdering at will?'

'Barry O'Brien committed suicide.'

'And I suppose Underwood threw himself out of his office window?'

Nightingale said nothing.

'Were you drinking before you went to see Mr O'Brien?'

'Of course not,' said Nightingale. 'It was first thing in the morning.'

'Because you do have a drink problem, don't you?'

'Bollocks.'

'You're due to appear in court on a drink-driving charge next month, aren't you?'

'I had a few beers and was stupid enough to drive,' said Nightingale. 'That doesn't qualify as a drink problem.'

Chalmers leaned forward and lowered his voice to a whisper. 'Look, Jack, I understand how you feel. I understand how you felt about Underwood, and I know there were no tears shed for him after what he did to his daughter. And I understand how you felt about

Robbie's death. He didn't deserve to die. He was a husband and a dad and a good cop, and some bastard who wasn't watching what he was doing ran him over. I understand that you'd be angry – hell, I'm angry. And I could see that you'd want revenge, because we both know the courts won't do anything. I can understand why you'd want to hurt O'Brien. Anyone could.'

'It was an accident, you said.'

'And you're okay with that?'

'Accidents happen,' said Nightingale.

'They do around you, that's for sure,' said Chalmers.

44

The Australian nurse carefully cut the chicken breast into pieces so small that they couldn't be choked on. The potatoes were mashed and the carrots had been boiled for so long that they had turned to mush, so the chicken was the only potential threat. The plate was on a tray over Rebecca Keeley's lap. She sat with her hands by her sides, frowning as she watched him cut the meat.

'That must have been nice, seeing your son after all these years,' said the nurse.

She didn't reply. She hadn't said a word since Nightingale had left. The nurse wasn't even sure that she'd spoken to her son.

'I hope he comes again – you could do with a regular visitor. He might bring you out of your shell.'

The phone in the hallway started to ring and the nurse cursed. He looked apologetically at her. 'Sorry

about the language, Miss Keeley,' he said. 'It's just that
it never rings when I'm not busy. Sod's law.' He put
the knife and fork on the tray and went to answer it.

As the nurse closed the door, the woman reached
for the knife. For the first time she smiled, showing her
raw, ulcerated gums. She placed the blade against her
left wrist, and splayed her fingers. She shuddered and
began to recite the Lord's Prayer as she hacked away,
sawing through flesh, veins and tendons. Blood sprayed
across the bed as she continued to work the knife.

45

Nightingale opened his office door and walked quickly to his desk. He pulled open the bottom drawer and took out the brandy he kept there.

'Jack?' asked Jenny, getting up from her computer.

'I've had a hell of a day.'

'And brandy's going to make it better?'

'It'll make me feel better,' said Nightingale. He unscrewed the top and raised the bottle to his lips, then stopped. 'Yeah, you're right,' he said. 'Booze has got me into more than enough trouble already.'

'Coffee?'

'Great.' He put the cap back on the bottle and the bottle back in the drawer.

'Where were you today?' asked Jenny, as she went to make the coffee.

'It's a long story,' said Nightingale, dropping onto his chair and swinging his feet up onto the desk. 'I went to see Barry O'Brien, the taxi driver.'

'And what did he have to say?'

'Nothing. He was dead.'

'What?'

'He'd killed himself. Sat in the bath and slit his wrists.'

'My God,' said Jenny.

'Must have done it a day or two ago. Maybe yesterday, while we were at Robbie's funeral.'

Jenny brought over two mugs of coffee and gave him one. 'You think he felt bad about what he'd done? Couldn't live with himself?'

'Chalmers thinks I did it.'

'He what?' She sat on the edge of his desk.

'He had me in for questioning, along with the two cops who came to tell us about Robbie. Evans and Derbyshire. The three bloody musketeers. They were firing questions at me for hours.'

'They can't seriously think you did it, Jack. Anyway, you were at the funeral or you were with me.'

'They do have a point, though,' said Nightingale. 'You know what's been happening to me. My father, my real father, blows his head off with a shotgun. My uncle kills my aunt and hangs himself. Barry O'Brien cuts his wrists before I can talk to him. It doesn't look good, does it? From their point of view. And that was before they mentioned Simon Underwood.'

'They're morons if they think you had anything to

do with any of those deaths. Sometimes people can be so bloody stupid.'

'Chalmers has always had it in for me,' said Nightingale. 'I don't think he seriously believes I killed O'Brien – he just wants to make my life difficult. And he's never forgiven me for the Underwood thing.'

'They never charged you, did they, for what happened to Underwood?'

'They couldn't. There were no forensics, no witnesses, no CCTV. And I didn't tell them anything.' He shrugged. 'What could I tell them? That I'd conveniently contracted a nasty case of amnesia?' He flashed her his little-boy-lost smile. 'I need you to do something for me, Jenny.'

'I am here to serve, O master.'

'I'm serious,' said Nightingale.

'So am I,' said Jenny.

'I need you to find someone for me. A guy by the name of George Harrison.'

'The Beatle? He's dead.'

'George Arthur Harrison,' said Nightingale. 'He'd be in his early sixties now. He was a truck driver in the nineties. He lived in south London then, but he could be anywhere now.'

'I'll get on to it,' said Jenny. 'What's he done?'

'He killed my parents,' said Nightingale.

'Jack,' said Jenny, 'are you sure you want to do this? It was a long time ago.'

'I know that,' said Nightingale, 'but it's unfinished business.'

'Unfinished in what way?'

'I need to know what happened, Jenny. I need to know why my parents died.'

'It was an accident. You should let sleeping dogs lie.'

Nightingale shook his head. 'I should have spoken to him then, but I was too young, just a kid.'

'What on earth do you stand to gain by confronting him now?'

Nightingale ran his hands through his hair. 'I just need to do it, Jenny. Can't you leave it at that?'

'It's because of Robbie, isn't it? And because of what happened to O'Brien.'

'That's part of it,' admitted Nightingale. 'Bad things are happening around me, Jenny, and it's all to do with Ainsley Gosling being my father. If I can find out what happened to my parents, maybe it'll explain what's happening now.'

'It was an accident.'

'That was what everyone said. But Robbie's death was an accident, too. Doesn't that seem a bit coincidental?'

'Coincidences happen.'

'Sure they do. And people commit murder and kill themselves. It's just that it seems to be happening to people I know a hell of a lot recently. Maybe I'm the key. Maybe Gosling had my parents killed – have you thought about that? Maybe he paid this guy Harrison to kill them.'

'And he paid O'Brien to kill Robbie from beyond the grave, is that what you think?'

'I don't know,' said Nightingale. 'But if I talk to Harrison maybe I'll find out.'

'You're starting to worry me, Jack.' The phone rang and she picked it up. 'Nightingale Investigations,' she said. She listened, then placed her hand over the receiver. 'It's Mrs Fraser at the Hillingdon Home. It's about Rebecca Keeley.'

'Now what?' said Nightingale.

'Jack, she's dead.'

46

M rs Fraser was sitting behind her desk when an assistant showed Nightingale into her office. The Australian male nurse was also there, his arms folded across his chest, his face a blank mask. Mrs Fraser didn't get up and waved Nightingale to a chair.

'What happened?' asked Nightingale.

'What happened, Mr Nightingale, is that after you visited her for the second time, your mother took a knife and slashed her wrists,' said the administrator.

'What was she doing with a knife?'

'She was eating her dinner. Your mother wasn't considered a danger to herself or anyone else, so the use of cutlery wasn't an issue.'

'Did she leave a note?' asked Nightingale. 'Do you have any idea why she did it?'

'She did it because you upset her,' said the male nurse. 'She was fine before you came along.'

'She was practically psychotic,' said Nightingale. 'According to you she never spoke, but she spoke to me.'

'And then she killed herself,' said the nurse. 'What did you say to her?'

The administrator raised a hand to silence him. 'Darren, please, let me handle this.'

'What's to be handled?' asked Nightingale.

'The thing is, Mr Nightingale, as things stand we have no confirmation that you are in fact Miss Keeley's son.'

Nightingale reached into his jacket pocket and took out an envelope. 'Here's the result of the DNA test I told you about,' he said. 'It clearly shows she was my mother.'

Mrs Fraser took the report out of the envelope and read it. 'I don't understand,' she said. 'How did you get a sample of her DNA?'

'I borrowed a hairbrush,' said Nightingale. 'The cells on the root of the hair are all they need these days.'

'You stole a hairbrush?'

'I borrowed it,' said Nightingale. 'And, as you can see, I'm quite definitely her son so there's no problem at all in my visiting her.'

'Your mother killed herself, Mr Nightingale,' said Mrs Fraser. 'Questions are being asked as to how that happened, and it might be that our level of care is called into question.' She gave the report back to him.

'My mother was upset. I don't see that anyone can blame you,' said Nightingale.

'She died in our care, which means we're responsible,' said Mrs Fraser.

'Have the police been informed?' asked Nightingale.

Mrs Fraser nodded. 'Yes, but purely as a formality,' she said.

'She died in my arms,' said the nurse. 'I was holding her while she bled to death.' There were tears in his eyes.

'Did she say anything?' asked Nightingale.

The nurse shook his head.

'The point, Mr Nightingale, is that it was clearly your visits that upset Miss Keeley,' said Mrs Fraser. 'I think we're all agreed that prior to your visits she was calm, albeit uncommunicative. And afterwards . . .'

'I understand,' said Nightingale. 'I certainly wouldn't be in disagreement with you on that.'

'That's good to hear, Mr Nightingale,' she said.

Nightingale leaned forward. 'I'm not looking to blame anyone, Mrs Fraser, and I hope that's your position. My mother was obviously very disturbed, and I know you were giving her the very best care possible.' He looked at the male nurse. 'Darren thought a lot of my mother, and I could see she really appreciated the way he took care of her. I agree that my suddenly turning up upset her, but I don't think that anyone could have foreseen that she would harm herself.'

They were more concerned about a possible legal suit or bad publicity than they were about why Rebecca Keeley had killed herself, Nightingale realised. The meeting was about avoiding blame, nothing else. 'As to what I said to my mother, it was just family stuff. I showed her photographs of when I was a kid, and we talked about them. I don't know why she got so upset in the garden, but as soon as Darren asked me to leave, I did.'

Mrs Fraser nodded, and even managed a smile. 'Thank you for your understanding, Mr Nightingale. You can imagine how upset we all are. One never likes to lose a resident, especially under such circumstances.' She picked up a pen and toyed with it. 'We have to make arrangements,' she said, 'for the funeral.'

'What normally happens?' asked Nightingale.

'It depends on whether the resident has family or not. If there's no one, we arrange a service at the local crematorium.'

'Can you do that for my mother?' said Nightingale. 'So far as I know I'm her only living relative, and it would be a big help.'

'Yes, of course,' said Mrs Fraser.

'I'll pay. Whatever costs there are, just let me know.'

'Mrs Keeley's fees were paid by the local authority, and they'll bear the cost of the funeral,' said Mrs Fraser. 'Now, what would you like us to do with her belongings? Her clothes and such.'

'What normally happens?'

'If there are relatives we give them everything. Otherwise we clean any clothing and send it to charity shops, along with electrical equipment and other articles that people might want. The rest we throw away.' She grimaced. 'It's sad, but most of our residents don't have much left by the time they come here.'

'Charity shops sound like a good idea,' said Nightingale.

'The crucifix,' said the nurse. 'Don't forget the crucifix.'

'Oh, yes, your mother always wore it,' said Mrs Fraser. 'It was a great comfort to her.'

Nightingale turned to the nurse. 'Would you like it, Darren?'

'Oh, that's not possible,' said Mrs Fraser, quickly. 'It's against company policy, I'm afraid. We're not allowed to accept bequests from our residents. Under any circumstances. We had a bad experience a few years ago.'

'I understand,' said Nightingale. He took out one of his business cards and gave it to her. 'You can send it to me here.'

Mrs Fraser studied the card. 'I didn't know you were a private detective,' she said.

'For my sins,' said Nightingale.

'That can't be a pleasant occupation.'

'It has its moments,' said Nightingale.

47

Nightingale was driving on auto-pilot, his mind more focused on the death of Rebecca Keeley than on the road ahead, which was why he didn't see the fox until a second before he hit it. The car slammed into the animal and Nightingale hit the brakes. The rear started to spin and Nightingale pumped the brake as he fought to control it. The road curved to the right, and the sky was obscured by the drooping branches of the woodland he was driving through. He straightened the MGB but realised he was heading for a beech tree. He spun the wheel to the right. The car skidded to a halt and stalled.

Nightingale sat where he was, his heart pounding, gripping the steering-wheel so tightly that his knuckles went white. He had chosen to drive back to London along B-roads rather than take the motorway because he wanted time to think, but his decision had almost cost him his life. He started the engine and carefully drove the car off the road, climbed out and lit a cigarette with trembling hands. The MGB had stopped just a few feet from the tree. If he'd been going any faster or been a fraction slower in braking he would have slammed into it and he was sure the impact would have killed him. He inhaled deeply and blew a plume of smoke skywards. The line between life and death was a fine one at the best of times.

He looked back down the road. There was no sign of the fox. He walked along to where he'd hit the animal. There was no blood on the Tarmac, no indication that there had ever been a fox. He checked the vegetation at the side of the road but found nothing. Had he imagined it? He shook his head, trying to clear his thoughts. There had been a fox in the middle of the road and he hadn't imagined the thud as he'd hit it. So where was it? Had it crawled off to die? He walked into the woodland, treading softly through the brambles and nettles, listening for any sounds of an animal in pain, but all he could hear was the territorial chirping of birds high in the trees.

He saw a church spire through the trees and headed towards it. It was surrounded by a dry-stone wall, moss-covered in places, and a sign at the entrance proclaimed it as St Mary's. It was small, stone-built, with stained-glass windows and a metal cross atop the spire. Nightingale walked towards the oak door. It opened silently, despite its bulk – the hinges were well oiled – and the wood had been polished until it shone. There were fresh flowers in the vestibule and the cloying smell of lilies.

There were a dozen rows of hard wooden benches with an aisle down the centre that led to a pulpit and behind it a stone font. Nightingale felt himself drawn towards the font and walked down the aisle, his hands in his pockets. The air was much cooler inside the church than it had been outside and he shivered.

The stone flags had worn smooth with the thousands of feet that had gone back and forth over the years, making the journey from pew to priest. There were thick oak beams overhead, and statues set into the walls depicting the agony of Christ's crucifixion. Candles flickered in alcoves, dripping wax onto the stone floor. Nightingale looked around but he appeared to be alone. To the left of the pulpit was a confessional box, the curtains on both sides closed. Nightingale stopped and listened but he couldn't hear voices.

He walked slowly up to the font and looked down at the water. It was holy water, blessed by the priest. Nightingale smiled to himself. Holy water was supposed to hurt vampires, and he wondered what it would do to a man whose soul had been promised to a devil. Would it burn his flesh, like it did in the movies? If he stuck in his hand, would it strip it to the bone and would he run from the church, screaming in pain? He rolled up his sleeve and held his hand just above the surface of the water. 'Our Father, who art in heaven,' he whispered. He plunged his hand into the water. It was cold, colder than he had expected, and he gasped. He flexed his fingers. At least he could touch holy water, which must mean something.

'Can I help you?' said a voice behind him.

Nightingale jerked as if he'd been stung. He swung around to find a young priest watching him with unabashed amusement. 'I was . . .' he began, but he wasn't sure how to finish the sentence. What exactly was he doing? Checking the potency of holy water?

'There's a washroom at the back,' said the priest. He was in his late twenties with a shock of red hair and freckles across his nose and cheeks. 'You're welcome to use that if you want to wash your hands.'

'I wasn't washing my hands,' said Nightingale. 'I just wanted to . . . To be honest, and I know it makes no sense, I just wanted to touch some holy water, that's all.' He shook the drops off his hand and rolled down his shirt sleeve.

'You look distressed,' said the priest.

'It's been a funny old day,' said Nightingale. 'I've just found out that my mother has killed herself, and I narrowly missed wrapping myself around a tree.'

'I'm sorry for your loss,' said the priest. 'Was she a Catholic, your mother?'

'I don't know,' said Nightingale. 'She wore a crucifix, if that counts for anything.' He took out his packet of Marlboro and tapped out a cigarette, but the priest wagged a finger at him.

'I'm afraid smoking isn't allowed on the premises,' he said.

Nightingale grinned. 'You can see the irony in that, can't you, what with all the candles and incense you burn in here?'

'Just one of the many regulations that make our lives so much more complicated than they used to be,' said the priest. 'Don't get me started on refuse collections from our church. Would you class unused communion wafers as a foodstuff? Because our local council does. And heaven forbid they find their way into the recycling bin by mistake.'

'Actually, I'd have thought communion wafers would have been the ultimate in recycling, from bread to the Body of Christ.'

The priest chuckled. 'I wish I'd thought of that,' he said. 'They weren't consecrated, of course. Once they've been consecrated they have to be consumed. These had gone mouldy so they had to be thrown away. But because they were edible they were classed as food so they were in the wrong bin and some jobsworth decided I had to pay a penalty or be taken to court.' He waved at the door. 'You can smoke outside and we can carry on our conversation there.'

They walked together out of the church and over to a wooden bench at the edge of the graveyard. A small brass plaque was fixed to the back: 'In memory of Mary, 1921–98, my soul-mate'. They sat on the bench and Nightingale lit a cigarette.

'Again, I'm so sorry for your loss,' said the priest. 'It's always difficult to lose a loved one, but the bond between a mother and son is the strongest of all, I think.'

'Thank you,' said Nightingale. The truth was that he didn't feel any sense of loss at the death of Rebecca Keeley, even though she had been his biological mother. She had given birth to him but that was all, and he had no more feeling for her than for a total stranger. But he knew that the priest meant well so he tried to look as if his mother's death meant something.

'You're not a churchgoer?' said the priest.

'No,' said Nightingale. 'Do you mind me asking how old you are, Father?'

'I don't mind at all,' said the priest. 'I'm twenty-seven, so you can drop the "father" if that makes you uncomfortable. My name's Peter.'

'I'm Jack. That's young to be a priest, isn't it?'

'It is, these days, that's for sure.'

Nightingale offered him a cigarette but he shook his head. 'I've never smoked,' he said.

'Do you drink?'

'Oh, yes,' said the priest. 'Definitely.'

'But no sex?'

The priest's eyes narrowed as if he suspected Nightingale was being provocative. 'That door is firmly closed,' he said.

'I didn't meant to pry, it's just that I can't imagine why anyone would become a Catholic priest,' said Nightingale. 'You have to give up so much.' He blew smoke, taking care to keep it away from the other man.

'But we get so much more back,' he said.

'But wasn't it a hard decision to make, to turn your back on everything to enter the Church?'

The priest smiled. 'You're looking at it the wrong way. I was turning to God, and that gives me everything I could ever want or need. There is no better way to live one's life than in the service of the Lord.'

'And you have no doubts?'

'I doubt the sanity of the idiots who run our local council, but no doubts at all about God.'

'And you talk to God?'

'Of course, all the time. That's what prayer is.'

'But does He talk back?' Nightingale took a long drag on his cigarette.

The priest chuckled. It was an old man's laugh, and he put up his hand to cover his mouth as if he realised that it was at odds with his appearance. 'I don't hear voices, if that's what you mean,' he said. 'It's not like Joan of Arc.'

Nightingale exhaled smoke slowly. 'But you have a conversation with God, and that's why you believe in Him?'

'It's complicated.'

'But He answers your prayers?'

'Of course.'

'So if you prayed to win the lottery, He'd give you the winning numbers?'

'I wouldn't pray for that,' he said.

'What about world peace? I'm sure Christians everywhere pray for that but the world is still a very dangerous place.'

'You're asking why God doesn't stop all wars, why He doesn't create heaven here on earth?'

'I'm asking what makes you believe in God when all the evidence is to the contrary.'

'Every day I see the evidence of God's hand, in the beauty of the world, in the people I meet.'

'Yeah, well, I was a police officer and I tended to see less of the beauty and more of the dark side. And a read through any newspaper will prove that bad things happen to good people all the time.'

'Again, it's perception. Maybe you should try talking to God. When was the last time you prayed?'

Nightingale dropped his cigarette butt onto the ground and stepped on it. 'It's been a while.'

'You should try it again,' said the priest. 'You don't even have to go to a church. Just find yourself a quiet place and pray.'

'Our Father who art in heaven?'

'Not necessarily the Lord's Prayer. Just tell Him what's troubling you.'

'And He'll talk to me? I don't think so.'

'You won't know unless you try,' said the priest.

Nightingale folded his arms and sat back. 'Here's what I don't get,' he said. 'God wants us to obey Him, worship Him and all that stuff. And church attendances are down because fewer people believe He exists. So why doesn't He provide definitive proof? Why doesn't He let us know once and for all that He exists? If He did that, the whole world would believe, right?'

'But He did that, didn't He?' said the priest. 'He sent

His son, and we killed Him on the cross, and God brought Him back to life. That was definitive proof at the time, and it still is.'

'It was a long time ago,' said Nightingale.

'A little over two thousand years,' said the priest, 'which in human terms is the twinkling of an eye. We can't keep asking for proof every twenty minutes. He gave us proof, and we have the Bible to remind us of that.'

'But it's not enough,' said Nightingale.

'For you, perhaps. But have you read the Bible?'

'No,' admitted Nightingale.

'And you're not a churchgoer, so how can you expect to hear God's message?'

Nightingale sighed and stretched out his legs. 'You're so sure, aren't you? You're sure that God exists, you're sure you did the right thing in becoming a priest.'

'I am,' said the priest. 'Tell me, Jack, can you say the same about the decisions you've made in your life?'

Nightingale grinned ruefully. 'Fair point,' he said. 'What about the devil? You believe in the devil?'

'Without a doubt,' said the priest. 'And if it's proof you want, I'd have thought you were spoilt for choice so far as evidence of the devil's concerned.'

'You believe that bad things are the result of the devil's work?'

'Don't you?'

'In my experience, bad people do bad things,' said Nightingale.

'But what makes people go bad? You don't think there could be some influence at work?'

'And that influence is the devil? Is that what you're saying?'

'The devil. Satan. The Antichrist. Yes, I really do believe that. I believe that Satan wants people to act one way and God wants them to behave in another. We have free will, so it's up to us to choose whom we serve.'

'How are you on geography, Peter?' asked Nightingale.

'Geography?'

'I was talking with a vicar a few days ago, asking him about hell.'

'Church of England?'

'I guess so,' said Nightingale.

'Then you were asking the wrong guy,' said the priest. 'The Church of England isn't great on heaven and hell – they're more interested in race relations, gay marriages and women bishops. You want to know about hell, you talk to the Catholics.'

'So you believe in hell?'

'Absolutely,' said the priest. 'And I believe that if you break God's rules you'll be punished.'

'In hell?'

'In hell,' repeated the priest.

'Fire, brimstone, devils with pitchforks?'

'Not necessarily, but a place where souls would be in eternal torment. The complete opposite of heaven.'

'And Satan presides over hell and everything that happens there?'

'That's what the Bible says.'

'And where is hell, Peter?'

The priest chuckled. 'The geography question,' he said. 'Hand on heart, I don't know where hell is. But that's not important. What's important is that you don't get sent there.'

48

Nightingale was making himself a coffee when his doorbell rang. He checked the intercom in the hallway and saw that Jenny was outside in the street, standing next to a brunette in a trench coat. He pressed the intercom button. 'Not today, thank you,' he said. 'I gave at the office.'

'Open this door, Jack Nightingale, or I'll huff and I'll puff and I'll blow your house down.'

'You swear by the hair on your chinny chin chin, do you?'

'Jack, it's bloody cold out here. Let us in, will you?'

Nightingale chuckled and pressed the button to open the door, then nipped into the kitchen to prepare two more mugs. When the inner door buzzed he went to open it. The girl with Jenny was in her late twenties, pretty with dark green eyes and long lashes.

'This is Barbara, a friend from uni,' said Jenny. 'We're

going to stay with my folks for the weekend but I wanted to see if you were okay first.'

'I'm fine.' He shook hands with Barbara and took their coats. 'Coffee's on in the kitchen,' he said, as he hung them in the cupboard where he kept the ironing-board and Hoover. He showed Barbara through to the sitting room and switched off the television. 'So, was Jenny a swot at university?'

Barbara sat down on Nightingale's sofa and shook her head. 'Actually she was one of those annoying students who never studied. She soaked up informa-tion like a sponge.'

'That's so not true,' said Jenny, carrying a tray of mugs in. She put it on the coffee-table and sat down next to Barbara. 'I studied, I just did it on my own. How did it go at the home? Did they say how she died?'

Barbara and Jenny looked at him expectantly and Nightingale realised that Jenny must have told her friend about his mother's death. He wondered what else she had told her.

'Everyone's in a state of shock. She was eating her dinner and just started slashing her wrists.'

Jenny's jaw dropped. 'She killed herself? You didn't tell me that.'

'I didn't know until I got there.'

'Jack, you should have called me.'

'There wasn't anything you could do,' said Nightingale.

She glared at him. 'That's not the point,' she said. 'You should have told me. For God's sake, Jack, your mother killed herself. That's not the sort of thing you should keep to yourself.'

'I'm sorry. She doesn't feel like my mother, she was just—'

'The woman who gave birth to you,' she finished for him. 'Which is what a mother is, actually.'

Nightingale shook his head. 'Irene Nightingale was my mother,' he said. 'The woman who killed herself was . . . I don't know what she was. Yes, she gave birth to me, but there's more to being a mother than that. She gave me away, Jenny, on the day I was born.'

'But still . . .'

'Jenny, it meant nothing to me. I mean, I'm sorry she's dead, but I did my grieving when my mother died. My real mother.'

'Did they say why she killed herself?'

'She'd been on medication for years.'

'At least you got a chance to talk to her before she passed away,' said Barbara.

'I guess so,' said Nightingale.

'Barbara's a psychiatrist,' said Jenny. 'I hope you don't

mind but I did give her some idea of what you've been through recently.'

'What I've been through?'

'Finding out you were adopted, meeting the woman who gave birth to you and then her dying. Your aunt and uncle. Robbie's death.'

'I'm not denying it's been an eventful few days,' said Nightingale, 'but I'm dealing with it as best I can. This is just a social call, right, because I hope you don't expect me to lie on my couch and unburden myself.'

'Would that be such a bad thing, Jack?' said Barbara.

Nightingale grinned at her. 'With the greatest of respect, I don't know you, and while any friend of Jenny's is a friend of mine I'm certainly not going to strip myself bare in front of a stranger.'

'Please, God,' said Jenny.

'Now, you see, you wouldn't say that if you'd ever seen me naked,' said Nightingale. 'I've got nothing to be ashamed of in that department.'

Jenny gave Barbara a knowing look. 'Told you,' she said.

'Told you what?' said Nightingale.

'Jenny mentioned that you might be a tad defensive,' said Barbara. 'It's understandable.'

'We just popped around to see if you were okay, after what happened and all,' said Jenny.

'I'm fine,' said Nightingale. 'There'll be an inquest, obviously, and you're both invited to the funeral.'

'Jack!' said Jenny.

'It seems that you're more worried about her than I am.'

'You felt no bond when you met?' asked Barbara.

'How could I?' said Nightingale. 'I'm almost thirty-three and this week I met her for the first time.'

'Sometimes when parents and children are reunited there's an immediate connection, as if the genes kick in and you recognise each other subconsciously.'

Nightingale shook his head. 'Didn't happen,' he said.

'Did you tell her how you felt?' asked Barbara.

'I wasn't there for an exchange of emotion,' said Nightingale. 'I was there because I wanted to know why she gave me away.'

'You wanted closure?'

'Barbara, please stop trying to psychoanalyse me. I didn't want closure, I wanted facts. Cold, hard facts.'

'And did you get them?'

'Not really.'

'And how do you feel now that she's dead?'

'That's such a psychiatrist's question.'

Barbara laughed and sipped her coffee.

'And that's an interrogator's trick,' said Nightingale. 'Leaving a silence and hoping the subject will fill it.'

'You're not a subject, Jack, or a patient. You're just a friend of a friend. We can talk about the weather if you'd prefer. Or sport. You're a Manchester United fan, aren't you?'

Nightingale smiled. She was good, all right. She had barely glanced at the photographs on his sideboard but had obviously spotted the one of him with his father and uncle outside the Old Trafford stadium, all wearing team scarves. 'I am indeed.'

'I've always followed Liverpool. That's where I was born.'

'You've lost the accent,' said Nightingale. 'I'd have placed you as home counties.'

'Well, an expensive private education does that for you,' said Barbara. 'Can I ask you about your memory loss?'

'My what?'

'Jenny said you were having problems remembering things from your past.'

Nightingale flashed Jenny a warning look. 'And what else did she tell you?'

'Just that,' said Jenny, and licked her lips anxiously. 'That's all I said, Jack. I thought maybe Barbara might have some thoughts.'

'Memory is a delicate thing,' said Barbara. 'You were a policeman, so you must have come across that.

You can have a dozen eyewitnesses to the same event and they'll all see it differently, even down to giving completely different descriptions of people and things.'

Nightingale nodded. 'Witnesses are the least reliable of all evidence,' he said.

'Exactly,' said Barbara. 'And, as the years pass, memories fade.'

'I'm not going senile,' said Nightingale. 'Crazy maybe, but not senile.'

'You don't seem in the least bit crazy,' said Barbara. 'Stressed, maybe, but that's hardly surprising.'

'Considering what I've been through?'

'Jenny didn't tell me everything, I'm sure, but what she did tell me left me in no doubt that you could be suffering from PTSD.'

'Post-traumatic stress disorder? I don't think so.'

'It would account for the memory loss, Jack. Sometimes people under stress blot out the memories that would cause them more anxiety. It's the subconscious protecting the conscious.'

'I'm fine,' said Nightingale. 'To be honest, I'm probably best not remembering.'

Barbara leaned forward. 'That's a very significant thing to say, Jack.'

'I was joking.'

'Jokes can often be a window into our psyche. We often use them to make light of our real fears.'

Nightingale threw up his hands and laughed. 'I can't win with you, can I? You're determined to psychoanalyse me, no matter what I say.'

'Jenny's worried about you, and sometimes a third party can offer a view that might not occur to those close to the situation. I think you're blotting something out, Jack. Subconsciously or consciously.'

'And?'

'And if you wanted, I could perhaps help you remember. There are various relaxation techniques we can use that will open up your subconscious and allow you to get to the memories you're repressing.'

'You mean hypnotise me?'

'Not necessarily. I'd help you reach a relaxed frame of mind in which you're less anxious about remembering.'

'Honestly, Barbara, if I need someone to talk to, I'll find someone.'

'Like who, Jack?' asked Jenny.

'Don't worry, I'll sort that out. Really.'

Jenny looked at her watch. 'We should be going.' She and Barbara stood up. 'If you need me over the weekend, call me.'

'I will, I promise,' said Nightingale.

'And think about what Barbara said. Maybe she can help you remember. And if you do remember, then maybe things'll become a bit clearer.'

'I'll think about it.'

'I'm serious, Jack. I'm worried about you.'

Nightingale hugged her. He winked at Barbara over Jenny's shoulder. 'I bring out her mothering instincts,' he said.

'She was always rescuing stray dogs when she was a student,' said Barbara. 'I can see that nothing's changed.'

49

Nightingale walked slowly through the cemetery – there was a full moon and the sky was cloud-less so there was plenty of light to see by. A soft wind blew through the conifers that bordered it. He was smoking a Marlboro and holding a Threshers carrier-bag. The earth had been shovelled back into Robbie Hoyle's grave and pounded down but there was still a slight curve. Soil settled over time, Nightingale knew. He'd once been on a search team in the New Forest, looking for the body of a woman who'd been strangled by her husband seven years earlier. The guy had turned up at a local police station claiming that his wife had come back to haunt him and wouldn't leave him alone until he confessed and arranged for a proper Christian burial. The detectives who had interviewed him didn't believe in ghosts, and neither did Nightingale, but they did believe in grief and guilt, and because the man was vague about where he'd buried his wife, more than fifty officers in overalls and wellington boots had been dispatched to the forest.

Nightingale was with the group who had found the remains, and two clues had pinpointed its location. There was a deep depression where the soil had settled, and the grass above the body was greener and lusher than the surrounding vegetation. Two hours before they'd found the murdered wife, another group had found the body of a child that had been in the ground for more than a decade. There was little more than a skeleton left, wrapped in a blood-stained rug, and the child was never identified. Again, the depression in the ground and lush grass had given it away.

There was no headstone on Hoyle's grave, but marble edging had already been put around the perimeter, white with dark brown veins. Nightingale flicked away his cigarette butt, spread his raincoat on the grass and sat down on it. 'How's it going, Robbie?' he asked. It was a stupid question. Hoyle wasn't going anywhere. He was in a wooden box six feet underground, his veins pumped full of formaldehyde, his best suit on and his tie neatly knotted, the way it had never been when he was alive.

He opened the carrier-bag and took out a bottle of red wine. 'I know you're a wine drinker, so I brought this,' he said. He grinned as he held up the bottle. 'I couldn't be bothered with a corkscrew so I got one with a screw top. The girl who sold it to me said it was a respectable red from Chile. Mind you, she was Romanian so I don't think she knew much about wine.' He poured a splash of wine over the grave. 'Cheers, Robbie,' he said, then took a long drink. He wiped his mouth on his sleeve. 'Respectable wine, long on the palate with a blackcurrant and raspberry aftertaste.' He chuckled. 'Yeah, you got me – that's what it says on the label. Perfect for red meat and pasta. What the hell do I know? I'm a beer drinker, right? Or whisky when there's serious drinking to be done.'

Nightingale had another swig, then poured more on to the soil. 'I know this is a bloody cliché, talking to your mate's grave and sharing a drink with him, but I couldn't think what else to do. Actually, I did think of doing the glass-and-letters trick but I'd feel a right twat if you told me to go and shag Jenny again.' He shook his head. 'And, no, I haven't shagged her. Doubt I ever will. Don't want to ruin what we have – or don't want to ruin what we don't have. Either way, we haven't. And probably won't.' He raised his eyes skywards. 'Yeah, I heard the "probably", too. Freudian slip?'

Nightingale sniffed the neck of the bottle. 'It's not bad, this, is it? But it doesn't give you the same warm feeling as a good whisky. Or a bad one.' He took another drink. 'My mum died, Robbie. My real mum. My genetic mum.' He frowned. 'I don't know why I said that because she doesn't feel like my real mum. She was just a sad woman who couldn't even feed herself and got conned into having me by a guy old enough to be her father. She slashed her wrists with a knife. They're arranging her funeral as we speak. I don't think it'll be as well attended as yours, mate. Did you hear Chalmers? Said some nice things, he did. For a moment I thought he'd turned over a new leaf, but then he had me in for a grilling because the moron who ran you over topped himself and Chalmers wants to put me in the frame for it.'

Nightingale cursed vehemently. 'Didn't anyone ever tell you to look both ways before you cross the road, you stupid bastard? How could you walk in front of a bloody taxi? And on Friday the thirteenth. Another stupid cliché.'

Nightingale drank again, then poured another slug of wine over the grave. 'Right, so here's the thing, Robbie. Here's why I'm sitting next to your bloody grave sharing a bottle of cheap plonk with you.' He took a deep breath. 'I need a sign, Robbie. I need you to let me know that there's something after death, that you're still out there somewhere, that it's not . . .' Nightingale closed his eyes and cursed again. 'What the hell am I doing?' he muttered. 'This is mad. Crazy.'

He opened his eyes. 'Am I crazy? Am I sitting here talking to myself? Or can you hear me? I need to know, Robbie. I really need to know. I need something. Some sign. Something to let me know that death isn't the end. You know what's important, Robbie. You know why I need to know. Just give me a sign. Please.'

A shooting star flashed overhead and vanished as quickly as it had appeared.

Nightingale laughed harshly. 'Is that the best you can do?' he said. 'A bloody meteor? One poxy bit of ice and rock? I need something real, Robbie. I need to hear your voice or see you or feel your hand on my shoulder. It's not much to ask, not considering all the years we've been friends.'

He swallowed some more wine. 'Someone else I know died the other day. Killed himself. Client of mine. He wanted me to follow his wife and when he found out she was having an affair he topped himself. He bloody well topped himself and now the wife's blaming me, calling me all the names under the sun and threatening to sue me . . . She won't, of course. It's just the grief and anger talking. When you lose someone you want to lash out. I wanted to kill the driver of the black cab that hit you when I heard. But he was just in the wrong place at the wrong time. Same as you. Just one of those things. One of those stupid bloody things. If you'd stepped off the pavement a second later or he'd taken another route or if he'd just been bloody well looking where he was going, then you'd still be here and . . .' Nightingale tailed off. He groaned, lay back on his raincoat and stared up at the night sky, the bottom of the bottle balanced on his stomach. 'He's dead, the guy that was driving the cab. He topped himself. Slit his wrists to the bone. God knows why. Grief, maybe. Guilt.' Nightingale sighed. 'The thing about suicides is that they don't really think about death, about what it means. You know that – you did the courses. They think that what they're doing will prove something, or hurt someone, and because they're not thinking straight they imagine they'll be around to see what effect their death has. They imagine that they'll be at their own funeral, seeing everyone crying and saying how sorry they are. If they really thought about what was going to happen, they'd hang on to every second of life because life is all there is, right? Tell me, Robbie, am I right?' He grinned. 'You can't, can you? Because if death really is the end then I'm wasting my time. You can't prove a negative, right? Or is the fact that you're not replying the answer to my question but I'm just too stubborn to hear it?'

An owl hooted. 'That doesn't cut it either, Robbie. Give me something bigger. What about those nuns who see statues bleed or make the lame walk or hear voices? If they can hear voices, why the hell can't you talk to me? Just whisper to me, Robbie – no one else need know. And if it's against the rules, sod it, because you and I are the same, we can bend the rules when we have to if it's for the greater good. Just whisper my name.'

The wind picked up and the conifers swished back and forth, murmuring like assassins.

'The trees don't count either, Robbie. Stop pissing around.'

The wind died down. Nightingale closed his eyes and listened to the sound of his own breathing. It became deathly still. There was no wind, no traffic noise, no hooting owls or barking foxes. Just silence. Maybe that was what death was like, he thought. Just nothing. Perfect silence, perfect blackness, nothing for all of eternity. He took a deep breath and held it. No sound, no light, no feelings, no thoughts. Nothing. He slowly exhaled.

'I don't understand what's happening, Robbie. I don't understand why you died. I don't understand why my uncle Tommy smashed his wife's head in with an axe and then hanged himself. I don't understand why my mother slashed her wrists. I don't understand any of it.' He sighed. 'So this is the way I see it, Robbie. If death is the end, if there's nothing beyond this life, there really is no point, right? Death sucks, Robbie, you know that. Anna's in bits and it'll be a long, long time before she's anywhere near okay. And what about your kids? The twins still think you're coming back – they've no idea what "dead" means. Shit, Robbie, all you had to do was look both ways when you crossed the road. It's the Green Cross Code, for God's sake.'

Nightingale opened his eyes and stared up at the moon. 'If you could, you'd talk to Anna, wouldn't you? You'd tell her not to worry, to give the kids a kiss from you. And I'm sure my mum and dad would have done the same for me. But you didn't and they didn't, so that means you can't, and the reason you can't is because you're dead and gone for ever.'

He closed his eyes again. 'So, if dead is dead and there's nothing after it, then all this nonsense about

Gosling selling my soul is just that. Nonsense. There are no souls to be sold. There's no God and no devil and no heaven and no hell so I should just stop worrying about what Gosling did or didn't do because the only thing I really have to worry about is that one day, sooner or later, I'm going to be dead and buried the same as you.' He smiled. 'Well, not buried. I'll either be scattered across Manchester United's pitch or sitting in an egg-timer in Jenny's kitchen. To be honest, Robbie, I don't know which is worse – to know I'm going to hell, or to know there's no such a place and that death is the end of everything.'

Nightingale heard music. The Rolling Stones, 'Paint It Black'. It was his mobile phone ringing in his coat pocket. Nightingale smiled to himself. 'If that's you calling, Robbie, I'll be well impressed.' He groped around for the phone and pressed the green button to take the call.

'Jack? Jack Nightingale?'

Nightingale didn't recognise the voice but it definitely wasn't Hoyle. 'Yeah?'

'This is Harry Wilde. I'm sorry to disturb you on a Saturday night and I'm sorry I didn't get back to you sooner, but I had a hell of a time trying to find my notebook. I'd left it at home and the wife had tidied it up, bless her.'

Harry Wilde. The police sergeant he'd spoken to at Gosling Manor. 'No problem, Harry,' said Nightingale. 'Any joy with the phone numbers?'

'The husband and wife lived in. They were given the day off on the night Gosling killed himself, but they turned up for work the next day and were interviewed at the house. There wasn't much they could say, obviously. They were paid off a couple of days later and moved out. I'm afraid we don't know where they went.'

'No need, because it was open and shut, right?'

'Exactly,' said Wilde. 'Once it was clearly suicide everyone throttled back. I've got their names, though. Millie and Charlie Woodhouse. Millicent and Charles. I had more luck with the driver. He discovered the body so he was of more interest, but again it was obviously suicide so we were just going through the motions. Have you got a pen there?'

Nightingale fished his Parker out of his pocket, along with a receipt from his local Tesco. 'Yup,' he said.

'His name's Alfie Tyler.' Wilde gave him an address and mobile-phone number and Nightingale scribbled them down.

'I shouldn't be talking out of school, but Alfie was a bit of a lad back in the day,' said Wilde. 'He used to work as a debt-collector for one of the north London mobs and did four years for GBH.'

Nightingale thanked him and put the phone away. 'Bloody hell, Robbie, I need a real drink,' he said. He stood up and poured the last of the wine over the grave. 'Red wine always gives me a rotten hangover,' he said, and tossed the empty bottle towards the conifers.

50

Alfie Tyler's home wasn't what Nightingale had expected. It was a six-bedroom mock Tudor house with tall chimneys on the outskirts of Bromley, with a double garage and a rock-lined pool in the front garden. A gleaming black Bentley was parked in front of the garage. Nightingale had checked the electoral roll and there was no Mrs Tyler. From a cursory look at the house Nightingale was fairly sure that no little Tylers were in residence. He'd driven down on Sunday morning, assuming it would be the best time to catch him at home.

Nightingale dropped the cigarette he'd been smoking onto the pavement and stamped on it. He'd phoned the land line and knew that Tyler was in. Unlike Gosling Manor, there didn't appear to be any CCTV cameras. The large black wrought-iron gates weren't locked so he pushed them open and walked up the driveway to the front door. It was painted black with a large brass knocker in the shape of a lion's head in the centre. A brass bell-push was set in the brickwork to the right.

Nightingale pressed it and a musical chime kicked into life. It sounded as if it might once have been classical. Then Nightingale heard footsteps on a wooden floor, and the door opened. 'Who is it?' growled the man, in a south London accent.

'Alfie Tyler?' asked Nightingale.

'Who wants to know?' asked Tyler, pulling the door wide. He was a big man, at least three inches taller than Nightingale, and Nightingale was a little over six feet. He had big forearms that strained at the sleeves of his polo shirt, and a trim but solid waist. He was sporting a gold Rolex on his left wrist, a thick gold chain on the right, and a full sovereign ring on the second finger of his right hand. As he stood on the threshold of his two-million-pound house with his arms folded across his barrel chest, Nightingale caught a whiff of very expensive aftershave.

'Jack Nightingale,' he said, slowly and carefully, watching for any reaction. There was none, no sign that Tyler had ever heard of him.

Tyler glared at him down his twice-broken nose. 'Are you a cop?' he asked.

'No, not any more,' said Nightingale.

'Then get the hell off my property before I throw you off,' said Tyler. His greying hair, with the wrinkles around his mouth and eyes, suggested he was in his fifties but his body was more in keeping with that of a thirty-something boxer and Nightingale was in no doubt that he was more than capable of carrying out his threat.

Tyler started to shut the door but Nightingale put his foot over the threshold. 'I just need a chat with you, Alfie,' he said. He took out his wallet and gave him one of his business cards.

Tyler held it between his thumb and forefinger and scowled as he read it. 'A private dick?' he said. 'I'm going to count to five, and if you haven't got the hell off my property I'm going to tear you a new arsehole,' he said, and tossed the card over Nightingale's shoulder.

'I'll take my car with me, shall I?'

Deep frowns furrowed Tyler's forehead. 'What?'

Nightingale gestured at the Bentley. 'That's my motor,' he said.

Tyler put a bear-like paw on his shoulder and squeezed, digging his thumb into the pressure point near the socket. 'You're starting to piss me off, private dickhead.'

'I'm the sole beneficiary of Ainsley Gosling's estate,' said Nightingale. 'I've seen the will, Alfie, and there's no mention of you or the Bentley. So, if I go along to the cops, the car will be back in my garage and you'll be back behind bars. Prisons are a lot more crowded than they were when you were last there, and I'm told the food's worse.'

Tyler squinted at Nightingale. 'How did you know I'd been in prison?'

'I don't care about your criminal record, I don't care about whose legs you did or didn't break, I just want to know about Ainsley Gosling.'

'Mr Gosling said the car was mine after he'd gone.'

'He came back from the grave to tell you that, did he?' said Nightingale.

Tyler frowned. 'What?' He released his grip on Nightingale's shoulder.

'When did he tell you the car was yours?'

'All the time. He knew how much I liked it, and he said I could have it. After . . . you know.'

'So he told you he was going to top himself, did he?'

'What? No, he bloody well didn't. What are you trying to do here? You trying to say I had something to do with him killing himself? That's bollocks.' He put his fists on his hips and glowered at Nightingale.

Nightingale lit a cigarette. He saw Tyler's nostrils flare and offered him the packet.

'I'm trying to give up,' said Tyler.

'One won't hurt,' said Nightingale. Tyler shrugged and helped himself. Nightingale lit it for him. 'Okay, here's the thing, Alfie. I'm not going to have much use for a car over the next year or two, and, anyway, I'm a fan of convertibles. I like the feel of the wind in my hair.'

'What?'

'What I'm saying is, I'm more than happy to let you keep the Bentley, free, gratis, whatever, but in return I want you to tell me what Gosling was up to in the weeks before his death.'

Tyler's eyes narrowed. 'What's the catch?'

'No catch, Alfie. I'll even sign a piece of paper here and now saying it's yours.'

Tyler's brow furrowed again. 'Give me another of them cards, yeah?'

'Only if you promise not to throw it away,' said Nightingale.

'What?'

'You say "what" a lot – you know that?' Nightingale gave him another business card.

Tyler pursed his lips as he read the card. 'Why did Mr Gosling make you his heir?'

'It's a long story.'

'Give me the short version.'

'I'm his son.'

'Mr Gosling never told me he had a kid.'

'Yeah, well, I'm the family secret,' said Nightingale. 'But Gosling Manor's mine now. And so's the Bentley. So, are you and I going to have a chat or what?'

Tyler took a long drag on his cigarette and nodded. 'Okay,' he said. 'What do you want to know?'

'It's going to take a while,' said Nightingale. 'Why don't you ask me in and we can talk over a drink? Or two.'

51

Tyler sighted down his cue, smacked the white ball against the number five and grinned as it shot into a corner pocket. 'That's another tenner you owe me,' he said, holding out his hand.

Nightingale took out his wallet and gave him a ten-pound note. 'That's the sign of a misspent youth,' he said.

Tyler had built a bar in his basement, complete with a full range of optics, draught-beer pumps, a pool table, a jukebox and half a dozen fruit machines. On one wall there were dozens of framed photographs of a younger Tyler with well-known villains, movie stars and even a few members of the Metropolitan Police. Nightingale recognised two senior officers from the Flying Squad, both of whom had left the force on medical grounds and now lived in palatial villas in Spain. Most of the villains had either retired or died, but as far as Nightingale could recall, none had served time behind bars.

'Not much else to do in prison,' said Tyler.

'How long did you get?' asked Nightingale.

'I did two stretches, eighteen months and four years,' said Tyler. 'It was when I came out the second time that I started working for Mr Gosling. He knew my probation officer and I went to see him. We got on like a house on fire.'

'Did you ever go into the basement at Gosling Manor?' asked Nightingale.

'Didn't know there was one,' said Tyler, as he racked up the balls again. 'How about twenty quid a game? Give you a chance to win your money back.'

'You conning me, Alfie?' he said.

'Wouldn't dream of it,' said Tyler. 'So, you're really Mr Gosling's boy?'

'He had me adopted at birth,' said Nightingale. 'How long did you work for him?'

'Fifteen years, pretty much,' said Tyler.

'And he paid you well, did he? Because this is one expensive place you've got here.'

Tyler grinned. 'I had this place long before I worked for Mr Gosling. I was pretty productive in my glory days.'

'So what were you doing driving for him if you weren't short of a bob or two?'

'He was a character, your dad,' said Tyler, putting

the white ball in position. He reached for Nightingale's
Marlboro and took a cigarette. 'Could charm the birds
from the trees. And the people he knew! Film stars,
businessmen, sportsmen. Everyone liked Ainsley
Gosling. They were like moths to a flame. He was on
first-name terms with half a dozen prime ministers. We
had Mrs Thatcher around three times at Gosling Manor.
She was a real lady. Took a shine to your dad, she did.'

'If he was that popular, why did I never read anything
about him? And Googling him doesn't throw up
anything. There's never been a newspaper article about
him and there are no photographs. He's the original
invisible man.'

'He had a team of spin doctors who did nothing but
keep his name out of the papers. And if someone did
start getting too close, well, let's just say that Mr Gosling
had a way of helping people to forget things.'

'Now it's my turn to look puzzled and say, "What?"'

'You never met him, right?'

'I only found out he was my father recently,' said
Nightingale.

'He wasn't like other men, your dad,' said Tyler. 'He
had a way with him. A strength.'

'You know he was a Satanist, don't you?'

Tyler shrugged. 'I'm not one for putting labels on
people.'

'He studied the occult – he spent millions buying books on witchcraft and devil-worship.'

'Can't argue with that.'

'Did you ever see him do stuff?'

'Like what?'

'Like summoning devils,' said Nightingale.

'You on drugs, Nightingale?' asked Tyler.

'He was a Satanist and that's what Satanists do, right? They serve the devil.'

'I never saw him do anything like that,' said Tyler. 'I was his driver, his personal assistant, his bodyguard. And I'd like to think I was his friend, too.' He hit the white ball and it shot into the triangle of numbered ones with the sound of a skull being cracked with a baseball bat. Two balls dropped into pockets.

'How did he make his money, Alfie?'

'He just made it. It came to him. I never saw anybody as lucky as Mr Gosling. If he bought gold, it went up in price. If he bought oil, it went up. Any shares he bought went through the roof.'

'Insider trading?'

'I don't think so. I reckon he was just lucky.'

'Lucky?'

Tyler potted three balls in quick succession. Then he straightened and rested the cue on his shoulder. 'We went to a casino once. He had two girls with him, model-slash-singers or singer-slash-actresses – bloody fit, legs that went on for ever. Couldn't have been more than nineteen, either of them. He was always lucky with the ladies, was Mr Gosling.'

'Yeah, rich men usually are,' said Nightingale.

'It wasn't about the money,' said Tyler. 'I mean, Mr Gosling was a generous man, don't get me wrong, but I've seen women fall for him even when they didn't know who he was or how much he had. It was like he had power over them, the sort of charisma film stars have. I mean, he was an old man and all but he had no problem pulling young flesh.'

He bent over the table and potted another ball, then picked up his pint of beer. 'Anyway, the girls wanted to go to a casino so I drove them all to Leicester Square. Mr Gosling won at every game he played. He sat down at the high-stakes blackjack table and he just won hand after hand. It was like he knew what cards were going to be dealt.'

'Maybe he was a card counter.'

Tyler shook his head. 'He was hardly even looking at them. He just sat there joking with the girls and chips kept piling up in front of him. Then they wanted to play roulette and he gave them thousands of pounds' worth of chips and they lost it all. But pretty much every time he placed a bet he won. It got so that a couple of the casino managers came over to see what was happening.'

'Did they throw him out?'

Tyler chuckled. 'You really didn't know Mr Gosling, did you?' he said. He sipped his beer. 'He looked at them and smiled, in that way he did, and they smiled and went away. Nobody ever gave Mr Gosling any trouble over anything. If a flight was overbooked, there was a seat for him in first class. If a restaurant was full, there was a table. He was like royalty. More often than not he didn't even have to ask. It wasn't money, it was . . .'

'Power,' Nightingale finished for him.

'Presence was what I was going to say,' said Tyler. 'People just wanted to help him, to make his life easier, happier, whatever. Maybe that's why I stayed with him so long. I can't explain it any other way.'

'Probably a gay thing,' said Nightingale. Tyler put down his pint and held his cue in both hands, his face tightening. Nightingale held up his hands. 'Joke,' he said.

'I'm not gay,' said Tyler.

'I was joking,' he said, 'trying to lighten the moment. Because what you're telling me is that Ainsley Gosling had power over people. And that's what I was told.'

'Who by?'

'Him. He left me a DVD, a sort of video last will and testament.' He smiled, trying to show that he wasn't intimidated by Tyler's menacing stare. 'Wasn't you that left the envelope on the mantelpiece, was it?'

'What?' said Tyler, his brow furrowing again.

'Someone left an envelope in Gosling Manor with my name on it. Inside it I found the key to a safe-deposit box and, in the box, the DVD.'

'And what did he say on it?'

Nightingale was there to question Tyler, not open his heart to him. 'Just the normal father-son sort of chit-chat. Basically apologising for giving me up for adoption. He never mentioned me to you? Not once?'

Tyler shook his head. 'Never.'

'Or my sister, his daughter?'

'Never talked about kids, never mentioned having them or wanting them.'

'I get the feeling he was different during the last few years.'

Tyler stopped holding his cue as if it was a club and picked up his pint. 'He changed, that's true,' he said. 'Starting travelling overseas more, meeting some very strange people. Buying books by the dozen. Expensive ones. Often in cash.'

'Books about the occult?'

'I didn't get to see them all but the ones I did see,

yeah, witchcraft and stuff. And he started spending more time on his own. Then last year he started getting rid of the staff, one by one. Then he sold his art collection and his furniture. I asked him what was going on but I don't think he ever explained to me what he was up to.'

'You don't think? Don't you know?'

Tyler sighed. 'You had to know him to understand what it was like. He had a way of, I don't know, looking at you that made you either forget or change your mind about something. Like, I'd be really tired and I'd tell him and he'd say something to me and it was like I'd just done a line of coke. Or I'd say I couldn't work on such and such a day because I had to do something and the next minute I'd forget what was so important and agree to drive him around.'

'He hypnotised you – is that what you're saying?'

'Nah, I was never in a trance and he never did any wavy-hand stuff or swung a watch.' He sat down on a bar stool. 'It was weird, though. Sometimes he'd mumble something that didn't sound like it was English. But then he'd smile and I'd forget about it.' He put a hand to his forehead. 'Even talking about it sounds stupid. Like I was imagining it. But I'll tell you, Jack, I would have taken a bullet for Ainsley Gosling, or a knife, or stepped in front of a train.'

'But have you never asked yourself why you felt that way? How he inspired that sort of loyalty?'

'It was just his way,' said Tyler.

'Charisma,' said Nightingale.

'Yeah, charisma.' Tyler put down his pint and potted the rest of his balls. He grinned and held out his hand. Nightingale sighed and gave him twenty pounds. 'Double or nothing?' enquired Tyler.

'Yeah, why not?' said Nightingale, and watched as Tyler set up the balls again. He'd asked for a Corona but the best Tyler could provide was Budweiser. 'You were the one who found him, weren't you?'

'Yeah. One hell of a mess.'

'He was alone in the house?'

Tyler nodded. 'He'd given the Woodhouses the night off.'

'The Woodhouses? That was the couple who took care of the house, right?'

'Millie and Charlie. They were with him even longer than I was. He had a big staff up until a few years ago but he let them all go.'

'Do you know why?'

'He was running out of cash. He always paid me and he never seemed short of cash for books, but I think he lost a lot when the stock market crashed.'

'How did you get into the house?'

'I had a key. I went to the kitchen, like I always did, for a coffee with Millie but she wasn't there. I waited until about ten and then I went up and found him.'

'Was there a note?'

'No.'

'You're sure?'

'You calling me a liar?'

'It's just that you and he were close, Alfie. Suicides usually want to explain themselves – to say why they did what they did. If he was going to say anything to anybody, it would have been to you, right?'

Tyler sighed and straightened up. 'There was a letter, but it didn't explain anything.'

'And you really didn't leave an envelope for me on the mantelpiece in the main room?'

Tyler shuffled uncomfortably.

'Alfie, you might as well tell me everything. It couldn't have been anyone but you. You found the body, and the police didn't see any envelope when they were there.'

Tyler nodded slowly. 'Fair enough,' he said. 'There was a letter for me and an envelope for you. In the letter Mr Gosling told me to wait until the police and everyone had gone, then leave your envelope on the mantelpiece and lock up.'

'And what did you do with your letter?'

'Burned it. That was what he told me to do.'

'And what else did it say?'

'Said I could keep the Bentley, for one. Apologised for the mess. Told me to call the cops. And there was some cash for the Woodhouses.'

'Where are they now?'

'No idea. They just went. I think they had a place in the Lake District.' Tyler finished setting up the table and picked up his cue.

'He was buying a lot of books over the year or so before he died, right?' asked Nightingale.

'Tell me about it,' said Tyler. 'He had me driving him all over the country and to and from the airport every week or so.'

'What about a diary written by a guy called Sebastian Mitchell? Did you ever see that? Big leather-bound book, written in Latin, back to front. I think it was the last thing he read.'

'Like I said, he didn't show me his books. But I went to Mitchell's house a few times.'

Nightingale's jaw dropped. 'You met him?'

'Never met him but drove to his house. Place up near Wivenhoe, in Essex. Big place, very heavy security.'

52

Nightingale drove up to a set of high, wrought-iron gates set into a ten-foot brick wall. He climbed out of the MGB, went up to a small brass speakerphone set into the gatepost on the left and pressed it. It buzzed, then there was static but no one spoke. Nightingale leaned closer to the grille. 'Hello,' he said. There was no reply, just static. There was a CCTV camera on a metal post on the other side of the wall, covering the gate. Nightingale grinned and held up his driving licence to it. 'Jack Nightingale,' he said. 'I'm here to see Mr Mitchell.' He had no way of knowing if anyone was watching him so he put it away and went back to the speakerphone. 'Jack Nightingale,' he repeated. 'I'm here to see Mr Mitchell.'

The static stopped abruptly and a woman spoke, her voice curt and official. 'Mr Mitchell doesn't see visitors. Please remove yourself from outside our property. Thank you.' The speakerphone went dead.

Nightingale pressed the button again and the static returned. 'My name is Jack Nightingale and I want to see Mr Mitchell. Mr Sebastian Mitchell.'

'Mr Mitchell does not receive visitors,' said the woman.

'Can you tell him it's about the book he wrote? His diary.'

'Mr Mitchell never sees visitors,' said the woman. 'If you don't go away immediately, the police will be called.'

There was more static. Nightingale leaned towards the speakerphone. 'Tell him my father was Ainsley Gosling.' The static ended and there was only the sound of birdsong from the trees on the far side of the road. The lock buzzed and the gates swung open. He turned and looked up at the CCTV, threw it a mock salute, then climbed back into the MGB and drove through the gates. The drive curved to the right in front of a three-storey concrete and glass cube. A flight of white marble steps led up to a white double-height door that was already opening as he got out of the car. Two men in black suits, wearing impenetrable sunglasses, walked down the steps towards him.

Nightingale knew instinctively that they were going to pat him down so he smiled amiably and raised his arms. One of the men, burly with a shaved head, slowly and methodically squeezed his legs and arms, then worked his way down from his neck to his groin. He found Nightingale's phone and examined it carefully before handing it back. 'Photo ID,' he said. He wasn't English, Nightingale realised. Serbian, maybe, or Bosnian.

Nightingale gave the man his driving licence.

'Business card.' The man held out his other hand. Nightingale took out his wallet and gave him one.

The second man was walking slowly around the car, checking it inside and out. Nightingale smiled and nodded but was ignored.

The heavy with his ID went back up the steps to where a woman had emerged from the house. She was wearing a black suit, the skirt ending just above her knees, a crisp white shirt and black high heels. Her blonde hair was tied back with a black ribbon.

As the man gave the driving licence and business card to her, a gust lifted the back of his jacket and Nightingale caught a glimpse of a black automatic in a leather and nylon holster. It looked like a Glock. The woman studied the licence and card and then waved at Nightingale to come up the stairs. He held out his hand to shake hers but she just gave him his licence and card. 'My name is Sylvia, Mr Nightingale. There are certain house rules that must be followed to the letter if you are to meet with Mr Mitchell.'

'I understand.'

'No, you don't,' she said. 'You will do everything I ask or you will not be permitted to speak with him.' She turned and walked back inside the house. Two more men in black suits and dark glasses were standing in the large white-marble hallway, their hands clasped over their groins. Two stainless-steel CCTV cameras covered the area.

A marble spiral staircase, also covered by a CCTV camera, led to the upper floors, and a glass-feature light, which looked like a waterfall that had frozen mid-flow, hung from the centre of the ceiling. Half a dozen jet black doors with glossy white handles led off the hall. Sylvia walked to the middle, her heels clicking on the marble, and stopped under the glass waterfall. She turned to him and pointed to a door. 'In there is a bathroom. You will remove all your clothing and you will shower, using the gel provided. You will use the same gel to wash your hair twice. You will use the brush provided to clean under your toe- and fingernails. There are no towels but there is an electric dryer in which you stand. When you are dry you will put on the robe provided and come back here. Do not touch your clothes once you have showered. Do you have any questions?'

'Just one,' said Nightingale. 'I said I was the son of Ainsley Gosling, but my name is Nightingale. Yet you showed no surprise at the different names.'

'Apparently Mr Mitchell was expecting you,' said Sylvia. She motioned at the door to the bathroom. 'Please, if you will.'

53

There were two stainless-steel CCTV cameras in the bathroom, which Nightingale thought overkill, considering the men with guns in the hallway. He was sure that the cameras were being monitored but didn't bother trying to protect his modesty. There were white plastic hangers on a set of stainless-steel hooks. He stripped off his clothes and placed them on the hangers. A pristine white cotton robe was hanging on one of the hooks. He rolled up his socks and put them into his shoes, took off his watch and stood facing one of the cameras, his arms held out from his sides. 'Happy?' he said.

The camera stared back at him. He walked into the glass-sided shower. There were multiple jets all around it and when he turned the control dial water squirted at him from every direction. There was a soap dispenser full of a bright green gel. Nightingale rubbed it into his hair and lathered it over his body. It smelled of mint and tingled on his skin. There was a brand new plastic nailbrush on a wire tray under the soap dispenser with which he methodically cleaned his nails. Then he rinsed off the lather and repeated the process.

The dryer was a stainless-steel box of the same size as the shower with a rubber floor. As soon as he stepped inside, warm air blew all over his body, caressing him like a soft summer wind. Nightingale raised his arms and let it play over his skin. In less than three minutes he was dry. He put on the robe, which reached almost to his ankles. There was no comb or brush so he stood in front of a floor-to-ceiling mirror and tidied his hair as best he could with his fingers.

Sylvia was waiting for him in the hall, flanked by two of the men in dark suits. 'Show me your hands,' she said. He held them out and she scrutinised his nails, then nodded. 'There are procedures that must be followed at all times,' she said. 'If at any time you break any of the rules I will give you, the meeting will end.'

'I'll be a good boy,' said Nightingale.

She ignored his attempt at levity. 'You will see that Mr Mitchell is inside a pentagram. You must not get within six feet of the perimeter.'

'Because?'

'There is no because, Mr Nightingale. There are only

rules that have to be followed. If you make any attempt
to get closer than six feet, my associates here will stop
you.'

'Stop me how?'

'By whatever means necessary.'

'They'll shoot me if I try to get inside the circle?'

'By whatever means necessary,' repeated Sylvia. 'You
must make no move to touch Mr Mitchell or to give
him anything.'

'So, no kissing, then?'

'This is not a laughing matter, Mr Nightingale,' said
Sylvia, disdainfully. 'If you refuse to take this seriously
I will have to ask you to leave.'

Nightingale's face hardened. 'I don't think that's
going to happen, Sylvia darling,' he said. 'Because the
way I see it, you're the hired help here. You dance for
Mr Mitchell and Mr Mitchell has decided that he wants
to see me. When I was outside you were all for calling
the cops and having me hauled away, but you changed
your tune when Mr Mitchell learned who I was. He
told you to get me in here, which means he wants to
see me, which means you're not going to ask me to
leave. So, do your job and let me in to see him and
stop playing the hard arse with me, because I've dealt
with some very hard people over the years and, believe
me, you don't even come close.'

Sylva's jaw tightened and if looks could kill Nightingale would have burst into flames on the spot, but he could see in her eyes that he was right. She didn't have the authority to keep him from the man he'd come to see. She walked past him, so close that he caught the delicate scent of her perfume. 'Follow me,' she said.

54

Sebastian Mitchell was in a ground-floor room over-looking the gardens at the rear of the house. The floor was of the same white marble that had been used in the entrance hall and the walls were painted white. He was sitting in a winged green leather armchair, an oxygen mask covering the lower part of his face and connected by a thin clear tube to a tall cylinder behind him to his left. To his right a heart monitor was connected to a sensor on his chest. He was an old man, at least ninety, with wisps of white hair and skin that was greying and speckled with liver spots. He was wearing a robe similar to the one that Nightingale had on, open at the front, and white cotton boxer shorts. There were pale blue slippers on his feet.

The room was large, almost as big as the main room in Gosling Manor. There were French windows leading out to a stone-flagged patio, which in turn led to lawns as smooth as a billiard table. A bodyguard stood at each corner of the room. Unlike the men outside they had taken off their jackets but kept on their sunglasses. Two had nylon shoulder holsters with Glock automatics, one an Ingram submachine pistol in a sling and the fourth was holding a shotgun across his chest. They were staring impassively into the middle distance.

Nightingale walked towards Mitchell, his bare feet slapping on the marble floor. Sylvia followed him, her high heels clicking like an overwound metronome. 'Not too close, remember, Mr Nightingale,' she warned.

A black circle had been etched into the floor, its edge bordering a five-pointed star. At first Nightingale thought that the design had been painted onto the marble but as he got closer he realised it was actually set into the white marble. There were other designs within the circle, strange markings and letters from an alphabet he didn't recognise. At each point of the star a large white candle burned, but there was no smoke, just a pure yellow flame. The only other furniture in the room was a hospital bed, in the centre of the circle next to the armchair.

'Thanks for seeing me,' said Nightingale.

Mitchell coughed, then pulled the oxygen mask away from his face. 'You have your father's eyes,' he said, 'and his jaw.'

'I don't think anyone else sees a family resemblance,' said Nightingale.

'He sent you?' asked Mitchell.

'He's dead,' said Nightingale.

Mitchell's eyes narrowed and he put up a hand to adjust the oxygen mask. 'How?'

'Suicide.'

'How?'

'Shotgun to the head.'

'When?'

'Last week.'

Mitchell began to laugh, but the laugh quickly degenerated into a cough. When he had it under control he took a tissue from a box and dabbed his lips. It came away spotted with red. He screwed it up and dropped it into a steel wastebin. 'How old are you?' he asked.

'I'll be thirty-three next Friday.'

Mitchell nodded slowly, a cruel smile spreading across his face. 'Today's the Lord's Day, so five days to go,' he said. 'He was trying to get out of the deal, you know that?'

'He left me a video, telling me everything.'

Mitchell laughed sharply. 'I hardly think he would have told you everything,' he said. 'But he was wasting his time. There was nothing he could do. And that's why you have come to see me, of course. But you're wasting your time, as your father wasted his.'

'He asked for your help?'

'I don't think your father asked for anything in his life. He demanded. He threatened. He bargained. But even if he had gone down on his knees and begged, even if I had wanted to help him, there is nothing that can be done. A deal is a deal.' He leaned over and adjusted the oxygen flow, took several deep breaths from the mask and settled back in his chair. 'You read my book?'

'Some of it.'

'You read Latin?'

'A friend helped me.'

'So you know what lies ahead for you?'

'I said I read it. I didn't say I believed it.'

Mitchell coughed and removed his mask again to dab at his lips. The blood-spotted tissue followed the first into the wastebin. 'It doesn't matter if you believe it or not. A deal is a deal.'

'Why my thirty-third birthday? Why didn't the devil he did the deal with take my soul straight away, at birth?'

'A soul that hasn't lived is no prize,' said Mitchell. 'There are seven cycles each of eleven years. The start of the fourth cycle is the most precious, when the body is at its peak.'

'And the deal would have been my soul for riches and power?'

'I don't know what your father asked for. But, whatever it was, he regretted it. Eventually.'

'And that was when he came to see you?'

'He kept coming. He was at my door every week. He knew I'd done a deal with Proserpine. He thought I could help him get out of the deal he'd done.'

'Proserpine?'

Mitchell grinned. 'You don't know anything, do you?'

'I'm on a pretty steep learning curve, yeah.'

'Proserpine is the devil that your father did the deal with. A bitch of the first order.'

'And you wouldn't help?'

'Wouldn't help, couldn't help, it amounts to the same thing. A deal is a deal and that's the end of it.' He chuckled. 'The end of you.'

'Why did you give him your diary if you didn't want to help him?'

Mitchell chuckled drily. 'Is that what you think? That I gave it to him? Your father stole it from me. He sent his people in at night. They killed two of my men and took it.'

'Why? What was so important about your diary?'

'He thought it would show him a way to get out of the contract. But he was wrong. The book contains many things, but getting out of a contract with Proserpine is not an option.'

'What about if I gave you the diary back?'

Mitchell stared at Nightingale. 'That would be the honourable thing to do,' he said.

'If I did,' said Nightingale, 'what could you do for me?'

'What do you want?'

'What I want, Mr Mitchell, is to forget about all this and get on with my life.'

'I'm afraid that's not an option,' said Mitchell. He began to cough again and bent forward to adjust the oxygen flow. He took several deep breaths to steady himself. 'Doing a deal with a devil, any devil, is easy enough. The information is out there. They want to be contacted, they want to deal. That's what they live for – to harvest souls. Even someone who is just dabbling in the occult will soon find out how to summon a devil. It used to be books that people turned to but now it's the Internet. Google will give you tens of thousands of sites that will tell you what to do. But once the deal is done, there is no going back. I told Gosling so, but he kept asking, kept pushing. He thought the answer lay in my diary, but it doesn't. The diary tells you how to summon Proserpine and her ilk, but not how to rescind a deal.'

'And what did you get? What did you bargain for?'

Mitchell sneered. 'That's between me and her,' he said.

'But you didn't try to back out?'

'I knew what I was getting into,' he said. 'I wasn't like your father. He was too eager. He didn't think through what he was doing. I knew exactly what I was doing and I did a deal I was happy with.'

'You sold your soul?'

'It's complicated,' said Mitchell. 'My soul is promised to a higher deity than Proserpine, though she would like to get her hands on it, I'm sure.'

Nightingale gestured at the circle on the floor. 'And what's the idea of the circle?'

'It's protection, of course.'

'I would have thought the CCTV and the men in black suits would have been protection enough.'

'Then you know nothing of the occult,' said Mitchell. 'The circle is the only thing that keeps her from me.'

'So you're just as scared as my father was,' said Nightingale.

'Your father wasn't scared of her – she had no interest in him. She already had what she wanted from him – the soul of his first-born son, promised to her at the moment of birth. The sweetest of souls. And the soul of his only daughter. Once she had them, he had nothing else to offer her.'

'But she wants you, is that it?'

'She wants my soul, yes.'

'So what's your plan? To hide in that circle for ever?'

Mitchell chuckled. 'I'm not hiding, Nightingale. You can't hide from a devil. She knows exactly where I am, I'm sure of that. And "for ever" isn't an option.' He coughed again, then moved his mask and spat bloody phlegm into a tissue. 'Cancer. I've a few months at most. Then I walk into hell of my own accord.'

'But either way you're dead,' said Nightingale.

'It's one thing to be dragged kicking and screaming into the eternal fire,' said Mitchell. 'If I walk in under my own steam, I take my place among the princes of hell.'

Nightingale folded his arms. 'So, what are my options?' he asked.

'You have none,' said Mitchell. 'Enjoy what little time you have left, and say your goodbyes.'

'There are always alternatives,' said Nightingale. 'Options. Choices.'

'Not in this case,' said Mitchell. 'Your soul is hers. Your father would have done the negotiation even before you were born. And at the moment of birth he would have carried out the ceremony. From that moment on, she owned your soul.'

'What if I were to do what you're doing? Make myself a protective circle and stay inside?'

'She owns your soul,' said Mitchell. 'She wouldn't have to enter the circle to take it.'

'And if I did what my father did? What if I stayed within a circle and killed myself?'

'You're thinking of suicide, are you?' Mitchell cleared his throat, slid his oxygen mask to the side and spat into a tissue. 'That would be ironic, wouldn't it? Father and son dying the same way. But you'd be wasting your time. Your soul is no longer yours. It has never been yours. It belonged to her before you were even born and there's nothing you can do to stop her taking it.'

Nightingale rubbed his chin. 'In your book, you say there should be a mark. A mark that shows that the soul has been sold.'

Mitchell nodded. 'A pentagram. Yes.'

'I don't have a mark anything like that.'

'If your father sold your soul, then you do. You just haven't found it yet.'

'And what if there isn't a mark?'

Mitchell chuckled. 'Then you've got nothing to worry about, have you?'

55

Nightingale followed Sylvia through the hall, flanked by two of the men in black suits. 'How long's he been in the circle?' asked Nightingale.

'It's a pentagram,' said Sylvia, archly.

'Fine,' said Nightingale. 'How long's he been inside the pentagram?'

'Two months.'

'And he never leaves it?'

'That's the point of the pentagram,' she said. 'If you leave, you're no longer protected.'

'But I don't understand why he has to stay there. What's he frightened of?'

'I'm sure there are a lot of things you don't understand, Mr Nightingale,' she said. She gestured at the bathroom. 'Please get changed and we shall escort you off the premises.'

Nightingale pushed his way into the bathroom. He

took off his robe and hung it on one of the hooks by the door. He caught sight of his reflection in the full-length mirror and instinctively sucked in his stomach. He stood facing it, his head cocked on one side, and grinned at himself. 'Not bad for a thirty-two-year-old,' he said. He wasn't as fit as he had been when he was in CO19, the Met's armed unit. The training was rigorous and never-ending and fitness was a must, so he'd worked out in the police gym three times a week and taken regular runs. He'd stopped exercising once he'd left the force but his body was still in good condition, considering the amount he drank and smoked. He patted his abdominals. Not quite a six-pack but it wasn't a beer gut either. And he still had all his own hair and teeth. But the one thing he definitely didn't have was a tattoo of a pentagram.

He turned to look over his left shoulder, then the right. No tattoo on his back. But he knew that. He knew every inch of his body and he had never seen a pentagram or anything like it. Neither had any of his girlfriends – a pentagram tattoo would have been mentioned. As he looked at his backside he had a thought that at first made him smile, then brought a frown to his face. There were some parts of your body you never looked at and nobody checked. He put a hand on each buttock and slowly pulled them apart.

He couldn't see much so he tried with his legs apart and his head between his knees, the pressure on his chest so tight that he had trouble breathing. There was nothing, but he hadn't expected there would be. As he straightened he saw the small red light flashing on the side of the CCTV camera opposite him. He winked at the camera. 'Just checking,' he said.

Nightingale put on his clothes and shoes and walked out of the bathroom. Sylvia and the two bodyguards were waiting for him. They took him outside and down the steps to his MGB. He tried to engage Sylvia in conversation but she had given up all pretence of civility. There was a look of utter contempt on her face that left him in no doubt that she had been watching his contortionist's act on her monitor.

Nightingale climbed into his car and started the engine. He gave Sylvia a friendly wave as he drove off but she stared at him impassively, her eyes as cold and impenetrable as the sunglasses her colleagues were wearing.

He headed for the road. The gates were already opening. He drove through, then turned right. In his rear-view mirror he watched them close behind him. His hands were shaking and he gripped the steering-wheel tightly but that didn't stop the tremor. Two miles down the road he pulled into a pub car park, climbed out of the MGB and lit a cigarette. Beyond where he stood there was a stream and Nightingale walked down to it. He watched the water burble by as he smoked. The wind blew through the trees on the other side of the stream and they swayed like lovers slow-dancing. Then, for the first time, Nightingale understood that one day he would die, that the sun would still shine and the stream would still flow and the wind would still blow through the trees, but he wouldn't be there to see or feel it.

He tried to blow smoke-rings but the wind whipped them away before they'd left his lips. The smoke-ring was a good analogy for life, he thought, or a metaphor. He was never sure what the difference was. Jenny would know – he'd ask her next time he saw her. Whether it was an analogy or a metaphor, the smoke-ring was like a human life. It came from nothing, existed for a short time and then was gone. Gone for ever.

Nightingale hadn't thought much about his own death before he had met Sebastian Mitchell. Death was something that happened to every living thing. That much he knew. It was part of the process. You were born, you lived, and then you died. But even when his own parents had been killed in a senseless car acci-dent, death had been something that happened to other people. He'd watched Sophie Underwood fall to her death from the apartment block in Chelsea Harbour, and he'd grieved for her but it hadn't made him think about his own mortality. Robbie Hoyle's death had been a shock but Nightingale hadn't imagined himself in his friend's place. During his years as an armed police officer, he'd been in situations where death was just a bullet away, but he'd never felt vulnerable. Mitchell had shown him what lay ahead for him even if he avoided bullets, looked both ways when he crossed the street, kept away from high places and wore his seatbelt every time he got into his car. If you lived long enough, you died anyway. That was the one simple fact about life. At some point it ended. Mitchell looked as if he didn't have more than a few weeks to live. Then he would die and that would be it. And as Nightingale had looked at the old man, gasping and wheezing and coughing up blood, he had grasped that one day he, too, would die. It was a horrible feeling, like a cold hand gripping his heart and squeezing. He'd never see Jenny again. Never drink a bottle of Corona or a good malt whisky. Never enjoy feeling the wind in his hair as he drove the MGB with the top down.

He took a long drag on his cigarette and held the smoke deep in his lungs. He'd never smoke another cigarette, smile at a pretty girl, eat a bar of chocolate. The world would go on, nothing would change, but he wouldn't be part of it. And he wouldn't be dead for a week or a month or a year. It wasn't like an illness when you went to bed and then you got better. Death was for ever. For ever and ever. Until the end of time, except that there was no end. You were dead for ever and Nightingale didn't want to die and he didn't want to be dead.

He shivered and gazed up at the clear afternoon sky, blue and cloudless. He didn't want to die but that didn't matter: it was going to happen, whether he liked it or not, sooner or later.

He flicked what was left of his cigarette into the stream. He shivered again and turned up the collar of his raincoat. There was no solution to what was troubling Nightingale. All he could do was accept the inevitable – that one day he would die. He looked up at the sky again. All the talk of his soul being sold to the devil didn't really worry him. He didn't believe in the devil and he didn't believe in souls. But he did believe in death, and that was what truly scared him.

He walked back to the pub. It was just after three o'clock and the lunchtime trade had gone. Two pensioners in cloth caps were sitting in a corner, one with a terrier asleep at his feet. Nightingale nodded at them as he went up to the bar. The publican was a jovial fat man with slicked-back hair, wearing a collarless shirt and red braces. 'Afternoon, squire, what can I get you?' he asked.

Nightingale thought of asking for a Corona but decided against it. He wanted something with more of a kick. 'A Bell's,' he said. 'With ice.'

'On the rocks, as our American cousins like to say.' The publican pushed a glass against the optic. 'You're not from around here.'

'Just visiting a friend,' said Nightingale, as the man raised the glass against the optic a second time. 'Just a single, I'm driving.'

'It's happy hour,' said the publican. 'Buy one get one free. BOGOF.' He put the glass in front of Nightingale. 'Be happy.'

'Do I look happy?'

'You look morose,' said the publican. 'But everyone does these days. With three million unemployed, house prices halving, the pound in a slump, there's not much to smile about. Which is why we've got the happy hour. We're doing our bit.'

Nightingale raised his glass to him. 'Cheers,' he said. He sipped his whisky, reached into his pocket for his cigarettes and put the packet on the bar. 'Every time I have a drink, I want to smoke. Reflex action,' he said.

'Me too,' said the publican. 'Still can't get used to not being able to smoke in my own bloody pub. I lost half my trade when the ban came in. The bloody nanny state, it is.'

'And for what?' said Nightingale. 'It doesn't save lives because everyone dies. Even if you never smoke a single cigarette in your whole life, you still die.'

'It's not about saving lives, it's about controlling the way we live,' said the publican. He helped himself to a brandy and clinked his glass against Nightingale's. 'You know, if we're not careful, the bastards'll be banning alcohol next. Then where will we be?'

'Do you ever think about the meaning of life?' Nightingale asked, as he swirled the ice around his glass.

'It's the number forty-two, innit?' said the publican. 'According to that movie, *The Hitchhiker's Guide to the Whatsit.*'

'The galaxy,' said Nightingale. 'Nah, forty-two was the answer to the ultimate question. It wasn't the meaning of life.'

'Ah, well, now you're asking,' said the publican. 'The meaning of life? It's got to be kids, right? That's all you leave behind, other than your debts. Your kids. Your DNA.' He leaned forward. 'My advice to you, have lots of sex and produce lots of kids. That bin Laden chappie, you know how many kids he's got? Twenty-six. Twenty-bloody-six. Doesn't matter who you are or what you do, good or bad, it's your kids that live on. Your kids and their kids and their kids' kids.' He jutted his chin. 'I've got four, and three grandkids. Two of my lads moved to Australia and I don't see them much, but that's not the point. They're the meaning of my life.' His eyes narrowed. 'You got kids?'

Nightingale shook his head. 'Nah.'

'There's your answer, then. That's why you're morose. Kids give your life meaning.' He grinned. 'Mind you, they also suck it out of you, but that's another story.'

Nightingale drained his glass and smiled. Maybe the publican was right. Maybe children were the answer. But it had been three years since he'd had a regular girlfriend and they weren't part of his immediate game plan.

'You're going to hell, Jack Nightingale,' said the publican, his voice cold and lifeless.

Nightingale's glass slipped from his fingers and smashed on the floor. 'How do you know my name?' he said.

The publican frowned. 'What?'

'How do you know my name?'

'Squire, I asked if you wanted another drink. There's no need to start smashing my glasses.'

'You said I was going to hell.'

'You're hearing things. I asked if you wanted a refill but it looks like you've had enough to drink already.'

Nightingale bent down to pick up the shards.

'Leave it!' said the publican. 'Health and safety. Customers aren't allowed to touch broken glass. The brewery'd have my job if they saw you do that.'

'Sorry,' said Nightingale. He reached for his wallet. 'I'll pay for the damage.'

'Forget it.'

Nightingale held up his hands. 'I'm sorry,' he said. 'I've had a rough couple of days.' He took a step back, turned and left the pub. The terrier lifted its head and growled at him, then settled back on the floor.

56

Jenny was tapping away on her keyboard when Nightingale walked in. 'There are some sick bunnies out there, Jack,' she said.

'Tell me about it,' said Nightingale. He flopped onto his chair and raised his eyebrows expectantly. 'Coffee?'

'I'd love one,' she said.

'I shall miss your sense of humour when I'm burning in hell.'

'That's not very funny, Jack,' she said.

'It's the best I can do at this time in the morning,' he said. 'What did you mean about sick bunnies?'

Jenny nodded at her computer screen. 'Do you know that you can buy a copy of *The Satanic Bible* on Amazon? With next-day delivery. And if you type "selling your soul to the devil" into Google you get more than a hundred and forty thousand sites? What sad bastards would want to know how to sell a soul to the devil?'

'My father, for one,' said Nightingale.

'Then there's ChurchOfSatan dot com. The guys there certainly believe in the devil.'

'There's a lot of rubbish on the Internet,' said Nightingale. 'Fifty per cent is plain wrong and ten per cent is malicious.'

'Those are official statistics, are they?'

'I read it on Wikipedia,' said Nightingale. 'How's my coffee coming along?'

Jenny flounced over to the machine.

'How was your weekend?' he asked.

'We had a great time,' she said. 'Bit of riding, bit of fishing, bit of shooting. Girl stuff.'

'I hope I wasn't too rude to her. I just didn't feel like opening up to a complete stranger.'

'Jack, you don't open up to anyone,' said Jenny. 'You're the original closed book, you are. But no is the answer to your question, she understood why you were so defensive and she wasn't offended by it. She's worked in Broadmoor so she can take care of herself.'

'She seemed a smart cookie, that's for sure.'

'Maybe she could help, Jack. You can't remember what happened with Simon Underwood. And the other times when you heard people saying you were going to hell. She could get you to relive those moments, and find out for sure what they said.'

'I'm not sure I want to remember,' said Nightingale.

'Nonsense.'

'Really? And what if she makes me remember that I actually did push Simon Underwood through the window? Do I turn myself in? Maybe I'm better off not remembering.'

Jenny didn't reply.

'And what if I've been imagining all these people telling me I'm going to hell? Then I'm crazy, right? Crazy, and maybe a serial killer. Hand on heart, I think I'm better off not knowing.'

'But she might prove to you that you didn't kill Underwood, have you considered that?

Nightingale shrugged.

'Please, Jack, give Barbara a chance. She's very good at what she does, I promise.'

'I'll think about it,' said Nightingale.

'That means no,' said Jenny.

'It means I'll think about it,' said Nightingale. 'Now, can we change the subject, please?'

'Okay, fine,' said Jenny. 'What did you get up to over the weekend?'

Nightingale explained about the phone call from Harry Wilde, meeting Alfie Tyler and driving to Wivenhoe to meet Sebastian Mitchell.

Jenny glared at him. 'I can't believe you didn't tell me any of this.'

'I'm telling you now.'

'Jack . . .' Words failed her. 'You should have called me.'

'Jenny, baby, I was on a roll. Wilde gave me Tyler's details and Tyler told me where I could find Mitchell. There just wasn't time to call you.'

Jenny carried his coffee to his desk and sat down. 'And Mitchell talked to you?'

'According to Mitchell, Proserpine is the real thing. He did a deal with her but somehow managed to piss her off. Apparently, my father could well have sold my soul to her.'

'That's nonsense.'

'Mitchell says it's possible. But he says that if my father did sell my soul I would have the mark, the penta-gram. No pentagram, no contract.'

'And you haven't, right?'

'I've checked and double-checked.'

'You could shave your head.'

'Yeah, so could you. I checked my head on the baby pictures, remember? Any tattoo would have been put there the day I was born.'

'So you're fine. Even if there is a devil called Proserpine and even if you can sell souls to her, none of that matters because there's no mark.'

'That's what Mitchell says.' He sipped his coffee.

'My father might have believed he'd sold my soul, but the fact that there's no mark says otherwise. So it's bollocks. It's all bollocks.'

'I was fairly busy myself,' said Jenny. 'In between riding and shooting I made a few calls.' She pulled a piece of paper from the pocket of her jeans. 'I tracked down George Harrison for you.' Nightingale stretched forward to take it but she held it out of reach. 'I want you to promise me something,' she said.

'You can have a pay rise when the business picks up.'

'I want you to promise you won't go and see him.'

'I can't promise that, Jenny.'

'Opening old wounds isn't healthy,' she said.

'Is that you talking or Barbara?'

'It's common sense, something you seem to be short of at the moment.'

'I have to talk to him, Jenny,' said Nightingale. He tried to grab the paper but she moved it away.

'Jack, I'm serious.'

'So am I,' said Nightingale. 'Give me the address.'

'If you go, and I don't think you should, I want to go with you.'

'Deal,' said Nightingale.

'Cross your heart and hope to die?'

'Yes to the first bit, no to the second. Dying isn't something I want to do just yet. But I'll take you.'

Jenny gave him the piece of paper. Nightingale looked at the address and phone number. 'Battersea? He's in London?' He gave it back to her. 'I need you to phone him.'

'And say what?'

'Ask him what mobile-phone service he uses, then tell him a sales rep will visit and give him a new iPhone for free, to test.'

'You mean lie to him?'

'Just humour me,' said Nightingale.

57

Nightingale climbed out of the MGB and looked up at the block of flats. 'What floor did you say?' It was a drab council building, the concrete stained by years of pollution and pigeon droppings, the windows grubby and cracked. There were colourful graffiti on most of the walls. A pack of mongrels watched them suspiciously.

Jenny grunted as she pushed herself out of the sports car. 'There's no elegant way of getting out of one of these things, is there?'

'It's a classic,' said Nightingale.

'I'm just glad I decided to wear jeans today.'

'What floor?'

'Ninth. Are you going to leave your car on the street here? The wheels'll be off by the time we get back.'

'Like I said, it's a classic. People respect classics.' He saw disbelief on her face and laughed. 'I'm serious.

When was the last time you saw a classic motor vandalised? It doesn't happen. They go for the flash cars, the ones owned by people with more money than sense. Plus they can see I don't have a CD player or anything worth stealing.' He nodded at the entrance. There was a stainless-steel panel dotted with dozens of buttons, and a CCTV camera covering the door. 'You should call him, tell him you're from the mobile-phone company.'

'Why me?'

'Because you're a girl, and a pretty one to boot.'

Jenny grinned. 'To boot?'

'You know what I mean. A girl is less of a threat than a guy.'

'Are you a threat, Jack? Is that what's happening here?'

'I just want to talk, that's all,' he said. 'Cross my heart.'

58

Nightingale leaned against the wall, his hand on the yellow metal handrail. 'What floor are we on now?' he panted. There were piles of rubbish on every staircase, cockroaches and a strong smell of vomit and urine that got worse the higher they climbed.

'Seventh,' said Jenny. 'And you wouldn't be so tired if you didn't smoke so much.'

'Smoking's good for you,' said Nightingale. 'It's packed with vitamins and minerals and has zero calories and fat.' He gestured at the stairs. 'It's exercise that's bad. Look what it's doing to me.'

'You should go to the gym more,' said Jenny. 'Maybe start running.'

'I don't need to lose weight,' said Nightingale. He patted his stomach. 'I'm not fat. You show me a fat smoker and I'll show you a smoker who's not inhaling.'

'What the hell does that mean?' asked Jenny.

'I have absolutely no idea,' he said, as he started up the stairs again. 'I was just feeling defensive.'

'When are you going to get over this lift thing?'

'Never.'

'Jack, lifts are just about the safest form of transport there is. You know how many people have died in lift accidents in the UK in the last twenty years? None. That's how many.'

'How do you know?'

Jenny grinned. 'I don't. I just made it up. But you never hear about lift accidents, do you?'

'That's because there's a conspiracy between the media and the big lift companies.'

'Nonsense.'

'Can we just leave it that I don't like lifts? It's no big deal, Jenny. Besides, get stuck in a lift here and you'd starve to death before someone came out to help you.'

They reached the ninth floor and Nightingale held open the door to let Jenny go through first. The smell of vomit and urine was even stronger on the landing. The floor was bare concrete and the pale green walls were streaked with dirt. A council notice warned residents not to leave their rubbish in the stairwell. 'That's the flat,' said Jenny, pointing at a door to their right.

'You knock, check it's him, then I'll step in.'

'Jack, are you sure this is a good idea? We've lied

our way into the building and he's not going to be happy to see us.'

'Please, Jenny. Just do it.'

Jenny walked to the door and pressed the bell. Nightingale flattened himself against the wall. The door opened and Nightingale held his breath.

'Mr Harrison?' asked Jenny.

'That's me,' said a male voice. 'You're from the phone company?'

'George Arthur Harrison?'

'I said already, that's me.'

Nightingale pushed himself away from the wall and put his hand against the door so that Harrison couldn't close it. 'Mr Harrison, I need a few minutes of your time,' he said.

Harrison was short and stick-thin, wearing a stained T-shirt that seemed to be several sizes too big for him, and brown cargo pants that had been turned up at the bottom. It was as if he'd shrunk within his clothes. 'Who are you?' He was balding with a greasy comb-over that barely concealed his liver-spotted scalp. From behind him came the sound of a TV show, *Jerry Springer* or *Trisha*. The audience were howling and jeering.

'My name's Nightingale, Jack Nightingale.'

Harrison tried to shut the door, but Nightingale was too strong for him. 'I'll call the police,' said Harrison.

'Jack,' said Jenny, 'maybe we should go.'

'Just a few minutes, Mr Harrison. Then we'll go. I promise.'

Harrison continued to push at the door but realised eventually that it wasn't a contest he was ever going to win. He stepped back, holding up his hands defensively. Nightingale saw that his nails were bitten to the quick. 'Please, just leave me alone.'

'You know who I am, then?' asked Nightingale.

'You're the boy, the Nightingale boy. Of course I know. You think I could ever forget?'

'I want to talk about what happened to my parents,' said Nightingale. 'The accident.'

Harrison's shoulders slumped and he turned to walk down the hallway.

Nightingale looked at Jenny. 'Do you want to wait outside?'

She shook her head fiercely. 'I'm coming with you,' she said.

'You don't have to.'

'I want to.'

Nightingale nodded and followed Harrison. The hallway was the same drab green as the corridor outside. A bare bulb hung from a frayed wire and there was a stack of unopened bills on a side table beneath a cracked mirror. As he passed it, Harrison adjusted his comb-over. Jenny shared a smile with Nightingale.

The living room was a mess. There were two red plastic sofas, one piled high with magazines, most of which seemed to be pornographic, and the other with old takeaway cartons. The only item of value in the flat was a large LCD television. Through an open door, Nightingale saw a filthy kitchen, with a greasy gas stove and a sink full of dirty dishes.

'How long have you lived here, George?' asked Nightingale. 'What brought you to London?'

Harrison shrugged but didn't answer. He went over to a door that led out to a small concrete balcony and pulled it open. A bicycle missing its front wheel was leaning against a box of empty vodka bottles.

Jenny stood watching the television. A young woman who must have weighed at least twenty stone was shrieking at a spotty-faced man, accusing him of fathering a child with her sister as the audience screamed and shook their fists.

Harrison went out onto the balcony, Nightingale behind him. The shabby council flat had a stunning view of the river Thames, with the Houses of Parliament ahead and the London Eye to the right. It was a cloudless day and they could see for miles. High overhead, passenger jets were lining up to land at Heathrow in the west.

The wind ruffled Harrison's comb-over but he didn't seem to notice. He wiped his face with his right hand. 'Why, after all these years?' he asked. 'Why now?' His comb-over flapped like a flag.

'I need to talk to you,' said Nightingale. He took out his Marlboro and offered one to Harrison. 'About what happened to my parents.'

'I don't smoke,' Harrison said.

Nightingale lit a cigarette. 'We're a dying breed, smokers,' he said.

'You're going to hell, Jack Nightingale,' said Harrison, his face a blank mask, his voice a dull monotone. He vaulted over the side of the balcony. Nightingale froze, the cigarette on the way to his mouth. He flinched as he heard the body slam into the concrete nine floors below.

Jenny appeared behind him. 'My God, Jack, what have you done?'

Nightingale backed away, the cigarette forgotten in his hand. 'He just jumped,' he said. 'We were talking and he jumped.'

'He jumped?' said Jenny. 'Why would he jump?'

'He told me I was going to hell and he jumped.' He turned to her. 'You heard him, right? You heard what he said?'

'I didn't hear anything. I just saw him go over the edge.'

'Jenny, he told me I was going to hell. You must have heard him say that! You were standing right there.'

'Jack, I'm sorry . . .' She was shaking as she folded her arms across her chest. 'I'm going to throw up,' she said.

'We've got to get out of here – now,' he said.

'You're not going to call the police?'

'And tell them what? That he took one look at me and jumped to his death? They're not going to believe that.'

'But it's the truth.'

'They'll assume I pushed him, Jenny.'

'But you didn't.'

'We have to go. We have to wipe everything we touched and then we have to go.'

'What?'

'Forensics. We have to wipe everything we touched to remove DNA and fingerprints and we have to do it now. Do you understand?'

Jenny stared at him blankly.

Nightingale grabbed her shoulders. 'Jenny, I need you with me on this. We have to clean up and go – now.'

'Okay,' she said.

59

Nightingale waved the barmaid over. 'A whisky – a double,' he said, 'with ice.'

'Any particular brand?' she asked. She had a South African accent.

'Bell's. Teacher's. Anything.'

'Jack, I don't see that drink is going to help,' said Jenny, putting a hand on his shoulder. They were in a pub close to the office. They had driven in silence from Battersea, too shocked to discuss what had happened.

'I need a drink,' said Nightingale. 'And so do you.'

'Make it two,' she told the barmaid. She put her head close to Nightingale's. 'What happened back there, Jack?'

'You saw what happened.'

'You were in the way.'

'You didn't hear him tell me I'm going to hell? Because that's what he said, Jenny, as clear as day. He said, "You're going to hell, Jack Nightingale." Those were his exact words.'

'The TV was on, I didn't hear him say anything.'

'We were talking on the balcony. You were right there.'

'And he said you were going to hell?'

'Yes.'

'So, think about it, Jack. Maybe it's your subconscious – maybe you were flashing back to what happened to Simon Underwood two years ago. Maybe you thought you heard him say that because the situations were so similar.'

'Similar in what way?'

'You know in what way,' she said.

'You don't think I pushed him, do you?'

'Who?' she asked. 'Underwood or Harrison?'

'Thanks a lot, Jenny. Thanks a bloody lot.' She reached over to touch his hand but he pulled it away. 'You don't want to get too close to me,' he said. 'I might push you out of a window.'

'Don't be ridiculous, Jack,' she said softly. 'Of course I don't think you killed anybody. It's not in your nature. But Harrison couldn't have slipped – the railing was too high.'

'I told you already. He jumped. He told me I was going to hell and then he jumped.'

'Why would he jump?'

'I don't know.' He drained his glass and gestured to the barmaid for another.

'Getting drunk isn't going to help,' said Jenny.

'I'm not driving, if that's what you're worried about,' said Nightingale. He handed her the keys to the MGB. 'You can drive me home.'

'I'm not your bloody chauffeur.'

'No, and you're not my mother either.'

His drink arrived. He raised the glass to her, then sipped.

'You can be an arsehole at times,' she said, and sat on a barstool.

'I'm sorry,' said Nightingale. 'I shouldn't have let you go with me.'

'That's what you're sorry about? You're not sorry that a man died, that we saw him jump to his death?'

'You told me you didn't see anything.'

'I saw him fall. I didn't see if you pushed him.' She raised her whisky to her lips, then put the glass down. 'I'm not drinking this.' To the barmaid she mouthed, 'Coffee, please.'

Nightingale picked up her glass and poured the contents into his own. 'Waste not, want not.'

'If the police come, it's not going to help if you're smelling of drink,' said Jenny. 'We should have stayed. We should have called them and stayed.'

'And said what? That he jumped to his death rather than talk about how he killed my parents? Chalmers already thinks I'm a vigilante killer after what happened to Underwood.'

'The police will come, Jack. There were CCTV cameras, remember?'

'They might not check if they're sure it was suicide.' He drained his glass. 'Another whisky, darling,' he called to the barmaid.

Jenny put a hand on his arm. 'Jack, come on, you don't have to do this.'

'Do what?'

'Drink like this. It isn't helping.'

'It's making me feel better, and that's what counts.'

'You should have stayed and talked to the police,' said Jenny. 'They would have believed you.'

'Only someone who's never dealt with the cops would say that,' said Nightingale. 'Cops make mistakes like everyone else and, as I said, Chalmers is already gunning for me.'

'You're not a killer, Jack. You couldn't kill somebody, not in cold blood.'

Nightingale smiled thinly. 'You don't know me, Jenny.'

'I know you couldn't deliberately kill somebody.'

'I was in CO19, Jenny. I carried a gun. I was trained to kill people.'

'There's a world of a difference between firing a gun as an armed cop and pushing someone off a balcony. The police would understand that.'

'Maybe,' said Nightingale.

'What's wrong, Jack?'

The barmaid put a fresh glass of whisky in front of Nightingale and he nodded his thanks. 'I don't know. Maybe I'm just going crazy.'

'You're not crazy,' she said. 'A bit confused, maybe. And knocking back double whiskies isn't helping.'

'My father was crazy,' said Nightingale. 'Ainsley Gosling claimed to have done a deal with a devil and blew his head off with a shotgun. My mother, my birth-mother, was in an asylum for most of her life and hacked her wrists over dinner. So I'm the product of two people who were both clearly deranged. With DNA like that, what are the chances that I'm going to be normal? Pretty bloody slim, I'd say.'

'You're stressed out, that's all.'

'People keep telling me I'm going to hell, Jenny.'

'It's an expression. It's just something people say. They don't mean it literally.'

Nightingale shook his head. 'No, they say it but it's not them saying it. It's like someone's using them to get the message to me. My uncle wrote the words in blood in his bathroom and so did Barry O'Brien, and that night in the Chinese restaurant it was written in the fortune cookie.' His words tumbled into one another, and he banged his glass on the bar.

'It's because Underwood said that to you before he died,' said Jenny.

'My subconscious is playing tricks with me? Is that what you really think?'

'What's the alternative, Jack? Messages from the grave? Spirits speaking through the living? The devil playing games with you?'

The barmaid glanced at them and Nightingale pointed at his empty glass. 'I'm starting to think that maybe Chalmers is right,' he said. 'Maybe it is me.'

'What do you mean?'

'I went to see Barry O'Brien and he's dead. I went to see my aunt and uncle and they're dead. Maybe . . .' He lowered his head.

'What, Jack? Maybe what?'

Nightingale sighed. 'Maybe I did kill them,' he whispered. 'Maybe I killed them and blocked it out. Maybe two years ago I did kill Underwood. And maybe I pushed Harrison off the balcony and I'm blocking it now. Hysterical amnesia. Or my subconscious is just refusing to admit what happened. Look at it from Chalmers's point of view. Barry O'Brien killed Robbie so I'd want him dead. George Harrison killed my parents so I'd want him dead. My uncle and aunt lied to me so I'd want to hurt them. I've got the motive, and I had the opportunity, and I was at all three crime scenes. And it started two years ago when Simon Underwood went flying through the window.'

'Except you didn't do it, Jack. You didn't do any of it.'

'But I don't know that for sure, Jenny. Don't you get it? The more I think about it, the more it feels like I might have done it.'

'Are you saying you remember killing them?'

Nightingale shook his head. 'No. It's a feeling, not a memory. Like maybe I could have done it.'

'Your mind's playing tricks on you. It's stress.'

The barmaid came over with another whisky and ice. Jenny ordered two black coffees. Nightingale reached for his glass but Jenny put her hand on his. 'Take it slowly, Jack, please.'

'You know what I'm thinking, don't you?'

She nodded.

'Maybe I've done this before,' he said. 'Maybe what's happening now is a rerun of what I did to Simon Underwood. I get angry, I lash out, and then I block out the memories.'

'I was with you today, Jack, remember?'

'But you don't know if I pushed Harrison or not.'

'I know you're not a killer, Jack.'

'You *think* I'm not a killer – it's not the same thing.' He pulled his hand away and picked up his whisky.

The barmaid brought over the coffees and placed them on the bar. 'You guys okay?' she asked.

'It's been a rough day,' said Jenny. She waited for the barmaid to leave, then leaned in to Nightingale. 'It'll work out, Jack. I promise.'

'Jenny, you don't know that. First rule of negotiating, don't make promises you can't keep. You don't know it'll work out. Look, today's Monday and my birthday's on Friday. Maybe at midnight on Thursday a devil's going to reclaim my soul in which case I burn in hell for all eternity. Or maybe Gosling was just mad and I'm mad too and I'm going to spend the rest of my life in prison. Either way, it won't work out.'

'You don't believe in this devil nonsense, do you?'

'I wish I did,' said Nightingale, 'because at least that would explain what's happening to me. Because if it isn't the devil screwing with my life then maybe I'm doing it myself.'

'You're not a killer, Jack.'

'I might be, Jenny. I might be. And that's what scares me.'

60

'You're going to hell, Jack Nightingale,' said Simon Underwood, his eye blazing with hatred.

'How do you know my name?' asked Nightingale. 'I didn't tell you my name. How do you know who I am?' Underwood was wearing a dark pinstripe suit that fitted so well it could only have been made to measure. There was a gold Rolex on his left wrist, a gold signet ring on his right hand and a pair of designer glasses on his nose. He was in his forties with a touch of grey at the temples. He was holding a mobile phone and pointing it at Nightingale as if it was a gun. 'How do you know my name?' repeated Nightingale.

Underwood turned towards the window behind him. It ran from the floor to the ceiling and gave a panoramic view of the tower blocks of Canary Wharf, home to some of the world's biggest financial institutions.

'No!' said Nightingale, knowing what would come next. 'No!' he screamed.

The phone that Underwood was holding began to ring. It was a regular ringtone, an insistent bell, and it got louder and louder until the sound was deafening. Nightingale opened his eyes and groaned as he groped for the phone on his bedside table and squinted at his bedside clock. It was eight o'clock in the morning. 'Mr Nightingale, this is Alice Steadman. I didn't wake you, did I?'

Nightingale sat up. His head was throbbing. He had drunk three double whiskies in the pub with Jenny and she'd driven him home where he'd finished off half a bottle of Macallan malt. 'Who, sorry?'

'Alice Steadman. From the Wicca Woman store in Camden.'

'Right,' said Nightingale.

'I did wake you, didn't I? I'm so sorry, I'm an early riser and I was asked to call you first thing to see if you'd be interested.'

'Interested in what?'

'I'm sorry, I'm not explaining this at all well, am I? I've sold two of your books for you, Mr Nightingale, at a very good price. The gentleman concerned is interested in another volume Mr Gosling has in his collection.'

'Who is this mystery buyer?'

'An American,' she said, 'from Texas. His name is Joshua Wainwright. Like your father, he's a collector. And apparently he was at several auctions where your father outbid him. Now he wonders whether you'd be prepared to sell at least one of the volumes to him. For more than your father paid, obviously.'

'Obviously,' said Nightingale. 'Which book is it?'

'It's called *The Formicarius*, and it's a first edition. Apparently your father bought it from a dealer in Germany.'

'I've seen the receipt,' said Nightingale. 'Sure, I'll be happy to sell it to him.'

'If you're agreeable, he'll fly over to meet you. He'll pay you in cash.'

'I'm certainly agreeable to that,' said Nightingale. 'Tell him to give me a call when he gets here.'

'Mr Wainwright said that if you were prepared to sell he'd fly over this afternoon.'

'Tell him I'll have the book ready for him.'

'And don't forget my commission, Mr Nightingale.'

'Heaven forbid.'

He put down the receiver and rolled onto his back. His alarm wasn't due to go off for another fifteen minutes and he was just wondering whether he was tired enough to doze when the phone rang again.

Nightingale sighed and reached for it, assuming that it was Mrs Steadman again. It was Jenny.

'Jack . . .' She sounded shaky as if she was close to tears.

'Jenny, what's wrong?'

'Jack, I'm at home – I've been robbed. Can you come, please?'

'Of course,' said Nightingale. 'I'll be right there.'

'They had guns, Jack. They said they'd kill me.'

61

Jenny lived in a three-bedroom mews house in Chelsea, just off the King's Road. The street was quaintly cobbled and the house bedecked with window-boxes. Outside the front door two massive concrete urns contained six-foot conifers. Nightingale parked his MGB in front of the yellow garage door and climbed out. Even after the property crash, Jenny's house must have been worth close to two million pounds. He had never asked her if it was hers or if she rented it, but either way he knew she couldn't have afforded it on the salary he paid her.

He pressed the bell, and a few seconds later the door opened on a security chain. He caught a glimpse of unkempt hair and then she closed the door to unhook the chain. She was wearing a dark green Cambridge University sweatshirt and baggy cargo pants and her eyes were red and puffy. 'What happened?'

She ushered him into the hallway, closed the door and bolted it. 'I was robbed, Jack. Three men broke in and took the diary.'

'Mitchell's?'

'Of course Mitchell's diary. Do you think they'd break in to steal my bloody Filofax?'

'Big men, black suits, sunglasses?'

Jenny nodded. 'Do you know who they are?'

'They're Mitchell's men, bodyguards, protectors – his house was full of them. Jenny, did they hurt you?'

She went through to the sitting room and dropped onto a flower-print sofa. 'No, but they scared the life out of me.'

Nightingale sat down opposite her. 'What happened?'

'I was leaving for work,' she said. 'I opened the front door and they were there. They just pushed me inside, one put his hand over my mouth and brought me in here, while the other two looked for the diary – not that they needed to do much searching. It was in my bag.'

'Did they say anything?'

'Not while they were looking for the diary. But when they found it, one pointed a gun at my face and said that if I called the police they'd come back and shoot me.'

'I'm sorry, baby.'

'It wasn't your fault, Jack,' she said.

'I should have figured that Mitchell would try to get it back. I should have warned you. He told me Gosling had stolen it from him.' Jenny's hands began to shake. 'I'll make you a cup of tea.'

Nightingale went to the kitchen, all stainless steel with state-of-the-art German appliances. He made the tea, stirred in three sugars and a splash of milk, and took it to her. She sipped it and winced. 'I don't take sugar,' she said. 'You know I don't.'

'It's good for shock,' he said, sitting down again.

'I'm not in shock,' she insisted.

'You are – you just don't know it,' he said. 'Do as you're told and drink it.'

'Yes, sir,' she said. 'What do you think, Jack? Should I call the police?'

'I'm not sure what they'd do, to be honest,' said Nightingale. 'There are no witnesses, no forensics, and they'll be back in the Mitchell house, which is like a fortress. I doubt they'll open the gates without a warrant.'

'They pointed a gun at me, Jack.'

'I know. You want me to have them shot? I know people.'

Jenny laughed uneasily. 'You're mad.'

'Tell me about it.' He stood up. 'Leave it with me, Jenny. I haven't finished with Mitchell yet.'

'I was so scared,' said Jenny. Tea slopped over the side of her cup into the saucer.

'Are you okay to go to work or do you want to stay home? We don't have much on, work-wise.'

'What are you going to do?' she asked.

'I've got to pick up a book from Gosling Manor and take it out to the airport later today. There's a buyer flying in from the States.'

'You're really okay if I don't go into the office?'

'Not a problem,' said Nightingale.

'I want to get a security company in,' she said, 'and have the locks changed.'

'They won't be back. They got what they wanted.'

'I'd just feel safer – you know?'

'I'm sorry, Jenny. It was my fault. I should never have given you the diary.'

'You weren't to know,' said Jenny.

Nightingale leaned over and kissed the top of her head. 'I'll make it up to you.'

'A pay rise?'

'I was thinking a bunch of flowers.' He ruffled her hair and headed for the door. 'Seriously, though, put all the bills through the office. The least I can do is to pay for your locks. And an alarm if you want it.'

'Thanks, Jack. But we're in the red as it is.'

'Not for long, hopefully,' he said, and winked. 'Wish me luck.'

62

If you'd asked Jack Nightingale what he thought Joshua Wainwright would look like as he climbed the stairs to the hatch in the Gulfstream jet, he'd probably have frowned and said that he never prejudged people but, if pressed, he'd have hazarded a guess that the man would be old, wearing cowboy boots and a Stetson and smoking a cigar, probably with a bodyguard or two in attendance.

He was wrong on all counts, except for the cigar. Joshua Wainwright was smoking a foot-long Cuban that would have had to be rolled on an especially large thigh, and was wearing a New York Yankees baseball cap. He was sitting in a white leather armchair with his bare feet on a matching leather footstool and looked as if he was barely out of his twenties.

Wainwright grinned when he saw the surprise on Nightingale's face. 'I'm guessing you were expecting someone older,' he said, his voice a lazy Texan drawl. 'And maybe whiter. That happens a lot. Take a seat.'

'Just don't tell me you're really two hundred years old,' said Nightingale, placing his briefcase on the table next to him. 'Or that you've a picture slowly going bad in your attic.'

Wainwright laughed. Two pretty blondes in matching charcoal grey Armani suits were standing behind him. 'Can I get you a drink, Jack?' he drawled.

'A whisky would be good.'

'A man after my own heart.' Wainwright twisted his head around. 'Two whiskies, darling,' he said. 'Glenlivet.' He looked at Jack. 'Okay with you?'

'In my experience, any malt beginning with a G or an M can't be faulted,' said Nightingale. 'Ice in mine, please,' he said to the stewardess, who flashed him a perfect gleaming white smile.

The plane was sitting on the Tarmac close to the private aviation terminal at Stansted airport. A black stretch Mercedes limousine had been waiting for Nightingale airside, and a uniformed chauffeur had driven him out to the Gulfstream. The plane was expensively outfitted with four white leather seats the size of armchairs, a three-seater white leather sofa, a large LCD television screen on the bulkhead, and oblong picture windows.

'Can I offer you a cigar, Jack?' asked Wainwright.

'I'm a cigarette smoker,' said Nightingale. 'Is it okay to smoke in here?'

'It's my plane, we can do what we want.'

Nightingale took out his packet of Marlboro and lit one. The second stewardess placed a large crystal ashtray next to his briefcase.

'So you're Ainsley Gosling's son?' asked Wainwright. 'How's that working out for you?'

'We weren't close,' replied Nightingale. The stewardess gave him his whisky and another beaming smile.

'But he left you his library?'

'He left me everything,' said Nightingale.

Wainwright jabbed his cigar at Nightingale's briefcase. 'Is that it?'

Nightingale nodded. 'It took some finding, I haven't worked out his indexing system yet. It's certainly not alphabetical.' He put down his drink and cigarette and picked up the briefcase. Wainwright licked his lips as Nightingale took out the book. It was almost two feet long, eighteen inches wide and a good two inches thick, the pages yellowing, the white leather binding cracked and faded. It had taken Nightingale almost three hours to find it in the basement. As so many of the books' spines didn't show the title he'd had to take them down and open them one at a time.

Wainwright put down his cigar and took the book from him reverently, as if he was holding a baby. His eyes were wide and he had a faint smile on his lips. It was a smile of triumph, Nightingale realised.

'Awesome,' said Wainwright. 'Do you know what it is, Jack?'

'*The Formicarius*,' said Nightingale, 'but that doesn't mean much to me.'

'This is a first edition, printed in 1475,' said Wainwright, stroking the cover. 'Written by Johannes Nider. It took him two years to complete and it was published eight years later. It was the second book ever to be printed that discussed witchcraft. Before *The Formicarius*, everyone thought only men served the devil.'

'And that's why it's so valuable?'

Wainwright shook his head. 'No, it's not what's written inside the book that's so important. I have a second edition, and a third, so I already have the words. It's the book itself I wanted. This book.' He ran his fingertips down the spine. 'Your father knew, too. That was why he was so determined to get it.' He grinned. 'It was supposed to be mine, you know? The bookseller in Hamburg had agreed to sell it to me but somehow your father got to him before I could wire the money. He was a very persuasive man, your father.'

'So I'm told,' said Nightingale.

'He paid a million and half euros, you know that?'

'I saw the receipt. So what is it about the book that makes it so special?'

'Are you sure you want to know, Jack?'

Nightingale nodded. 'Why not?'

Wainwright smiled, relishing the moment, then he kissed the book's front cover. 'This isn't leather,' he said. 'It's human skin.'

Nightingale tried not to look surprised but he could see from the satisfaction on the American's face that he hadn't succeeded. 'You don't say.'

'Your father paid a million and a half euros, so what say I give you two?'

'Two sounds good,' said Nightingale.

Wainwright smiled at a stewardess and she took a small aluminium suitcase from a cupboard and placed it on the table next to Nightingale's chair. She opened it for him, then went to the rear of the plane. Normally Nightingale would have turned to glimpse her legs but he couldn't take his eyes off the bundles of banknotes. 'Wow,' he said.

'You've got to appreciate the euro,' said Wainwright. 'That five-hundred note makes moving cash around so much simpler. If I'd had to use hundred-dollar bills, we'd have needed another suitcase.'

'It's not a problem I'm normally faced with,' said Nightingale.

'Well, it could be,' said Wainwright. 'There's a few other books in your late father's library that I might be interested in buying. When you get the chance, can you give me an inventory? There's not many I haven't got, but your father was buying books before I was born. I'd be interested to see what he has in his collection.'

'No problem,' said Nightingale. He was still staring at the money. Two million euros. He tried to work out how many years he'd have to work to earn that sort of money. Thirty? Forty?

'Do you want to count it, Jack?' asked Wainwright.

'Do I need to?'

Wainwright laughed. 'If it's short, give me a call, but it won't be.'

Nightingale closed the case. 'Can I keep the case? I don't think it'll all fit into mine.'

'We'll do a swap,' said Wainwright. He put the book back into the briefcase that Nightingale had brought with him. 'Any objections?'

'I can always buy a new one,' said Nightingale.

The stewardess who had given him the case stepped forward with a clipboard and a pen. 'I'll need you to sign an invoice and a receipt. I've copies of both for you,' said Wainwright.

Nightingale took the pen, a Mont Blanc the size of a small flashlight, and signed his name four times. He frowned when he saw that he was signing in red. 'Please tell me that's not blood,' he said.

'I like red ink,' said the American. 'It's a quirk of mine. Red is my lucky colour, always has been. Humour me.'

The stewardess took the pen and the clipboard from Nightingale, then gave him a copy of the invoice and the receipt.

'My cellphone number is on there,' said Wainwright, 'and my personal email address. Soon as you have an inventory, I'd like a look. I'll pay top dollar, cash on the nail.'

Nightingale folded the papers and put them into the inside pocket of his raincoat. He nodded at the brief-case. 'This stuff works, does it?'

'Some of it does, some of it doesn't. It's a process. It's something you become better at the more you do it.' He grinned. 'That's why they call it witchcraft. Because it's a craft.'

'It seems weird, sitting in a state-of-the-art jet with a suitcase of cash and talking about magic.'

'So?'

'So it's weird, that's all. Why didn't you fly over on a broomstick?'

'You're thinking Harry Potter. Besides, have you ever tried joining the Mile High Club on a broomstick?'

'I guess not,' said Nightingale. 'So flying broomsticks are bollocks?'

'Of course they are. But if I wanted to move around the world without the benefits of a Gulfstream, yeah, that's doable. Astral projection. It's not easy and it takes a lot of practice, but I can do it. And remote viewing, seeing things at a distance. It's easier than astral projection, but not as useful.'

'You're winding me up,' said Nightingale, 'or shitting me, as you Yanks are so fond of saying.'

'No, I'm serious,' said Wainwright. 'Let's say you're as good at astral projection as I am. We could arrange to meet somewhere, and at the appointed time we both go into a trance and meet on the astral plane, face to face.'

'You've done that?'

'I've done that with your father, Jack. Many times. He was a master at it.'

'So how does it work?'

'Now you're asking,' said the American.

'I'm interested.'

'I can see that.' He swung his feet onto the footstool and picked up his cigar. 'You've got a cellphone, right?' He peered at his cigar and frowned when he realised it had gone out.

'Sure.'

'And you know how to use it, right?' He picked up a box of matches and relit his cigar.

Nightingale wasn't sure what he was getting at.

'So, can you tell me how fifty people in a room can have fifty separate cellphone conversations with fifty other people all around the world, and how those fifty people could get into fifty different cars and drive off in fifty different directions, all the time continuing their conversations without a single overlap or lost word?' He sucked at his cigar and blew smoke without inhaling.

'I guess not,' said Nightingale. 'But you're not saying that cellphones are magic?'

'No, I'm saying it's technology, and we don't have to understand technology to use it. The occult operates on the same principle.'

'And anyone can use it?'

'There are different levels,' said the American. He patted the copy of *The Formicarius*. 'This is a tool, and in the right hands, like mine or your father's, it can accomplish great things. But give it to a child and it's just a book. You have to know how to use the tools, and that knowledge separates the greats from the wannabes.'

'But how do you separate the wheat from the chaff, knowledge-wise?'

'You have to know your source,' said Wainwright. He pointed at Nightingale's briefcase. 'A book like that you can rely on. First editions are best because often there's information in the illustrations that gets left out if they go on to mass production. Handwritten books, illustrated manuscripts from the Middle Ages, that's the real gold.'

'And what about talking to other . . .' He hesitated, not knowing what word to use. 'How do I describe guys like you?' he said.

'Young, gifted and black.' He chuckled. 'That works for me. And with a black man in the White House, it can only get better.'

'I meant what you guys do,' said Nightingale. 'Satanist sounds a bit . . .' He shrugged. 'I don't know. But I guess it's better than devil-worshipper.'

'There are all sorts of descriptions,' said Wainwright. 'There are straight-up Satanists – theistic Satanists, we call them – there are Luciferians, LaVeyans, Setians, Diabolotors, Demonolators . . . There's even the Slaytanists.'

'The Slaytanists?' echoed Nightingale.

'Slaytanists,' said Wainwright. 'That's what we call the dabblers, the weekend Satanists who are more interested in the devil-worship than the process.'

'What process?'

'The magik. And that's magik with a K not the sort of magic you see on TV.'

'So what do you call yourself?'

'I tend to avoid labels,' said Wainwright. 'They're so limiting.'

'But do you guys talk to each other, share secrets and stuff?'

'Chefs don't give their recipes to other chefs, stage magicians don't go showing their tricks to their rivals. We guard our secrets jealously. Why do you ask, Jack?'

'I need information about my father. What he did, what he was capable of, that sort of thing.'

'You could try the Order of the Nine Angles,' said Wainwright. 'You know he was a member?'

'I know almost nothing about him,' said Nightingale. 'Who are they?'

'They're a Satanic sect here in England. They're best known for saying that human sacrifice isn't necessarily a bad thing, which always guarantees them a bad press. And they're one of the groups that believe Satan exists.'

'You said angles, not angels?'

'A lot of people make that mistake,' said the American. 'They figure it's a group involved with rogue angels, but it's not. The name comes from their emblem, which has nine lines connecting the seven planets with the seven lower sefirot on the cabbalistic tree of life.'

'You've lost me,' said Nightingale.

'It's a complicated subject,' said Wainwright. 'Becoming adept can take a lifetime, which is why men like your father are always looking for shortcuts.'

'And all these groups worship Satan?'

Wainwright shook his head. 'Far from it,' he said. 'They don't all even acknowledge that Satan exists. You can believe in Satanic power without believing in Satan. It's the cellphone analogy again. It's not why it works that matters, it's what the effects are.' He sucked at his cigar. 'There are some practitioners who call themselves Atheistic Satanists. They believe that a dark force uses entropy to destroy all things, and that force can be used by us here on earth. But they don't believe that Satan exists as an entity.'

'And you, what do you believe?'

Wainwright grinned. 'Me? In the words of the Monkees, I'm a believer.'

'In the devil?'

'In God, the devil, the whole nine yards.'

Nightingale blew smoke. 'I'm told that calling up a devil is fairly easy.'

'It's Occult 101,' Wainwright said. 'Use any search engine and type in "calling up the devil". You'll get thousand of hits.'

'And selling your soul is easy, too?'

Wainwright winced. 'You've got to know what you're doing, Jack. You've got to make sure you're protected and you have to know how to handle them. They're not lapdogs, they're the masters of hell. You make one wrong move and they'll rip your soul out.'

'You've heard of Proserpine?'

'Of course. One of the greats. Definitely not amateur material. You wouldn't want to go calling her up unless you really knew what you were doing.'

'And what about selling her the soul of an unborn child? Is that doable?'

Wainwright's eyes were suddenly as hard as flint. 'What's going on, Jack?' he said. 'What is it you really want to know? You're dancing around it whatever it is.'

Nightingale smiled tightly. 'Even saying it sounds crazy,' he said.

Wainwright's cigar froze inches from his lips and he narrowed his eyes. 'Gosling did it, didn't he?'

Nightingale said nothing. Wainwright's eyes bored into his and Nightingale had to look away.

'Ainsley Gosling sold your soul to Proserpine before you were born?'

'That's what he told me, yeah,' said Nightingale. 'He left me a DVD saying just that.'

'You've got the mark? The pentagram?'

'I don't think so.'

Wainwright leaned forward. 'If there's no pentagram, there's no contract,' he said. 'That's an absolute fact.'

'I've looked everywhere,' said Nightingale.

'Then you're okay,' said Wainwright. 'What happened to your father?

'He killed himself.'

'How?'

'Shotgun.'

'But he was inside a protective circle, right? A pentagram.'

Nightingale nodded. 'How did you know?'

'Because that's the way I'd do it. Something quick and sure.'

'And the pentagram?'

'So they can't get at you before you die. So that you can choose your own time.'

'But you still go to hell, right?'

'That depends.'

'On what?'

'On whether you've been naughty or nice. Bit like whether or not you get a gift from Santa.' He laughed at his own joke.

'What I mean is, if you're going to hell and you die within the protective pentagram, do you still go to hell?'

'Yes, but you'd be going in under your own terms.'

'I don't understand,' said Nightingale.

'I wouldn't expect you to,' said Wainwright.

'You see, I can't work out why my father, my genetic father, went to all the trouble of protecting himself with the pentagram and then he goes and kills himself.'

'Because he wanted it to be his decision,' said Wainwright. 'He wanted to choose the time and place of his passing. That's not unusual.'

'And if my soul was sold, what are my options?'

'Zero. But, like I said, if there's no mark on you, your soul's your own.'

Nightingale ran a hand through his hair and down the back of his neck. He could feel the tendons there, as taut as steel wires. 'I need to talk to this Proserpine.'

'No, you don't, Jack. She's a devil. She'd eat you for breakfast.'

A middle-aged man in a crisp white shirt with black-and-yellow epaulettes opened the cockpit door. 'We're about to fire up the engines, Mr Wainwright,' he said. 'We're going to have to get our wheels off the ground within the next ten minutes or we'll lose our slot.'

'Ready when you are, Ed,' said Wainwright. He smiled at Nightingale. 'Looks like our time's up, Jack,' he said.

The pilot went back into the cockpit and closed the door behind him. Wainwright stood up and held out his hand. 'Good luck,' he said.

They shook. 'Have a safe trip,' said Nightingale.

'You too, man,' said Wainwright. 'But remember, if there's no mark there's no deal and you have nothing to worry about.'

As Nightingale walked away from the plane towards the waiting Mercedes, he heard the stairs retract, the door thump shut and the engines start to whine. The chauffeur already had the door open for him. 'Shall I put that in the boot, sir?' asked the chauffeur, indicating the metal suitcase.

'I think I'll keep it with me,' said Nightingale. He climbed into the back and put it on the seat next to him.

63

The bank manager rubbed his chin as he stared at the suitcase full of money. 'Mr Nightingale, this is very, very unorthodox,' he said.

'Tell me about it,' said Nightingale.

'There are money-laundering regulations, customer-identification protocols, procedures.'

'I understand that, Mr Collinson, but that's how the money came to me and that's how I'm giving it to you.'

'But no one carries around two million euros in cash,' said the bank manager, dropping into his high-backed executive chair. 'My head office is going to be asking all sorts of questions. You're not even a customer of the bank.'

'But my father was, and I'm his sole heir. And I'm sure I don't have to remind you that I'm responsible for the mortgage on Gosling Manor.'

Collinson pursed his fleshy lips, like a toddler about to

burst into tears. 'Very irregular,' he said. 'We're not even geared up for having this much cash on the premises.'

'It's perfectly legitimate,' said Nightingale. 'I sold some of the books in my father's collection.'

'For cash?'

'For cash,' said Nightingale. 'I was as surprised as you are.' He reached into his jacket pocket and took out two sheets of paper. He gave them to the bank manager. 'There's the receipt that the buyer gave me. And the invoice from the bookstore in Hamburg that sold the book to my father.'

Collinson scrutinised both pieces of paper. 'A substantial profit.'

'Especially when you consider how much the euro has risen in value,' said Nightingale.

'You do understand that if you lodge these funds with our branch, we'll be duty-bound to inform the Inland Revenue?' said Collinson.

'I didn't, but I do now.'

'There will probably be a capital-gains tax liability, and you'll have to fill out a form explaining where the money came from.'

'Not a problem,' said Nightingale.

'So, tell me, what do you want to do with the money?' said the bank manager, running the fingers of his right hand along the bundles.

'I'd like to open an account with you, convert this to pounds and pay it into the account, then use that account to continue paying the mortgage my father took out. Does that make sense?'

Collinson nodded.

'I'll get my accountant to give you a call to arrange any paperwork.'

'We'll need a copy of your passport, two recent utility bills, and a reference from your current bank,' said Collinson.

'Easy peasy,' said Nightingale.

'Will you be planning to sell more of your father's books, Mr Nightingale?' asked the bank manager.

'Possibly,' said Nightingale. 'I'm going to draw up an inventory and see what there is.'

'They must be very interesting volumes,' said Collinson. 'Perhaps you could show me some time.'

'They're an acquired taste, Mr Collinson,' said Nightingale. 'I wouldn't have thought they'd be of much interest to you.'

Next door to the bank an optician was offering free eye tests and fifty per cent off all frames. A young woman in a white coat with long black hair tied back in a ponytail was standing behind the counter, showing a range of frames to a housewife with two small children. There was an eye-test chart behind her and Nightingale read the letters all the way down to the bottom line. He'd always had perfect vision. A buzzer sounded as he pushed open the door and went inside.

64

Nightingale was already at his desk when Jenny walked into the office. He had his feet on the desk, his keyboard on his lap, and was staring intently at his screen. 'You're in bright and early,' she said, then noticed the bottle of whisky next to the overflowing ashtray. 'Or did you not go home last night?'

'Couldn't sleep,' said Nightingale. 'You okay?'

'I had new locks fitted to the doors and windows and Banhams are putting in a motion-sensor alarm system later this week.'

'They won't be back, Jenny. They only wanted the diary.'

'I'd feel more secure.' She took off her coat and hung it on the back of the door. Nightingale picked up the whisky and took a long swig. 'What's wrong, Jack?'

'Why should anything be wrong?'

'It's half past eight in the morning and you're drinking whisky.'

'Do you believe in hell, Jenny?'

'Of course not.' She sat down opposite him and moved the whisky out of his reach.

'Because?'

'Because how can there be a place called hell? Where would it be? We're mapping the universe and there's nowhere that hell could be. It can't be a planet or a star or a black hole.'

'So you don't believe in heaven either?'

'As a place, of course not. Angels sitting on clouds playing harps. How ridiculous is that?'

'So when we're dead, we're dead, is that it? Just nothingness? The great abyss?'

'Life will go on, whether I'm here or not, so it's not blackness. What's wrong, Jack?'

Nightingale shook his head. 'I guess I want to know what happens when we die, and it's the one question no one can answer. That's the paradox, isn't it? We all die, it's the one thing we have common, yet no one knows what it really means.'

'It depends on what you believe, Jack. Some people truly believe that when they die they go to heaven. Others believe they'll be reborn, that our time here is just part of a process.'

'Reincarnation?'

'I guess. Atheists think there's nothing. We're born, we live, we die, it's over.'

'Which is pretty depressing.'

'You think hell is a better alternative?'

'Oh, Jenny, I don't know. I don't know what to think any more.'

'You think it might be true? You're starting to believe that Ainsley Gosling sold your soul to the devil.'

'To *a* devil. Proserpine. I'm sure he did, yes. Or, at least, I'm sure he believed he did. The big question is, do I have a soul to sell? Is the soul something tangible that can be traded? It's nonsense, right? There's no such thing as a soul.'

'Are you asking me or telling me, Jack?'

'That's the thing, isn't it? We can talk about it until the cows come home but we'll never know for sure.'

'That's what makes us human,' said Jenny. 'We're the only animal that knows it will die one day. No other creature thinks about death.'

'But most of us do everything we can not to think about it,' said Nightingale, 'because it's the scariest thing imaginable.'

'Life is what you should be thinking about,' said Jenny. 'Enjoy it while you have it. Relish every moment. Every second.'

'But one day it'll be over.'

'Maybe.'

'Maybe?' echoed Nightingale.

Jenny shrugged. 'I don't know, Jack – I don't know any better than you. But I have a gut feeling there's more. That's all it is, a gut feeling. Jack, what's brought this on? Has something happened?'

'You're not religious, are you?'

Jenny smiled. 'No, but religion has nothing to do with life after death, has it? You can believe in that without believing in God. Maybe we just move on to something else.'

'Like what?'

Jenny sighed. 'I have no idea, Jack. Nobody does.'

'That's the point, though, isn't it? If there was something else, wouldn't those who have passed on come back and tell us what lies ahead? Why didn't my mum and dad? The last time I saw them they were on the doorstep, waving me off to university. Then, bang, they're killed in a car crash. If there was life after death, wouldn't they have come back to say goodbye? Just to let me know that everything was okay?'

'Sometimes people do get messages from beyond, don't they? And lots of people say they've seen ghosts.'

'Have you?'

'No,' admitted Jenny.

'And neither have I. And my parents died suddenly and violently, and so did my aunt and uncle, and if you believe what you read, those are the most likely circumstances to produce a ghost. I got nothing from them, Jenny. Not from my mother and father and not from my aunt and uncle. They died and that was the end of it.' He sighed. 'You know, when I buried my mum and dad, I expected to feel their presence at the funeral but there was nothing. Just the coffins.' He reached for the whisky but didn't make it.

'Maybe they couldn't come back. Maybe that's not how it works,' said Jenny, picking up the bottle. 'I'll make you a coffee.'

'And what about my so-called genetic father? He died violently but I haven't seen him floating around. He left me a DVD apologising for what he'd done, and you'd think he might have come back and apologised in person. Or in spirit. And if there is life after death, don't you think he'd get in contact and tell me what to do? And what about Robbie? Remember the message he left on my phone? He had something to tell me, something important.'

Maybe it's a one-way journey with no coming back. Like caterpillars.'

'Caterpillars?'

'Caterpillars spend their lives crawling over leaves

until one day they turn into a chrysalis and then the chrysalis bursts open and there's a butterfly. Now, does the caterpillar know that one day it'll be a butterfly? I doubt it. So far as the caterpillar is concerned, the chrysalis is death. The end of the caterpillar. And does the butterfly remember being a caterpillar?'

'Who knows?' said Nightingale.

'Exactly,' said Jenny. 'Who knows. But do you ever see butterflies hanging out with caterpillars? No, you don't. They've nothing in common. Maybe that's what happens when we die. Part of us moves on and there's no looking back.'

'Our spirit, is that what you mean?'

'They say that when you die, you lose twenty-one grams. It just goes. You weigh a person before they die and you weigh them afterwards and twenty-one grams have disappeared.'

'Says who?' asked Nightingale.

'I did a philosophy course in my final year,' said Jenny. 'It was an American doctor who did the experiment, back in the nineteen hundreds. Duncan MacDougall, his name was. He designed a special bed that was built on a set of scales and he had six dying patients who agreed to help him. By weighing the entire bed he was able to take into account sweat and urine loss, everything physical. With all six patients there was an immediate weight loss of twenty-one grams at the moment of death.'

Nightingale narrowed his eyes. 'And that's the weight of a human soul, is it? Twenty-one grams?'

'The weight of a humming-bird, give or take,' said Jenny. 'That was MacDougall's theory. He repeated the experiment with fifteen dogs. Tied them to the bed and put them to sleep. With the dogs, there was no change in weight as they died. His theory was that people had souls and dogs didn't.'

'And why has no one done the experiment since?'

'Weigh dying people? I'm not sure you'd get away with it these days.' Jenny put a hand on his shoulder and squeezed. 'What's wrong, Jack? What's brought all this on?'

'Give me the whisky and I'll tell you.'

'Jack . . .'

Nightingale held out his hand. Jenny gave him the bottle.

'You know there's supposed to be a pentagram mark?'

'If your soul is sold to the devil, yes. But you haven't got a mark, remember?'

'There was an optician next to the bank in Brighton. I went there to deposit the money and the optician was offering free eye tests.'

'You don't need glasses,' she said. 'Eyes like a hawk's.'

'I went to get my retinas scanned,' he said quietly. 'I figured it was one of the parts of the body you never get to see.'

'And?'

Nightingale slid a manila envelope across the desk. She opened it with trembling hands and slid out the photograph inside. There were two images on it, retinal scans of his right and left eyes. On the left eye, down at the four o'clock position, there was a small black pentagram.

65

'That's impossible,' said Jenny, staring at the scan in horror.

'Yeah, that's what the optician said.'

'It's a pentagram.'

'Isn't it just.'

'On the back of your eye?'

'Apparently. He did the scans twice, thought there might be a problem with the machine.'

'Jack . . .'

'I know.'

'Oh, my God.'

'My thoughts exactly.' He raised the bottle in salute. 'Now you understand why I'm drinking. It's Wednesday morning. Tomorrow night at midnight . . . blah, blah, blah.'

'That's your plan?' said Jenny in disgust. 'You're going to drink yourself to death?'

'My plan is to talk to Proserpine. I just can't work out how to do it. I've been trawling the Internet but there isn't much about her.'

'Please tell me you're joking,' said Jenny. 'I'm making you a coffee whether you want it or not.' She went over to the machine. 'Is that what you're doing, looking for an email address for Proserpine?' She forced a smile. 'Hotmail, probably.'

'Ha ha,' said Nightingale. 'The guy I saw at the airport yesterday said it's all true, that you can sell souls and there are devils out there who'll buy them.'

'Then he's a loony,' said Jenny, sitting on the edge of his desk.

'A very rich loony, who gave me two million euros for one of the books in my father's library. He wants me to give him an inventory of the rest.'

'Get away,' said Jenny.

'I'm serious. I paid the money into the bank – here's the credit slip if you don't believe me.' He held up a piece of paper.

Jenny took it from him and stared at it with wide eyes. 'Oh, my God,' she said again. 'Who is this guy?'

'According to Google, he doesn't exist,' said Nightingale. 'Young guy, looks like a rap star, flies around the world in a Gulfstream jet when he's not on the astral plane, and he reckons that if I have the mark, the pentagram, then my goose is well and truly cooked.'

'Jack, it's nonsense and you know it.'

'That's what I thought until I saw the pentagram.'

'There are no such things as devils and demons, Jack. Same as there's no Father Christmas or Tooth Fairy. Waiting for a devil to come and claim your soul is as stupid as sitting by your fireplace waiting for Santa to bring your presents.'

'I don't have a fireplace.'

'Exactly.'

'Exactly? What does my not having a fireplace prove?'

'This isn't about Father Christmas,' said Jenny. 'Stop changing the subject.'

'You brought him up.'

Jenny groaned in frustration. 'As an example – as a way of showing how ridiculous you're being by even entertaining the idea that your father did a deal with the demon.' She saw him opening his mouth to speak and held up a hand to silence him. 'A devil,' she corrected herself. 'A female devil. It's all in Mitchell's diary, how he thinks he called up this Proserpine and did a deal with her.'

'Yeah, it's a pity we don't still have it because I need to talk to her.'

'I made notes,' she said.

'They didn't take them? Mitchell's men didn't take your notes?'

Jenny went over to her desk and pulled open the bottom drawer. She took out an A4 ring-backed notebook. 'They only wanted the diary. This was in my bedroom.'

'You wrote down everything?'

'The bits I'd read.'

'Including how to call up Proserpine? You wrote that down?'

Jenny nodded. 'There's a few words I need to look up, but I got most of it.'

Nightingale took the notebook from her. 'You're a star, Jenny. An absolute star.'

'It's nonsense, Jack. The ramblings of a deranged mind. Mitchell is as crazy as your father was.'

'Does that mean you don't want to help me?' asked Nightingale.

'Help you?' asked Jenny. 'How?'

'Help me talk to Proserpine. Help me find a way out of this.'

'Jack . . .'

'It's my only chance, Jenny. 'He tapped the scans. 'This proves that my father was telling the truth. He did sell my soul. Tomorrow night at midnight a devil is going to come to claim it and I'm damned if I'm going to let that happen.' He smiled without warmth. 'Damned if I do, damned if I don't. Now, will you help me or not?'

66

Alice Steadman was dusting a display of crystals when Nightingale walked into her shop. She smiled brightly when she saw him. 'Mr Nightingale, so nice to see you,' she said. 'Did everything go all right with Mr Wainwright?'

'Everything went perfectly,' said Nightingale. He took an envelope from his jacket pocket and gave it to her. 'I wanted to drop by and give you your commission. I hope a banker's draft's okay.'

She took the envelope from him and opened it. She slid out the cheque and her eyes widened. She gasped and leaned against a display case. 'Mr Nightingale, this is a fortune. I can't accept it. I really can't.'

Nightingale waved away her objections. 'It's the commission we agreed.'

'But this is . . . this is . . . I never expected . . .'

'It's fine. If you hadn't put me in touch with Mr Wainwright I wouldn't have sold the book, so you've earned that.'

She blinked at him. 'I can't thank you enough, Mr Nightingale,' she said. She looked up from the cheque. 'If there's anything I can ever do for you, please, just ask,' she said.

'Actually, there is,' he said. 'I want to draw a magic circle on a wooden floor. Is there a special chalk or something I should use?'

'Of course, and I have it in stock,' she said. 'I use it myself for making sacred circles.'

She went over to a display of Tarot cards. Next to it were a dozen or so boxes about the size of cigarette packets, but instead of government health warnings they were adorned with stars and moons. 'On the house,' she said, and handed him one.

'And consecrated salt water,' said Nightingale. 'This is a protective circle, is it?'

Nightingale nodded. 'I'm told that a chalk circle reinforced with consecrated salt water is the strongest defence.'

'Defence against what, exactly?' she asked. 'What are you planning to do?'

Nightingale ignored her questions. He took a list from his pocket and gave it to her. 'There are a few other things here that I'm told I need to open and close the circle.'

She took the list from him and ran her eyes down it. Her lips tightened. 'Oh dear, Mr Nightingale. Are you sure about this?'

'I'm sure. Can you sell me those items?'

'Oh, yes, they're all very straightforward. But I do hope you know what you're doing.'

'So do I, Mrs Steadman. So do I.'

67

Nightingale was mopping the wooden floor of the main drawing room when Jenny walked in with her briefcase. She smiled. 'That's a first.'

'It's got to be clean,' he said. 'Any dirt will compromise the circle. That's what Mitchell wrote.'

'You're really not going to go through with this, are you?'

'Tonight's the night,' he said. 'I spent all yesterday getting everything. I've got the special chalk and the consecrated salt water, and the herbs you said I needed. Mrs Steadman sells all that sort of stuff.'

'Did she ask what you were planning to do?'

'I think she sort of guessed. Can you do me a favour? Can you go down into the basement and bring up five of the church candles, the really big ones?'

Jenny handed him a small padded envelope. 'It came

in the post this morning,' she said. 'From the Hillingdon Home.'

As Jenny headed down to the basement, he opened the envelope. Inside was his mother's crucifix and a handwritten note from Mrs Fraser, repeating what she had said in her office, that she was sure his mother would have wanted him to have it. He put the chain around his neck. The crucifix nestled at the base of his throat.

Nightingale continued washing the floor until Jenny returned with the candles. She put them by the door and watched as he got down on his hands and knees and dried it with paper towels. Jenny opened her brief-case and took out her A4 notebook. 'Mitchell says you can outline the circle with chalk, but for it to be really effective you need to inscribe it with a sword,' she said.

'There are swords in the basement,' said Nightingale, 'lots of them.'

'It has to be a magic sword,' said Jenny. 'That's what it says here. *Veneficus mucro*. Magic sword.'

'How the hell am I supposed to know which of them are magic?' asked Nightingale. He gathered up the used paper towels and put them into a rubbish bag.

Jenny ran her finger down the page of her notebook. 'He says you can use the branch of a birch tree.'

'Now that's more like it,' said Nightingale. 'We've

got our own forest out there. Now, please tell me you know what a birch tree looks like.'

'I'm a country girl, remember?' She laughed.

Nightingale put the rubbish bag by the door. 'One of these days I'm going to have to read your CV,' he said.

68

Nightingale used the chalk he'd bought from Alice Steadman's shop to draw a circle in the middle of the room, about twelve feet in diameter. 'Are you sure it doesn't have to be a particular size?' he asked.

Jenny looked up from her notebook. 'Mitchell says it can be as big or as small as you want,' she said.

Nightingale grinned at her. 'Funny, that,' he said, 'because before you said size was important.' He straightened and used the birch branch they'd taken from a tree in the garden to outline the circle.

'Once you've gone around it with the branch, you draw the pentagram. A five-pointed star. Make sure there are two points at the top of the circle and one at the bottom.'

'Which is the top and which is the bottom?' said Nightingale.

'That's up to you,' said Jenny. She frowned as she

read her notes. 'Okay, here it is. You have to draw a triangle around the circle. Once the devil has been summoned, it will be confined to the area between the circle and the triangle. And the apex of the triangle has to point north.'

'Okay,' said Nightingale, hesitantly.

'So you make the apex of the triangle point north, and two points of the pentagram should point north, with one pointing south.'

Nightingale looked through the windows and across the lawn, trying to visualise the way he'd driven to the house. He gestured across the grass. 'London is that way, so that's north,' he said.

'I think we should be more accurate than that,' said Jenny. 'I saw some compasses downstairs. I'll get one.'

As she headed back down to the basement, Nightingale sprinkled consecrated salt water around the perimeter of the circle.

Jenny returned with a brass compass. She stood at the edge of the circle and showed Nightingale which way was north.

'I wasn't too far off,' he said.

'Well done, you,' she said. She watched as he drew the pentagram inside the circle, and a large triangle outside.

When he had finished the triangle, he looked at her. 'Now what?'

'Now you have to write in the three points of the triangle. You write "MI" and then "CH" and then "AEL".'

'Michael?'

'The archangel,' said Jenny. 'Don't blame me if it sounds ridiculous. I'm just telling you what Mitchell noted in his diary.'

Nightingale wrote the three sets of letters, then put the chalk down and dusted his hands. 'Is that it?' he asked.

'That's the circle done. When you're ready you put the candles at the points of the pentagram, light them and burn the herbs.'

'Okay,' said Nightingale.

'Then you have to recite this.' She showed him a passage in Latin that she had written down. 'I'm pretty sure you'll have to say these words as they are and not the translation. Then when you've finished you say, "*Bagahi laca bacabe.*" And before you ask, I've no idea what that means. It's not Latin.'

'And that's it?'

'According to Mitchell, once you've said those three words, Proserpine will appear. But I've had enough Delia Smith recipes go wrong to know that sometimes it's not enough just to have the right ingredients.'

He took the notebook from her. 'You know what I don't understand, Jenny?'

Jenny sighed. 'I could draw up a list, but it would take months.'

'Why do you stay with me?'

'What do you mean?'

'You're way overqualified, the work isn't demanding, I'm an idiot most of the time.'

'All true,' she said.

'So why do you work for me?'

'I haven't really thought about it,' she said.

'You must have. You must think about changing jobs sometimes. Everyone does.'

'I like working with you, Jack.'

'I could never figure out why you came for the job in the first place.'

'It was pure luck,' she said. 'It's not as if I was looking for a job with a private eye.' She paused. 'I never told you what happened the day I came for the interview.'

'I thought you were a spy for the Inland Revenue at first,' he said. 'You seemed too good to be true.'

'I was shopping in New Bond Street,' she said, 'and popped into Costa for a coffee. I was waiting to hear if I'd got a job I'd been interviewed for, assistant to the marketing director of a big advertising agency.'

'Nice,' said Nightingale.

'Yeah, well, I was sipping my latte and thinking all was well with the world, when the director of human resources called me and said I hadn't get the job, blah, blah, blah. As he was saying that, I was looking at a free newspaper someone had left on the table. He'd been doing the crossword but had screwed it up, big-time. Couldn't even spell Esperanto. Anyway, under the crossword there were situations-vacant adverts, and yours had been circled. So as the human resources director was telling me I wasn't quite right for the position, I was looking at an advert asking me if I wanted a job that would never be boring.'

'I wrote the copy for the ad,' said Nightingale.

'I know,' said Jenny. 'But if I hadn't gone into that coffee shop, and if the paper hadn't been left open at the page your advert was on . . .'

'Maybe my guardian angel wanted you with me,' said Nightingale.

'Jack!'

'I'm serious, Jenny. If it wasn't for you, I'd never have known about any of this. I mean, who reads Latin, these days?'

'It was serendipity, Jack. A fortunate set of circum-stances.'

'It's my clumsy way of saying thanks. Thanks for putting up with me, and thanks for sticking with me.'

'Somebody has to,' she said.

'Well, I'm glad it's you.' Nightingale checked his watch. 'You have to go now, Jenny.'

'No way.'

'I have to do this on my own.'

'I'm staying, Jack.'

Nightingale folded his arms. 'I don't know what's going to happen, but I do know that if it goes wrong I don't want you around.' He smiled confidently. 'I'll call you when it's over.'

'They've got phones in hell, have they?' she asked.

Nightingale went to hug her but she shook her head and walked away.

From the bedroom window, Nightingale saw Jenny walk towards her car, then stop and look back at the house. Their eyes met. He gave her a small wave but she shook her head sadly and turned away. Nightingale lit a cigarette as she got into the car and drove off.

He smoked slowly, then stubbed out the butt. He was in the master bedroom, the place where his father had killed himself. He stripped off his clothes and walked through to the bathroom. The large tub was already filled with water and he slid into it. He held his breath and submerged himself, sliding down the cold enamel and staring up through the tepid water. He stayed under until his lungs started to burn, then pushed himself up and exhaled. He scrubbed himself clean with a small plastic brush and a bar of soap. He washed and rinsed his hair twice, then climbed out of the bath and towelled himself dry. He put on clean underwear, socks, a pale blue polo shirt and cargo trousers. He took his cigarettes and lighter from his suit, stuffed them into one of the knee pockets in the cargos and put on a pair of brand new Nike trainers. He looked at the padded envelope, then took out the crucifix and hung it around his neck. Finally he combed his hair, checked himself in the mirror over the wash-basin and walked slowly downstairs.

He went to the drawing room and lit the five candles. Then he stepped inside the pentagram. He took several deep breaths to compose himself, then went over the chalk outline with the birch branch. He sprinkled more consecrated salt water around the perimeter of the circle, then set fire to the contents of a lead crucible. The herbs and bits of wood in it hissed and spluttered and filled the room with cloying smoke.

He picked up Jenny's notebook and began to read the Latin words she'd shown him, stumbling over the strange language. A wind blew through the room, even though the windows and door were firmly closed. The candle flames flickered and the smoke pouring up from the crucible began to form a circle. Nightingale coughed and continued to read, running his finger beneath the words so that he wouldn't lose his place. When he finished, he coughed again and said out loud,'*Bagahi laca bacabe.*' He closed the notepad.

The room was thick with smoke, as dense as a pea-souper fog, sickeningly sweet but acrid enough to make his eyes water.

What happened next, Nightingale was never able to explain to anyone, not even to himself. He wasn't sure that he remembered it properly. The only way his mind could come close to interpreting what he'd seen was to picture it as space folding into itself, a series of flickering flashes. Then the air blurred and she was standing within the apex of the triangle. It was a girl, in her late teens or early twenties, white-faced, with heavy mascara, a black T-shirt with a white skull on it, a black leather skirt, black boots and a studded collar around her neck. She looked at him through narrowed eyes. 'Jack Nightingale,' she said, her voice a throaty whisper. 'Are you in such a hurry to join me? You have only six hours left. Why are you wasting them?'

Now Nightingale saw that a second figure had folded out of the air. A dog, a black-and-white collie, that sat at the feet of his mistress. 'I know you,' he said. 'We've met before.'

'Our paths have crossed from time to time,' she said. Her eyes were black and featureless, the irises so dark that they merged seamlessly into the pupils.

'I have an investment in you and I watch over my investments.'

'Are you Proserpine? Princess of hell?'

'So formal,' she said. She laughed and the floor shook. The dog at her side growled menacingly. She reached down and stroked it behind the ears. 'Do you want to see my ID, Nightingale?' She laughed again, and this time the whole building vibrated. 'You expected what? Horns? A forked tail? The stench of brimstone? I can give you that, if that's what you want.'

'But you're a girl,' said Nightingale.

'I am what I am,' she said. Her eyes narrowed as she looked at his neck. 'Nice crucifix,' she said.

'It belonged to my mother.'

'I know,' said Proserpine. She smiled. 'I'm not a vampire. Crucifixes are only good against the Undead.'

'That's not why I'm wearing it,' said Nightingale. 'Did you kill her? My mother?'

'She killed herself.'

'And my uncle? And Barry O'Brien? And George Harrison?'

'I always thought he was the weakest member of the band,' said Proserpine. 'I mean, "My Sweet Lord". What the hell was that about?'

'You know what I mean,' said Nightingale. 'Did you kill them?'

'They killed themselves.'

'What about Robbie?'

Proserpine shook her head solemnly. 'A tragic accident.'

'Uncle Tommy? Auntie Linda?'

'You have been unlucky on the relatives front, haven't you?'

'You killed them all, didn't you?'

'Is this how you used to interrogate suspects when you were a cop?' she said. 'It's not very subtle, is it?'

'Did you kill them?'

'No.'

'I don't believe you.'

'Ask them yourself,' said Proserpine. She waved a languid hand and four figures appeared behind her, flickering at first, then becoming solid. Rebecca Keeley was on the right, wearing a long grey nightdress, blood dripping from her wrists, her eyes wide and staring. Next to her, Barry O'Brien was naked and soaking wet, his arms cut open to the bone. Blood and water dripped to the floor. Uncle Tommy stood next to O'Brien, his neck at a grotesque angle, his lips drawn back in a snarl. Just behind them Auntie Linda was crawling along the floor, her skull in pieces, blood and brain matter trailing behind her.

Proserpine's hand moved again, forming a gnarled

fist. Harrison appeared, the left side of his body mashed and bloody, one eyeball hanging from its socket. And next to him was Robbie, blood trickling from between his lips, a white bone sticking out from his left elbow, his right leg buckled and twisted. He was staring at Nightingale, his shattered jaw moving soundlessly.

All six figures moved slowly towards him.

Proserpine looked over her shoulder and frowned. 'We're missing someone,' she said. 'Who are we missing? Ah, of course . . .' She waved again and Sophie Underwood appeared. Unlike the others, she didn't bear the marks of her death but was exactly as Nightingale had seen her on the balcony of her apartment, her blonde hair tucked behind her ears, the Barbie doll clutched to her white sweatshirt. She looked at Nightingale, her lower lip trembling. 'I don't like it here,' she said. 'I want to go home.' She took a step towards the protective circle. 'Please help me, Jack.'

Nightingale forced himself to look away. He knew she wasn't really there. Sophie was dead and buried and there was no way she could be standing in the bedroom at Gosling Manor. 'I want to go home, Jack,' said Sophie, and began to sob.

Nightingale glared at Proserpine. 'Don't do that,' he said.

'Don't do what?' asked Proserpine. She put a finger

up to the side of her mouth and smiled girlishly. 'Am I being bad? Do you want to punish me?'

'Don't use others to get to me,' said Nightingale. 'Fight your own battles.'

Proserpine's eyes hardened and she waved her hand again. The figures vanished. She crouched and put a hand towards the chalk circle. 'Consecrated salt water,' she said, and nodded approvingly.

'What are you? A devil? A demon? Are you here or am I imagining all this?'

'I am what I am, Nightingale,' she said, as she straightened.

'I don't understand,' he said, folding his arms. 'I don't understand any of this.'

'With respect, you're no Stephen Hawking, are you? Now, *there* was a book. How can you write about the creation of the universe without discussing heaven or hell? And how can you get away with telling people that one moment there's nothing but the void and the next there's an expanding universe heading out to infinity?'

'I couldn't finish it,' said Nightingale. 'If there is a hell, then where is it?'

'Hell is everywhere – you just can't see it.'

'And heaven?'

'The same.'

'The same place?' Nightingale shook his head. 'Maybe you're not even here. Maybe this is some sort of stupid delusion, brought on by the crap I burned in the crucible.' He took out his pack of Marlboro. 'Do you want a cigarette? I'm guessing cancer isn't one of your worries.' He took out a cigarette and slipped one between his lips. He held his lighter to the end and was just about to flick it, but hesitated. He looked at Proserpine with narrowed eyes. 'Cigarette smoke's an impurity, isn't it? It'll weaken the pentagram.'

Proserpine shrugged carelessly. 'Maybe,' she said. 'Try it and see.'

Nightingale slid the cigarette back into the packet.

Proserpine studied the pentagram, the candles and the still-smouldering crucible. 'Where did you learn this?' she said.

'I read a diary written by Sebastian Mitchell.'

Proserpine's black eyes snapped. 'And how did you come across it?'

'My father had it,' said Nightingale.

'It won't do you any good,' she said, putting her hands on her hips. 'It didn't do your father any good, it didn't do Mitchell any good, and it won't do you any good either. Your father sold your soul to me on the day you were born. The contract is inviolable, written in his blood. And you bear the mark.'

She stalked around the pentagram, occasionally moving closer to him but never touching the chalk mark. It was as if she was testing his defences. Nightingale kept turning so that he was always facing her. She looked like a punk teenager, but she was a devil from hell and not to be trusted. 'Deals can be broken,' said Nightingale, quietly.

Proserpine threw back her head and laughed. The noise was like a thousand wolves howling, a blood-curdling scream that chilled him. The sound went right through him and he shivered. The dog sat up and stared at him. The animal's eyes were as black and featureless as the girl's. 'Not this one,' said Proserpine. 'Your soul is mine. There's nothing you can do to change that.'

'Why do you want it?'

'It's what I do. I take souls.'

'Why?'

'The why doesn't matter. It's what I do.'

'But what good is my soul to you?'

'It's how we keep score,' said Proserpine.

'It's a game?'

'No, Nightingale, it's not a game. It's a struggle between the dark and the light, between good and evil.'

'Between God and Lucifer?'

'Whatever,' she said.

'If you're a demon, or a devil, or whatever you call

yourself, why do you look as if you've just walked out of Camden Lock market?'

'It's my style – it's what I'm comfortable with.'

'But you don't really look like that, is that what you're saying?'

'I do and I don't,' said Proserpine. 'I'm here and I'm not here. You're never going to understand it, Nightingale. Energy, matter, light, it's all connected. You're human, you only see a small part of it. I see everything. If I try to explain it to you, it would be like you explaining nuclear physics to an earthworm.'

'And why my soul?'

'Because it was offered to me by your father.'

'But that's not fair. It's my soul, what right did he have to trade it?'

Proserpine laughed, her voice louder and deeper than any sound Nightingale had ever heard. 'Fair?' she said. 'You want fairness? Nothing in life is fair. Haven't you learned that yet?'

'So anyone can sell a soul, is that what you're saying?'

'Your soul was promised to me by your father before you were born. Before it was yours.'

'And there's nothing I can do to stop you taking it?'

She shook her head. 'Nothing.'

'Mitchell seems to think you can be beaten.'

'Mitchell is wrong.'

'He says that so long as he stays within his penta-gram, he walks into hell on his own terms.'

Proserpine smiled. 'Yeah, well, the fat lady hasn't sung on that one yet.' She nodded at the packet of Marlboro. 'Maybe I will have a cigarette.'

Nightingale threw the packet to her and she caught it one-handed. She tapped out a cigarette, tossed it high in the air and caught it between her lips. 'Got a light, mister?' she asked, in a sing-song little-girl voice. She winked and held out her right hand. It burst into flames and she lit the cigarette. She blew smoke at the ceiling, shook her hand and the flames vanished.

'I saw a conjuror do that once,' said Nightingale.

'I shall miss your sense of humour,' she said.

'When I'm in hell?'

'When your soul is in hell,' she said. 'You'll be dead.'

'I've a question for you,' said Nightingale.

'This isn't phone-a-friend, Nightingale. You can't summon devils simply to question them.'

'Actually, I'm pretty sure I can,' said Nightingale. 'The spell means that you have to appear and that you have to stay between the circle and the triangle. And you have to stay until I release you.'

'So that's your plan, is it? You think you can keep me trapped here? Well, that may be right, Nightingale, but you're trapped too. And I reckon I can go a lot longer than you without food or water. And it won't make any difference anyway, because at midnight your soul is mine, pentagram or no pentagram.'

'I didn't do this to trap you,' he said, 'and what I have in mind won't take long. I just want to ask you a question. Why is Sebastian Mitchell so scared of you?'

'He said that? He said he was scared of me?'

'He's sitting in a magic circle waiting to die because he knows that if he sets foot outside it you'll drag him down to hell, so I sort of inferred it. What did he do?'

'He cheated me,' said Proserpine.

'How?'

'It doesn't matter how.'

'Just humour me,' said Nightingale. He looked at his watch. 'In a few hours you're supposed to be condemning me to eternal damnation. The least you can do is satisfy my curiosity.'

'I don't owe you anything, Nightingale.'

'I know that,' he said. 'What did he do that's got you so riled?'

Proserpine glared at him, then smiled. 'Are you planning to write a book? I have to point out that you probably don't have enough time.'

'I just want to understand the situation I'm in,' he said.

'Mitchell promised me four souls,' she said. 'Young girls. Virgins. They were novices at a coven of his. He promised me their souls but then he went behind my back and gave them to someone else.'

'Another demon?'

Proserpine nodded. 'He was leading them along the path, getting them ready to offer themselves to me, but then he negotiated a better deal.' She smiled thinly and took a drag on the cigarette. 'What he thought was a better deal.'

'But why does that matter? Are you in competition with the other demons, is that it?'

'You wouldn't understand, Nightingale. He made me look . . . incompetent. He made me look a fool, as if I wasn't in control.'

'So you want revenge?'

'They were my souls,' she said, 'promised to me, but he reneged. I can't let him get away with that.' She took another long drag on her cigarette, then flicked it away. It bounced off the wall and hit the floor, still glowing. 'Just get on with it, Nightingale.'

'With what?'

'Begging for your soul. I assume that's why you summoned me. To plead for me to leave you alone, to allow you to continue your miserable existence.'

Nightingale smiled. 'Actually, you're wrong,' he said. 'I didn't call you here to beg.'

'Why then?' she said. 'Why did you summon me when you have so little time left?'

'To do what I do best,' said Nightingale. 'To negotiate.'

70

Nightingale climbed out of his MGB and looked at his watch. It was eleven o'clock. One hour to go before midnight. He pressed the speakerphone button. It buzzed and he waved up at the CCTV camera covering the gates. 'Mr Nightingale, if you do not leave the property immediately we will have no choice other than to call the police.'

Nightingale bent down to the speaker. 'Nice to talk to you too, Sylvia,' he said. 'Tell Mr Mitchell it's important. Tell him I know how to deal with Proserpine. Tell him I have the answer to his problems.'

'You're wasting your time, Mr Nightingale. He doesn't want to see you.'

'Just give him the message, Sylvia.' The moon was full and dark clouds moved slowly across its face. 'Nice night for it,' he muttered to himself. The gates buzzed and began to open. Nightingale climbed back into the MGB.

When he arrived at the house Sylvia was waiting for him with four of Mitchell's heavies. Nightingale got out and went to the boot. He opened it and took out the metal suitcase Wainwright had given him.

'We'll need to check that,' said Sylvia.

'It's locked,' said Nightingale. He handed it to her. 'You can keep hold of it until I need it.' He smiled at her look of apprehension. 'If it was a bomb, sweetie, I'd hardly have been driving it around in an old banger like my MGB, would I?'

Sylvia turned on her heel and walked up the steps to the entrance. The four heavies moved aside to allow Nightingale to follow her, but he stayed where he was. 'Which one of you scumbags pointed a gun at my friend?' he asked.

The four men stared at him, their eyes hidden behind the dark lenses. One drew back his jacket to reveal a submachine pistol in a nylon sling.

'Cat got your tongues?' said Nightingale, looking at them one by one. 'You were very chatty when you were scaring a young woman, but now you're coy, aren't you? When this is over, we're going to have a chat about what you did to her and I'll explain the error of your ways.' He smiled brightly. 'Right, let's go and put the world to rights, shall we?' He jogged up the stairs after Sylvia.

She took him into the hall and pointed at the bathroom door. 'You know the procedure, Mr Nightingale.'

71

When Nightingale walked out of the bathroom in the robe, Sylvia was waiting for him with two of the heavies. They escorted him to Mitchell's room. He was in exactly the same position as he had been when Nightingale had last visited, though this time he was wearing royal blue silk pyjamas. Sylvia made Nightingale stop ten feet away from the edge of the pentagram. He nodded at Mitchell. 'You got your diary back, then?' he said. 'You only had to ask, you know. I would have given it to you.'

Mitchell pulled the oxygen mask away from his face. 'What do you want, Nightingale?'

'I get asked that a lot these days.'

'Haven't you got better things to do? You've got, what, an hour before she comes for you?'

'That's what I wanted to talk to you about.'

'There's nothing I can do, Nightingale. I told you

that already.' He began to cough and he pressed the mask over his mouth.

'I've found a way,' said Nightingale, 'to stop Proserpine.'

Mitchell shook his head, still coughing. He regained his composure and took the mask away from his mouth. 'She can't be stopped. She has too much power.'

'Do you know Joshua Wainwright? American guy. I get the feeling he's embraced the dark side.'

'I've heard of him,' said Mitchell.

'Wainwright owes me a favour.'

'I doubt that,' said Mitchell.

'I sold him a book he's wanted for years. My father snatched it from under his nose but I got it back to him.' Nightingale grinned. 'I made a tidy profit, but he was still grateful – grateful enough to help me.'

'No one can help you,' said Mitchell. 'One minute after midnight and it's all over for you.'

'Not according to the book Wainwright's lent me.'

Mitchell was coughing again. He dabbed at his lips with a tissue, then threw it into the bin by his side. 'What book?' he said.

'It was written by an Iranian Satanist back in the eighteenth century, but he only showed it to a few people. When he died it went missing but it turned up in Paris in the 1930s and was translated into French.

There are only three copies in English, and Wainwright has one, which he's lent to me.'

Mitchell frowned. 'This book, what's it called?'

'It has no name, no title,' said Nightingale, 'but it has a chapter on killing devils.'

'You can't kill a devil,' said Mitchell.

'Not so much kill as destroy,' said Nightingale. 'There's a spell that ends them.'

'Nonsense,' said Mitchell. He coughed again and spat bloody phlegm into a fresh tissue. 'Proserpine sits on the left hand of Satan. She's beyond all attacks.'

'The book tells of a spell that weakens a devil's power. Then you can use a dagger. A dagger that has been given but not thanked for.'

'And where did you get the dagger?' asked Mitchell.

'Have you heard of the Order of the Nine Angles? Nasty little group that goes in for human sacrifice? My father was a member.'

'The Order gave you a dagger?'

'And I didn't say thank you. How rude was that?'

'So why are you here? Why not just do it?'

'I need your help,' said Nightingale.

Mitchell shook his head. 'I'm not leaving the circle,' he said.

'You don't have to,' said Nightingale.

Mitchell put the mask over his mouth. He continued to stare at Nightingale with unblinking eyes as his chest heaved.

'Here's the thing,' said Nightingale. 'I can't summon Proserpine to do this. That won't work. For the spell to be effective, she has to come of her own accord and she has to be in human form. And at midnight, she'll come for me.'

'How do you know she'll be in human form?'

'Because I've already summoned her.'

'And she came?'

'My assistant, the girl your heavies terrorised, made notes from your diary, including the section on summoning Proserpine.'

Mitchell chuckled. 'And you performed the spell?'

'Couldn't find a magic sword, but we made do with a birch branch.'

'And when she came, what form did she take?'

'A girl. With a dog.'

Mitchell nodded. 'He's always with her. Her protector.'

'Seemed like a regular sheepdog to me.'

'They choose their appearances, Nightingale. But she came to you the same way that she appeared to me.'

'But don't you see? That's her weakness. She appears

as a human, and when she's in human form, she can be killed. With the dagger.'

'So why are you here, Nightingale? Why don't you just do it?'

'Because when she comes, she'll be focused on me, which means I won't get the chance to get close to her. But you'll be a distraction. And when she's distracted, I can get to her.'

'I'm not leaving the circle,' said Mitchell.

'I already told you, you don't have to,' said Nightingale. He pointed at the terrace outside the french windows. 'I'll do it there. She'll come at midnight. You keep the lights off until you see me reading the spell from the book. As soon as I close the book, you turn on the lights. She'll see you, and that's when I'll do it.'

Mitchell coughed. 'You're mad,' he wheezed.

Nightingale shook his head. 'No, I'm not mad,' he said. 'I'm desperate.'

72

Nightingale walked out of the bathroom. He had changed back into his suit and had on his raincoat. Sylvia was waiting for him with the metal suitcase. Two of Mitchell's heavies were standing behind her. 'If you do anything to compromise Mr Mitchell's security, you will be dealt with immediately,' she said.

'Don't worry, Sylvia, I've his best interests at heart,' said Nightingale. 'Once I've dealt with Proserpine, he can go back to living a normal life.'

Sylvia flashed him a cold smile. 'Mr Mitchell's life has never been normal,' she said. 'We will walk around the house to the patio,' she said. 'Mr Mitchell says that I am to give you anything you need.'

Nightingale patted the suitcase. 'I've got everything I need right here.'

They went outside and around the house, flanked by the two heavies. The gardens were illuminated by floodlights and beside the wall Nightingale saw another heavy walking with a Rottweiler on a leash.

When they reached the terrace, he put down the case and lit a cigarette. Sylvia looked at her watch. 'It's half an hour until midnight,' she said.

'I know,' said Nightingale. 'But I figure that the condemned man deserves a last cigarette.'

73

Sebastian Mitchell kept the oxygen mask over his mouth as he took deep breaths, his eyes on Nightingale, who was slowly chalking a pentagram on the stone slabs. There was a clock on the wall and he squinted at it. Eleven forty. Twenty minutes before Proserpine would come to take Nightingale's soul.

Sylvia walked into the room, her high heels clicking on the wooden floor. 'I've stationed extra men around the house, and we have three dogs in the garden now, sir.'

'Thank you, Sylvia,' wheezed Mitchell. 'But there's no danger for us. It's Nightingale she wants.'

Nightingale placed the metal suitcase in the centre of the pentagram. He took out an ornate gold dagger and held it up. It glinted in the spotlights covering the terrace. He waved the knife over the five points of the pentagram, then slid it into the inside pocket of his raincoat. 'You're wasting your time, Nightingale,' Mitchell muttered. 'Knives are useless against devils.'

Nightingale took a piece of a branch from the case and slowly went over the chalk outline with it. Then he sprinkled water from a small bottle around the perimeter. 'Consecrated salt water,' Mitchell wheezed, 'but it will do you no good. It will keep her out but you will still lose your soul.'

Nightingale put the branch and the bottle back into the case and took out a small leather-bound book. Mitchell frowned. 'What's that? Sylvia, can you see what book he's holding?'

Sylvia walked over to the french windows and peered through the glass. 'No, sir,' she said. 'There doesn't appear to be a title but it looks old.'

'What are you up to, Nightingale?' muttered Mitchell.

Nightingale sat cross-legged in the centre of the pentagram with the book in his lap, staring out over the garden.

'Now what's he doing?' said Sylvia.

Mitchell looked up at the clock on the wall. 'He's waiting,' he said. He looked back at Sylvia. 'Turn the lights off,' he said. 'We might as well give him a chance.'

74

Nightingale could feel his pulse racing and kept his breathing slow and even. Behind him, the lights in the drawing room went out. The spotlights around the terrace were still on and he was bathed in a clinical white light. There were lights around the perimeter wall, too, casting long shadows from the trees that dotted the garden.

He didn't have to look at his watch to know that there were still ten minutes to go. There was nothing he could do to speed up the process. Proserpine would come exactly at midnight because that was when his soul would be forfeit. There was no point in trying to summon her. All he could do was wait until she showed up of her own accord.

An owl flew overhead, its wings beating silently in the still air. Then it swooped down to a patch of grass under an oak tree, grabbed something small and furry in its claws and flew up towards the roof.

Nightingale closed his eyes. He could hear a far-off rumble of traffic but other than that the night was silent. There was no sound from the house behind him but he was sure that Mitchell was watching. He tried to visualise him sitting in his chair, the oxygen mask pressed to his mouth, staring out of the window. Sylvia would be there, too, close to Mitchell's protective pentagram, watching and wondering.

The seconds ticked by. Then the minutes. A breeze blew from the north, ruffling Nightingale's hair. He opened his eyes. The trees were swaying in the wind, their shadows writhing on the grass like living things.

His knees cracked as he got to his feet. He held the book to his chest and licked his lips. He wanted a cigarette desperately but that was impossible.

A mist had gathered around the lawn, patchy at first but soon thickening, and the security lights around the walls became glowing balls that grew dimmer with each second that passed. A dog barked in the distance but the sound was cut short as if its leash had been pulled harshly.

Nightingale stared ahead. He could no longer see the wall surrounding the garden, or the trees. He could see the terrace but only a few dozen yards of lawn before it was swallowed in the mist. Then the air in front of him cleaved apart, folded in on itself, shimmered – and she was there, standing about twelve feet from the pentagram, a sly smile on her face. Her eyes were dark pits, her lips black and glossy. She was wearing the same black skirt and boots as before but a different T-shirt, black with a gold ankh cross on it. Her collie circled her, his eyes continually watching Nightingale, tail twitching from side to side. Proserpine grinned. 'Time to pay the piper, Nightingale,' she said.

He ignored her. He had already marked the page he was to read. He opened the book and read the Latin words slowly and precisely, his eyes fixed on the page. The wind was getting stronger now and he held on to the book tightly, fearful it would be whipped out of his grasp.

'You're wasting your breath,' said Proserpine. She took a step towards the pentagram. 'It's midnight. Time for me to take what is mine.'

75

Mitchell took the oxygen mask away from his face. 'What's he doing?' he croaked. 'No spell can stop her – she's too strong.'

'What's going to happen, sir?' asked Sylvia.

'She'll take his soul,' said Mitchell. 'Nightingale's got balls all right, but he's as good as dead.'

He pushed himself out of his seat to get a better look at what was happening on the terrace. Proserpine was moving closer to Nightingale. She was saying something to him but Mitchell couldn't make out what it was. Nightingale was being buffeted by a strong wind, his hair in disarray, his coat whipping around his legs like a living thing, but Proserpine was totally unaffected by it.

Nightingale was reading from the book, his head down as he concentrated, ignoring the devil that was now only feet away from the pentagram.

'He's wasting his time,' muttered Mitchell. 'It's over.'

'The lights, sir,' said Sylvia. 'Nightingale said we should turn on the lights.'

'It won't make any difference,' he said. He dropped the oxygen mask onto the chair. Proserpine was next to the pentagram now, her black eyes glaring at Nightingale, her fingers curved into talons, bent forward at the waist like a wild animal preparing to spring.

Nightingale stopped reading and closed the book. He held it out to Proserpine.

'No, never allow contact!' said Mitchell.

'The lights, sir,' said Sylvia.

'Yes, okay,' snapped Mitchell. 'Put the lights on, but it won't make any difference.' He stared at Nightingale, who was still holding out the leather-bound book to Proserpine.

Sylvia's heels clicked on the wooden floor as she hurried to the switches. She placed her hand against the panel and flicked the three together. The room was flooded with light.

Proserpine's head jerked and she stared at the french window, snarling when she saw Mitchell standing there. 'Mitchell!' she screamed, so loudly that the glass rattled. Mitchell took a step back and his leg banged against the chair behind him.

Nightingale dropped the book and the dagger was

in his right hand. He brought it down in an arc towards Proserpine's chest. There was a flash of lightning, then another, and a howl from Proserpine as she staggered backwards. Black blood gushed from the centre of the golden ankh, pulsing out in a stream that splashed over Nightingale's legs. The lightning flashed again and there was a clap of thunder so loud that the ground shook.

Nightingale stepped out of the pentagram and stuck the knife into her chest again and again, his face contorted. He was screaming at her but the wind was tearing the words from his mouth and ripping them away.

'No . . .' said Mitchell, clutching the chair for support. 'It can't be.'

Proserpine's dog ran away, tail between his legs, ears flat against his head, keeping low to the ground as if he hoped to escape unnoticed.

Proserpine fell back, arms flailing. Lightning flashed again and again, with simultaneous booms of thunder. Nightingale straddled her and used both hands to slam the knife down into her chest.

She bucked and kicked, and then lay still.

'I don't believe it,' whispered Mitchell. 'He's done it.' He glanced at the clock. It was barely two minutes after midnight. He looked back at the terrace. Nightingale was standing up, the dagger in his right hand, the wind tugging at his coat. 'Sixty years I've studied, and I couldn't have accomplished that.' He looked at Sylvia, who was still standing at the door, her hand on the light switches. 'Nightingale's worked a miracle. Did you see that, Sylvia? Did you see what he did?'

'I saw, Mr Mitchell.'

'He killed a demon. He killed a demon from hell.' He stood with one hand on the armchair, shaking his head in bewilderment.

76

Nightingale stood looking down at the body, his ears ringing from the thunderclaps. The knife dropped from his nerveless fingers. His body was drenched in sweat and the strength had drained from his legs. Lightning flashed and the earth shook with another rumble of thunder.

He heard the French windows open behind him, but he didn't look around. 'You did it, man!' shouted Mitchell.

He heard Mitchell step out onto the terrace, and only then did Nightingale turn. He was standing there, his blue silk pyjamas rippling in the wind, with Sylvia behind him, her hands clasped as if she was in prayer, and four heavies, guns at the ready.

'I wouldn't have believed it if I hadn't seen it with my own eyes,' said Mitchell. He walked unsteadily across the flagstones and grabbed Nightingale's arm, his fingers digging into him like talons. 'You killed her. How did you do it? How in God's name did you do it?'

'God had nothing to do with it.' The voice was a deep growl that came from behind Nightingale.

Mitchell stiffened, and Nightingale stepped away from him, leaving him standing alone with his arms outstretched. They both stared down at Proserpine. She was smiling. As they watched, she pivoted upright, the wounds on her chest vanishing.

Mitchell took a step backwards, his mouth working soundlessly, his hands clutched to his chest.

'Nice to see you, Sebastian,' said Proserpine, in her little-girl voice. 'It's been a long time. But not as long as you're going to burn in hell.'

Mitchell threw up his hands to cover his face. 'You set me up,' he hissed at Nightingale.

Nightingale shrugged. 'I did a deal,' he said. 'Your soul for mine.'

'You bastard!' screamed Mitchell.

'Sticks and stones,' said Nightingale.

Mitchell started to turn. Proserpine laughed and waved her hand. Mitchell's feet sank into the stone slab he was standing on. He swayed unsteadily. 'Where do you think you're going, Sebastian?' she asked.

'Shoot her!' screamed Sylvia. The four heavies fanned out across the terrace. The one on the left, holding a machine pistol, was the first to fire. Bullets smacked into Proserpine but she smiled. She made a motion with her left hand and a bolt of lightning hit the man in the chest. He fell back, smoke belching from a gaping wound.

The other three fired their weapons. Nightingale heard a growl and turned to see the collie running across the grass out of the mist towards the terrace. It leaped into the air, and as it did so it rippled and doubled in size. It was as big as a tiger, and its fur had become hard and scaly. Its four massive paws hit the terrace and it sprang into the air again, passing so close to Nightingale that he felt the rush of wind as it went by. It had three heads now, dog-like but with massive fangs and forked tongues, and there were bony spikes down its spine. It hit the flagstones and now it was the size of a large car. Two of the heads bit into one of the men and the third ripped an arm off the other. The last turned to run, but the dog, or whatever it had turned into, jumped onto his back and ripped him into a dozen bloody pieces.

Sylvia screamed, but Proserpine made another motion with her hand and the woman fell silent. 'Am I going to have a problem with you, Sylvia?' she asked.

Sylvia shook her head.

'What do you think, Nightingale? Does she live or die?'

'It's up to you,' he said. 'None of them means anything to me.'

Proserpine looked at him suspiciously. 'Are you trying to play me, Nightingale? You think if you pretend not to care then I'll spare her?'

'I'm not that devious,' he said.

'Where's your chivalry, then? She's a woman. You don't care if she lives or dies?'

'I think you've made up your mind already,' Nightingale said quietly. 'I think that nothing I do or say matters any more. I'm just a spectator. Do what you have to do and be done with it.'

'Die, then,' said Proserpine flatly. She made another motion with her left hand and Sylvia burst into flames. She screamed and ran off the terrace towards the garden but barely made half a dozen steps before she fell onto the grass in a smouldering heap.

The dog had reverted to a collie and was sitting at Proserpine's feet, his tongue lolling out of the side of his mouth.

Proserpine walked towards Mitchell, hands swinging, head up. 'I have a deal,' said Mitchell, his voice a raspy croak. 'I can get you whatever you want.'

'I have what I want,' said Proserpine. 'I have you.'

'I can get souls for you, all the souls you want.' He coughed and bloody spittle frothed between his lips. 'Just listen to—'

Proserpine waved her hand and Mitchell fell silent. His mouth worked but he made no sound. Proserpine smiled. 'Go to hell, Mitchell,' she said.

There was a ripping sound and the air behind the old man split and folded in on itself. Figures moved about him, rippling like dark mirages. Mitchell screamed and coughed more blood, and things with scales and red eyes, tails and claws reached for him, things that smelled of decay and death, sweat and fear, things that hissed and growled and grunted. Mitchell was dragged away, screaming and crying, and the air folded again and it was as if he had never been there. Proserpine turned to Nightingale. She smiled. 'I do hate long goodbyes,' she said.

'This was planned from the start, wasn't it?'

She shrugged carelessly. 'It worked out all right in the end, didn't it?'

'You got what you wanted.'

'And you got your soul back. So all's well that ends well.' The collie made a soft woofing sound. 'Yes, baby, soon,' Proserpine whispered to him. She patted his head as she continued to smile at Nightingale.

'You used me to get Mitchell,' said Nightingale.

'It was your idea, Nightingale. Remember? You summoned me. You negotiated.'

'Which is what you intended, right from the start. All those people telling me I was going to hell, it was to put the frighteners on me. Then anyone who might be able to help me, they died. Except Tyler. Because he pointed the way to Mitchell, and Mitchell was who you wanted all along.'

'I'm just glad you're a better negotiator than you are an interrogator,' she said.

'The key to a good interrogation is only to ask questions to which you know the answers.'

'But doesn't that rather defeat the point?'

'All those people dead,' said Nightingale. 'My aunt. My uncle. Robbie. What about my parents? Did you kill them?'

'Do you want to deal, Nightingale? How about you offer me your soul and I'll tell you everything?'

Nightingale stared at her but didn't say anything.

'Many happy returns, Nightingale.' She blew him a kiss and turned to go.

'Wait!'

She stopped and looked at him over her shoulder. The dog growled, hackles rising. 'Do not try my patience, Nightingale,' said Proserpine, her voice deeper now and more menacing.

'My sister?'

Proserpine shook her head. 'Not my problem.'

'My father sold her soul, too.'

'Not to me.'

'To whom, then?'

Proserpine laughed. It was a deep, booming sound that echoed off the house and reverberated around the garden. Nightingale shivered. 'Who gets my sister's soul?' he shouted.

Proserpine winked at him. 'Unless you want to put your eternal soul on the table, you've got nothing left to bargain with, Nightingale. We're done. Catch you later.'

She walked away, the dog following in her footsteps. She waved without looking back. Then reality shimmered, bent in on itself, and they vanished. The wind gradually died down and the trees stopped whispering. The mist had cleared and he could see the gardens again. Two of Mitchell's heavies were standing by a willow tree close to the perimeter wall, scratching their heads. One was holding a leash but there was no sign of his dog.

Nightingale took out his packet of Marlboro and lit a cigarette. He held the smoke deep in his lungs and relished the feel of the nicotine entering his bloodstream, letting him know that he was still alive. He blew a smoke-ring towards the moon, and smiled to himself. 'That went well,' he muttered. 'All things considered.'

77

There were five candles spaced around the circular table and Nightingale lit them one by one. 'Very romantic,' said Jenny.

'If you don't take this seriously, I'll do it myself,' said Nightingale.

'How can you use a ouija board yourself?' said Jenny, scornfully. 'The whole point is that it's a joint effort.'

Nightingale went up the stairs, switched off the lights and came back down into the basement. He had found the ouija board in the bottom drawer of Gosling's desk. It was made of oak that had cracked with age, the words 'Yes' and 'No' in the top corners and the letters of the alphabet embossed in gold in two rows across the middle. Below the letters were the numbers zero to nine in a row and 'Goodbye'.

The planchette was made from ivory or bone, cool to the touch and as smooth as marble. He had put the board on a circular table in the middle of the basement with a crystal vase containing freshly picked flowers and a crystal glass of distilled water. He had placed the five large church candles around the table. He took a small bowl of sage and sprinkled it onto the burning candles, then smudged some over the board and the planchette. He had also prepared bowls of consecrated salt and lavender, which he sprinkled over the board before taking two high-backed wooden chairs and putting them together at one side of the table. He waved for Jenny to sit down. 'Are you sure this is a good idea?' she asked.

'We won't know until we try it,' said Nightingale, taking his seat. 'Come on, sit down. It won't bite.'

'I wish I had your confidence,' she said, and sat. She looked at the candles. 'Shouldn't we have a protective circle or something?'

'This isn't about raising demons,' said Nightingale.

'That's right,' said Jenny. 'All we're doing is talking to the recently departed.'

'Relax,' said Nightingale.

'That's easy for you to say,' said Jenny. 'Why the salt and herbs and stuff?'

'It's what you're supposed to do.'

'And the flowers and the glass of water?'

'Spirits love flowers and water.'

'What about the ones with hay fever? Or the ones that died of rabies?'

Nightingale looked at her sternly. 'You've got to take this seriously or it won't work,' he said. 'The table has to be free of all negative energy or the spirits won't come.'

'It's a kids' game, Jack.'

Nightingale shook his head. 'I've read some of Gosling's books on it, and it's deadly serious,' he said. 'Over the years it became a game, a bit of a laugh, but the ouija board is a genuine way of conversing with spirits.' He reached over and took her hands. 'Close your eyes,' he said.

'You've got to be joking.'

'Jenny, just do as you're told. If nothing else, do it to humour me.'

Jenny closed her eyes. Nightingale began to speak, clearly and loudly so that his voice echoed around the basement. 'In the name of God, of Jesus Christ, of the Great Brotherhood of Light, of the Archangels Michael, Raphael, Gabriel, Uriel and Ariel, please protect us from the forces of evil during this session. Let nothing but light surround this board and its participants, and let us only communicate with powers and entities of the light. Protect us, protect this house, the people in this house, and let there only be light and nothing but light. Amen.'

He squeezed her hand. 'Amen,' she said.

They opened their eyes. 'Now, this bit is important,' said Nightingale. 'You have to imagine that the table is protected with a bright white light. First you imagine it coming down through the top of your head and completely surrounding your body. Then push it out as far as you can go. Can you do that?'

'I'll try,' said Jenny.

'Good girl,' he said. 'Now we put our right hands on the planchette. If anything goes wrong, we move the planchette to "Goodbye" and we say it firmly. Then I'll recite a closing prayer.'

Jenny took her hand off the planchette. 'What might go wrong?' she said.

'A malicious spirit might try to come through, that's all.'

'Oh, that's all?' she said.

'Jenny, it'll be fine, just trust me. Now put your hand back.'

Jenny slowly reached out with her right hand and touched the planchette.

'Now visualise the white light. Okay?'

Jenny nodded.

Nightingale took a deep breath and looked up at the ceiling. 'We're here to talk to Robbie Hoyle,' he said.

The candle flames flickered.

'Robbie, are you there? Please talk to us.'

Jenny looked around the basement, then back at Nightingale. 'Jack . . .'

Nightingale ignored her. 'It's Jack, Robbie, and Jenny. Are you there? We need to talk.'

He took another deep breath, then exhaled slowly.

'This is a waste of time,' said Jenny.

'I have to try,' said Nightingale. 'He said he knew something about my sister.'

'He's dead, Jack. Robbie's dead.'

'I know that.'

'So this isn't going to help.'

Nightingale glared at her, then looked up at the ceiling again. 'Robbie? Robbie, are you there?'

Jenny was just about to take her fingers off the planchette when it twitched. Her mouth opened in surprise.

Nightingale smiled. 'Robbie,' he said, 'is that you?'

The planchette slid slowly across the board until its point was resting on 'Yes'.

STEPHEN LEATHER

Dead Men

Former SAS trooper turned undercover cop Dan 'Spider' Shepherd knows there are no easy solutions in the war against terrorism.

But when a killer starts to target pardoned IRA terrorists, Shepherd has to put his life on the line to protect his former enemies. Whilst he is undercover in Belfast, a grief-stricken Saudi whose two sons died under torture in the name of the War On Terror is planning to avenge their deaths by striking out at two people close to Shepherd.

As the Muslim assassin closes in on his prey, Shepherd realises that the only way to save lives is to become a killer himself.

'He explores complex contemporary issues while keeping the action fast and bloody' *The Economist*

Out now

HODDER

STEPHEN LEATHER

Live Fire

Mickey and Mark Moore are hard men who live by their own code and leaders of a gang that has made millions at the point of a gun. Now they're enjoying a life in the sun in Thailand.

Dan 'Spider' Shepherd is sent to infiltrate the team of bank robbers. But when he does, he discovers that he has more in common with them than he first thought. While he and his Serious Organised Crime Agency colleagues are plotting the downfall of the Moore brothers, a far more sinister threat is stalking the streets of London.

A group of home-grown Islamic fundamentalist fanatics embarks on a campaign of terror the like of which Britain has never seen. Car bombs and beheadings are only the beginning . . .

And Shepherd is the only man who can stop them.

'Pacy read . . . totally convincing' *BBC Radio 5 Live*

Out now

HODDER